THE MAN BURNS TONIGHT

A Black Rock City Mystery

DONN CORTEZ

POCKET BOOKS

New York   London   Toronto   Sydney

An *Original* Publication of POCKET BOOKS

 POCKET BOOKS, a division of Simon & Schuster, Inc.
1230 Avenue of the Americas, New York, NY 10020

ISBN-13: 978-0-7434-7699-7
ISBN-10:   0-7434-7699-9

First Pocket Books printing August 2005

10 9 8 7 6 5 4 3 2 1

POCKET and colophon are registered trademarks of
Simon & Schuster, Inc.

Cover art and design by Carlos Beltran

Manufactured in the United States of America

For information regarding special discounts for bulk purchases,
please contact Simon & Schuster Special Sales at 1-800-456-6798
or business@simonandschuster.com.

This book is dedicated to all the Burners,
past and present,
I have had the honor of sharing the Playa with.

ACKNOWLEDGMENTS

I'd like to thank each and every citizen of Black Rock City for helping create the most amazing metropolis on the face of the planet. I don't have room for all of you (and frankly, some of you are kinda blurry, if you know what I mean), so here's a few in no particular order: Liam, Molly, Matt, Nick, all the members of Yoga Granola, the Vancouver Burner community, Sheriff Marty and the gang at the Starlust Lounge, the superheroes of Justice Intense, the Bad Mintons (who serenaded me), and of course Larry Harvey, who started it all.

AUTHOR'S NOTE

This is a work of fiction. While Burning Man certainly exists, it is a place as surreal as it is real, as much an imaginary kingdom made of myth as it is a city built from rebar, sweat, and miles of duct tape. Most of the theme camps, art and performances in this book are also real—though they may have been shuffled a little in time and space—and a few were born of plot demands or sheer artistic indulgence. As a general rule of thumb, the more outrageous the description, the more likely it is to be accurate. The characters in this book are either composites or original creations—any resemblance to actual persons, famous or otherwise, is strictly ironic. If any Burners recognize some elements of themselves in one of my depictions, I offer my thanks and hope you consider their inclusion as my gift to you.

See you on the Playa.

THE
MAN
BURNS
TONIGHT

BURNING MAN 2003
ADMIT ONE HUMAN

YOU VOLUNTARILY ASSUME THE RISK OF SERIOUS INJURY OR DEATH BY ATTENDING.

Your use of this ticket confirms your agreement to the following terms: You must bring enough food, water, shelter, and first aid to survive one week in a harsh desert environment. Commercial vending, firearms, fireworks, rockets, and all other explosives are prohibited. You agree to read and abide by ALL rules in the *Survival Guide.* You agree to follow federal, state, and local laws. This is a LEAVE NO TRACE, pack-it-in, pack-it-out event. You are asked to contribute 2 hours of playa cleanup in addition to that of your own camp before departure. You appoint Burning Man as your representative to take actions necessary to protect your intellectual property or privacy rights, recognizing that Burning Man has no obligation to take any action whatsoever. All vehicles including trucks, trailers, and RVs entering and exiting Burning Man are subject to search by the Gate staff. This ticket is a revocable license and it may be revoked by Burning Man for any reason. Commercial use of images taken at Burning Man is prohibited without the prior written consent of Burning Man.

CHAPTER 1:

DUBIOUS REALITY

I must be out of my mind, Dex Edden thought.

The RV lurched as it bounced over another pothole in the rough desert surface, but his boss seemed oblivious of any damage he might be doing to the rented vehicle. Wade Jickling gripped the steering wheel tightly with one fist, a can of beer in the other. A huge grin stretched across his apelike face, making it only slightly less menacing than usual. "Almost there," he said gleefully. "Almost there, almost there . . ."

Dex sighed, and tried to concentrate on the laptop on the Winnebago's little fold-down table. *It's not like I had a choice,* he reminded himself. *Not really.* The last place in the world Dex wanted to be was in the middle of the Nevada desert at the end of August, but his employer had seen things differently—and apparently so had a few other people.

Thirty thousand of them, in fact.

Dex could understand that many people going to Nevada to gamble, or see Wayne Newton, or even attend a plumber's convention—but these people weren't going to Vegas or Reno. They were going to the Black Rock Desert, where the nearest town was a speck twelve miles away called Gerlach. Out here there was no water, no power, no stores, nothing except what you brought with you. Besides food, water, and booze, Wade had brought a huge plastic sack of fortune cookies and Dex. Dex still wasn't sure which was the more bizarre choice.

He wouldn't have gone at all if he hadn't needed the money so badly. Since the dot-com bubble had burst, things had been tough in the IT world; coders like Dex had to scramble to find even temporary contracts. Wade was one of the few who'd gotten out at the right time, selling his company while it was still worth a fortune and devoting himself to the serious pursuit of partying. He'd ridden out the crash on a wave of beer and smugness, laughing as everybody else's money swirled down the drain. Wade himself knew very little about software—he'd owned a restaurant in Seattle when one of his waiters had convinced him to bankroll a dotcom start-up he was developing.

Now Wade was planning to reenter the business world as an online restaurant-supply wholesaler, and Dex was designing his Web site. Dex didn't really like him much . . . but he needed this job, and saying yes seemed the safest thing to do. Wade wasn't comfortable with the concept of *"no."*

Dex unfolded his lanky body from behind the cramped table and stood up carefully. He stretched, feeling the muscles in his neck cramp. They'd been driving for hours since picking up the RV in Reno; the last time Dex had glanced out the window, the sun had just been setting. It was full dark now, and he couldn't see much outside other than headlights and swirling white dust.

No, wait—there was a sign up ahead. The upper half proclaimed BURNING MAN in large, neon-green and pink letters; below that, BLACK ROCK CITY was done in a red-and-yellow flame motif. There was a wide arrow pointing to the right.

"We are *here*," Wade exulted. "Burning Man. We're at fucking *Burning Man!*"

Dex started to sigh, and sneezed instead. The dust tickled his nose.

They were stopped by a balding man in a brown uniform, who stepped inside, took their tickets, and did a quick inspection of the inside of the RV, including the bathroom. "Just making sure you don't have any stowaways," he said. "Take the lane on the right, and keep it slow." He left.

Dex went back to his laptop. The RV continued to bump along. A few minutes later they stopped again; Dex assumed they were parking.

"Hey," Wade said. "Somebody wants to talk to you."

"Hmmm?" Dex got up and walked to the front. "Who?"

"Her," Wade said with a grin.

They were stopped at one of many entrances that led through a fence of bright orange industrial netting. The banner overhead proclaimed BURNING MAN 2003; beside the gate was a vaguely pyramidal ten-foot-high framework with a large brass bell suspended from the peak.

In front of that was a Catholic schoolgirl.

She was in her twenties, her hair in pink pigtails,

and smiled at him in a way that would have made Britney Spears blush. When she crooked her finger, Dex swallowed and stepped outside.

He was shocked at how cold it was—the wind poked through his T-shirt with frozen fingers, needled his face with dust. He sneezed again, took a lungful of dust on the inhale and started coughing. He had to duck his head and cover his mouth and nose with both hands before he could stop.

"Sorry," he croaked, looking up. *Just great, my first moment here and I look like a total spaz in front of a gorgeous—*

Six-foot-five, bearded, grinning—

—Schoolgirl.

For a second, his brain refused to process the incongruity; what he saw in front of him was a tall, hairy man wearing a plaid skirt and knee socks, with his hair in pigtails. Then his mind adjusted . . . and he realized he *was* looking at a tall, hairy man wearing a plaid skirt and knee socks. With his hair in pigtails.

"Aha!" the man bellowed triumphantly. "Abel, we have us a virgin!"

"I saw him first, Boytoy!" the girl yelled back. She was handing a sheaf of papers to Wade through the window of the RV. "I get to spank him!"

"Well, why don't we let *him* decide?" Boytoy shot back. "What's it gonna be?" he asked Dex.

"Um," Dex said.

"Me! Me! Me!" Abel yelled, sprinting around the front of the RV. She slid to a stop in front of Dex and produced a Ping-Pong paddle from thin air. She rubbed the stippled red rubber surface with the palm of one hand and raised an eyebrow. "I guarantee you'll remember it for a long, long time . . ."

He glanced from one to the other, considered trying to make it back into the RV and locking the door, and finally said, "Her?"

"Turn around and assume the position!" Abel said gleefully.

Hesitantly, Dex did so, leaning against the wall of the RV with both hands. "Not too hard," he said, looking back over his shoulder. She gave him a soft pat on the rear of his jeans and smiled reassuringly.

And then Boytoy pulled his pants down. His briefs went with them.

An icy gust of wind hit his privates at the same second the paddle cracked his buttocks. He yelped, and only the fact that his jeans were bunched around his ankles prevented him from bolting like a rabbit. She swung the paddle three more times, and he couldn't help making the same high-pitched cry every time. By the last one, Boytoy was making it with him.

"Done!" Abel said. "Welcome—"

He was already back in the RV, pants half-on, not looking back.

"—home," Abel said. "Hey! You have to ring the bell!"

Dex locked the door and refused to come out. Wade drove on, but he didn't stop laughing for another ten minutes.

"The thing you gotta understand about Burning Man," Wade said, opening another beer, "is that people come out here to screw, get wasted, dance naked and set shit on fire."

Dex took a sip of his own beer, shifted slightly in his seat and winced. "For a whole week?"

"Hell yes, for a whole week. Some of these guys are here for two weeks beforehand building stuff, and six weeks afterward cleaning up. I promise you, man— you're gonna see shit here that will blow your *mind.*" Wade paced up and down the narrow confines of the RV restlessly, gesturing with his can of beer. He was a short man, with a thick, barrel-chested body, muscular arms, and bandy little legs; with the millimeter of orange stubble on his thick-browed, flat-nosed head, he reminded Dex of a shaved orangutan. "Wild, crazy shit. Shit I can't even *describe.*"

"Great," Dex said, trying to sound enthusiastic. "Uh—what exactly are they building?"

"A whole goddamn *city,* Dex—Black Rock City. Streets, businesses, radio stations, post office—everything! Except . . ." He gave a snort of laughter and shook his head. "Except the businesses ain't businesses, the streets change every year, and the post office is more about performance art than anything else. . . . I just can't put it into words and do it justice. You're gonna have to see it for yourself."

Dex ran a hand through his short brown hair. "Uh, yeah. Looking forward to it."

Loud techno music from outside had provided a soundtrack to their conversation ever since they'd arrived; Dex couldn't tell how far away the source was, but it was close enough that he had to raise his voice to be heard. "How late does the music go?"

Wade looked at his watch. "Well, it's almost eleven

PM on Sunday night," he said. "So they'll turn it off sometime around . . . seven days from now."

He grinned and raised his beer. "Hope you brought earplugs . . ."

It's not as if I don't enjoy a good party, Dex thought as he lay in bed and tried to get to sleep. *I just don't like* chaos.

Wade had claimed the RV's bedroom, leaving Dex with the sleeping space over the vehicle's cab. Not that his boss was sleeping—he'd gone to "check out the neighborhood," as he put it. Dex wondered if he'd be back before dawn.

He stared up at the off-white plastic ceiling, only two feet above his head. He'd thought it would be darker—and quieter—in the middle of the desert, but the people parked next to them were running a generator and lights while they set up camp; enough illumination spilled through the RV's windows to let him see little drifts of dust sway through the air.

I can handle this, he thought. *Let Wade show me around a little, have a beer or two, make my excuses, and head back to the RV. Stay inside, run the air-conditioning, get a bunch of work done. Wade'll forget all about me once he gets into full party-mode.*

That was the thing about Wade—obnoxious and overbearing as he could be, he knew how to have a good time. It was a skill Dex had never really mastered himself, not in college or in the decade since; he always felt vaguely guilty at social functions, like there was something more important he should be doing.

He recognized this as a simple avoidance behavior,

but so far the knowledge hadn't done him any good—he still chose to keep to himself rather than going out. Fortunately, he was perfectly happy with his own company; it was other people he wasn't sure about. They tended to be so . . . *unpredictable.*

Maybe, he reflected, he should try to spend a little time observing Wade at the festival. Dex prided himself on his ability to analyze and solve problems; couldn't the same skills he used to learn new programs be used to learn new behaviors? Wade could be loud, crude, and tactless, but he still had a large circle of friends. Almost all of Dex's friends were online—and he hadn't had a girlfriend in years.

Not that he hadn't had offers, he reminded himself. He was only thirty, in good shape, reasonably attractive—as near as he could tell, anyway—intelligent, and well-mannered; he drew his fair share of female attention. Somehow, though, it never went any further than that. He never felt comfortable making the first move, and he felt even more awkward around the women who did so themselves.

It was like juggling, he thought. It looked easy, even fun, but he just couldn't keep his balls in the air.

When he finally got to sleep, he dreamt about jungles: tribal drums pounded, while somewhere, deep in the undergrowth, a giant, redheaded ape crashed about with an entire keg of beer in one knuckly fist.

Dex woke up with a hangover.

It wasn't *his* hangover, he thought muzzily, sitting up and rubbing his eyes; he'd only had a single beer last night before turning in. But there was no mistaking the cottony taste in his mouth, the slight ache behind his eyes, the queasiness in his belly. Wade's hangover, Dex surmised, must be so epic he was broadcasting.

He hadn't slept well. He didn't know if it was the music, the RV's mattress or the overall strangeness of the situation, but he'd woken half a dozen times during the night. He got up, drank some water and took some Tylenol. He didn't know what time his boss had gotten in, but the snoring in the bedroom had to be him. Dex took a quick shower, grateful for even the minimal pressure of the RV, brushed his teeth and started to floss.

Wade pounded on the door when he was half done—Dex traded places with him quickly, hoping he wouldn't have to listen to an extended bout of vomiting before his first cup of coffee. Wade was only in the bathroom for a minute though, and when he came out he seemed fine.

Dex made coffee while still in his robe. He'd get dressed once Wade returned to the bedroom, but for now his boss was apparently comfortable lounging around in only his underwear, a pair of baggy red boxers that had seen better days.

"How'd things go last night?" Dex asked. He took some eggs out of the small fridge.

"They went—okay," Wade said. His voice suggested otherwise; it sounded more baffled than anything, like that of a man who'd taken a slug of whiskey that tasted like chicken noodle soup.

Dex hesitated. "Anything wrong?"

"No. *Fuck* no," Wade snapped. "Make me some of those eggs too, willya?"

"Sure," Dex said. That was more like the Wade he

knew—and even a surly Wade was better than an uncertain one.

"Somebody's gonna be coming over later," Wade said. "Somebody I want you to meet. Gonna be here after dark—make sure you're around, all right?"

"Of course," Dex said, cracking an egg into a frying pan.

Where would he go?

That first day, most of what Dex saw of the festival was from the windows of the RV.

That didn't mean what he saw wasn't bizarre. Every so often he'd look up from his laptop to observe, say, a nine-foot-tall electric tricycle driven by a woman dressed only in green paint, or a double-decker bus covered in elaborate white scrollwork with a full gospel choir riding on top. He assumed they were a gospel choir, anyway; despite the robes, he wouldn't have been surprised if they'd started belting out old Led Zeppelin numbers.

What did surprise him was the number of police vehicles he saw, slowly driving past. Their presence cheered him considerably; he realized one of the reasons he'd been reluctant to go out was the half-admitted fear that he'd be accosted by loud, drunken attendees who would demand to know why he wasn't enjoying himself—loud, drunken, schoolgirl attendees, carrying Ping-Pong paddles.

He still wasn't sure how he felt about that, so he tried not to think about it. Much.

Wade had left right after breakfast and made only a halfhearted attempt to drag Dex along, accepting his excuse that he wasn't feeling well without an argument. Truth was, Dex wasn't feeling that great; along with the hungover feeling he'd started with, his sinuses had been plugged up all day and he felt exhausted. He hoped he wasn't getting sick.

He'd expected relentless sunshine and high temperatures, but the sky stayed a sullen, chilly gray all day. A few drops of rain even spattered against the window in midmorning, though it didn't last long. He had a sandwich for lunch, a can of beef stew for supper. He even tried to take a nap in the afternoon, but despite feeling overtired he couldn't get to sleep. He finally gave up and went back to work.

Wade didn't get back until after seven, and wolfed down a can of chili without even heating it up. Dex tried to show him how the website was shaping up, but Wade just grunted, "Yeah, yeah," and opened another Coors. He leaned against the counter and chugged back half the beer in one pull, paused, scowled, then polished off the other half. He crushed the can in one hand and tossed it onto the counter without looking.

"You get along with your folks?" he asked abruptly. The question was so unexpected that it took Dex a moment to formulate a reply.

"Uh, yeah, pretty much," he said. "They moved to Florida a few years ago, so I don't see them that much."

"Easier to get along with someone that ain't there, right?"

"That's not what I meant, actually—"

"Whatever. Never did too well with my own. Scrapped with my mother all the time and never knew my dad—he took off before I was even out the chute. Can't say I ever really gave a shit."

Wade paused, but Dex didn't know how to respond; he settled for just looking expectant.

"Know what I saw today? This old geezer, must have been in his sixties or seventies, wandering down the street buck-naked. His mouth was open and he was shaking like he was gonna have some kinda fit. Looked like a fuckin' zombie from an X-rated version of *Night of the Living Dead.*" Wade shook his head. "Man, seeing all that wrinkled skin flappin' around was rude. Hope someone puts me out of my misery before I ever get that bad." He belched, loudly and unself-consciously. "He did have a helluva tan, though . . ."

"I'll bet."

"I gotta say, that's one of the things I like about this place—you never know *what* the fuck is gonna pop up. People compare it to Woodstock all the time, but that's bullshit. It's more punk than hippie, you ask me."

Dex hadn't, but he wasn't about to disagree, either.

"*I* was a punker, you know?" Wade said. "Back in the late seventies, early eighties. Man, it was wild. Everybody tryin' to be crazier and more fucked-up than everybody else, stickin' safety pins and fishhooks and whatnot through their faces. . . . I knew this one guy, he stuck fuckin' *knitting needles* through his ears. Skewered 'em top and bottom, just like shish kebabs."

Wade shook his head and chuckled. "But it gave the whole scene this *charge,* you know? Like anything could happen, anything was possible. None of us would admit it—hell, we woulda stomped the crap outta anyone who suggested it—but even though we had this whole fuck-the-world-everything-sucks-we're-all-gonna-die attitude, there was somethin' else there. A kind of—braveness, maybe. I don't know."

"It must have been an—interesting time to live in," Dex said.

Wade snorted. "Yeah, me and the fuckin' dinosaurs, right?"

Hastily, Dex said, "I didn't mean—"

"Nah, that's okay. I know it was a long time ago—it just doesn't seem like it."

Wade got two more beers from the fridge, handed one to Dex and opened the other himself. Dex didn't really feel like a beer, but he took it and said, "Thanks," anyway.

"Y'know, people get this idea of what somethin's like, especially if it's something outta the ordinary, and it's real hard to shake that idea outta their heads. It's like they're threatened by it, so they have to find some way to put a label on it they understand. But that's *fucked-up,* 'cause if it's weird enough to be scary, it's too weird to be just one thing. You know?"

Dex took a sip of beer. "Well . . . I guess things are always more complicated than they seem."

"Bullshit," Wade snapped. *"Some* things are really fucking simple. What I'm talkin' about is the stuff that looks simple and ain't. *People,* you know? I'm talkin' about *people."*

Dex had thought they were talking about punk rock, but he nodded anyway.

"Like the people here. You see a guy dressed in a cocktail gown and high heels, and you think you know what he's like. But then you talk to him, and you find out he's a Green Bay Packers fan and he works on a ranch and drives a Harley. See what I mean?"

"Sure."

"That's just how the punk scene was. Everybody thinks it was all about anger and despair and giving the world the finger, but we were just people. Just kids. We were having a good time. We partied and laughed and hung out. We listened to a lot of music, and we fuckin' *danced*. You like dancin', Dex?"

"I'm not much of a dancer," Dex said. He tried to imagine Wade on the dance floor and couldn't.

"Yeah, well, back then you didn't have to be. You just got out there and jumped up and down a lot. And maybe slammed into whoever was next to you." He pulled a booklet out of his back pocket and waved it at Dex. "They got all kinds of dancing here, lemme tellya. You got Celtic, swing, hip-hop, belly dancing . . . everything from goth raves to fucking roller disco." He took another long drink and stared out the window over the sink for a moment.

"Well," Dex said, "I really should get back to work—"

"And then there were the *girls*," Wade continued, as if Dex hadn't spoken at all. "I tellya, for a group that liked to make itself ugly, there sure were some hot women. There was this one at a concert in Jersey— man, was she somethin'. Bloodred Mohawk a foot high, black stripe across her eyes like that chick in *Blade Runner*, dressed in combat boots, ripped fishnets and cutoffs. Two perfect little breasts with nothing but *X*'s of black electrical tape on 'em. And man, could she *slam*—she bounced around in front of the stage like a fuckin' pinball, off guys must have weighed three times what she did. I swear, sometimes her feet never even touched the floor. . . ."

He trailed off, staring into the distance, then snorted and shook his head. "Anyway, I asked her if she wanted to do some coke and we wound up fucking in the bathroom. Romantic, huh?"

Dex took a drink of beer and didn't reply.

Wade looked down at the booklet in his hand, started leafing through it. "Hey, you checked this out yet?"

"Uh, no. I've been concentrating on the website—"

"I can't believe some of the shit they've got going on. The world's biggest game of Pong, the world's biggest game of Ski-ball. Naked croquet. Tricycle jousting. Something called the Turnilympics Turnip-Toss, for Christ's sake." He shook his head, but he had a wide smile on his face. "It's like nobody here ever fuckin' grew up."

"Everybody needs a place to blow off steam, I guess."

"Yeah? Even you?"

Too late, Dex saw the trap he'd stumbled into. "This isn't really my sort of thing—"

"Bullshit. This place has somethin' for *everybody*, I'm tellin' you—they got camps where you can catch anything from *The Muppet Show* to old episodes of *Space: 1999*. They got poetry slams, strip contests, and karaoke. They got a drive-in that shows cartoons, old kung-fu movies, and *Rocky Horror*. And let's not forget the *porn*—Christ, Amsterdam's got nothin' on this place. The people that aren't fucking on-screen are probably doin' it on the couch right next to you."

"That's—uh . . ."

Wade laughed. "Little too much, huh? Sorry, didn't mean to freak you out—I know I get kinda carried away. But just 'cause something's new and scary doesn't mean it's *bad*, right?" Under the joking tone was something else—a note of pleading.

"Of course not," Dex said. "I just like to take things a little slower, is all."

"Sure, sure. Look, I'm gonna go freshen up—that visitor I mentioned should be here soon."

"All right," Dex said. He was tapping away at the laptop before Wade shut the bedroom door—but stopped a few seconds later, a thoughtful look on his face. There was something distinctly odd about the conversation he and Wade had just had, but he couldn't quite put his finger on it.

Then he realized what it was. He'd never heard Wade use the word *sorry* before. . . .

About half an hour after the sun had set, somebody knocked on the door. Wade was still in the bedroom, so Dex answered it.

It was Darth Vader.

The costume was perfect in every detail, except for two things: first, the helmet sported a pair of long bunny ears; and second, the entire outfit was a bright, shiny pink.

"Uh . . . yes?" Dex said.

"I'm—uh, I'm looking for Wade?" Darth Bunny said. His voice sounded strange—almost like someone trying to make his voice deeper than it actually was. He looked around, one hand on the pommel of the lightsaber stuck through his belt, as if expecting

Day-Glo Rebel fighters to appear at any moment.

"I'll get him—come on in," Dex said. He stepped back and rapped on the sliding panel that separated the bedroom from the rest of the camper. "Wade? You have company."

The weight of the camper shifted as the Sith Lord stepped aboard—he wasn't quite as tall or broad as the cinematic version, but he was still a big man. *Though the hot pink,* thought Dex, *suggested not so much* Sith *as* Sithy.

The panel slid open. Wade, freshly shaved and dressed in khaki shorts and a Hawaiian shirt, looked almost presentable. He didn't say anything for a moment, though, just stood there with an expression on his face Dex had never seen before; somewhere between apprehension and elation, as if their visitor were delivering a subpoena engraved in solid gold.

There wasn't much room in the RV in the first place, and Dex was trapped between them in the narrow passage from the bedroom to the front door. He solved this by sliding behind the fold-out table and sitting down on the bench seat against the wall. "Hi. I'm Dex," he said, sticking out his hand across the table.

The stranger hesitated, then shook it with a pink-gloved hand. "Hello," he said. "I'm—"

"This is Rafe," Wade said abruptly.

The hand in Dex's suddenly gripped it much tighter, then let it go and stepped back.

There was a moment of strained silence. "Great costume," Dex said. It was the first thing that leapt to mind; it was either that or *I sense a disturbance in the Force—a great big* pink *disturbance.*

"Thanks," Rafe said. There was an edge of nervousness in his voice. "I thought you were going to come alone," he said to Wade, fidgeting with the handle of his lightsaber; the blade, Dex saw, was a short length of rebar painted the same shade as the rest of the costume.

"It's okay," Wade said. "Dex is the first person I've told, and I guarantee he hasn't told anyone else."

"Okay, sure, that's cool . . ." Abruptly, Rafe pulled the lightsaber from his belt. The rebar made little rippling noises as the ridges in the iron bumped over the leather. "Pretty cool, huh?" he asked Dex. "Here—check it out." He proffered the weapon handle-first.

"Uh—"

"Go ahead—try the balance."

Dex took it by the handle and hefted it. The hilt was wrapped in black duct tape around foam, giving it a sure grip. It wasn't that heavy—the blade was shorter than an actual lightsaber's would be. "Nice," he said, and handed it back.

"How about a beer?" Wade asked. He knelt down, opened the door of the half-size fridge and reached inside. "You want a can or a bottle?"

"Can," Rafe answered. "Shouldn't bring glass out to the desert—it's easier to recycle aluminum." He took a firm, two-handed grip on the handle of his sword, and spread his legs ever so slightly.

"Wade?" Dex said.

He was suddenly terrified, but he wasn't sure why. He was about to either embarrass himself horribly . . . or witness something horrible.

"What?" Wade said, looking up.

And then Rafe brought the lightsaber around in a tight, deadly arc, and Dex knew.

The rebar connected with Wade's temple with a crunch that reminded Dex of a beer can being crumpled. There was no blood; Wade just suddenly slumped to the floor, his body blocking the fridge open. A bottle of Corona rolled from his limp left hand and stopped against Dex's bare big toe—he hadn't even bothered putting on shoes that day.

After that, things happened very quickly.

Dex yelled, "CHRIST!" He threw as many of his limbs up in defence as he could, which meant both arms and one leg. His knee cracked into the folding table, flipping it up at the precise second Rafe took a swing at Dex's head. The rebar *chunked!* into the side of the cheap pressboard hard enough to embed itself, and Dex took the opportunity to dive, low and fast, past his attacker's pink leather boots and toward the front door.

There was a frozen instant while Dex was on his knees, fumbling with the latch, when he expected to be hauled back—by telekinesis, maybe—and be either beaten or throttled to death; but Rafe wasted it trying to get his weapon (apparently not as frictionless as your standard-model lightsaber) unstuck from where it was lodged.

The door opened and Dex spilled out into darkness. He scrambled to his feet and ran.

CHAPTER 2:

RIDICULOUS CREED

File A (Fratboy Yahoo): So me and JD and Cody and Mario came down 'cause we heard all the booze was free and there was naked tail everywhere, right? All these hippie chicks running around, havin' sex right out in the open? Too good to pass up.

It was kinda expensive. Three hundred apiece for tickets at the gate. Cody thought it was only two fifty, but it turns out the later you go in the week, the more the tickets are—which don't make any sense to us. I mean, the fewer days you're there, the more it costs? What about the people who don't *wanna* spend a whole week in the desert, who maybe only want to drop by and check it out for a few days?

Anyway, we blew more than that for spring break, and we'd saved some cash by borrowing JD's parents' camper to stay in. It was also the first week of September, so we miss some classes, but what the fuck. Gotta fight for your right to party, y'know?

And man, it was fucking in*sane*. *Sick* fun. We get there Wednesday, get stoked on a few joints, and start roaming around. I never *seen* such crazy shit—it was like they let all the inmates outta the asylum at once, y'know? I saw this one guy riding this thing like a trike, except it didn't have no pedals or anything—just these levers. He stood on this little platform between the rear wheels, and there was this female mannequin on the front. He made the thing go by hanging on to the levers and pumping his hips—you had to *do* the dummy to make it go, man! And he had a speaker mounted with porn samples playing, all these moans and whimpers and stuff, so he had a soundtrack as he fucked his way across town.

I don't know if we fucked our way all over town, but we sure got fucked *up* right across it. We started in this place called the Paddy Mirage, a little Irish pub way up in one corner of the city. Live music and beer on tap—great way to start the night. When we got tired of that, we went out and caught the Dave Train, which is like this mobile bar that gets towed all over the place. That was pretty cool, but Mario got this girl all pissed off because he kept asking her to get naked, and finally we jumped off at this rave. They weren't serving booze, though, so we decided to go to this place we heard about called Pinky's. Problem was, it was on the other end of the city and we didn't feel like walking—so Cody just grabs one of the bikes lying outside the rave and rides away, and after a second we all do the same. None of 'em was locked up or anything—guess their owners were too high on E to give a shit.

We wound up in this bar that was giving away fresh strawberry daiquiris, but they got a little cranky when we didn't give 'em anything in return.

"Hey, I thought everything was supposed to be free," JD says. "No vending, right?"

The guy running the bar says he doesn't want money. When JD asks what he does want, the guy says, "I want you to *participate*. Know any good jokes?"

So I told him the one about being stranded on a desert island with Cindy Crawford, and that seemed to make him happy. Wish I woulda known what that joke was worth sooner—I been giving it away for years!

After that, we hit the Barbie Death Camp and Wine Bar, knocked back a few glasses of vino and did some seriously fucked-up shit to plastic dolls . . . ditched the bikes, got on a tiki bar on wheels, and roared around for a while drinking playa margaritas—that's tequila and Gatorade—then got off and stumbled over to the Green Fairy Bar Camp. I thought we were gonna run into a bunch of queers dressed like leprechauns, but JD tells me the Green Fairy is this chick they used to put on bottles of absinthe, like that blonde on cans of Pauli Girl.

You ever had absinthe? That is one serious mother-fuckin' pop. Made outta this stuff called wormwood, makes mescal look like Earl Grey tea. These people brewed up their own, too—not that watered-down stuff you can buy legal. Couple shots of that, you're ready to go out and howl at the goddamn moon—and we had more than a couple shots.

Things got a little blurry after that. We never did make it to Pinky's.

Slept most of the next day, but got up in time for happy hour, which is around five. You stroll down the street, and people call you over and stick a cocktail in your hand. Long as the sun's up, there's still plenty of eye candy walkin' around naked. I was a little hung-over, but it was still pretty sweet.

The whole weekend was like that, more or less. At one point we hooked up with this older guy named Wade—man, he made us look like amateurs. Guy drank like a sponge, said *fuck* every other word and didn't give a shit about anything. He was kinda enter-taining at first, but partying with a guy like that is like holding a hand grenade with the pin pulled; after a while, waiting for the thing to blow gets on your nerves. We ditched him at the Porta-Johns and kept going.

Problem was, he caught up with us—and he was *not* happy. We're at this camp doing the limbo— y'know, that dance where you go under a pole?—for martinis, and he comes outta nowhere and clocks Mario when he's just about to go under the bar. Nails him right in the face, grabs the pole, starts waving it around yelling about how nobody ditches *him*. Went after Cody next, gave him a nasty whack on the head before JD and I jumped him. Even wasted, the guy could fight; he was built like a fuckin' gorilla, for one thing. We finally kicked his ass and he took off, but he broke JD's nose and knocked out two of Cody's teeth first.

"I ever see that guy again," Cody says to me, "he's a fucking dead man." 'Course, we never did—place this size, you're lucky to see the same person twice. Maybe next year . . .

Y'know, there's one thing I never did figure out. Every once in a while, usually while we were taking a picture of something, I'd hear somebody say, "No spectators." It took me a couple times to figure out they were talking about us, which makes no fucking sense to me at all. I mean, they bring all this amazing shit out to the middle of nowhere, dress up in these wild costumes and do all these crazy things, and they don't want people to take pictures? Why the fuck not? I mean, that's like telling people not to take pictures at Disneyland, y'know?

I just don't get it.

CHAPTER 3:

ABSURD THEORY

Afterward, Dex would reflect on a single, simple truth, over and over: *Murder makes you stupid.*

It wasn't the act itself that was stupid—though it could certainly be argued that destroying a life was always a bad idea—it wasn't even the psycho in the Evil Overlord Space Bunny outfit that he considered moronic. *The moron,* Dex thought, *is me.*

At first he'd just been driven by blind terror. He hadn't even thought of calling for help, just ran flat-out as fast as he could down the street, throwing wild glances behind him every few seconds to see if he was being chased. When the notion of screaming "Murder!" penetrated the fear, it was immediately crushed by two bigger and more irrational fears: first, that *everyone* here was violently insane, and once they knew he was Not One of Them, he would be run down, tied up, and beaten to death with Ping-Pong paddles.

Second, that he was going to embarrass himself.

This last idea, so absurd in and of itself, refused to

go away. When Dex finally slowed to a jog, his lungs on fire, he finally realized why the idea was persisting.

Maybe he hadn't seen a murder at all.

He stopped, looked back the way he'd come. He'd changed directions a few times during his sprint, cutting around vehicles and tents and structures, and though he'd blurred past groups of people, there wasn't anybody in sight now. Other than the distant, omnipresent thudding of techno, he was alone.

He bent over, breathing hard, and rested his hands on his knees. "Just a joke," he told himself between pants. "That's all, it was, that's why, no blood. Big joke, my expense. Like the, spanking."

Sure. He could even make himself believe that they'd faked that horrendous crunching noise when the rebar bit into Wade's skull. Sure. But . . .

His breathing was starting to slow. He straightened up and looked around again, paying more attention this time. He saw a big RV to his right, a cluster of tents to his left, two pickups and a tent-trailer across the street. He was suddenly aware he was dressed in only a pair of shorts and a T-shirt—he wasn't even wearing shoes. The ground was cold under his feet, and the air wasn't exactly toasty, either.

He had no idea where he was, or how to get back to the RV. Or if he *should* go back.

He didn't even know the name of the street the RV was *on*.

Murder, he thought. *It makes you stupid.*

Eventually, he did the only thing he could think of: he struck out for the biggest, best-lit structure he could

see, a tall structure framed in red neon glowing in the
distance—though it was hard to say just how tall or
far away it was. Its shape suggested a skinny pineapple
on top of a pole, or an art deco microphone; maybe it
was a radio tower.

The street he walked down was as wide as a three-
lane highway and covered in a fine, powdery dust that
felt like cool talcum powder on his feet. The stars
overhead were bright and numerous in a cloudless sky,
and ahead of him he could hear the *pop-pop-pop* of fire-
crackers.

The street reached an intersection, and there was a
signpost at the corner. ABSURD, read one; THEORY, read
the other. Dex squinted up at the stars and wondered
about God's sense of humor.

He headed up Absurd.

There was a figure ahead, walking toward him.
Maybe I should just ask for directions, he thought. *But—*

But there was something *wrong* with it.

Not in asking for help—he wasn't *that* stubborn—
but with the figure itself. Its body was too blocky, its
head the wrong proportions; was it wearing a helmet?

And then it stumped closer, and he realized he was
looking at Lego.

Specifically, one of the tiny figures that came with
Lego kits, blown up to life-size: squared-off torso and
limbs, C-shaped hands, a bright yellow cylinder for a
head with a raised disk on top where you could snap
on a plastic wig or hat . . . Dex suddenly knew there
was no way he could look into the blank, smiling face
painted on the head and make anything that resembled sense. He let the Lego-man walk past, and tried
not to stare.

At the end of the block, a car was parked with its nose toward him and the hood up. Somebody was poking around the engine with a flashlight; the occasional swear word or clank echoed off metal.

"Hello?" Dex said.

"Fuck! Goddamn piece of *shit!*"

"Uh—excuse me?"

The light stopped bobbing around and swiveled to shine directly into Dex's eyes. It wasn't a flashlight but a headlight, strapped to the man's forehead; its owner was only a vague shape behind its glare. "Yeah?" the man snapped.

"I—I just wondered if I could ask you a question."

The light dipped as the man looked him up and down. "I'm a little busy for tourist shit," he said. "Y'wanna know where the Porta-Johns are, I got no fuckin' idea." He turned back to his vehicle.

"No, I—I don't know where I am," Dex said. Which wasn't really true—he knew he was on Absurd, he just didn't know where Absurd *was.* "I need to get back to my RV," he finished lamely.

The man slammed the hood shut, giving Dex a good view of the car for the first time. It wasn't so much a vehicle as a weapon on wheels—*if the Batmobile had offspring that grew up listening to nothing but punk rock and heavy metal,* Dex thought, *it might look like that.* Jagged metal fins ran down its back and roof, coming together at the immense fanged skull that served as a hood ornament. A row of dolls' heads with steak knives through them adorned the dash. The entire thing was dimly illuminated by the small flame guttering at the end of a thick pipe sticking up from the rear, flanked by two large propane tanks.

Though he'd never seen one up close, Dex recognized it as a flamethrower.

The man stuck something in his mouth and lit it with a tiny butane torch; the brief flare of light was enough to show Dex the man had long black sideburns and a tatto of a scorpion across one cheek. Dex didn't get a good look at what the man was wearing, but it all seemed to be made of leather. Something silver glinted in his left hand, down by his side; some kind of tool.

The man took a long drag of his cigarette. He let the smoke out with his reply.

"RV. Lemme guess. Big white boxy thing, nice soft bed inside, air-conditioning that you run all the goddamn time because you *can't* be hot out in the *desert,* and since that takes power you run the *generator,* which spews carbon monoxide all over the people in tents camped next to you—may as well put 'em in fuckin' *killing jars*—as well as making a huge goddamn racket but what the fuck do *you* care? You're in your big insulated cratemobile eating microwaved burritos and watching porn on DVD while bitching about the fact that you can't get a signal on your goddamn CELLPHONE!"

"Uh," Dex said.

The man was waving the tool around now, his voice getting louder and louder. "You don't get it! You don't *belong* here! You're not even wearing *shoes,* for fuck's sake! Where do you think you are, poolside at the goddamn *Sheraton?* This is the *Black Rock Desert,* you moron, and it's trying to kill you *right fucking now.* And you know what?"

He leaned in close, and poked Dex in the chest with

the tool—a monkey wrench. "I hope it *does,*" the man growled.

Dex swallowed. "Okay," he said. "I'm going to leave now. . . ." He backed up slowly, then turned around and walked away.

When he'd taken about twenty steps, his fight-or-flight reflex abruptly switched sides with a surge of adrenaline. He stopped and looked back.

"Hey!" he called out angrily. "Maybe I *don't* belong here—but your car *sucks!*"

The monkey wrench just missed his head.

Murder, he thought as he ran. *It makes you stupid. . . .*

The driver chased him for over a block, but Dex was able to lose him fairly easily by ducking into a warren of tents and parked vehicles. He hid underneath a panel truck, trying to breathe shallowly and hoping the dust he'd kicked up wouldn't give him away. The driver stomped through a few seconds later, and kept on going.

When he hadn't come back after five minutes, Dex thought he'd probably given up and gone back to his deathmobile. Dex crept out from beneath the truck and headed in the opposite direction.

He didn't try talking to anyone else.

The blocks were long ones, and he'd gone three of them when the exhaustion hit him. He was cold, his feet were sore, and his stomach was tied in knots; all he wanted was to sit down someplace for a few minutes without someone trying to crack his skull open.

And there, miraculously, was a big, open tent full of couches.

He peered inside cautiously. A small halogen lantern in the far corner illuminated a three-walled canvas structure roughly twenty by twenty, with a ten-foot ceiling held up by a central pole. A half-dozen couches in varying condition were scattered throughout, and several huge Persian-style carpets covered the floor. Backpacks and coolers lined one wall, but nobody seemed to be at home.

He took a cautious step inside, and almost sighed at the softness of the rug underfoot.

I'll just sit down for a second, he thought. *If someone shows up, I'll apologize and leave.*

He sank onto a chesterfield that had once been white. Foam was bulging from a few rips along its top edge, but it was still extremely comfortable. There was even a blanket draped across one arm; he hesitated, then grabbed it and wrapped it around himself. *Just until I warm up a little.*

He was asleep in under a minute.

He opened his eyes groggily, not sure where or when he was.

A gigantic, purple panther stared back.

"Hello," Dex croaked. He was *tired* of being surprised; frankly, he just didn't have the energy. Once he'd had coffee he might be able to manage the whole jumping-up-in-startled-amazement thing, but until then the universe would have to settle for stunned detachment. If Wade had walked up at that moment with a piece of rebar jutting out of his head, Dex would have nodded, wished him a good morning and asked where he could find the nearest bathroom.

"Sounds like you could use some water," the panther said, stroking its whiskers thoughtfully. It extended a furry purple paw with a water bottle in it; Dex took the bottle gratefully, drank deep, and tried to give it back.

"Finish it," the panther said. "I've got a camelback." He straightened up from his crouch—and while he was wearing a knapsack, he looked all panther to Dex. All six purple feet of him.

"Have a good day," the panther said cheerfully. Dex noticed he was also carrying a sign on a stick; the placard read ANIMAL CONTROL ARE A BUNCH OF WUSSES. "Gotta go," the panther said. "My message must be heard!" He marched out into the bright sunlight and down the street, holding the sign in both paws.

"Thanks," Dex said belatedly.

"Well, well, Sleeping Beauty awakes," said a voice behind him.

Dex turned, still not quite awake. He saw that several other people were asleep on couches, some singly, some in pairs. A plump young woman in a sarong was eating a banana and studying him curiously. "You a friend of Shannon's?"

"Uh—no," Dex said. He was a terrible liar, so he avoided it whenever possible. "I don't know anyone here, actually—I just sort of fell asleep. I'm sorry, I'll get out of here—"

"Whoa, slow down," the woman said with a chuckle. "Nobody's gonna mind if you crashed—that's what the couches are *for*, man. You want a banana?"

"No, thanks," Dex said. He tried to stifle a yawn and failed. "Excuse me. Can I use your bathroom?"

This time she laughed out loud. "Sorry, we don't

have one. I can give you directions to the Porta-Johns, though."

"Sure," he said. "That'd be great, thanks."

She told him to go left down the street, take another left at the corner and go up two blocks. He thanked her again and left, blinking his way into late-morning brightness.

It had still been cool in the shade of the tent, but the air was heating up fast; he saw more than one person wearing only sandals and sunglasses. Most of them seemed to be going to the same place he was, too—there was a long line when he got there. Two lines actually; the row of sky-blue Porta-Johns, twenty or so, had a queue of people waiting patiently at either end for a door marker to switch from a red OCCUPIED to a green VACANT. Dex joined the nearest one.

At least here he didn't look out of place; several people were dressed much as he was. Not all, though—there was a woman clothed only in bright purple paint and a man wearing a sundress and flowered hat, among others. None of them, he noted gratefully, had a scorpion tattooed on their face.

He took mental stock while waiting, something he normally did over his first cup of coffee, and found the situation was just as bad as he remembered. Either (A) his boss had been murdered in front of his eyes and he was lost in a very strange and hostile place, or (B) he was lost in a very strange and hostile place and he was going to murder his boss himself for doing this to him.

He suddenly saw the pink rebar sinking into Wade's skull again, as surreal and vivid as a fever dream, and option B came apart like a cheap toy. His stomach churned, he gasped, "Excuse me!" to the people in front of him and bolted for a door just swinging open. He barely made it inside before he threw up.

Outside, someone said, "Better in there than on the playa . . ."

"Hey, I gotta barf, too! Lemme in!"

Laughter. His head spun.

He came out a few minutes later, feeling marginally better. *What I really need,* he thought, *is, is . . .*

And then he saw it, in the hands of a hairy-chested man dressed in a kilt and motorcycle boots. He marched right up to him, tapped him on one furry shoulder and said, "Pardon me. Where did you *get* that?"

The man took a sip out of his paper coffee cup and said, "Center Camp Café, of course."

"Of course," Dex said. "And you would get there from here *how?*"

The man grinned and pointed. "Straight down this street. Big-ass tent right in the middle, you can't miss it."

"Thank God," Dex said.

Unbelievably, it was just that simple.

It took him about fifteen minutes to get there. He was not accosted by leather-clad, tattooed lunatics, cross-dressing giants or pink assassins. He passed or was passed by many strange things, but determinedly kept his eyes straight ahead; he would not be distracted by anything as trivial as a bicycle that moved sideways like a crab, or a man carrying a huge gourd painted like a gigantic green penis.

He was going to get *coffee*.

The street—he was on Dogma, apparently—ended at something called the Karmic Circle. In the dark this might have confused him, but he understood quickly that Karmic Circle was an avenue that ringed Center Camp. And in the middle of that, clearly visible, was the "big-ass tent" that housed the café. It was huge, a circular structure a good thirty feet high at its peak; it must have covered almost an acre. It had multiple entrances, each of them large enough to ride an elephant through, and bike stands between them crammed with dusty cycles. He made his way across the wide plaza that surrounded the café, dodging hordes of people on foot or wheels, and entered the shade of the nearest entrance gratefully.

Inside, it was divided into multiple lounging areas, much like where he'd spent the night but on a much larger and more varied scale. The apex of the tent was an open ring thirty feet in diameter, with a huge metal ball suspended from an intricate web of steel cables. It glinted in the sun, throwing shards of light onto the maze painted on the floor beneath it.

And against one wall, exactly what he was looking for: a long counter emitting the *ffffsssshh!* of steamed milk, the aroma of fresh-ground beans, the glint of chromed equipment.

There was a second of panic as he groped for his wallet, but it was still there. He joined the shortest line he saw, and two minutes later he was pouring sugar through the foam of an extra-large latte.

He looked around, spotted a vacant couch, shuffled over and sank into it.

He leaned back and took a long, slow sip.

He closed his eyes, tried to think . . . but that brought back visions of Wade's head, so he opened them again. *Focus, Dex, focus. Time to figure out what to do.*

He couldn't concentrate—the caffeine hadn't made its way into his bloodstream yet. He took another sip and looked around.

Panels of some tough industrial fabric made up the skin of the tent, black twenty-by-five-foot lengths alternating with long wedges of green, attached to each other by rows of black plastic zap straps. The purpose of the structure was obviously to provide shade rather than shelter—the zap straps left wide gaps between panels, and the fabric itself was a wide-weave mesh.

Then his eyes fell on a piece of paper lying next to him on the couch—some kind of newsletter?

The headline read: "MURDER IN BLACK ROCK CITY."

A second passed. Dex stared at the paper but made no move to pick it up; he was desperately hoping it would go away. Stubbornly, it continued to exist.

"Shit," Dex sighed, and picked it up.

At least he could eliminate option B. . . .

BLACK ROCK GAZETTE, August 26 Edition (Tuesday): The Washoe County Sheriff's Office is investigating what appears to be a homicide committed sometime on Monday in Black Rock City.

Officer Pete Sempel said a body was found late Monday night after a mysterious fire started in an RV at Dubious and Reality. The fire, apparently set to destroy evidence, was quickly put out by alert members of a nearby camp. The RV is currently considered a crime scene, and the police are asking Burners to stay clear while they investigate. They are withholding the identity of the victim pending notification of next of kin, but will say he was a white male in his forties.

The police are also asking for your help: if you saw anyone running from the vicinity of Dubious and Reality between nine and eleven PM last night, please go to Playa Info at Center Camp and ask to talk to an officer. Police say they're also interested in talking to a Dexter Edden, who may or may not be a suspect; if you know the whereabouts of this person, tell someone at Playa Info and they'll put you in touch with the authorities.

Dex read the story three times. He stopped himself after that, realized he was becoming compulsive. There was nothing else to be learned, not from this flimsy sheet of paper.

Wade was dead.

He knew that already, of course; he'd just been trying to deny it, in the hope that all this would go away. Now he could admit to himself this was real, that Wade wasn't going to show up and laugh in his face. He felt a weird sort of relief wash over him, partly because he now had at least one concrete fact to work with—and partly because he wasn't being made a fool of.

Or was he . . .

There was no mention of Darth Bunny. Nobody was on the lookout for a big, pink murderer . . . which meant maybe no one had seen him. Actually, according to what had almost been Wade's last words, Dex was the only other person who even knew Rafe was going to be there . . . a fact Rafe obviously had serious problems with.

Here—check it out. Along with the voice came a sudden sense-memory of duct tape, warm and plasticky against his hand as he grabbed the hilt.

Rafe had been wearing gloves. Pink ones.

"Oh, *crap,*" Dex whispered.

He'd been set up. Wade's murder had been planned—isolated location, head-to-foot disguise that would minimize even traces of DNA, custom-made murder weapon—but a suspicious Wade had brought Dex along as insurance. That hadn't stopped Rafe, though—he'd not only tried to kill Dex, he'd created his own insurance policy on the spot by getting Dex's prints on the murder weapon first.

This was looking worse and worse. If the whole thing was premeditated, Rafe must have had an escape route and an alibi worked out, too . . . he wouldn't have left any evidence behind at all, except for the lightsaber. That he would have left outside, where it would be sure to be found—with Dex's prints all over it.

And where was Mr. Dexter Edden? Why, he'd been seen running away from the scene. He wasn't running away because he was *guilty,* oh no—he was running away from a big, pink Lord of the Sith.

Let's not forget the bunny ears, Dex thought gloomily. *Nothing like those little details to add credibility to a story . . .*

Murder, it seemed, didn't make *everyone* stupid.

Just him.

• • •

Two lattes later, he still didn't know what to do.

He was definitely awake, though. His stomach rumbled, but he didn't feel hungry—actually, he was a little nauseous. The insistent pulsing behind his eyes threatened to become a pounding, and his body was feeling achy and—unbelievably—a little chilled. He'd gotten up to go to the bathroom twice already; luckily, there were Porta-Johns only a block away. He'd come back both times, having no idea where else to go.

He could go to the police, turn himself in; he'd walked right past a big sign reading, PLAYA INFO, on his way to the john. But the more coffee he drank, the worse the idea seemed—even though nothing else came to mind.

"Excuse me?" The speaker was a mid-thirties man with spiky blond hair and a goatee, wearing a red cape, sunglasses, sandals and nothing else. He had the words *CAPTAIN FUN* painted on his chest in red and held a canteen in one hand. "Can I ask you a question?"

"I guess," Dex said. The last thing he wanted was to be dragged into another weird encounter—but it just wasn't in his nature to be rude.

"Do you have a headache?" Captain Fun asked.

"Beginning to," Dex said warily. He waited for the punch line.

"Stomach queasy? Body aches, maybe even chills?"

"Uh—yes, actually," Dex said, puzzled.

"You like helicopter rides?" The man sat down next to him.

"Not particularily," Dex said with a frown. "Why?"

"Because you're suffering from dehydration," the

man said. "And if they have to put more than two bags of saline into your arm, they'll airlift you to Reno. Here." He handed Dex his canteen.

Dex hesitated, then took it and drank. Something in his body responded; he found himself gulping water so hard he had to stop just to catch his breath.

"Easy," the man said gently. "Do you know where the medical tent is?"

Dex shook his head, panting.

"I'll take you over there. When was the last time you drank something other than coffee?"

Dex thought back. "I had a few sips of water when I woke up," he admitted.

Captain Fun whistled and then shook his head. "Usually, by the time you get really thirsty it's already too late," he said. "Drinking coffee just makes things worse—it's a diuretic."

"A what?"

"Makes you pee. Come on, I'll show you where it is."

Medical tent. Paramedics, doctors, legal forms.

"I—I can't go."

"Don't worry, it doesn't cost anything—"

"That's not it. Just—just let me drink a little more water first, okay?"

"Sure," Fun said with a shrug. "Finish the whole thing—just don't gulp it, all right? You'll give yourself water cramps."

Dex nodded and took another drink, slowly this time.

"You need to cool off, too," Fun said. "Dump some of that over your head—don't worry, I have plenty more."

Dex hesitated, then did as he said. The cool water sluicing over his head was a shock at first, making him gasp—then it felt wonderful. He emptied half the canteen that way, soaking his clothes and the couch as well.

Fun grinned. "Bet that feels good . . . of course, the docs have a trailer with actual air-conditioning they stick heat-cases in. Imagine how good *that* would feel . . ."

Dex looked at him, took another drink, then asked, "What are you, some kind of roving paramedic?"

The Captain laughed. "No, all my prescriptions are strictly under-the-counter. I was just playing a game of orgasmic pinball and noticed you sitting there. No water bottle, no sun hat, not even sunglasses . . . drinking coffee, rubbing your temples, looking kinda pale and shaky. When I actually saw you shiver, I had to come over and say something."

"Thanks," Dex said. "I . . ." He trailed off. "Thanks," he said again.

"No problem. You need some help?"

The question caught him off-guard; he answered without thinking. "Yeah," he said quietly. "Yeah, I think I do. . . ."

He didn't tell Captain Fun about the murder—instead, he made up a plausible story about getting separated from the people he was traveling with. "I was pretty drunk," he said. "I woke up on a couch in a tent, and managed to find this place. I don't even know where my camp is."

The last statement was close to being true—Dex

hadn't known where the RV was parked until he'd read the location in the *Black Rock Gazette.*

"Well, you can put up a sign on the message board," Fun said. "And one on Playanet—if your friends check either of those, you can hook up."

"Playanet?"

"Sure—the whole festival's networked. Long as you've got a wireless card and a laptop, you can log on—"

Dex's eyes widened, and he missed the rest of what Captain Fun was saying.

Laptop.

Not his . . . *Wade's.*

Wade had always been a little paranoid, and the first thing he'd done after they'd rented the RV was find a cubbyhole to stash his laptop. "Fucking RV," he'd said. "Goddamn aluminum everything—doors, latches, locks. A ten-year-old with a pair of pliers could break in here."

And Dex had seen where he'd hidden it.

"—still be easier if we got the Rangers to help, but I can see you've got this thing about authority," Captain Fun said. "Which, frankly, I can relate to . . . so, *screw* authority, we'll find your friends on our own. Although if you don't keep drinking water every few minutes, I *will* drag you down to the REMSA tent myself, understand?"

"Sure. Absolutely."

"Okay, then," Captain Fun said, standing up. "First things first. Let's get you something to *eat.*" He looked down at Dex, frowned, and scratched his pubic hair unself-consciously. "And some protective gear—you aren't even wearing *sunscreen,* are you?"

Dex shook his head.

Fun sighed. "Follow me. . . ."

He led Dex to another couch, pulled a green canvas knapsack from beneath it, and took out a bottle of sunblock. "Be generous, and don't forget your ears," Fun said. "I'll be just over there." He pointed to a pinball machine a few feet away.

Dex poured some lotion into one hand, started to spread it down his arm—

"Mmmmm. Ooh. Ooh."

Dex looked up sharply, thinking he was being mocked . . . then realized the sound had come from the pinball machine.

"Orgasmic pinball," he muttered to himself. "Right."

"Oooooooooh. Uh. Uh. Uh."

It *was* more interesting than buzzers and bells, he thought . . . but it wasn't what he wanted to hear as he smeared a white, slippery liquid all over his body. By the time he was finished, the machine had climaxed a hundred times and he felt like everybody in the room was staring at him.

He approached Captain Fun, who was watching someone else play. "I'm, uh, ready."

"Just in time, too—you're already looking kinda red," Fun said. "Your face, anyway . . . okay, now we gotta get you a hat."

"You're not wearing one."

"*I'm* not suffering from dehydration. Drink some more water."

Dex did so, feeling like a child who'd been told to eat his vegetables.

"Look, I can tell this is your first time here," Fun said. "And your first time can be Heaven, or it can be Hell. Depends on a lotta different factors—but the two most important, in my opinion, are preparation and attitude. Preparation, you clearly don't got."

"I guess not," Dex said neutrally. What he wanted to do was scream, *I never wanted to be here in the first place!* . . . but at the moment, Captain Fun was the only friend he had.

"No problem. Hey, I've seen lots of people go through the same thing you are right now . . . they feel overwhelmed, out-of-place, completely lost. Well, maybe not *quite* as lost as you are. But close." Fun smiled. "Don't worry—it gets better."

It can hardly get worse, Dex thought. He forced a smile onto his face and said, "I'll try to work on my attitude."

"Work on your *attitude?"* Fun shook his head. "I can see that Captain Fun is sorely needed here . . . c'mon. We got places to go." He strode off, motioning for Dex to follow him.

They left the café, and walked across the dusty plaza to one of the camps that ringed the edge. This one was a shade structure open on three sides, with a cluster of bikes parked in front and more beneath the canopy, being tinkered with by a dozen or so men and women. Tools and boxes of parts were strewn about; the atmosphere was relaxed but focused.

"They'll let me borrow a hat?" Dex asked.

"More important than a hat, actually. Wait here a second, and stay in the shade." Fun walked up to a young guy with grease stains up to his elbows and smoking a cigarette. He talked to him for a moment, then pulled something small and shiny out of his backpack and handed it over. He followed the guy inside an adjacent tent.

Dex looked around. The medical tent was right next door, a couple of guys in shorts and bright yellow shirts lounging around the entrance; even though he knew they weren't cops, Dex quickly looked away.

Fun came out a minute later, wheeling a bike with him. He walked up to Dex and said, "You don't have a bike, do you?"

"No," Dex said, dismayed. He could see Captain Fun getting bored with his dull, uninteresting problems and riding away—

"Well, now you do," Fun said cheerfully. He pushed the bike forward and Dex reflexively grabbed the handlebars. "Mine's parked outside the café—hang on a sec and I'll get it."

"You got someone to lend me a bike?" Dex said. "Tell him I'll take good care of it—"

"You better—it's *yours* now," Fun said. " 'Pack it in, pack it out'—when you leave the site, that bike's going with you."

"But—you mean you got someone to *give* me a bike?" Dex said carefully.

"No, I got them to give *me* a bike, and now I'm giving it to you. That's the way a gift economy works." He saw the confusion on Dex's face and said, "You really have no clue, do you? Leave No Trace? Welcome Home? Piss Clear?"

"Excuse me?"

"Did you even *glance* at the *Survival Guide?* No,

wait, forget I said that—I just remembered how we met, a whole ten minutes ago. Okay, this is how it works—you see that big white tent across the way?" Fun pointed at a large structure on the other side of the plaza; it had a big sign that read, ARCTICA. "That's where you can buy ice, at two bucks a bag. That—and the coffee you were sucking back in the café—are the only two things in Black Rock City you can actually *buy*. With money, anyway."

"But—aren't there bars?"

"Sure. Bars, restaurants, casinos, hair salons . . . but none of 'em take money." Fun started walking; Dex followed.

"Then what *do* they take?"

"It's not *about* taking—it's about *giving*. Like I said, that's how a gift economy works . . . it's basically capitalism in reverse. Instead of everybody trying to grab what they can out of the system, everybody puts in instead."

"That—wouldn't work," Dex said.

"On a large scale, for an extended period of time, of course not. But for a week, in a self-contained system? You'd be—correction, you *will* be—amazed at just how well it works." They stopped by a bike rack outside the café, and Fun fished a key out of his pack. He unchained a fat-tired mountain bike covered in holographic tape, a plastic velociraptor wired to its handlebars. "Anyway, the BRC bike shop always brings a few spares to give away. I just gifted one of the mechanics to give me one in half-decent shape."

"What did you give him?"

"Just a few extra 'shrooms I had," Fun answered.

"Chocolate-covered. Figured I should get rid of 'em before they melted and made a mess, anyway."

"Ah," Dex said. *Great. Now I'm involved in drug dealing, too . . . or was it drug dealing if you gave them away?*

They mounted their bikes and rode off.

CHAPTER 4:

KARMIC CIRCLE

File B (Santa Crusty): Yeah, I've been going to Burning Man for thirteen years now—since before it was out in the desert, in fact. I wasn't there the first time Larry Harvey burned a wooden man on a San Francisco beach—that'd be in '86—but I was there the last time he tried, in 1990; eight hundred people had gathered to see him do it, and they were having problems with the Park Police. They decided to move it out to the middle of nowhere, and I was one of the fools that went along. It was just such a crazy idea I wanted to see what they'd do with it.

Only ninety of us followed him out to the Black Rock Desert for the first burn, but a couple hundred came the next year, and twice as many the year after that—actually, the population more or less doubled every succeeding year until it reached around eight thousand in '96, then slowed down a bit. Still, after seventeen years we're up to almost thirty thousand, and still growing. In all that time, I've only missed one year.

Felt *exactly* like missing Christmas.

I guess the whole Santa thing started off as a joke—what environment could be more different from the North Pole than the middle of a desert, right? Except that anybody who's spent a night in the desert knows how bloody cold it can get, and when the sun goes down you're suddenly glad you're wearing that big red suit.

But that's not the only reason people join Santa. We Santas are a permanent fixture in Black Rock City because it's *great* being Santa. It's even spread to other cities; every December packs of roving Santas descend upon bars, malls, and hotels all over the world to bring cheer to the holiday season. Cheer usually involves naughty Christmas carols, occasional nudity and lots and lots of drinking, but Santa has a strict set of rules he abides by. Never abuse the public, keep everything friendly, and leave whenever mall security asks you to. Santa's all about being jolly, not being arrested. And, of course, gifts.

Now, some people might try to tell you *they* came up with the whole gifting thing, but they're just trying to steal Santa's thunder. I mean, come on—giving stuff away is Santa's *bag*. Christmas Camp was the very first theme camp, started by Peter Doty back in '93. Gave away spiked eggnog, but you had to eat some fruitcake first. God-awful stuff, that fruitcake . . .

Things are a lot different now. People give away all sorts of things you'd never expect to find in the desert, the more incongruous the better. One group brought one of those refrigerated trucks they use to haul meat cross-country down here, turned it into a little night-club called Antarctica. People'd go inside and dance in parkas. Or Freezing Man, an ice-cream truck that drove around with a reggae band on the roof; you had to have a special coupon to get a frozen treat. Back then a lot more bars ran on barter instead of donations, so one of those coupons was pretty close to hard currency.

Sure, we started with a barter economy, but that's kind of out-of-fashion these days. I have to say I'm glad. Barter has its place, but the real spirit of Black Rock City has always been about giving—and I'm not just talking about generosity, either. See, one of the great things about getting a present from a total stranger is that plunge into the unknown. You never know what's going to be under the tree—maybe something useless, maybe something great. Maybe something that'll change your life, or at least the way you think. Some of the best gifts I've ever received were ideas.

And a really good gift isn't about trying to outdo anybody else—it's a little piece of you. Maybe it's you trying to be funny, or sexy, or smart—maybe it's just you asking people to *like* you. Whatever it is, it creates a little connection between you and someone else.

Is there an element of competition to it? Sure. But think about that for a second. I heard someone say once that the perfect marriage is two people trying to see who can make the other one happier. That's what a gift economy is about—people competing to make each other happier. A whole city, doing that for a whole week? Sounds like Heaven to me.

Most first-time Burners don't truly get the phrase, "Welcome Home," at least not right away. But if you really embrace this experience, let it become part of you, you will. Black Rock City becomes *your* city—you may only get to live here a week out of every fifty-two, but it's still your home.

You know, no matter how long some people live in a particular place, if they visit their parents for the holidays they still call it "going home for Christmas." Well, once you become a citizen of Black Rock City, that's what coming back here feels like: going home for Christmas. Not the Christmas you have now, with twenty-four-hour-a-day marketing and crowded malls and an overstressed credit card, but the Christmas you used to have as a kid. The one full of magic.

Think back. Christmas morning. You've been looking forward to this moment for *months.* The tree is all blinking colored lights and shiny ornaments. And under that tree might be *anything* . . . anything at all. It's a perfect moment, anticipation and excitement and unlimited potential, all wrapped up in a giddy sense of wonder.

That's Burning Man.

That's what it means to Santa, anyway. Of course, you'll get a different answer from every Santa you ask. Santa is large; he contains multitudes. Does Santa contradict himself? All the time. Santa is many things to many people, and all he asks is that you keep the spirit of giving alive. And drink enough to keep those cheeks nice and red.

Problems? Sure. Santa may be a saint, but not everyone loves him. The Evil Klowns, for instance—they *hate* Santa. Santa and the Klowns have had many a rumble, yes sir. The pies and the eggnog have flown thick and fast out on the playa. . . .

Does anyone take it seriously? Of course not.

Well . . . there was this *one* guy, okay? But he wasn't a Santa. He was with the Klowns, and I got the feeling he took everything a little too far. He had this big wooden mallet with him, and I thought it was just a prop—the Klowns are big on props. I was driving my sleigh—it's an art car the Santas made, looks just like a sleigh being towed by eight Grinches—and I parked next to the café and went inside for a minute. When I come out, this maniac is smashing the hell out of the sleigh with the mallet, screaming, "Death to Santa!" I was so freaked I didn't know what to do—I mean, he was going *apeshit*. Looked kind of like an ape, to tell the truth; short guy with a really beefy chest and arms.

Anyway, his own crew finally pulled him down and took away the mallet. They apologized to me, told me he was new, and stripped him of his Klown status right there. The guy just laughed, swore at us and took off.

He's *still* on Santa's naughty list.

CHAPTER 5:

REVEALED EVIDENCE

The first place Captain Fun took him was four blocks away, a small geodesic dome covered in white and silver triangles of fabric with a big pink sign out front that read, KOSTUME KULT. He told them Dex needed a hat, and Dex soon found himself looking at a huge pile of assorted headgear. He chose a relatively tame white cap with a row of bones hot-glued across the brim. Fun gave the man and woman running the camp each a temporary tattoo mounted on a piece of paper, and both happily accepted his offer to apply them with his tongue. Dex spent several minutes pretending to adjust his new hat in a mirror.

Then it was off to a place called Barter Bob's Forgotten Supplies, a kind of trading post offering just about anything. There were no tables, or even a tent—just heaps of stuff laid out on the ground like a garage sale where the furniture had sold first. Dex had no problem finding a pair of sunglasses.

He thought for a second, then fished in the pocket of his shorts and pulled out his key ring. He took off the nail clippers attached to it and handed them to the bearded man running the place—Bob, he supposed. "Uh, here."

"Thanks," Bob said. "I'm sure somebody will really appreciate these."

"You're welcome," Dex said. The clippers were gold-plated, given to him as a joke years ago at an office party—still, he was sure they were worth ten times what the cheap pair of plastic sunglasses were.

For some reason, he felt oddly pleased with himself.

Captain Fun located a water bottle for him, and even got it filled. "Okay, you have the basics," Fun said. "Now, how about some food?"

Dex still felt a little nauseous, but he had to admit food sounded like a good idea.

They went back to Center Camp, to a place called the Pancake Playhouse. A few minutes later Dex was seated on a bench at a long table, wolfing down hotcakes smothered in blueberry syrup and washing them down with gulps of water from his own bottle.

"Well, you've been fed, watered, and outfitted," Fun said, stroking his goatee. It was shaped like an hourglass, Dex noted, a little triangle under his lower lip connecting to the top of another on his chin. "Let's see if we can find you shelter."

Dex swallowed his last mouthful of pancake before answering. "I really appreciate this," he said. "But about the RV I was staying in—there's something I didn't tell you."

"Let me guess. You can't really go back there, right?"

Dex blinked. "Uh . . ."

"Because it's not really *there*, is it?"

Dex's heart began to hammer. *He knows. He's figured it out.*

"I figured it out," Fun said. "The clothes, the lack of preparation, not knowing where your camp was . . . obvious, really."

Dex put his plate down on the table carefully. He wondered if he should just bolt and take his chances.

"You snuck in without paying, didn't you?" Fun said.

"What?"

"Don't worry, I'm not going to turn you in . . . there never was an RV, right? You got past the gate staff somehow, got into the booze, and you've been wandering around ever since. That about right?"

"More or less," Dex said, thinking hard. "I *did* come in an RV—they picked me up hitchhiking. Once we were inside, they said they wanted, uh, sexual favors if I was going to stay with them. So I left."

Fun shook his head and grinned. "Man, oh, man . . . look, I don't approve of what you did, okay? But since this *is* your first time here, let's see if I can educate you properly. I do my job right, next year you'll be happy to pay full price."

"Oh, I will, I will," Dex said. "Believe me, I'm going to pay . . ."

"I think I can find you a spot in Aetheria," Fun said. "It's a bit of a ride, but a nice neighborhood."

They went back out into the sun, got back on their bikes. "We'll take the Esplanade," Fun said. "Just stay close."

Fun led him around the Center Camp Café and past an immense multicolored sphere mounted on a scaffolding at least three stories high. As they rode by, Dex saw that the sphere had several layers, each one made of transparent colored panels; the layers were rotating around each other, turning the whole thing into a huge kaleidoscope . . . and there were people inside, standing on a little platform and gazing out over the city.

The Esplanade appeared to be a main thoroughfare of sorts, with the city proper on one side and some sort of huge, mainly empty space on the other. Dex noticed two things almost at once: first, the empty space allowed him to see that the street wasn't straight—it curved away from Center Camp in both directions; second, that another, straighter avenue led directly from Center Camp to some sort of Aztec-looking pyramid with a statue at its peak.

"What's that?" Dex asked.

Fun glanced over. "What?"

"That," Dex said, pointing.

Fun looked again, looked back sharply at Dex, then slammed on his brakes and came to a dead halt.

"You're *kidding*," he said.

"How big *is* that thing?" Dex said, staring. At first he'd thought it was just another tent structure with a life-size sculpture of a person on top, but now his eyes were adjusting to the perspective. Those little dots at the base were people . . . and the temple itself was at least half a mile away.

"Including the base, the whole thing stands around eighty feet tall," Fun said. "That's the *Man* . . . man. Hey, what *is* your name?"

"Lyle," Dex said, still staring. "*That's* the Burning Man?" Somehow, he hadn't expected there to be an actual figure involved.

"Not yet," Fun said. "Not until Saturday night. *Then* he burns . . . along with a whole lotta other stuff."

The temple the Man stood on was at least four stories tall. *Must have taken a lot of time and effort to build,* Dex thought. "How do they keep the base from catching on fire?" he asked. "Something that size, it can't be made of metal or brick . . ."

Fun stared at him—then whooped with laughter. Dex stared back, confused.

"Oh, Lyle . . . thank you, man. Really," Fun said when he got himself back under control. "Being able to tell people what you just said is *more* than adequate compensation for everything I've done for you. And to answer your question . . . no, the base isn't fireproof. Exactly the opposite, in fact."

"But—oh. Really?"

"Don't take my word for it, Lyle—on Saturday night, you can see for yourself."

They pedaled on.

Aetheria, it turned out, was not just a camp but an entire village, composed mainly of angular white structures Fun called pods. They were made of triangular panels of white cardboard, joined at the seams with strips of white plastic. Smaller, translucent triangles set into the cardboard provided light. Each pod was roughly spherical and about the size of a small cabin.

The village was spread over most of a block, with vehicles and tents clustered around its edges. Fun led Dex to a pod on the far side of the village, leaned his bike against the wall and entered without knocking.

Inside, sleeping bags and duffels were strewn about in a semiorganized way. A card table against one wall held an electric lantern, a roll of duct tape and a bottle of massage oil. A woman sat cross-legged on a rug in the middle of the pod, wrapping fluorescent orange tape around the tubing of a hula hoop. She looked up when they came in, and smiled.

"Hey, Captain," she said. "What's up?"

"Lorilei, this is Lyle," Fun said. "Lyle, Lorilei."

"Hello," Dex said.

Lorilei was in her twenties, with long brown dreadlocks interwoven with strips of brightly colored yarn. She had thick eyebrows over green eyes, freckles over a snub nose, and slightly crooked teeth in a wide and dimple-framed mouth.

If Dex could have been said to have a fetish, it would have to have been a woman's smile. It was always the first thing he noticed, and it wasn't just the mouth he paid attention to—a smile involved the entire face, not just teeth and lips. Lorilei's eyes, for instance, crinkled up at the corners at the same time.

She beamed at Dex and said, "Hey, Lyle—great hat!"

"Thank you," he said reflexively. Maybe he was just in a particularily emotional state, but she had one of the loveliest grins he'd ever seen—even that one off-kilter tooth was somehow endearing. It was at least a full five seconds before he noted what Lorilei was wearing *besides* that terrific smile . . .

Nothing at all.

"Ulk," Dex said. He said it quite clearly, and with perfect enunciation. If anyone present had been asked to spell what he had just said, Dex was sure they could have done so without difficulty. Fortunately, neither of them seemed to notice.

"Dex needs a place to crash," Fun said. "Got any room?"

"We have enough floor space, sure. How much gear does he have?"

"You're looking at it."

She raised an eyebrow. Dex stared at it desperately, trying not to let his gaze wander any lower. Her skin was a golden brown, with sprays of freckles in the most interesting places . . .

"I guess I can dig up some spare bedding. Food and water, too?"

"I'm really sorry," Dex said. "I can pay for whatever I eat—"

"Huh?" Lorilei cocked her head to one side and cupped a hand to her ear. Tiny silver rings glinted in a row of piercings that ran all the way from the lobe up to the slightly pointed tip. "What was that word? Did you catch that, Captain?"

"Sounded like . . . *bay?*"

"More like *pray.*"

"No, no, it was closer to *play.*"

"Well," she said, looking Dex in the eye, "if you want to bay, pray, *or* play for your food, you're more than welcome."

"Thanks," Dex said. "I'll keep that in mind." He tried his best to sound as relaxed and whimsical as they were, but his delivery fell somewhere between sarcastic and unhinged.

And then she was standing up, and Dex saw that she had *tattoos* . . . tattoos in places freckles were afraid to go.

"If you clean up after yourself, you can hang out as long as you like," Lorilei said. "Also, you have to be at least mildly interesting. He's interesting, right, Captain?" She looked him up and down frankly as he tried not to do the same to her. Was that a butterfly?

"Hidden depths. I can tell," Fun said. "Besides, I know how much you love strays."

"This is *not* the Black Rock City Pound and Lyle here is *not* a puppy and did you *really* say 'Ulk'?"

"Not, *no*," he blurted.

"Well, 'Not no' would be *yes*, wouldn't it . . . ?" she said, and did something with her eyebrows that made her smile take a sharp turn from sweet to wicked.

Dex was suddenly very glad he wasn't naked.

Fun was staying in a tent-trailer on the edge of Aetheria, a rickety old Lionel that was probably older than Dex; Fun showed him where it was, then told Dex he was going inside for a nap. "Siesta time," he said. "Important tip from Captain Fun—get your rest when you can. I'd advise you do the same."

"I think I will," Dex said.

He got back to the pod just as Lorilei was leaving, hula hoop slung over one shoulder. "Gonna get a little practice in," she said. "I laid out a bedroll over there if you want to catch some z's."

"Thanks," Dex said. "I guess I'll see you later?"

She laughed at the look on his face. "Don't worry, I'm not going far," she said. "You need anything, I'll be on the other side of the Esplanade." She'd put on a pair of dusty, knee-high leather boots, and now stood as tall as he did. When she turned and walked away, he couldn't help himself; how could anyone not watch *that?* She had the most incredible, superb—

She spun around and caught him.

His face burst into flames. He was glad; maybe, if he was lucky, it would kill him fast. Then he wouldn't have to hear her say—

Nothing. She just grinned, spun back, and kept going.

"Ulk," Dex said.

He went inside, lay down, and tried to think.

Wade's laptop. If the fire hadn't destroyed it, it might hold information that could clear him—or at least point toward some other suspect. All he had to do was alert the authorities to its existence, and then— what?

Then they could trip any number of security pre-cautions, erasing vital evidence. Dex had very little confidence in the technical skills of public sector em-ployees; he'd dealt with too many civil servants that treated computers as if they were jukeboxes that would work properly if you just hit them in the right place.

And why should the police search for another sus-pect when they had him? His prints on the murder weapon, him running away . . . He had to see what was on that laptop *himself.*

Which meant going back to the RV, somehow get-ting past the cops, and retrieving the laptop. Then, as-suming he could pull some kind of relevant data off the thing, he'd have to find a way to get that informa-tion into the hands of someone who would take it seri-ously.

It seemed hopeless. The laptop could have been destroyed in the fire, or maybe Rafe had found it and taken it with him. And who *was* Rafe anyway?

He tossed and turned, unable to get comfortable on the thin foam pad. He was hot, worried, and he'd drunk too much coffee. After a while he gave up, drank some more water, and realized he needed to use the bathroom again. Luckily, Captain Fun had pointed out the nearest row of Porta-Johns as they'd arrived.

He put on his sunglasses and hat, slung his canteen over his shoulder, and stepped outside. *Let's see—he said they were straight up Revealed, between Dogma and Evidence* . . .

And then he saw Lorilei.

She was standing just across the broad expanse of the Esplanade, arms raised above her head, eyes closed. Both her feet were planted firmly on the ground . . . but she was dancing. The hoop didn't so much circle her body as embrace it, caressing her hips, her belly, her neck . . . and then it had traveled up past her head, out to the end of one outstretched arm and around her wrist, where it spun for five or six heartbeats before descending gracefully once more to orbit her torso. It seemed as if the hoop moved on its own, that her muscles were responding to it rather than the other way around; as if she were undulating her way through some ghostly tunnel, only the thinnest ring of it made visible by her touch.

He told himself to look away before she opened her eyes, to not get caught twice . . . but he couldn't. He found himself *wanting* to be caught, to be favored with that amazing smile again; but she never opened her eyes, just kept moving in that easy, sinuous way, a brown-skinned serpent swimming up an unseen river.

After a moment, he forced himself to walk away.

Looking back on it later, he would recognize the moment as the first time he'd seen anything at Burning Man as other than threatening or bizarre. Such a simple thing, a woman playing with a hula hoop . . . but the thing that had stood out, more than her lack of clothing or the backdrop she danced against, was the look on her face. Joy? Peace? He couldn't quite put a word to it—it was something of both, but something else, too.

He was so distracted, he almost walked right into the robot.

"Uh, sorry," Dex said, stepping back. The robot in question was large, blue, and eerily familiar; it wasn't until Dex saw his bright-red partner that he realized he was looking at the Red Rocker and Blue Bomber. They belonged to a game called *Rock 'Em Sock 'Em Robots* Dex had owned as a child. He'd always played the blue one.

"No sweat!" the Bomber said. "Snack?" He proffered a bowl filled with pretzel sticks and toasted Cheerios, a mix Dex hadn't seen in years. It was called—

"Nuts and Bolts," Dex said. "Thanks." He took a small handful.

"Gotta keep your salt intake up," the Red Rocker said.

"I guess you do," Dex agreed. He suddenly felt embarrassed; not because he was conversing with two people in robot suits, but because he had nothing to offer them in return. Dex hadn't really noticed the music playing on a nearby camp's boom box until it picked that moment to end, turning a moment's awkward silence into an eternity.

"You're listening to 94.5, Burning Man Information Radio," a woman's sultry voice announced. "More music in a minute—but first, a *very* interesting update on that possible murder in Black Rock City. Sources close to the investigation tell me that Dexter Edden, seen fleeing the scene, is definitely the prime suspect in this case. All vehicles leaving Burning Man are being checked by the police, and patrols of the city perimeter have been stepped up. So if you're going out to party by the Trash Fence, be warned . . . they don't want this guy leaving without answering a few questions, that's for sure. Even the airport is being watched, just in case he tries to steal a plane. . . . Hey, anybody out there remember the movie *The Warriors*? Came out in the late seventies, about a gang from Coney Island that gets stranded in New York City and has to *fight* their way home? If you do, you're gonna understand why I'm playing this next song . . ."

The opening bars of "Nowhere to Run" boomed out.

"Excuse me," Dex said with a glassy smile.

He left the robots standing in the bright sun, and managed to find his way back to the village, the pod, and the foam pad with the sleeping bag.

He curled up and lay there, eyes wide open, for a long, long time.

He finally went to sleep because it was the only safe place left to go.

In his dream, he woke up. He raised his head from the pillow, still groggy, and looked around.

Motel room. Motel bed. Motel furniture, motel television, motel art on the motel walls.

Panic.

He ripped the covers off, his heart pounding and his breath coming in choking gasps. He sat up, then stood up, trying to get his bearings. Where was he? What was going on? What was *wrong*?

He stumbled to the bathroom, turned on the light, tried to get himself under control. He looked in the mirror; he looked like himself. He ran some lukewarm water, splashed it on his face. Finally, his breathing slowed and he felt a little better. His head was still all unfocused, though; it was like coming out of anesthesia. He still wasn't quite sure of the situation—concepts of *where* and *when* were like wet bars of soap.

He went back and stood in the dimness of the bedroom. Felt the carpet under his toes. Looked down and noticed for the first time that he was naked, not wearing the boxers and T-shirt he usually slept in. For some reason, this made the panic come back. He looked around wildly, searching for . . . what?

There was something wrong with the wall.

He licked suddenly dry lips. The wall looked completely ordinary, painted a flat, mundane off-white . . . but there was something *wrong* with it, just the same. He reached out with a tentative hand, touched it with his fingertips.

It moved.

Not like a living thing, but like tightly stretched fabric, giving under pressure. And from beyond the wall a rising sound, wind building from a moan to a howl. The wall rippled, fluttered, strained against itself. Dex took a step back, his panic replaced with a horrible sense of dread. He knew where he was.

A tent.

Cleverly made up to look exactly like a motel room . . . but it didn't fool the wind. It ripped off the ceiling and tore away the walls in a roaring instant, exposing Dex to the world.

He was in the middle of the desert, in the middle of the day. Despite the wind, there was no dust; he could see very clearly. And around him, hundreds of feet high, were robots and rabbits and pillars of fire, statues and vehicles and buildings; and they were all so intricate and immense and perfect that he felt astonished and terrified at the same time.

The last thing he realized before he woke up was that he wasn't in the desert after all—he was sitting in a sandbox. And someone was calling his name, but it wasn't his name, really . . .

"Lyle? Hey, you still with us?"

He opened his eyes blearily. Captain Fun was standing in the doorway, a coconut in one hand. There was a paper umbrella sticking out of the coconut, and a long, loopy purple straw that ended between the Captain's lips.

"Sorry to wake you up," Fun said, "but I wanted to make sure you were feeling okay."

"I—I don't know," Dex said. "I don't know what to do—"

"Hey, take it easy," Fun said. "You don't *have* to do anything. You can relax here all week if you want to—nobody'll mind."

"You don't understand," Dex said quietly. "My

name isn't Lyle." And before he could stop to think about it, he blurted, *"I'm Dexter Edden."*

There was a long pause.

"Um," Captain Fun said. "Who?"

Dex sighed.

And then he told him.

"Holy Jesus Fucking Crap," Captain Fun said thoughtfully.

"Yeah," Dex agreed.

"Let's get one thing straight right off," Fun said firmly. "I believe you."

"Why?"

"Because no one could plan such a perfect murder, screw it up so completely, and then make up a cover story that ludicrous. Too many internal contradictions. I mean, luring someone to Burning Man to kill them is brilliant—traveling in the same RV to do it is not. A head-to-toe disguise is well thought out—running into the desert with no food, water, or supplies is not. And you're just too straight to come up with something as deranged as Darth Bunny. No, I think we're dealing with someone a lot more dangerous."

"Who?"

"An experienced Burner. Someone who understands the way this place works and is using it to his advantage." Fun scowled. "A Burner that's gone over to the dark side—well, the dark pink side, anyway."

"So I'm completely screwed, right?" Dex said miserably. "Rafe obviously knows exactly what he's doing—"

"Hold it right there," Fun said. "You are *not* completely screwed. Most killers act alone; in that case, Rafe is now outnumbered."

"I don't—"

"You and me. Two versus one. You don't think I'm gonna throw you to the wolves, do you? *Fuck* that."

Dex didn't know what to say for a moment; he'd half expected Fun to try to convince him to give himself up. "But the police—"

"Forget the police. There's no way they can find you if we take a few elementary precautions—which means we have a week to find Rafe and prove your innocence."

"Find him? He's probably a hundred miles away from here by now!"

Fun smiled. "No, he's not. Either he's worried that you're still on the loose and can screw him up, or he thinks that he got away with it and everything's fine. If he's worried, he'll stay and try to finish the job."

Dex swallowed; he hadn't thought of that. "And if he's not?"

Fun shrugged. "He's a Burner—if he thinks he's in the clear, he'll stick around to celebrate. No way he leaves before the Burn on Saturday night."

Dex had also told Fun about Wade's laptop. "I don't know what's on it," Dex said. "But it might tell me who Rafe is. I have to get my hands on it—somehow."

Captain Fun nodded. "And I think I know just the person who could help us do that. . . ."

"Lyle," Fun said, "this is Sundog."

Sundog was in his thirties, with a full black beard

and a tan so deep it looked unnatural. He wore an an-cient straw cowboy hat with the sides rolled up, a greasy T-shirt with the word *FUCK* on it, and a black skirt. He leaned back in his lawn chair, crossed two hairy arms across his broad chest, and glared at Dex.

"Hello," Dex said. He was going to offer his hand, but thought better of it.

Captain Fun had brought him to a place a few blocks off Center Camp called DPW, which stood for Department of Public Works. "These are the people that actually build the city," Fun had told him on the way over. "They drag chains over the playa to make streets, post signs, put up the streetlights, do all the heavy lifting." Dex hadn't even noticed the street-lights, but sure enough, there were tall wooden stands spaced at regular intervals, each with four red kerosene lanterns hanging from the top. He wondered how they kept them filled.

Fun had also warned him that DPW workers were, in his words, "A bunch of crazy fucks . . . they spend most of their time smoking dope, drinking beer, and welding. They're equal parts biker, roadie, engineer, and redneck—but they're who you go to if you want something built, torn down, or hauled away. If the po-lice are going to take the RV away as evidence, they'll know when and how."

DPW headquarters was a cluster of wooden shacks, each about the size and shape of a house trailer. Dex, Fun, and Sundog were sitting on lawn chairs beside one, under military camouflage netting. "So, Fun said casually, "What do you know about the RV that guy got killed in?"

Sundog glowered at them with bloodshot eyes. He

took a swig from his can of Tecate, belched, and said, "CSI guys finished looking it over about an hour ago. Another hour, it's outta here; got a truck-'n'-trailer comin' to pick it up. Meat wagon took the body this morning."

Fun nodded. "You hear anything else? About the murder?"

"Some guy named Jickling—Wayne, I think. Severe head trauma. Didn't see the body, but I know someone who did. Said he probably got clocked from behind."

"How bad was the fire?" Dex asked.

Sundog stared at him for a second before answering. "Barely got started. Smoke and surface damage, mainly."

"The cops take anything interesting out of there?" Fun asked. "You know—suitcases full of opium, crates of machine pistols?"

Sundog pulled a pack of cigarettes from his hatband and a Zippo from a pocket in his skirt. "Not that I heard of. Just the usual cop stuff—fingerprints, hair samples, that kinda shit. I heard they bagged and tagged a piece of rebar, though—*pink* rebar. That part might be bullshit."

"How about a laptop?" Dex asked.

This time, Sundog stared at him and didn't answer. Fun took a deep breath and said, "Look, Sundog—we need some help. *Serious* help."

"Yeah?" Sundog said. He opened the Zippo with a snap of his fingers, sparked it the same way, and lit his smoke.

"We need to take a look inside that RV before it leaves the site," Fun said. "For *exactly* the reason you think we do."

Dex held his breath. Sundog gave him a long, blank look. Then he said, "You're Edden?"

Before Dex could reply, Fun said, "Yes."

"You do it?"

"No," Dex said.

"Framed," Fun added.

"You sure?" Sundog asked.

"Yes," Fun said.

Sundog's frown deepened. He reached up and scratched his beard.

"Okay," he said.

And that was all the justification Sundog apparently required to subvert a criminal investigation. "Details later," he told them. "We're on the clock. This is gonna be tricky, but I got an idea. . . ."

Which is how, twenty minutes later, Dex found himself four floors above Black Rock City.

He was in the bucket of a cherry picker, a mobile crane with a small platform mounted on the end of an extendable arm. "We use it for all kinds of shit," Sundog told them. "Rigging tents, moving stuff . . . but that's mainly beforehand. During the event, it just makes for a great view."

The plan was relatively simple. The RV was being guarded by police at the site, but once it was loaded on a flatbed it was unlikely they would follow it. The truck would have to creep through the streets of Black Rock City, and at some point the cherry picker would pull out in front of it and fake engine trouble. At the same time, they would deposit Dex on top of the RV from above—a spot the truck's mirrors wouldn't cover. It would be up to him to get inside without being seen, and then get out again.

He was wearing a paper dust mask and tinted goggles that covered his face; Fun was sure the police must have a picture of him by now. Dex was still amazed at the speed everything was happening—in less than twenty-four hours he'd gone from Web-page designer to a wanted fugitive suspended forty feet above the desert.

He had to admit, the view was incredible. For the first time, he got a visceral sense of the size and shape of the city: it was a vast semicircle, a curving grid bent around a largely empty, disc-shaped middle. Art installations, some small, some huge, were scattered throughout the disc; and at the very center, atop his temple, stood the Man. Beyond the desert itself, craggy mountains rose in the distance.

Dex didn't have time to appreciate it, though. Sundog had supplied him with a walkie-talkie and told him he'd have to double as lookout; Dex had watched as the RV was put on the flatbed and secured, and now the truck was starting to move.

"Dex—uh, Lyle to Sundog," he said. "It's rolling."

"Which way?" Sundog crackled back.

"Straight ahead. Down, uh, Reality."

"Keep an eye on 'em. Long as they take Reality to Certain, we're okay. If they decide to cut over on Dubious and head up Vision, I'm gonna have to do a little fancy drivin'."

Dex had to clutch the railing of the bucket as the cherry picker lurched forward. He wasn't afraid of heights, but a wave of vertigo swept over him all the same.

"Hang in there," Fun's voice said over the walkie-talkie. "Any sign of an escort?"

"No," Dex replied. "I can see two officers getting into their cars, though. The truck is still heading down Reality . . . it's past the corner."

The cherry picker sped up. They were heading for the next corner, Certain and Reality. He could see the truck, a big eighteen-wheeler, coming toward them and churning up a cloud of dust in its wake.

The cherry picker roared into the intersection just ahead of the truck, cutting it off. The bucket shuddered as the picker slowed, sputtered, and died a convincing death. The truck stopped with a squeal of air brakes and an angry blast of its horn.

The bucket began to descend, the arm angling down from the articulation point in its middle. It was squarely over the roof of the RV when the flatbed's driver jumped out of the semi.

Dex paused, frozen with one leg already slung over the guardrail of the bucket. All the driver had to do was look back—but his attention was focused on Sundog. He stalked forward a few steps and made an angry *What-the-hell?* gesture.

Dex had no time to think about it. He dropped onto the roof of the RV as quietly as he could, wincing at how hot the metal was under his bare feet. The plan was to get in via the sun roof—it had a nominal latch but no lock. Sundog had given him a tire iron to pry it open, and he found it popped up with hardly any pressure at all. He stuck the tire iron in the waistband of his shorts and clambered inside.

He dropped down into a smelly, monochrome mess. The walls and furnishings had been blackened by smoke and then frosted via fire extinguisher; here and there were little bright pink explosions of color that on closer inspection turned out to be dustings of finger-print powder. The place stank of melted plastic and burnt fabric. The curtains on the windows were drawn, but enough light filtered through to see by.

He made his way gingerly to the rear, where the panel that divided the bedroom from the rest of the camper stood open. The top of the bed was a charred ruin, but Dex could see that the fire hadn't burned all the way through the mattress. That was a good sign.

He got on his hands and knees. The cubbyhole Wade had used wasn't a real storage space—he'd pried one of the cheap pieces of veneer off with his bare hands and found a thin gap between the closet and the wheel well. And in it—

The laptop.

Dex pulled it out, checked for fire damage. It was a cheap model with a gray plastic case, its power cord wrapped around it. It seemed to have survived un-scathed. He wouldn't know for sure until he'd booted it up, of course—

The truck lurched forward.

"What?" Dex whispered. For a second he was sure it was some kind of cruel joke Fun and Sundog were playing on him—*Let's see what he does now, huh?*—but the thought was only a short-lived hybrid of paranoia and wishful thinking. They must have been forced to move out of the way, which meant—

He took a careful peek out the back window. There was a patrol car inching along behind them.

He forced himself to breathe. The patrol car must have pulled up right after he'd dropped in. They'd probably follow the truck right up to the highway, and maybe after that. He was totally and completely—

"Fuck it," he said out loud. He wasn't caught yet.

He just had to *think*. All he had to do was get out before the truck picked up speed. The roof was out—the cops would spot him. Same with the door on the side. There was a window in the berth above the cab, but it didn't open.

How about the doors on the cab? He considered it. The body of the camper was wider than that of the cab, enough to hide him from the patrol car if he was careful. If he unrolled the window, he might be able to get onto the hood. Of course, the truck driver might spot him—but only if he glanced in his mirrors. Even so, the center of the RV's hood would be in a blind spot; and from there he could crouch down between the RV and the back of the semi's cab. If he waited until the truck was making a turn, he could probably jump off without being seen.

Once again, there was no time to ponder—there was only one turn between here and the highway. Keeping low, he pulled aside the curtain that divided the driver's compartment from the rest of the camper. He reached over and cranked down the passenger side window; dust immediately billowed in, making him cough despite his dust mask.

He got on the seat, holding the laptop under one arm. With his free hand, he gripped the edge of the doorframe near the top, then scrunched his body up and climbed into the window itself. When he was wedged into the opening, feeling ridiculously exposed, he swung his right leg around and onto the windshield. There was nothing to grab and no way to grab it, but he did his best with his bare foot and the windshield while clutching the laptop tight to his body. He realized what he was going to have to do, and made himself do it before he lost his nerve: he pushed off with his other foot, letting go of the doorframe and spinning around in midair to land on the windshield on his back. He slid down the glass, a hood ornament amazed to still be alive.

He scrabbled down quickly, half falling off the front of the vehicle. He banged his elbow and a knee on landing, but protected the laptop. Now he was on the oil-stained bed of the flattop itself, between the RV and the cab of the semi.

The truck was starting to turn. He realized in a flash that what he'd thought was a blind spot would in a second be exactly the opposite; the driver of the truck would be able to see him clearly in his left-hand mirror as the position of the cab changed.

He scrambled for the right-hand edge of the flatbed, and jumped without looking.

CHAPTER 6:

PROFANE AUTHORITY

File C (Pain Priestess): Everything has a price.

I think that's the biggest misconception about Burning Man—that everything is free. We don't use money, but that doesn't mean there's no cost; it just means you pay in other ways. You pay with sweat, you pay with time, you pay with energy. You pay with *commitment*. Burning Man isn't the kind of place you just jump in a car and go to on the spur of the moment—and if you're stupid enough to do so, you *really* wind up paying. I've seen more than one bliss-bunny show up thinking this was nothing more than a big party and wind up cold, sunburned, and sick as a dog because they couldn't be bothered with elementary precautions.

And you know what? That's just as it should be.

Burning Man isn't just about hedonism—it's about *consequences*. This place is Saturday night *and* Sunday morning, all wrapped around each other. It's a week-long, object lesson in responsibility. Radical self-expression, followed by the ramifications thereof.

This isn't a theme park. Nothing here has been "sanitized for your protection." It's dirty, it's dangerous, it's *real*. And that's just how I like it.

At the Temple of Atonement, we take our pleasure *and* our pain very seriously. Some don't even use the word "playing" when it comes to S and M—they don't think that's the proper attitude. "Purging" is closer to the truth. When a dom and and a sub trust each other enough to do a really intense scene, it goes way beyond the erotic. There are people here that let their masters tie them up in the hot sun and leave them to bake. We monitor that kind of thing very closely, but it's still tremendously intense.

Risky? Of course. It says so right on your ticket: you voluntarily assume the risk of death or serious injury. First-timers always think that's just the usual bullshit legal disclaimer you can't get away from in America, but it's not. They mean it—you can *die* out here. People overdose, or roll their vehicle, or even crash their plane. It's a real shock to the system when you realize that for the first time—it's like the first time you're in a big crowd and Daddy isn't holding your hand. Some people can't handle it.

I get really turned on.

People love to rave about how nice everyone is in Black Rock City, and all the sharing and caring and blah-blah-blah—like it's all sweetness and light. Me, I like a little salt. . . .

Danger is the ultimate aphrodisiac. Nothing gets the old sex urge going like the knowledge this might be the last orgasm you ever have. Just being around it is enough to get me all charged up, and Burners *love* to mess around with that kind of energy; there's a huge

S and M contingent out here. This one camp—the Headless Maiden, I think it was called—wouldn't give you a drink unless they could mark you first. They'd put a little cardboard cutout with their camp logo on your bare behind, then paddle you with a wooden spoon until you had a welt of the proper shape. Or the Spank-O-Tron—some genius hooked up paddles to a variable-speed motor, then set it up out on the Esplanade. You flick the switch and bend over—the harder you push back, the harder you get spanked. That one gets me wet just thinking about it. . . .

Really, the whole festival is about staring Death in the face. I mean, where do you think the expression, "playing with fire" came from? There've *always* been adrenaline junkies, people who just have to push their luck all the way to the edge. I know this guy who likes to use a flaming bullwhip on people—and I know people who'll *let* him. Black Rock City is just a big old buglight for all sorts of extremists . . . which means that everybody here is *not* your best friend. Some of the people you'll meet are just plain bad news.

Case in point: I was whipping this girl at the Temple one night. We'd never played together before, but she seemed like she knew what she wanted. I tied her down, selected a nice single-tail, and went to work. She'd asked for a gag, so we were using the drop method: instead of choosing a safe word, you let the bottom hold something in their hand; if it drops, you stop.

Normally, I don't do more than one scene at a time. I mean, part of the attraction for a lot of subs is having the dom's whole attention focused just on them—but in a public space like the Temple, things are a little different. The situation is more fluid, more chaotic. Plus, the Burning Man ethic is all about participation rather than observation, so people are more likely to join in, or move between scenes. When another couple interrupted me to ask about whip technique—and invited me to demonstrate—I patted my girl on the head, blindfolded her, and told her I was going to get something special. In retrospect the blindfold may have been a mistake, but I was trying to preserve the illusion I was only there for her.

You have to understand, the Temple has people who monitor all the ongoing scenes just in case something gets out of hand. Even though I was over on the other side of the Temple—and, I'll admit, thoroughly distracted—I thought she'd be okay. I was only gone a few minutes.

But when I get back, there's this *ape* standing behind her. He's whaling away on her backside with this flogger like there's no tomorrow, and I can tell at a glance she's going to have nasty bruises for the next two weeks. She's dropped the ball, and is trying her best to scream through the gag that this is *not* okay— but she's not the only one making those kinds of noises, and so far nobody else has noticed.

Well, I ran over and grabbed the flogger from his hand and started screaming at him. He started screaming back—accused *me* of being out of line! The monitors came over and tried to get things sorted out, and he started screaming at *them.* . . . It was the most bizarre thing. He wasn't being arrogant; he was genuinely confused and frustrated. He didn't seem to understand the scene, the rules, how any of it worked. It was like he was taking everything at face value, that he assumed anyone that was there and tied up must be some kind of offering to the general public. Crazy motherfucker . . . but you know, at least he was *trying*. I'd rather deal with genuine lunatics like him than a bunch of tourists who just want to gawk.

Unfortunately, the girl he was beating didn't see it that way. When we released her, she went after him like you wouldn't believe—tried to kick his balls in, for starters. We had to hold her back until he left, or there would have been *serious* bloodshed. . . .

CHAPTER 7:

RATIONAL DOGMA

Dex knew he was going to die.

Hurtling through the air, laptop tucked against his body, he had an epiphany: he was sure, *completely* sure, that he would strike the ground at the precise angle to break his neck. Whatever information the laptop held would be forever denied to him. His story would end here.

He would remember that flavor of utter certainty later; in fact, he would pull out the memory whenever he needed to remind himself that *nothing* was set in stone—not even the Ten Commandments.

They were made, apparently, out of foam rubber . . . or at least that's what it felt like as Dex crashed face-first into them. The Commandments toppled over, Dex on top of them, with a puff of dust and a startled cry of, "Jesus *Christ!*"

"What?" Christ said.

Dex rolled off the Commandments, gasping an apology. The police car tailing the flatbed was just rolling past, but the officers in it apparently hadn't seen Dex jump; they took no more notice of him than of the person he'd just knocked down, who Dex quickly helped to his feet. His costume was fashioned to resemble a large stone tablet, with the Commandments painted on the front. Most of them had also been crossed out.

Christ didn't offer to help. Instead, he lit a cigarette and adjusted the cross strapped to his back—it looked like it was made of foam, too. "I *told* you that thing would be impossible to walk in," he said.

"I didn't trip!" the Commandments said indignantly.

"I knocked him over," Dex said. "I'm really, really sorry."

Christ chuckled. "Look, you're supposed to break them one at a time," he said. "Not all at once. . . ."

Captain Fun sprinted up, with Sundog a few steps behind. "You okay?"

"Yeah, I'm finc," Dex said. He noticed there was a large, dusty mark on the Commandments where his head had struck—right in the middle of "THOU SHALT NOT STEAL," except "STEAL" had been crossed out and replaced with "VEND."

"No harm done," the Commandments said. He and Christ shuffled off.

"We got out of the way when we saw the cops coming," Captain Fun said. "We thought they might have seen you get on."

"If they looked like they were going in, I wanted to be in a position to ram," Sundog said. He didn't sound like he was joking. "Create a diversion, let you get away."

"Really? Well, I'm glad it didn't come to that. I got it, anyway. . . ." Dex showed them the laptop. "As long as it's still working."

"Then let's go somewhere and find out," Fun said. "Aetheria has a generator."

"I gotta return the cherry picker," Sundog said. "I'll drop by your camp later, okay?"

"Sure. Burn on," Captain Fun said.

"Burn on," Sundog said.

The laptop hadn't been damaged—Dex had no trouble getting it up and running. He sat cross-legged on his sleeping roll with the machine in his lap and searched through files.

Captain Fun was outside, making supper in Aetheria's communal kitchen. People wandered in and out of the pod now and then, but Dex was too absorbed to pay much attention.

He did look up to see if any of them were Lorilei, though.

The laptop was a junk heap of badly organized files: old business letters, MP3s, games, and porn ranging from banal to ludicrous. He finally found what he was looking for buried in a subdirectory of miscellaneous text files, a folder simply labeled "BM."

He read every file in it, pausing only to dig into the chili that Captain Fun showed up with. Dex thanked him, gobbled it all—he hadn't realized how starved he was—and went back to reading.

When he was done, he turned off the laptop, got up and stretched, and went outside. The sun had just finished sinking behind the mountains, and Captain Fun had changed into a costume that covered a lot more skin. He still wore the red cape, but now he sported a black plastic chest-piece molded into a muscular chest and abs, black bikini briefs, red-and-black leather boots, and fishnet stockings. Black shoulder pads and gauntlets finished off the outfit—and he was talking to Lorilei.

She was wearing more than last time, Dex noted gratefully; a sarong with a bright flame design wrapped around her hips. She smiled at him as he walked up.

"Hello, Ulk," she said sweetly.

"Hi—What?"

"It's a much better name than Dex. Or maybe it should be the Incredible Ulk?"

"Technically, it should be the N'credible Ulk," Fun pointed out.

"Or you could just say it in an English accent. Oim the encredible 'ulk, oi am."

Dex was starting to realize that once they got going it could take a while for them to wind down—he wondered, suddenly, if they were more than just friends. The thought depressed him even further . . . and then he realized what she'd said.

"Did you just call me Dex?" he said.

"Hey, she's cool," Fun assured him. "Besides, she's already seen your real face. Once the cops start showing a picture around—and they will—she would have figured it out anyway."

"The Captain told me the whole story," Lorilei said. "Don't worry, nobody in Aetheria is going to turn you in. So what did you find on the laptop?"

"I have good news," Dex said gloomily, "and bad news."

"Bad news first," Fun said.

"I found a bunch of personal files dealing with Burners. I don't know exactly how Wade got hold of them, but most of them concern incidents from last year's festival where he managed to piss somebody off. If these stories are true, he was a one-man, weeklong wrecking crew."

"How bad was he?" Lorilei asked.

"About as bad as Wade used to get," Dex said. "He got into fights, he vandalized art, he was loud and obnoxious and stupid. I'm amazed someone didn't try to kill him then."

"But they didn't," Fun said. "They were smart about it. They took a year to plan."

"And got him to come back," Lorilei pointed out. "So, Mr. Ulk—how many suspects are we talking about?"

"Eleven."

"Eleven?" Lorilei and Fun said.

"Eleven," Dex repeated sadly. "How am I supposed to even *find* eleven people here, let alone figure out if one's a killer?"

"You do what a Burner always does when he's in trouble," Lorilei said softly. "You ask for *help.*"

They moved the laptop to Fun's tent-trailer. It had two double beds, one at either end, with a narrow corridor between them lined on one side with a long bench and the other with a counter, sink, and stove. A small fold-down table abutted one of the beds; the table was littered with camping supplies. One of the beds was piled high with costumes.

Lorilei and Fun took turns reading the files, and whichever of them wasn't reading sat down with Dex and gave him a crash course in Burning Man. Sundog showed up about half an hour later with a bottle of whiskey; he found glasses and poured them all shots without asking.

Dex learned very quickly that he could have avoided a lot of his problems if he'd just read the materials he'd been handed at the gate. They included, among other things, a map and a *Survival Guide*—one both Lorilei and Fun insisted he read from cover to cover.

"The easiest way to navigate in Black Rock City," Lorilei said, "is to look for the Man. He's the tallest thing here, and he's located right dead center. All the avenues point at him, and at night he's lit up with neon."

"The streets have different names every year, but they generally follow a logical pattern," Fun added. "The Esplanade is always the first one, on the very inside. This year, after that we have Authority, Creed, Dogma, Evidence, Faith, Gospel, Reality, Theory, and Vision. Roughly alphabetical, though they skip a few letters."

"Y'might also notice that some of the street signs have times on them," Sundog said. "From two o'clock to ten o'clock."

"I did notice that," Dex admitted. "I didn't get it, though."

"Think of Black Rock City as a huge clock," Fun said. "With the Man at the center. Straight down between his legs is six o'clock. To either side is three and nine o'clock. Space becomes time—once you wrap your head around that, getting around becomes a lot simpler. Blocks are half an hour long. Addresses are a little rubbery, but they work—if I say my camp is at seven-forty and Vision, you can probably find it."

"Leads to some fucked-up conversations, though," Sundog said. He poured himself a shot of whiskey with one hand and slammed it back with the other. " 'Where are we?' 'Two-thirty.' 'Shit, I was supposed to meet my girlfriend by three o'clock at seven-fifteen.' 'That's okay, it's only one.' "

Dex looked down at the map spread out on the table. There were streets called Promenades connecting the Man to the rest of the city at six, three, and nine; the one at six ran straight down to Center Camp, while the ones at three and nine ended in keyhole-shaped plazas named Absurd and Real, corresponding to the streets at three and nine o'clock. There was another Promenade at twelve that ran up to something marked on the map only with a mandala.

"What's that?" Dex asked.

"The Temple of Honor," Fun said. "A shrine to the dead. It burns Sunday night."

"For some people it's more important than burning the Man," Lorilei said.

"And other people just go 'cause it's the last big thing to set on fire," Sundog said. "Either way, I don't think the dead give a shit. . . ."

Dex wondered if Wade would have cared. As long as there was a party involved, he'd probably have been all in favor. "Go ahead—throw my body on the fire!" he would have yelled. "Then stand back, 'cause I'm gonna go up like a rocket!"

Dex sighed. Wade had hardly been a friend, but there was something terribly sad about his dying on the very first day of the festival. Of course, considering the swath of destruction he seemed to have cut last year, there were no doubt a large number of Burners who'd be glad to never see him again.

And at least one who felt a darker kind of joy.

"You've got to be kidding," Dex said.

"It makes *perfect sense,*" Fun insisted.

"Actually," Lorilei said, "I think it's kinda *hot.*"

Dex blushed. Captain Fun had dug through his pile of costumes and come up with a gray trench coat, fedora, black socks, and a pair of beat-up black sneakers that fit. With shorts and T-shirt on underneath and the coat belted shut, Dex's bare legs made him look like a flasher on the prowl.

"Look, the dust mask and sunglasses will protect your identity," Fun said. "The hat and coat will protect you from the sun *and* the cold. But best of all, it gives you an excuse to go around and ask people questions—you're just *in character.* A playa detective: half gumshoe, half pervert. It's *perfect.*"

"Just remember to keep your coat open when you're talking to a suspect," Lorilei said. Dex still wore the T-shirt he'd been wearing the night of the murder; it was a faded yellow, with the logo of a defunct software company on the chest that resembled a stylized *L.* "You want the killer to recognize you, without anyone else knowing who you are."

"If the killer *does* spot you" Fun said, "he's not gonna attack you in public. He's not gonna yell for the cops either, 'cause then you'll accuse *him.*"

"Nah," Sundog said. "He'll act all innocent, then rat you out to the cops as soon as he can get away from you. One of us can shadow him after you talk, see what he does. He tries anything and *wham!*" He smacked the bottle against the table. "We're all over the sumbitch."

"But I don't even know where to *start*," Dex said. He wasn't much of a drinker—the two shots of whiskey he'd had were making his head swim.

"Ann Atomic," Lorilei said. She was seated with the laptop in front of her; she tapped a few keys and read from the screen: " 'Last year, this idiot almost got himself *and* me killed. . . .' "

"Really?" Fun asked. He leaned against the counter, his arms crossed over his plastic chest. "She wouldn't be my first choice for the killer."

"Maybe not," Lorilei said. "But Dex said Rafe's voice sounded like he was disguising it—he might be a she. Besides, we have to start somewhere . . . and I know where to find her. She's performing with Carnivale Diablo at the Chandelier in half an hour."

"But—what am I supposed to *do?*" Dex said. "It's not like I'm a real detective or anything—she doesn't *have* to talk to me."

"Actually, she sort of *does,*" Fun replied. "Burning Man is all about participation. If she's guilty and blows you off for no good reason, it'll look suspicious; that means she *has* to talk to you just to keep things looking normal."

"But—"

"And we can hide you as soon as you're done," Lorilei added. "Don't worry—we'll keep you safe."

Dex felt his control of the situation slipping away. He had been on firmer ground when they were looking at maps and reading files, but suddenly even that aspect seemed surreal; it was like they were all twelve, hiding in a tree house and figuring out how to get revenge on the school bully.

They looked at him expectantly. Finally, he belted the trench coat tightly, tried his best to smile, and said, "Okay. Let's give it a shot. . . ."

The bike ride there was only ten minutes long, but it took them the better part of half an hour before they were ready to leave camp; canteens had to be filled, costumes adjusted, gifts pulled out. Lorilei was giving away sequined pasties she'd made herself, the kind old-time burlesque dancers used to wear—she modeled a pair for Dex and grinned at his reaction.

Dex stashed the laptop in Captain Fun's trailer and hoped it would be safe—his door didn't have even a perfunctory lock.

The art installation was past the Temple of Honor, in an area the map referred to as "the Wholly Other." The actual name of the piece was "Cleavage in Space," but Dex could immediately see why they called it the Chandelier; that's exactly what it was, an enormous light fixture resting on the surface of the playa. Four spindly metal arms tipped with bulbs curved out from a central body that resembled an enormous red Japanese lantern. The entire structure was canted at an angle, as if it had come to rest only moments ago after ripping loose from the ballroom of a *Titanic*-size zeppelin passing overhead. A huge chain trailed from the chandelier's top to the round white base of its ceiling fitting lying a hundred feet away, bits of plaster and lath still clinging to the edges.

It was already full dark when they pulled up, but

Dex wasn't cycling blind; Sundog had duct-taped a small but powerful penlight to Dex's handlebars. When Dex had thanked him, Sundog had just grunted and said, "Remember—safety third."

Dex laid his bike carefully down on the ground at the edge of the crowd that had already gathered around the Chandelier. "Here," Lorilei had said. "You can lock it to mine." Hers was an old-style Mustang with long, curving handlebars and an extended banana seat, all of it painted a Day-Glo green. She unwrapped a plastic-coated chain from the frame and ran it through her spokes and his.

A fireball *whoofed* into the air. Dex joined Fun, Lorilei and Sundog as they found an empty spot at the front of the crowd, and got his first look at Carnivale Diablo.

There were five of them. In the center, a man wearing only dusty leather pants was taking a drink from a plastic bottle, a flaming torch held in his other hand. He held the torch a short distance from his lips and spewed liquid at it, producing another fireball.

Behind him, a man and woman on stilts juggled flaming torches, passing them back and forth to each other in whirling arcs of fire. Off to one side a woman in black latex spun fire: short cables ablaze at their ends swinging in tight little circles and figure eights, flame-bolas crisscrossing each other in an intricate, everchanging pattern. Dex had seen fire-breathers and fire-jugglers before, but the fire-spinner was hypnotic; the flames left blue and orange tracers behind them as they whirled, creating a flickering mandala that was always moving, always different. They gave the taut, shiny-black curves of her suit a wet, rippling gleam.

"Beautiful, isn't it?" Lorilei murmured.

"Is that her?" Dex asked.

"No," Lorilei said. *That's* her." She pointed.

Another woman strode out as the fire-breather withdrew; the stilters stopped their juggling and the fire-spinner stopped her whirling. The newcomer was tall, muscular, with short-cropped hair of bright orange. She wore thick-soled black boots, a leopard-skin loincloth and a metal bustier of brushed aluminum. She carried a metal cage, about the size of a bucket, suspended from a lengthy chain that dragged behind her on the ground. As soon as she appeared, the crowd began to move back, giving her plenty of room.

The fire-spinner approached and touched a torch to the cage. When it ignited, Ms. Atomic began to spin like an Olympian preparing for a hammer throw—but she didn't let go. Instead, she paid out more and more of the chain, until the flaming cage at its end was roaring around the radius of a circle at least thirty feet in diameter. That was the limit at which she could keep it aloft; its orbit became erratic, dipping down so the cage kissed the earth, sparks exploding on contact. The crowd roared in approval. The woman was a whirling dervish orbited by a dying comet, muscles standing out in cords on her arms, teeth clenched in a strained but exuberant grin. The cage touched down again and again, generating its own fireworks every time, until finally both it and she ran out of fuel. She let it tumble to a stop, and gave the crowd an exhausted smile as they broke into applause and cheers.

That apparently marked the end of the performance; the crowd began to break up and drift away as the performers gathered their equipment.

"Go," Lorilei said. Dex wished briefly that he had time for another shot of whiskey—and found Sundog beside him, handing him the bottle. He took it, had a swig, grimaced . . . and made himself step forward.

"In character, in character," he whispered to himself. *Sure. No problem.*

"Ann Atomic?" he said. His voice sounded a lot more authoritative than he felt.

"That's me," she said. She was cleaning her hands with a rag.

"I'm—"

"He can't call himself Lyle."

"Why—"

"Nope. Dumb name."

"Stupid fucking name."

"Doesn't sound like a detective. How about Inspector something?"

"Inspector Something? 'Hi, I'm Inspector Something, can I ask you a few questions?' I don't know."

"Not Inspector Something, Inspector *something*. Inspector Inspector?"

"*Stupid* fucking name."

"I just—"

"I know! Inspector Ulk!"

"How about Dick something?"

"That isn't—

"You're *always* thinking about dicking something, Captain."

"Inspector Dick? Private Dick? Dick Private? Dick Inspector?"

"Sure, Dick Private, the Dick Inspector. Why don't

we just send him over to Penetration Village with some poppers and a box of condoms."

"I am *not*—"

"*Incredibly* stupid fucking name."

"The Questioner? The Inquisitor? The Puzzler?"

"What is he, Batman's archenemy?"

"Curious Urge," Dex said.

"—What?"

"—What?"

"*Fucking* stu—huh?"

There was a long pause.

"That," Lorilei finally said, "is *brilliant.*"

"—Curious Urge," Dex said. "I'm *conducting* an *investigation.*"

She met his eye and laughed. *"Are* you?" she said. She had the raspy voice of a heavy smoker. "Great name. Well, I'm Ann Atomic—How can I help you, Mr. Urge?"

"I was *wondering* if I could *ask* you a few *questions.*" He sounded, Dex realized, ridiculous—but he seemed unable to stop *placing* the *emphasis* on certain *words.*

"What do you want to know?" She started to gather up the length of chain.

"There was an *incident* last year. Involving you and a, uh—*uninvited* collaborator."

She stopped what she was doing, gave him a sharp look. "You mean the guy that spiked my cage? Yeah, I won't forget *that* asshole any time soon. . . . Hey, who the fuck *are* you, anyway? You from the insurance company?"

She took a step closer, the chain dangling from one

sinewy, grease-stained hand. Dex glanced nervously at the Chandelier, where Fun, Sundog, and Lorilei were standing and pretending to admire it. Or maybe they really were admiring it—they seemed oblivious to his situation.

"I'm not from the insurance company," he said hastily. "I'm—" A sudden idea struck him. "I'm a journalist," he said. "I'm doing a story on the festival."

"You and about a thousand others," she said sourly, but she stopped advancing. "What's the jerkwad have to do with it?"

"That's my angle. Jerkwads who come here and—and ruin other people's fun."

She snorted. "Well, you picked a good example. Guess it was my fault for leaving my stuff unattended, but you never figure someone's going to fuck with your stuff—not until afterward. Since then, I've been a lot more paranoid."

"What happened, exactly?"

She resumed gathering up the chain, looping it between her wrist and elbow. "Guess the bastard thought my show wasn't exciting enough. When I wasn't looking, he crammed some fireworks into the cage. They went off when I had about half the length let out—skyrocket came straight back at me, almost took my eye out." She tapped a spot above her left eyebrow. "Caught me right here. Didn't break the skin, but freaked me so bad I let go of the chain. Had enough momentum built up to send the cage right into the crowd, throwing fireworks in every goddamn direction. People got out of the way in time, but it made me look like an incompetent idiot."

"How did you know who did it?"

"It wasn't hard. He was standing right at the front, with this big, shit-eating grin on his face. When I started to spin, he started to laugh. I was just starting to wonder what his fucking problem was when everything blew up. Wish he'd caught the cage right between his fucking eyes."

"And then?"

"And then the asshole disappeared." She shook her head. "You know, I never thought I'd say this, especially at Burning Man, but I wish he would've been happy to just stay a spectator. I mean, I get the whole participation thing, I really do, but there's gotta be a line somewhere. At some point you have to say, '*This* is the performer, and *this* is the audience.' It's like the whole thing with cameras."

"The thing with cameras?"

She slung the looped chain over one broad shoulder—it rattled loudly against the aluminum of her chest-piece. "Yeah. As a Burner, I don't like 'em. Our whole culture has this fetish about capturing images— it's like we think something's more real if we see it on a screen, when all you're doing is turning an event into an object. We do it because it's easier to distance yourself from an object—it's harder to ignore something that's actually *happening.*"

"You think that's why he did it?" Dex asked. He stuck his hands into the pockets of the trench coat, found his hand bumping into something he couldn't identify.

"Who the fuck knows? Probably he was just an insecure toad who needed a little attention and decided to steal some of mine. And see, as a performer, I can understand that; attention is what we get paid in return for the images they take away—in their heads or in their cameras, whatever. But if somebody takes a really good picture of me, then they're creating art at the same time I am—and that's good, right? Only then I bounce back to the whole 'observing isn't interacting' thing . . . you can experience something or you can record it, but you can't do both at the same time."

"Quantum physics," Dex said. His fingers explored the object in his pocket. It was smooth, metallic, and cylindrical.

"Yeah," she agreed. "You can't know the position and velocity of a particle at the same time, right? It's always one or the other. That's why I have this whole love/hate thing with cameras—I keep flipping back and forth."

"That's a very interesting theory," Dex said. It was more than that, though—it was familiar. She'd said much the same thing in file M: (Ann Atomic), and Dex thought he knew why. Having formally collected and organized her thoughts, she was reluctant to discard them after a single use. Dex had once worked with an office manager who'd done the same thing: having written one brilliant memo in her entire career, she quoted it whenever she could.

"Excuse me for asking," Dex said, "but have you ever expressed your theory in print? I'd like to put it in my article, and I have to know for copyright reasons."

She gave him a smile that was almost shy. "Well, only online. I post on some of the Burning Man groups, and I went on this whole rant last year after it happened. Do a search in the archives for 'Ann Atomic'; it'll come up. You can quote from it if you want."

"Thanks," Dex said thoughtfully. "That's very helpful. . . ."

"The files were downloaded from an online discussion group," Dex said. He'd rejoined Lorilei and Captain Fun, and they were riding slowly back toward the city. Sundog was hanging back to see what Ann would do, but Dex thought he'd be disappointed—while she was tall enough to be the killer, he didn't think it was her.

"Aha!" said Fun. "So that means . . . hmmm. What *does* that mean?"

"It means Wade was lurking in e-groups, posing as someone else and getting the people he pissed off to talk about it," Dex said. "I just don't know *why.*"

"To rub it in?" Lorilei suggested.

"But he didn't," Dex said. "Not in Ann Atomic's case, anyway, or she would have mentioned it."

"Unless she's the killer," Fun pointed out.

"I don't think she is. For one thing, she's left-handed—the killer wasn't."

"You sure?"

Dex saw the rebar arcing toward Wade's skull again, and shuddered. "Yeah. I'm sure."

"Where to now?" Lorilei asked.

"Well, Sundog's going to give me a call on the walkie-talkie if Atomic goes to the cops," Fun said. "But in the meantime, I was thinking we should try the Earth Guardian next."

"If we're going to, we should do it now," Lorilei said. "Before everybody hits the party trail."

"Good idea. What do *you* say, Inspector Urge?"

"Call me Curious," Dex said.

The Earth Guardians, as it turned out, were the ecological side of Burning Man; Dex had learned a little about them from the *Survival Guide*. He knew they were located in Center Camp, and were involved in both educating the public and recycling. He'd been a little surprised at how much emphasis the *Survival Guide* had placed on the environment—he hadn't thought of a flat, alkali plain as having much to protect.

They rode toward Center Camp, but turned left just before the entrance; the Earth Guardians were located on the outer edge, where the Karmic Circle met the Esplanade. Passing beneath the rotating shadow of the elevated Kaleidosphere, Dex could hear it creaking as it turned.

As they got off their bikes, a police car slowly rolled past. Though he'd taken off his sunglasses, Dex was glad he was still wearing his dust mask.

He wished he had a printout of the files—his memory was good, but it would still be nice to have something concrete to refer to. A sudden thought struck him, and he said, "Wait a minute. How are we going to identify this guy? I don't even remember what he was called."

"I do," Captain Fun said. "Stay here." He strolled into the tent.

"What's he going to do?" Dex asked.

"Captain Fun has a way with people," Lorilei said with a grin. "Give him a few minutes, he'll get the guy's favorite color and sign. You warm enough?"

"Yeah. You?"

"Oh, I'm a hot-blooded girl. Comes from growing up in a cold place."

"Where's that?"

She uncapped her water bottle, took a long drink before answering. She gave him a pointed look, and after a second he grabbed his canteen and drank, too.

"*That's* better," she said. "I'm from Alaska, originally."

"What was that like?"

"Oh, you know—bears, wolves, putting Grandma out on an ice floe. The usual."

"Right."

"What about you?" She capped her bottle, and took out a small yellow vial.

"Uh, Washington State. Still live there, actually."

She took the lid off the vial, dipped her finger inside and then rubbed it over her lips. "Here," she said, offering him the vial. "Chapping is another thing you have to watch out for."

He took a little bit of balm, rubbed it gingerly around the edges of his mouth; it was smooth and slippery and tasted of peppermint. "Thanks," he said.

"Can't have a detective with cracked lips," she said.

Dex slipped his hands into his pockets. His fingers bumped up against the metal object he'd been playing with while talking to Ann Atomic; he pulled it out and looked at it. It was a cylinder about three inches in length, aluminum, with one end round and the other tapered to a short neck; it looked like a cartoon version of a missile minus the fins. The tapered end had a hole punched in the top.

He glanced up at Lorilei, but she wasn't paying attention; her eyes were fixed on a man riding what appeared to be a robot dog. He was pushing and pulling on two levers, which somehow propelled the thing forward in an undulating motion.

"Lends a whole new meaning to the phrase 'doggystyle,' " she said.

"Uh, yeah," Dex said.

He slipped the cylinder back into his pocket as Captain Fun strode back out of the tent. "His name is Green Grover," Fun said. "He's not here at the moment—but I know where he's gone."

"Where?" Lorilei asked.

Fun picked up his bike. "Recycle Camp," he said. "Just on the other side of the café."

They hopped on their bikes and followed the Captain. This was the first time Dex had entered Center Camp after dark, and it seemed like a very different place. There were fewer naked people but more elaborate costumes; vehicles and people alike glowed, flashed or twinkled in every color. He saw a man and woman walking hand in hand in perfect *Tron* outfits, white jumpsuits and helmets outlined by neon circuitry; a sultan dressed in harem pants, a brocaded vest and a turban, sailing past on an electric scooter cunningly made into a wavy flying carpet; a man in a red tracksuit and seventies blow-dried hair running in slow motion on a moving treadmill, while the theme song from *The Six Million Dollar Man* played from hidden speakers.

Recycle Camp was right next to the place Fun had gotten Dex's bike from. Dex had thought it was just an extension of the same camp, but now he noticed that the single bike in the center of the shade structure was attached to a frame that kept it stationary and an extended chain system that turned two closely spaced car tires behind it in opposite directions. As one person pedaled, another fed aluminum cans between the car tires; the tires crushed the cans, spitting flattened discs into a crate below. "That's him on the bike," Fun said.

Dex took a deep breath. "Okay. . . ."

He walked up and cleared his throat; the rider glanced at him. He was in his twenties, lean, with a long, clean-shaven face and shaggy brown hair pulled back in an untidy ponytail. "Yeah?" he panted.

"I was wondering if I could ask you a few questions," Dex said.

"Sure, go ahead." Behind him, the tires crunched steadily away as a woman in a long black cloak fed can after can between them.

"It's about an altercation you had last year? The assault?"

"Oh, yeah. That guy *sucked.*"

"I was just wondering if you'd had any contact with him since then."

"Why? He fuck *you* up, too?"

"Not exactly. I'm looking for him on behalf of someone else . . . someone he *did* fuck up. I'm collecting statements from people he interacted with—anything you could tell me would strengthen our case against him." Dex was amazed at how easily the lie spilled from his lips; normally, he couldn't come up with a good excuse for being late. "We believe he may have even tried to contact you via e-mail."

"Huh. Maybe. I got a message a few months ago, guy claiming to be a writer. Said he was doing research on violence at big festivals, wanted to hear my story. I sent it, but haven't heard from him since."

"What did he ask you, exactly?" Dex asked.

"Only two things. He said he wanted to hear what happened to me, in my own words—and he wanted to know what Burning Man meant to me."

Dex frowned—he couldn't remember exactly what

Green Grover's response had been. "And what did you tell him?"

Grover smiled, and slowed his pace a little. "I told him I thought it was elemental. Fire, earth, air, water—you're just so *aware* of them here. The wind is so strong it can rip apart your whole camp; you don't drink water *constantly,* you'll get sick; somebody's always setting *something* on fire; and the dust . . . well, the dust gets into fucking *everything.*" He shrugged. "You ignore any of them, you get into *big* trouble. 'Course, sometimes you got to pay attention to *people,* too."

Dex nodded. "Sure. How bad were you injured, exactly?"

"A sprained wrist, bruises. It was the humiliation more than anything, you know? I was in the middle of taking a crap when he knocked over the Porta-John."

"Any idea why he did it?"

Grover shook his head. "None. Maybe he always *planned* to steal an art car and use it to drag a Porta-John around the playa; maybe he just took the car for a joyride and the second part was pure *inspiration.*" He laughed.

"You don't sound that angry about it."

"Well, it might sound weird, but getting bashed around and covered in my own shit was kind of a wake-up call, you know? I mean, the universe doesn't slap you in the face with something like that at *random.* It made me do some serious thinking, realize that my life was *already* exactly like that. I was trapped in this little box, so concerned with my own shit I couldn't think about anything else. You know?"

Dex hesitated. His first day at the festival—how

many times had he even looked out the window before returning to his laptop?

"Yes," he said. "I suppose I do."

"Sometimes, when you're stuck, what you really need is a *sudden jerk*. Well, that's just what I got. . . ." He chuckled. "It got my attention. I realized I needed to make some changes in my life, do things differently. I wanted to give something *back,* so I got involved with the Earth Guardians. I'd always heard Burning Man was careful about the environment, but *man*—I had no idea. You know we go over *every square inch* of the site afterward? We pick up fucking *feathers,* individual *sequins.* And when we're done, there's *nothing* left. Think about that for a minute." He released one of the handlebars and gestured with his free hand. "All this, all gone. Like you threw the party to end all parties and afterward you couldn't even tell you'd had house-guests. It's the world's biggest vanishing act—from a city of thirty thousand to empty playa in no time at all. We're one of the most environmentally sound festivals in the country, and that's not just bragging; every year, we get graded by the Bureau of Land Management. They come in, they check out the job we do with a fine-tooth comb."

"What happens if they're not satisfied?"

"They can turn down our permit. But that's never happened, and it never will—'cause we're actually getting *better* at this as we go along. Did you know the first year Recycle Camp got started they pulled in twenty thousand cans?"

"Impressive," Dex admitted.

"Yeah? Well, by their third year they were doing over a hundred thousand. They used to even have a smelter on site, melt the cans down and make bicycle racks, but the process was too toxic. Lotta paint and other stuff getting burnt off."

"So what do they do with them all?"

"Make art out of some of it. The rest they sell, give the money to the high school in Gerlach. Helps buys 'em band uniforms, that kinda thing."

"That's admirable."

"Nah." He grinned. "That's Burning Man. . . ."

Afterward, they decided Captain Fun would hang back and keep an eye on Grover in case he went to the cops. "Lorilei doesn't have a walkie-talkie, so if he does go, I'll have to come tell you personally," Fun said. "Stay put until you hear from me—I'll keep an eye on Grover and in touch with Sundog. If nothing happens with either one after an hour or so, we'll move on."

The rendezvous point they agreed on was called Cosmonaut Camp, a geodesic dome made from a frame of white PVC tubing covered with parachute fabric. Black light provided the only illumination; psychedelic wall hangings fluoresced in unearthly greens, pinks, and oranges, while anything white shone as if lit from within. They sat on transparent inflatable furniture that looked like it was made from ectoplasm, and drank gin-and-tonics given to them by their hosts, a couple in blindingly white space suits with crimson hammer-and-sickle logos on the back. The two moved in the slow, exaggerated fashion of zero gravity, smiling behind the faceplates of their helmets. Even his drink, Dex noticed, seemed to be emitting a faint, bluish glow.

"Two down, nine to go," Lorilei said. "What about Green Grover?"

"I doubt it," Dex said. "He actually seemed *grateful* for what Wade did."

"Could have been an act to throw you off. How are you at reading people?"

"Not very good. I'm not that . . . *perceptive* with other people. Not very empathic, I guess."

"Really? I don't get that from you at all," she said thoughtfully. The yarn woven through her dreadlocks stood out in brilliant symmetrical helixes, as if rogue strands of her DNA had suddenly grown enormous and radioactive. "It's not your perceptions, Dex—it's just how you *react* to them."

"How am I *supposed* to react?" He took a long drink. "I mean, I feel like I'm on a roller coaster—no, I feel like I'm in a roller coaster car that's being chased by *another* roller coaster car, and they're firing at us with bazookas and the tracks are made out of spaghetti and after a few really sharp curves it leads straight down Godzilla's *throat.*" He paused. "And then there's an earthquake."

She chuckled. "And the people in your car are all lunatics, right?"

"Mmmmmm . . . no. Actually, they seem pretty nice."

"Well, Fun is a sweetheart. I've always been a sucker for a man with a superhero fetish."

"So, you two are . . ."

She leaned forward, looked him right in the eye. Dex wondered what it looked like when someone blushed under a black light—was it invisible, or did he look *twice* as embarrassed?

"Nope," she said. "Just friends. Although he *is* pretty good in bed."

"Ah," he said. "I wouldn't know."

"It's all those superpowers, you know? Orgasm vision, superstamina, cybernetic genitals . . ."

"You enjoy doing that *way* too much."

"What?" she said innocently.

"Teasing me."

"Oh? You think I'm a tease?" She took a sip of her drink and peered at him, wide-eyed, over the rim of the glass.

"No. I think you're lovely." Somehow, the words came out of his mouth without ever going near his brain. "And you seem very—*at home* here. But I'm not, and I don't think I ever *will* be, and I can't believe I'm about to say this but I wish you wouldn't—do that. So much."

"Mmmm. Is it because you find it distracting?"

"Yes," he blurted. "I'm not used to *any* of this—actually, it feels like I'm on another *planet* or something, most of the time—and I don't want to offend you or anything but—"

"I understand. It's a bit much for you, right now."

"Yes," he said, relieved.

"I'm sorry. And no."

"Thanks. It's just—What?"

She smiled. "Radical self-expression. That's a phrase that gets tossed around a lot here, but all it really means is that this is a place where people can communicate in any way they want. Now, if that means actually *hurting* someone else, it's not okay . . . but if it just makes someone *uncomfortable*, it is. The best art usually has that affect . . . and if it makes you *really* uncomfortable, you can always leave. That's one of the nice things about the playa—there's plenty of room for everyone."

"But—"

"Look, you're not going to accomplish *anything* here by retreating. You need to be aggressive, you need my help—and *I* need *you* to feed my blush fetish."

"Your *what?*"

"Well, you know what a blush is, don't you?" She gave her lips a slow, exaggerated lick. "It's just blood rushing to your *head* . . ."

He groaned, and tossed back the rest of his drink as she giggled.

An Asian woman in a belly-dancing outfit strolled up and joined them, sinking gracefully to a cross-legged position on the carpet beside Dex. "Hey," she said.

"Uh, hi," Dex said. The woman took a small tin box from the bag slung over her shoulder, opened it, and offered it to him. "Turkish delight?"

"No, thanks."

"I'd love one," Lorilei said. "These are made with rosewater, aren't they?"

"The pink ones," the woman said with a nod. She handed the box to Lorilei, then took it back, selected one herself and popped it into her mouth. She gave Dex a curious look as she chewed.

"So," she said. "Did you *really* kill Wade Jickling?"

CHAPTER 8:

INSPIRED VISION

"What did you just say?" Dex managed.

The Asian woman studied him for a moment before answering. She was in her twenties, with a determined look on her face and a sunburned nose. "Don't worry, I'm not going to turn you in," she said. "My name's Jimmy. I'm a reporter for the *Black Rock Gazette*."

"What makes you think I'm—who am I supposed to be?"

"Dexter Edden," Jimmy replied. "I'd keep that dust mask up and learn to drink through a straw if I were you. We're going to run a picture of you tomorrow, and then *everyone* will recognize you."

Dex quickly pulled the mask up, glancing around as he did so.

"He didn't do it," Lorilei said. "Actually, we're in the process of trying to prove his innocence."

"Oh?" Jimmy said. "Tell you what—you give me *your* side of the story, and I won't tell the cops a thing. Confidential source, right?"

"But you'll tell the whole *festival?*" Dex said. "No

way. Uh-uh. How am I supposed to clear my name if—"

"Look," Jimmy said firmly. "This works in your favor. If you're really innocent, this gives you a chance to tell the world what really went on. I don't have to reveal any details that might compromise where you are or who you're hanging out with—just tell me what happened on Monday night."

Dex glanced at Lorilei helplessly. She shrugged.

"Bazookas. Spaghetti. Straight down Godzilla's *throat,*" Dex muttered.

"Excuse me?"

"Okay, okay," Dex said wearily. "Just tell me one thing—how'd you know where to look for me?"

"Oh, I didn't," Jimmy said with a grin. She fished in her bag and pulled out a notebook and a pen. "I just like hanging out at Cosmonaut Camp. Isn't the lighting *great?*"

Captain Fun showed up just as Dex was finishing his story, Jimmy scribbling furiously in her notebook.

"—and then I fell asleep on a couch," Dex said. Fun signaled cautiously to Dex from behind Jimmy, pointing and making a *what's going on* gesture. Dex shrugged; Fun hesitated, then went over to the bar and started talking to one of the cosmonauts.

"How've you been surviving since then?" Jimmy asked.

"We've been taking care of him," Lorilei said. "And by we, I mean my camp."

"The identity of which I don't need to know," Jimmy said quickly. "Better if I don't, actually. . . .

Wow. Thank you, Dex—this has got to be the most amazing story I've ever covered."

"You believe me?" he asked her.

She gave him a long, considered look. "You know . . . I do. It's just too crazy not to be true." She tucked her notebook and pen back in her bag. "One last question. What are you going to do now?"

"Find the real killer," Lorilei said. "Wait. That makes him sound like O.J. Simpson, doesn't it? But we really *are* looking for the killer—we even have evidence the police don't have."

"Shouldn't you turn it over to them?"

"I don't know," Dex admitted. "Maybe I should. I just don't know if they'll take it seriously."

"I wouldn't worry about that," Jimmy said. "After tomorrow, they'll *have* to."

"What do you mean?" Dex asked.

Jimmy got to her feet as gracefully as she'd sat down. "Black Rock is a city *built* on stories," she said. "A really good one propagates through the population faster than the common cold. *This* one's going to spread like flesh-eating disease at a fat farm. . . . Come tomorrow, there's going to be thirty thousand Burners wanting to know how it all comes out. That's a lot of public pressure; the cops will *have* to take it seriously."

Dex swallowed with a suddenly dry throat, then grabbed his canteen and took a long drink. When he was done, he said, "Are—are you sure you want to run this?"

She slung her bag over her shoulder and grinned. "You should thank me. Remember—O.J. *walked*. See you around."

She took two steps, then stopped and turned back. "Oh, and, Dex—I wouldn't come back to this camp if I were you."

When she was gone, Captain Fun came over and sat down. "What was that all about?"

"Dex is about to be famous," Lorilei said. She told Fun what had happened.

"Well, your picture was going to run tomorrow anyway," Fun pointed out. "Jimmy was right—at least this way you can tell your side of the story."

"I guess," Dex said doubtfully. "It's not like I had much of a choice."

"Well, you *could* have smacked her upside the head with a piece of rebar," Fun said cheerfully. "But you didn't even consider it, which is definitely a point in your favor."

"Maybe we should have just run away," Lorilei said. "Tried to lose her, met back at camp."

"Ah, but then you would've had to wait for *my* news," Fun said. "I surveilled the dastardly-but-environmentally-conscious Green Grover from a safe distance, and I don't think he ever knew I was there. He pedaled the can-cruncher for another ten minutes or so—and then he took off."

Dex leaned forward. "Where did he go?"

"Jiffy Lube."

"So he was . . . getting his oil changed?"

"In a manner of speaking," Lorilei said. "Jiffy Lube's kind of like a gay bathhouse, minus the bath. One stop service."

"Right," Fun said. "Maybe that's how Rafe lured Wade here—sex."

"Except Wade wasn't gay," Dex said. "Although

somebody posing as a woman online might have worked. Wade was always . . . promiscuous."

"He thought with his dick, you mean," Lorilei said. "No offense, but if *half* of what was in those files is true, Wade Jickling was a world-class asshole."

"That's . . . fair enough," Dex said. "Uh—how about Sundog?"

"Ann Atomic went back to her camp, changed, and hit a party at the Canadian Consulate. He's there right now, keeping an eye on her and slugging back Canadian Club. She doesn't seem terribly nervous, though."

"So one suspect goes to a party, the other to have sex," Dex said. "Doesn't sound like either has a guilty conscience, does it?"

"Hey, we're just getting started," Captain Fun said. "Sundog said he'd dig up two more walkie-talkies for us tomorrow, so we can keep in touch better."

"Yeah . . . look, I'm pretty tired. Think we can call it a night?"

"Sure," Lorilei said. "It's going to be almost impossible to track anyone down at this point, anyway—everybody's out partying. We'll have a much better chance of finding people at their camps during the day."

"Well, you two can head off to bed," Fun said, "but I'm not ready to shut down for the night just yet."

Lorilei laughed. *"There's* a surprise. . . . Try to get at least a few hours sleep, all right?"

"Speaking of which—I think Inspector Urge and I should swap beds. Come tomorrow, he's gonna need the privacy."

Lorilei hesitated, then said, "Fine with me." Dex nodded.

They thanked their hosts for their hospitality and got on their bikes. Dex glanced back as they rode away; the cosmonauts were waving good-bye in slow motion, their suits glowing as white as twin full moons.

They cut across the playa to get home. A school of angelfish swam past in the distance, each at least a yard across, outlined in neon; they seemed to be floating around six feet above the ground, though none were at exactly the same height. They darted back and forth in front of each other like an aquarium sign in a fever dream, pursued by an art car shaped like a huge lunar crescent. Dex felt as if he'd fallen into a nursery rhyme gone horribly wrong.

And then he glanced over at Lorilei, and thought it might not be that bad after all.

Back at Aetheria, they locked their bikes together outside the pod. "I'll try to find you a lock of your own, tomorrow," she said.

"No hurry."

She grinned. "You *do* know there's all kinds of things I could say about locks and keys and maybe even chains right now?"

"Do your worst. I'm starting to get used to it."

"Really? I must be slipping . . . guess it's time to raise the bar." She looked at him and blinked once, very slowly. "I'm going to go inside," she said softly, "and take off all my clothes. Then I'm going to get into bed . . . and *think.*" She leaned infinitesimally closer, but suddenly Dex could smell the sweetness of her hair. "I'm going to think really, really *hard.* About you."

Dex tried to say something, but nothing came out. He was almost glad; it probably would have made "Ulk" sound like Shakespeare.

"You can think about me, if you want to," Lorilei whispered. "I find that a good hard *think* helps you fall asleep, especially when you're tense. I may need to think about *you* several times before I drift off. . . ."

And then she opened the door, stepped inside, and closed it again.

Dex stood outside for a full minute before leaving. It wasn't that he was steeling himself to knock on the door; he just felt sort of dizzy, and was worried he might get lost between the pod and the trailer.

Totally, completely lost.

He slept poorly. His nose was still stuffed up, and his thoughts ricocheted from death to sex to imprisonment and back again. Every time he heard a noise outside he would bolt upright, thinking it was either the police, the killer, or Lorilei; every time it proved to be nothing. He had to leave twice to stumble to the Porta-Johns with a flashlight.

Despite what she'd said, he didn't take Lorilei's advice. He was just too nervous.

He finally got up, clicked on the batttery-powered lamp, and reviewed Wade's files again. He made notes, again wishing he had access to a printer. Still, he felt an obscure sort of pride in the notes themselves; despite being written with borrowed materials from a stolen source, they belonged to him—the first thing he'd actually made with his own hands since he'd arrived. They might not be art, but they were *his*.

He finally nodded off around four, and woke eight hours later covered in sweat, brightness leaking through the unzipped edges of the window flaps. He levered himself out of bed, yawning, and wondered blearily if his next shower would take place behind bars.

It took him a minute to notice there was something hanging on the doorknob that hadn't been there the night before.

His heart stumbled, fell flat on its aorta, and leapt up again. The object in question was a small cloth bag, with a piece of paper pinned to it with "CURIOUS?" written on it in flowing purple script. Realizing who must have left it, he looked inside and found:

A toothbrush.

Toothpaste.

A hotel bar of soap.

A square piece of brightly colored cloth.

A waxy, floral-scented lump in the shape of a semi-oval, which he eventually realized was half a deodorant stick.

"This," he said reverently, "might just save my life."

Twenty minutes later, feeling a lot cleaner and more awake, he slipped on his dust mask and sunglasses and stepped out into the sun.

"Hey, Inspector," Captain Fun said. He was adjusting the chain on his bike, wearing nothing but sandals and a cape again. "You get Lorilei's care package?"

"Yes," Dex said. "I used some of your water to wash up—hope that's okay."

"Sure. Help yourself to some food—I just made lunch."

Lunch turned out to be gnocchi with a tomato and artichoke sauce and freshly ground Parmesan. Dex helped himself to a large bowl, but stopped when he realized he'd have to take off the mask to eat; there were two other people sitting in lawn chairs eating already, and he didn't know either of them.

Captain Fun solved the problem for him. "I'd like you to meet the newest members of Tribe Curious," he said. "This is Cromagg and Sigma Jen. Guys, you *know* who this is . . . but please, call him Mr. Urge."

Dex glanced at Fun unbelievingly. "You *told* them?"

"Hey, it's cool," Cromagg said. He was in his twenties, with long brown dreadlocks and a neatly trimmed beard. He wore a tan-colored loincloth and had a happy face with devil horns shaved into his chest hair. "Fun explained the situation. We're onboard."

"Absolutely," Sigma Jen said. She had bright red hair pulled back into a single long braid and was dressed in a toga almost as pale as her skin. A crown of green leaves circled her forehead. "You'll never be able to track down all those suspects without help."

The wobbly, out-of-control feeling in his stomach was starting to feel eerily familiar. "Uh, thanks," Dex said. He sank onto an unused chair, pulled down his mask and started to eat.

"By the way, thanks for those temporary tattoos," Fun said to Cromagg. "They're coming in real handy."

"Well, it wasn't like I could use them," Cromagg said. "Not on *this* hairy body, anyway."

"So," Sigma Jen said, leaning forward and addressing Dex, "did he crap himself?"

Dex stopped with the spoon halfway to his mouth. "Excuse me?"

"The guy that got killed," Sigma Jen said. "I heard that's what happens when somebody dies."

Dex's appetite vanished. He put down the spoon. "I didn't notice," he said quietly.

"*Jesus,* Jen," Cromagg said. "Why don't you just hit *him* with a piece of rebar? I'm sorry, man."

"It's all right," Dex said.

"I was just *wondering,*" Sigma Jen said. "I never met anyone who saw somebody get killed."

The arrival of Sundog spared Dex from a reply. The DPW man came striding up, dressed in the same black skirt he'd worn the day before—but it *wasn't* a skirt, Dex suddenly noticed; it had multiple pockets and "UTILIKILT" stenciled on a tag along the waistband.

"Hey," said Sundog gruffly. Then, "You tell him yet?" to Fun.

"Tell me what?" Dex said.

"Sundog lost Ann Atomic last night," Fun said.

"Yeah," Sundog said. "Gave me the slip over at Carnevil around midnight. Went in but never came out. Think it was deliberate, too—she left her bike behind."

"So she figured out you were following her," Sigma Jen said. "Could be she was just creeped out."

Fun shook his head. "Have you *seen* Ann Atomic? If she thought Sundog was tailing her, she'd probably just pound on the top of his head till she turned him into a fence post."

"Wait," Dex said. "I thought you were only going to watch her for an hour or so."

"Yeah, well," Sundog said, "I kinda got into it. Thought I might find out something useful."

Great, Dex thought. *I'm inspiring stalkers.* "Look, it doesn't mean anything. If she was the killer, she would have gone straight to the cops."

"Perhaps not," Cromagg said. He scratched one hairy leg absently. "Where would she have sent them? You didn't give her this address, right?"

"Well—no," Dex admitted.

"So maybe she decided to think about it, weigh her options. Come up with a plan. Only thing is . . ." Cromagg frowned. "She'd need to know where you are. So her wandering off doesn't make any sense, unless she has some way to find you later."

"Or if she's innocent," Dex pointed out.

"Did I just hear the word 'innocent'?" The voice was Lorilei's, and came from behind Dex; he turned to find her standing there with a newspaper in her hand. "That *would* be the word of the day . . ."

She held up the paper for everyone to see. It was a copy of *The Black Rock Gazette*, with a headline that read: "ACCUSED KILLER CLAIMS INNOCENCE." Beneath it was a picture of Dex, apparently taken from his driver's licence.

"Well?" she asked Dex. "What do you think?"

"I think," Dex said, "that I *really* need a cup of coffee."

The article, Dex discovered, wasn't as bad as he'd feared. It gave away no clues to his whereabouts or possible activities, and described the murder exactly as he'd told it to Jimmy. The way it ended was a bit of a surprise, though:

> As most of us know, sometimes the truth is a slippery concept in Black Rock City. As long as we're just playing, that's fine—but now, the truth is a matter of

life and death. Is Dex Edden a murderer, or a victim? If his story is true, the police have little or no chance of catching the real killer—he or she has obviously put a lot of thought into this. Like it or not, the chaotic nature of BRC makes it the perfect place to stage this crime. But there's one thing "Rafe" didn't count on:

Us.

It's always the first-timers that need help, and no matter how clueless or misinformed they are, Burners help them out. We give them food, we give them water, we educate and enlighten until they finally get it. And that's a wonderful moment, isn't it? When the lightbulb comes on and they finally understand that they *belong* here? I can still remember the instant I realized I was a BRC citizen, that this was *my* city, and I'm not ashamed to admit it still makes me a little teary.

I don't want to take that moment away from Dexter Edden.

Please. Get involved. Keep your eyes and ears open. Let's find out what really happened in that RV . . . and let's show the world that nobody comes into *our* city and gets away with murder.

Dex looked up and saw that Sundog, Captain Fun, Cromagg, and Sigma Jen were all reading their own copies; Lorilei had brought a stack of *Gazette*s to share.

He turned, walked back to the tent-trailer, and went inside without saying a word.

Lorilei followed him. Of course. She found him sitting at the table inside, staring at the screen of the laptop.

"You all right?" she asked from the doorway.

"No," he said flatly. "No, I'm *not* all right. I hate to

ruin everybody's good time, but I don't find this as—as *entertaining* as you all seem to."

She came inside, closed the door behind her. "You don't think we're taking this seriously."

"I don't know if you people take *anything* seriously. A man is *dead,* for God's sake. Maybe he wasn't a very *good* man, but he didn't deserve to have his *skull* caved in."

"No. No, he didn't." She came over, sat down on the bench beside him.

"And you're all treating it like a *game.* You treat *everything* like a game. When I first got here, I thought this whole place was just anarchy, people running around doing whatever they wanted—but I was wrong. You *do* have rules. *Leave No Trace, No Vending, No Spectators. Do Not Pass Go Without Sunscreen.* Of course you have rules—you can't play a game without them, can you? Even if you're just making them up as you go along."

"Piss Clear," she said.

"—What?"

"It's one of our 'rules.' If your urine has no discernable color, it's a sign you're drinking enough water. Piss Clear."

He sighed. "I have more important things to worry about right now than the color of my urine—"

"Really? So I guess you're really looking forward to that nice air-conditioned cell?"

"Of course not."

"Then you *better* pay attention to the color of your pee—because if you get sick, you'll lose what little control over this situation you have." She sighed, and took his hand. "Look, Dex, I know you're feeling kind of overloaded—that's perfectly natural. Even people who *aren't* wanted fugitives go through this, their first few days here. Everything's weird and distorted, none of the usual social conventions apply . . . you just have to ride it out."

"But I don't *want* to ride it out," he said miserably. "I want to go *home*. I want to sleep in my own bed, and watch crappy TV, and pay some faceless kid to bring me pizza. I want to take a *bath*. I want everything to be *normal* again."

She gave him a sad smile. "Oh, sweetie . . . you *know* there's no such thing, don't you?"

"I don't know what I know anymore."

"Well, let me tell you a few things *I* know. First off, your whole game analogy? Dead-on."

". . . It is?"

"Absolutely. Some of us refer to Burning Man as 'playing city for a week.' Burners love games—hell, we love *playing*. But just because we get enjoyment out of something doesn't mean we don't take it seriously. You don't believe me, I'll take you down to the Thunderdome and introduce you to a few Death Guilders.

"Second—I know you're scared. But you're not in this alone anymore. . . . and that article is going to shake all *kinds* of things loose."

"Just what I need," he said morosely. "More shaking. . . ."

When they rejoined the others, they were already in the middle of debating strategy; Tribe Curious, it seemed, was of the opinion that they needed a new plan. They retired to Lorilei's pod for privacy—Cromagg and Sigma Jen, as it turned out, were her other two roomies—and kicked around ideas for over an hour. They passed around Dex's laptop, drank coffee, made suggestions. Cromagg took notes. It wasn't really all that different from many other meetings Dex had sat through, aside from the lack of overhead projectors and the fact that it was his own fate they were discussing.

In the end they came up with a three-pronged approach. Dex would continue to approach and interview possible suspects, and direct each one to a different decoy camp. All the camps were in sight of a four-story tower with a platform on top called Olymplatypus; one of the Tribe would stay up there with a walkie-talkie and watch for a police presence at any of the decoys. Other members would spread out, searching for people mentioned in Wade's files.

A lot of the ideas had been Cromagg's; he seemed to have a natural gift for tactics, and Dex told him so.

Cromagg laughed and said, "Well, that's probably my background—it's sort of what I do."

"Oh?" Dex said. "How's that?" He couldn't imagine Cromagg being in the military.

"I write source books and adventure modules for RPGs—role-playing games. You know, generate the stats for the monsters and environment. How many hit points can a Frost Giant take before it goes down, stuff like that."

"Huh," Dex said. "I'm not sure I see the connection."

"That's probably because you play video games as opposed to ones where you actually roll dice. See, in most video games you have about as much personality as—well, you. It's all about immediate physical action and reaction: running, shooting, driving, flying. But in a role-playing game, you actually *become* a different person. That person has a specific history, and an attitude that's informed by his or her experiences. It has a lot more to do with mental adaptability than it does with eye-hand coordination."

"I can see how that would come in handy for someone like an actor," Dex said.

"Sure. But see, RPGs are about more than taking on a different persona; they're about problem-solving. Once the Game Master sets up the situation and tells you what resources are available, it's up to you to figure out what to do."

"So it's a simulation. Like a computer model."

"Exactly. It's why so many corporate seminars use role-playing as a teaching tool. Of course, they tend to use scenarios like, 'How to deal with an unsatisfied customer,' while the stuff I play is more about 'How can we storm a well-fortified castle with only three dwarves, a catapult, and fifty feet of rope'; but really, it's the same mental process. Once you get used to doing it, you can apply it to anything . . . ever hear of a game called Top Secret?"

"No, I don't think so."

"Came out in the early Eighties, was all about espionage. Had lots of stats on guns, disguises, getaway vehicles. Couple of teenagers wound up using it to rehearse gas-station stickups."

"Really? How'd they get caught?"

Cromagg grinned. "Who says we did?"

● ● ●

They decided the smart move would be to start with a Lamplighter named Glow Shtick. "We can probably find him at Lamplighter Village," Fun said. "If he isn't there now, he'll show up by dusk."

"Okay," Dex said nervously. Knowing that his face was plastered all over the city wasn't making going out in public easy, despite Lorilei's assurances. He took one long, final drink of water and pulled up his dust mask. "Let's go."

Lamplighter Village was at Creed and Karmic Circle, just off Center Camp. Dex, Captain Fun, and Lorilei stopped half a block away. Sundog had managed to dig up two more walkie-talkies; he had one, Cromagg and Sigma Jen had one, and Fun, Lorilei, and Dex had two between them.

"Break a leg," Captain Fun said.

"Go get 'em, Ulk," Lorilei told him. "We'll be right across the street if you get into trouble."

"Wait a minute. What if I do get into trouble? What if he recognizes me and starts yelling for the cops?"

"You run," Lorilei said. "And we run interference."

"How? Ram a police cruiser with your bike?"

"If neccesary," Fun said. "Nothing slows down a high-speed chase like an innocent bystander bouncing off a fender."

"All right, all right," Dex said. "Here I go."

He headed for a large, peaked-roof shade structure; it was at least twenty feet tall and probably a hundred feet in length. The floor was covered in hurricane lanterns, the same kind he'd seen suspended from the wooden streetlamps. People were busy filling them with fuel then moving them outside, where dozens of poles were balanced down the length of a long, narrow table. Each pole had a dozen hooks embedded in it, six on either side; the first thing that came to Dex's mind was a group seesaw for hanging ferns.

That's just crazy. They're for carrying the lanterns.

The wind, Dex noted, was starting to kick up, raising billows of dust at random. Good; it made keeping his dust mask on more plausible. He made himself approach the most normal looking person he saw, a white-bearded man wearing a T-shirt, shorts, and a brown cowboy hat. The man had never heard of Glow Shtick, but suggested he talk to a woman wearing a white robe with a gold-and-crimson flame design reaching up from the hem.

"Glow Shtick?" She laughed and put down the lantern she'd been inspecting. She was a blonde, round-cheeked woman in her late thirties, wearing sunglasses covered in gold glitter. "Sure—you're talking to him."

"I'm sorry," Dex said. "From the email that was forwarded to me I assumed you were male."

"Hey, sometimes when I'm online I *am* male," she said with a grin. "Which email in particular are you referring to?"

"The open letter to the vandal."

Comprehension dawned on her face. "Ah, that. What did you want to know?"

"I'm working on a story for the *Black Rock Gazette*, about people who come here and . . . well, go crazy. I was just wondering if you'd mind talking about it face-to-face."

"Depends."

"On what?"

"On whether or not you give me a hand while we

talk. These lanterns aren't going to fill themselves, you know." She held out a jerry can of kerosene and a small plastic funnel; after a second's hesitation he took them.

She inspected and trimmed wicks while he filled. "You know, I still can't believe it happened. People tell me, 'Well, with thirty thousand freaks out in the desert, some of them are bound to be badass crazy.' And while I know that in my head, I just don't feel that way in my heart. The idea that anyone would deliberately wreck something beautiful and useful . . . it doesn't just seem wrong, it seems blasphemous. You know?"

"Yes," Dex said. "What was the final tally?"

"Well, there are four lanterns to a stand, and he darkened eighteen of them . . . so seventy-two."

"That's a lot."

"Not as many as you might think. We're pushing a thousand lanterns this year, seven hundred and fifty the year it happened."

"How did he get away with it? You'd think somebody would have stopped him."

"He used a BB gun—you know, one of those CO_2-powered ones? Blew out the glass from a distance and the wind did the rest."

"Personally," Dex said, "I think people like that should be punished."

"You know, I used to think so, too. But now, I'm not as certain."

"Oh? What changed your mind?"

She inspected a lantern critically, then popped off the top. "I couldn't stop thinking about why he'd do such a thing. It took a certain amount of perseverance. The amount of rage he must have had . . . I just wondered why he did it. So I tried to find out."

"By posting an open message to a Burning Man bulletin board."

"Yes. I'm sure you've read it, as well as most of the replies—but not all of them. Somebody calling themselves Duststorm got in touch with me privately, seemed very interested in talking about what happened. He never admitted it—but I know it was him."

Dex had, in fact, read the very reply she was talking about, but he couldn't say that without telling her how he'd gotten it. "What makes you so sure?"

"There was an . . . incident. After the first story about the vandalism was published in the *Gazette*. This man showed up in the Lamplighters' Lounge, making jokes about blackouts like he thought the whole thing was funny. Needless to say, he wasn't very popular—but I was the one that talked to him the longest, and I was the one he blew up at."

"What happened?"

"He tossed a mug of sangria at me. I knew the stain would never come out, so I just integrated it into the design. See?" She tapped her chest, and Dex saw that what he'd thought was a random flame pattern did look a little like a splash. "Red wine may as well be red dye. Just added a little edging to it."

"Why'd he do it?"

"I was trying to explain to him about the importance of ritual. That's what the Lamplighters are all about, really; we're not the only camp here based around that kind of thing, but we do it every year and we do it pretty much the same. We keep getting bigger, but one thing never changes: as the sun goes down we hit the streets, carrying fire."

"And that made him angry?"

"It was more involved than that. See, he was taking a very typical 'us versus them' attitude—because the Lamplighters provide an essential service, he was equating our camp with some kind of central power structure. I tried to explain that we were all volunteers—that everybody here is 'us' . . . but he just didn't get it. To be honest, I think it scared him. Like a kid who'd been rebelling against authority his whole life and suddenly didn't have anything to fight anymore."

Dex tightened the cap on a lantern, moved on to the next. Despite the smell of kerosene, he was finding the work strangely centering. "And you think this man was the same one who contacted you later?"

"Yes. He was a lot less confrontational online, but he steered the discussion along the same lines as our earlier conversation, about ritual and the role it plays here."

An image of Darth Bunny popped into Dex's head. Bizarre though it was, the costume could be said to have a certain ritual significance. "And what do you think that role is, exactly?"

"Depends on which ritual. The people over at the Temple of Atonement are all about control and surrender; the people who bring things to burn at the Temple of Honor are usually trying to let something go. Anger, love, grief . . . expectations. It's different for everyone. I guess that's what's so unusual about ritual out here. Historically, it's been used to unify belief; on the playa, you're encouraged to interpret a ritual in any way you want."

"Doesn't that—well, dilute its power?"

She stopped what she was doing, paused. "Let me

ask you a question. What's more powerful—the universe talking to a crowd that you're part of, or the universe talking directly to you?"

"I see your point."

"The more personal it is, the more profound it is. On the surface, ritual might seem to be about repetition . . . but it's really about transformation. Connecting with something in a way that changes you. Almost like bone and muscle."

"I don't follow."

"Muscles are what move us, but they couldn't do their job if they didn't have bone to anchor to and push against. That's how I think of ritual—the bone that the muscle of change pushes against."

The skull was just another bone, Dex thought. And what would that make the rebar that crushed it? The ultimate act of transformation?

"So why did this Duststorm contact you? To gloat?"

"No, that wasn't it. I think he honestly wanted to understand. . . . I just don't know if he did." She gave Dex a strange look, somewhere between intrigued and confused. "You know, I talked to a reporter from the *Gazette* last year . . . do you know Jimmy?"

"Yes," Dex said. "She's the one who asked me to follow this up, actually. She's a little preoccupied with another story at the moment."

"Of course. The murder."

Dex's stomach tightened. "You read the interview?"

"Me and every other Burner. Did you hear what *Piss Clear* is calling him?"

"Uh, no," Dex said.

"It came out a few hours after the *Gazette* did—hang on, I've got a copy around somewhere." She walked over to a bike, fished around in a saddlebag slung over the back fender. "Ah. Here it is."

The banner of the newspaper she held out proclaimed: "PISS CLEAR—*Black Rock City's Favorite Alternative Newspaper.*" Beneath that was an obviously Photoshopped picture of Darth Vader with a pair of long furry ears added, holding a gigantic mallet instead of a lightsaber. To one side was a cartoon corpse with Xs for eyes; to the other, a picture of the Road Runner zooming away, with Dex's head pasted on the skinny neck. The caption read: *"Whodunnit? Darth Bunny or the Rogue-Runner?"*

"The 'Rogue-Runner'?" Dex said.

"They're more or less calling for his head," she said. "Posting a reward for his arrest, setting up a hotline for tips, organizing a search of every tent and vehicle in the city . . ."

Dex's head swam. It was suddenly very hard to breathe; he had the sudden urge to rip the dust mask away from his face and scream, *Here I am! Come and get me!*

"Really," he managed.

"Sure." She chuckled. "It ends with them suggesting a lynch camp that could pass out pitchforks and torches, and have everyone dress as irate townsfolk. You can always count on *PC* to go as far over the top as possible."

His heart shifted into a slightly lower gear. "Yeah. Funny stuff. We love 'em over at the *Gazette.* . . ."

He gave her the address of the decoy camp and told her she could get in touch with him there if he wasn't at the *Gazette,* just in case "Duststorm" showed up; she gave him the e-dress the man had used, so he could contact him directly. Dex didn't think Wade would be checking his email anytime soon, but he thanked her anyway, got on his bike, and rode off.

Fun and Lorilei caught up with him a block away. "How'd it go?" Fun asked.

"Unless she has an accomplice, it's not her."

"Her?"

"Yeah. Wrong build for the killer, plus I can't see someone committing murder over a few broken lanterns and a wine stain."

"She sounded pretty vehement in the file," Lorilei said.

"Well, she's mellowed in the last twelve months. Seems to be leaning more toward understanding than retribution."

"One more down, anyway," Lorilei said. "Who's next?"

"Playa Fiya," Dex said.

"Actually," Fun said, "I've got something else I have to take care of. Okay if I take the extra walkie-talkie and catch up with you later?"

"What's up?" Lorilei asked. "Got a hot date or something?"

"Something like that," Fun said with a grin. "Shouldn't be too long—maybe an hour."

"I guess we'll see you later," Dex said. He felt a sudden brief flash of paranoia—*is he going to the police?*—but pushed it away firmly. Fun had gone to great lengths to help him, and it made no sense for him to turn Dex in now.

After Fun rode off, Lorilei and Dex stopped at the Porta-Johns. There was a short line, but someone had set up a table and chair next to it with a sign that read:

GRATITUDE BOOTH. The wide-faced man seated there wore a bathrobe and a bright green bowler hat; he was giving out Jolly Rancher candies.

"And what do you have to be grateful for?" he asked Lorilei.

She unwrapped a pink one, carefully tucking the plastic into her bag before popping the candy into her mouth. "I'm grateful for . . . new friends," she said.

"And you?" the man asked Dex.

Any friends at all was the first response that came to mind, but he left it there; it sounded pathetic. "I guess I'm just grateful to be alive," Dex said.

"I know what you mean," the man said. He closed his eyes and raised his face toward the sun. "Aren't we lucky?"

"Some of us more than others," Dex said.

And then, apparently, their luck ran out.

Sigma Jen and Cromagg called in to say they hadn't been able to find the person they'd been searching for, a woman camped with the Temple of Atonement. Sundog reported no police activity at any of the decoy camps. And when Dex tried to locate a BRC postal worker, he encountered a level of weirdness that was both entirely new and eerily familiar.

The Black Rock City Post Office appeared to share an impressive-looking two-story building with the PedEx delivery service and something called the INSS, but appearances were deceiving; it was only a plywood front, and hiding behind it were an ordinary-looking cluster of tents.

There was a wicket set into the facade, with a man

behind it. He wore a loud Hawaiian shirt and a scuba mask, and was reading a magazine. Dex walked up and said, "Excuse me."

"Dake a number, blease," the man said without looking up. The scuba mask made him sound like he had the worst cold in the world.

Dex glanced around. There was a hook on the wall beside the wicket, with square plastic tags hanging from it. The tag on the top had a large red *J* painted on it.

"Uh—these?"

"Do you see any *udder* numbers?"

"No," Dex said, feeling foolish.

"Den take onc of dose and go stand in line."

"But there isn't any line," Dex pointed out.

The man looked up from his magazine. He peered carefully around Dex, and sighed heavily. "You're right. Blease fill dis out." He pulled a form from under the counter and slapped it down in front of Dex with a pen. The form read:

FORM 1775B—Registering A Complaint In Regard To The Nonexistence Of A Line

Name:

Real name:

Name you answer to when dressed as a naughty little schoolgirl:

Are you a naughty little schoolgirl?:

I knew it, call me Daddy:

Bad Girl! Naughty little girl! (Check one):
< > Bad < > Naughty < > Pickle

If you checked Pickle, please explain:

Sweet, Gherkin, or Dill:

How do you feel about condiments? Be honest:

A train leaves Boston at 10:15 heading East. A Greyhound bus leaves Cleveland at 7:00 heading Northwest. How about that?:

Do you feel the previous question was an accurate portrayal of an overused setup, and if so, was the punch line telegraphed in advance? Do you have any idea what a telegraph is, or did you feel a lost and desperate urge to look it up on Google? Are you a *complete* dumb-ass, or do you just play one on TV? Are these questions becoming abusive?

If you answered yes to ANY of the above questions, please see a Service Representative.

"Bress down hard—you're making three goppies," the clerk said. "Den go stand in line."

"But there isn't any line—"

"Well, of *gorse* dere idn't. Dad's why you're filling oud da *form*, idn't it?"

Dex opened his mouth, then shut it again. He took the plastic tag from its hook. He turned around and walked a short distance to the sign stuck in the ground that proclaimed, LINE BEGINS HERE. He waited.

After thirty seconds or so, a voice from another wicket called out, "Number twelve! Number twelve, please!"

He looked down at the *J* in his hand, sighed, and approached the wicket. It was the same clerk, but he'd taken off the scuba mask.

"Number twelve?" he asked pleasantly.

Dex held up the *J*.

"That," the clerk said, "is not a number twelve."

"But—"

"It's a number eleven." The clerk rolled his eyes. "Honestly, it's a simple system—letters equal numbers, *A* equals one and so forth. What are you, *drunk?*"

"In that case, *J* should equal the number *ten*—"

"The letter *C* was eliminated by the Reduction of Consonants Act of 1991, making *J* the number nine— as anyone who doesn't have 'Moron' embossed on their personal stationery already knows. Now, ma'am, I'll have to ask you to go wait until it's your turn."

"There's no one else in line—"

"Really? Then I'll have to ask you to fill out one of—"

"I've already *got* one of those. Can't you just see me next?"

"Would you like to take another number?"

Dex looked at the next tag on the hook. It had a picture of a duck on it.

"No," he said wearily, "I don't think so. Look, I'm just wondering if I can talk to somebody on your staff."

"Somebody *on* my *staff?*" The man's eyes went wide. "Is that some sort of *sexual innuendo?* Are you *harassing* me?"

"No, no—"

The man's voice went up a note in pitch. "You *are*! You said *staff* when you clearly meant *penis,* and *some-*

body when you clearly meant *a skanky, disease-ridden whore.* You are obviously implying that I spend my time behind this wicket indulging in illicit sex with *hookers!*" He glared at Dex in righteous indignation.

Dex sighed. "Yes," he said. "That's what I'm saying."

"Oh. Well, don't go telling everyone; they'll get jealous. Now, how can I help you?"

"I'm looking for somebody called Playa Fiya."

"Why didn't you say so? He's out on his route, delivering mail. Won't be back until tomorrow."

"Oh. I don't suppose you could tell me what his route is?"

The man's eyebrows went up. "First you mention my *staff,* now you want to talk about somebody else's *route?* Honey, you don't have enough vodka. Or any, for that matter. Do you?"

"Uh, no."

"Well, come back when you do. Next!"

"But there's—oh." Now there actually were several people behind him; he got out of their way. "Good luck," he muttered as he left.

Lorilei was waiting for him at a little café just behind the Post Office, lounging on a pile of pillows and sipping a cup of tea. Soft jazz played in the background. "How'd it go?" she asked him with an innocent look on her face. "Were they prompt, courteous, and helpful?"

He threw himself down with a scowl. "You knew that was going to happen."

"That what was going to happen?"

"I'd tell you, but you'd have to fill out a form first."

"Actually, I could hear quite a bit of it from here.

Not everything, though . . . for instance, *what* did you say about his penis?"

Dex groaned. "Don't start. If you overheard, then you know Playa Fiya is not currently available."

"Onward, then. After I finish my tea."

"Take your time. I need to take a bathroom break, anyway."

"Head toward the Man—there's a couple of Porta-Johns on either side of the six o'clock Promenade, about halfway up. And here, take my bike lock."

He transferred the chain from her bike to his own, and she tossed him the key. The wind was really starting to pick up, he noticed; visibility was rapidly decreasing, vehicles and people blurring into indistinct outlines all around him.

"You might want to wait a few minutes," Lorilei said.

"Can't," he said. "I've been drinking so much water I'm starting to grow gills."

"Well, if it gets too bad just find shelter and wait it out. I'll be right here until you get back."

"I'll be fine," he said.

And he was, all the way out to the Porta-Johns—but in the minute or so he was inside, the wind rose from a moan to a howl. When he stuck his head outside, he was stunned; all he could see was a wall of white. Even his bike, not ten feet away, was invisible.

Suddenly, there was a tall, triangular shape beside him. "Hey!" a voice called out. "Can you give me a hand?"

The shape was a sail—a windsurfer's sail, to be exact; it was attached to some sort of large-wheeled skateboard, its rider struggling to get it under control.

Dex jumped out, grabbed hold of the frame, and tried to keep the bow pointed into the wind.

"Thanks!" the rider shouted. "I'm gonna try to lash it to the Porta-Johns!" Before Dex could suggest a more reasonable course of action—like laying it flat—he was trying to hang on to the sail by himself while the rider fumbled with rope.

He was only alone for a second, though—the rumble of an engine cut through the wind as a vehicle pulled up. Dex could only make out something vaguely car-shaped, but the driver hopped out and rushed over to give him a hand.

The spirit of cooperation, Dex had to admit, was alive and well at Burning Man. There was nothing like the threat of imminent disaster to get people to pull together—

Which is when he noticed the scorpion tattoo on the driver's face. It was the man who'd chased him the night of the murder.

He froze, then caught his breath and forced himself to concentrate on keeping the sail under control. *You're wearing a mask,* he told himself. *He only saw you once, in the dark—*

He caught the driver staring at his chest. At the T-shirt visible beneath his unbelted trench coat, now flapping wildly in the wind. The driver looked up sharply, stared him straight in the eye.

"Dexter. Fucking. Edden," he snarled.

CHAPTER 9:

REAL FAITH?

The man with the scorpion tattooed on his face, his eyes filled with a savage glee, shouted, "I'd recognize that stupid-ass T-shirt anywhere! You are *busted,* assho—"

Dex shoved him, hard. Caught off guard, the man stumbled backward and went down. It was probably the most impulsive, unthought-out act of Dex's adult life—and he topped it a split second later.

He jumped on the windsurfer's board and pushed off.

He did it because he had, several summers ago, actually done some windsurfing. He'd won a free lesson as a prize at the company Christmas dinner—back when the company could afford such things, before they'd downsized his entire department down to zero—and he'd actually enjoyed taking it. He was no surf-dude, but by the time the lesson was over, he could at least keep the board upright most of the time.

It was dumb luck that the board didn't immediately flip over; instead, the wind caught the sail at just the right angle to launch Dex like a cannonball into the howling mouth of the storm.

It was a short trip. The rope tied to the mast snapped taut as it reached its end, almost sending Dex sprawling; he caught his balance just in time. He couldn't have traveled more than twenty feet, but he could no longer see the Porta-Johns—just a wall of dust. Of course, all Scorpion-face had to do was follow the rope. . . .

The line was attached to the mast by a carabiner snapped to a metal ring. All Dex needed was a little slack to get it off—but the wind was keeping the rope stretched tight. He pulled on the sail as hard as he could, but it was like trying to rein in a hurricane.

Run. Just run—he'll never find you in this storm. You can hunker down and wait it out—

And then, above the roar of the wind, he heard the unmistakable sound of an engine revving.

A second later, an eddy in the dust storm provided a sudden clear patch; he could see the outline of the car, not fifteen feet away. It was creeping closer.

Frantically, he angled the sail to provide the least wind resistance, stepped off the board, and pushed instead of pulled. It worked; he was able to unsnap the carabiner, dropping the line to the ground.

He jumped back on, shifted the sail, and hung on for dear life as the wind catapulted him forward.

If not for the sail in front of him, he would have thought he'd gone blind. The whiteout was total, a howling, stinging creature trying to invade his mouth and nose, wanting to devour all his senses. At the same time, the sensation of speed was incredible—despite the bumpiness of the ride, he still felt like he was rocketing into an endless void.

But it's not *endless. This part of the playa is pretty empty, but there are still structures out here—BIG structures, made of steel and two-by-fours and God-knows-what-else, and if I run into one at this speed—*

And then he heard the throaty rumble of an engine, coming up behind him fast.

Is he insane? *Unless he has radar in that thing, he's risking the life of everybody in his path—*

Dex understood, suddenly, why he hadn't taken off on foot. Scorpion-face wouldn't abandon his death-mobile any more than Genghis Khan would abandon his horse, and he would have used it to run Dex to ground in much the same way. Dex might have been able to use the near-zero visibility to evade him . . . but it could have just as easily resulted in his being struck and killed.

It still could, he thought. He yanked the sail savagely to the right, changing course sharply. Almost immediately, he heard the car's engine get farther away . . . and suddenly, he was out of the storm. He'd breached the far wall of the cloud, and was now bumping across mostly empty playa.

He glanced around quickly, trying to get his bearings. He couldn't see the Man, but that was the city off to his right, still hazy through a veil of dust. At his current heading he would cross one of the promenades that ran from the Esplanade to the Man, lampposts evenly spaced down its length. He started wondering about how he was going to stop.

And then the deathmobile roared out of the billowing edge of the storm front, a hundred feet ahead of him. Its matte-black body dragged a dust plume behind it like smoke from a smoldering fire, and it slammed to a skidding, sideways halt as soon as the driver spotted him.

Dex had no choice. He dove back toward the storm, plunging blind into dusty chaos once more. As long as he was unseen, he had a chance; out in the open, the deathmobile could easily cut him off and run him down.

But the driver had a fix on him now. He'd seen how fast Dex was moving and at what angle; it wasn't like Dex could make the Windsurfer pivot a hundred and eighty degrees. Maybe a more experienced rider could, but Dex was more or less at the mercy of the wind. Which meant Scorpion-face already had a rough idea of his position . . .

Dex angled back toward the storm's edge again, just in time to hear the roar of the car coming at him. There was a frozen instant when he was sure the next thing he would feel would be the crunch of impact— and then the car shot past him, slamming on its brakes a second too late. Dex immediately changed course again, knowing that zigzagging was his only hope of throwing his pursuer off.

Suddenly there was a lamppost right in front of him.

He tried to swerve, but the edge of the sail clipped the wooden standard anyway. The sail swung hard into Dex's shoulder. He almost lost his balance and his grip, but managed to hold on. A second later he'd crossed the promenade—narrowly missing the post on the other side—and was heading out into the Wholly Other.

This, Dex realized almost immediately, was not good. As big as it was, Burning Man had borders; borders that were currently being guarded by the police. Sooner or later he'd hit them, and then he'd be screwed . . . or the dust storm would die down, and the deathmobile would get him.

He needed cover. Black Rock City had plenty of that, but it lay in the opposite direction and was getting farther away every second. He might be able to find an art installation to hide in, but the Windsurfer would act like a big triangular sign pointing right at him; it was too big to hide. He could try to let it blow away on its own, but it would probably just topple over. That would at least make it less visible. . . .

While he was pondering, an apparition materialized in front of him.

At first, he didn't believe what he was seeing. Even after all he'd witnessed, he just couldn't process what his eyes were telling him.

Before him, its bulk rising out of the dust like a wraith, was a Spanish galleon.

Her stern towered at least thirty feet in the air. Her two masts had their sails tightly furled; she moved through the storm as if obeying another set of natural laws entirely, a ghost ship gliding through a fogbound purgatory.

It was traveling slower than he was, which meant he had to swerve to the side to avoid ramming it. He had a brief glimpse of its name, painted on the stern— *La Contessa*—and then he was alongside. Two battered lanterns hung from the weathered brown wood of her flank, about halfway up; Dex could see a railing lining the deck, but no crew.

He had the idea even before he saw the rope trailing

down. He knew immediately that he'd have only one chance to grab it, and he'd have to let go of the Windsurfer's sail to do so; whether he managed to hang on or not, the board would certainly wipe out.

Somewhere behind him, he heard the sudden WHOOF! of a fireball. He'd forgotten the deathmobile had a flamethrower mounted on its back. The driver was probably trying to use it for extra illumination in the storm, which wouldn't work very well . . . but it would work just fine for setting a Windsurfer's sail on fire.

Dex jumped.

Actually, it was more of a grab-and-swing; he had to let go of the Windsurfer and pivot in order to reach the rope, and once he had hold of it, his feet on the board kept going. It wound up giving him just enough momentum to toss him a few feet up the side of the ship before swinging back down again, his knees bumping against the smooth wooden planks. The Windsurfer, freed of both weight and control, took a sharp nosedive into the playa.

It only took Dex a few seconds to pull himself up the rope; with his trench coat billowing behind him in the wind and his feet braced against the ship, he felt absurdly like Adam West in the TV version of *Batman*. He almost expected some semicelebrity to stick his head out of a porthole and make a bad joke, except the ship didn't seem to have any.

Portholes, that was. *As far as semicelebrities go*, Dex thought, *now it's got* me.

There were no ghostly pirates to greet him as he pulled himself over the railing; he assumed the crew was below, out of the storm. He could see light issuing from a square opening in the deck between the two masts, and hear a murmur of voices. He hesitated, then decided that whoever was down there was better than Scorpion-face.

He made his way slowly down the steep wooden steps, into an interior crammed with people. There were benches down the length of the ship, a pair of wooden berths in one corner, and a bar in another. It was lit by lanterns, and looked as authentic as the outside of the ship had. The only anachronism Dex had noticed so far was the use of steel cables for the rigging as opposed to rope.

No one took much notice of him; people were engaged in drinking or talking or necking, and the person Dex assumed was the captain—he was certainly dressed for the part, in a buccaneer's coat, hat, and boots—was busy behind the bar. Dex found a spot on one of the benches, and sank down gratefully.

From overheard bits of conversation, Dex was eventually able to piece it together; the ship was built on the frame of a bus. There was a small compartment beside the bar, behind a black velvet curtain, that housed the driver. Apparently *La Contessa* sometimes even hosted spoken-word performances of Coleridge's "Rime of the Ancient Mariner" while sailing the dry and dusty playa sea.

When the ship finally stopped ten minutes later, Dex cautiously joined everyone else on deck. The dust storm was over; the sky was blue and the sun was bright overhead. The deathmobile was nowhere in sight—but a whale was. A great white whale on wheels, built to scale, with a tail that moved up and down and a blow-hole that released an enormous fireball as he watched. It and *La Contessa*, it seemed, had been playing tag in and out of the dust storm.

They were parked right on the Esplanade, just outside of Center Camp. Dex disembarked with everyone else—there was a door right on the stern at ground level, which he'd somehow missed before—and walked back to the café he'd left Lorilei in.

"What took you so long?" she asked when she saw him. "And where's your bike?"

"Back at the Porta-Johns. I think maybe you better go get it. . . ."

Captain Fun's voice crackled over the walkie-talkie just as Dex was finishing his story. "Hey, Cap'n," Lorilei said. "We're in the Jazz Café in Center Camp. Come on down."

"I'll be there in a few—I'm not that far away."

"I'm beginning to think," Lorilei told Dex, "that your 'Curious Urge' is more like a 'Curious Death Wish.'"

"It just sort of *happened*," Dex said. He took a long drink of water. "But at least it worked. I got away."

"Yeah, but now Mr. Death Race knows what you look like in that getup—we're gonna have to find you a new disguise. I think you need one anyway, to go with your new image."

"As what? Surf-jacker?"

"More like antihero. Somebody came along a few minutes ago, passing these out."

She handed him a sheet of paper. It read:

SUPPORT THE ROGUE-RUNNER!
Will you let the *Boulder* of *Injustice* crush the *Spirit* of
Running Away?

Is it fair to be targeted by the *Exploding Dynamite
Darts* of *False Assumption?*

Should you be forced to eat the *Birdseed* of
Destruction just because your legs turn into a *Whirling
Blur* at the first sign of danger?

FUCK NO!
We, the *Acme Rogue-Runner Guardians,* believe in the
Innocence of **The Rogue-Runner.**

Join ARG in a *Candlelight Vigil* at *the Man* to show
your support.

Wednesday Night, Nine O'Clock

No Coyotes, Please

**this paper will self-destruct as soon as you finish read-
ing it and throw it in a fire**

"Is this good or bad?" Dex asked. "I can't tell anymore . . ."

"I don't know—but it'll probably be entertaining.
We should go."

"Sure. Why not. I can do a striptease while somebody in a fish costume reads me my rights."

She laughed. "That's pretty good. I think you're getting the hang of this . . . and as far as the stripping
goes, I don't think you should wait. Lose the coat and
hat."

He tossed her the hat, then stood up and shrugged
out of the trench coat.

"And the shirt."

"What?"

"C'mon—you said he recognized it. It's gotta go,

at least until we find you another layer to go over top." She grinned up at him. "What, do you need music?"

He blushed.

"Oooh, *baby*," she said. "That's the stuff, right there. Does it stop at your neck, or does it go *all* the way down? Show Momma."

"Very funny," he muttered, but underneath his dust mask he was smiling.

He pulled the T-shirt off, ignored her exaggerated gasp, and sat back down again.

"I was expecting a third nipple, at the very lea—"

He balled up the T-shirt and threw it. It bounced off her forehead.

"Aha!" Captain Fun said as he rolled up and dismounted. "Dissension in the ranks! Or maybe some sort of Strip Frisbee Tag—it's hard to tell."

"Hey, Captain," Lorilei said. "Hope you have some interesting stories to share, 'cause *we* sure as hell do."

Fun sank down onto a cushion, and uncapped his water bottle. "Well, you know how much I love a good story. Hit me."

Dex told him what had happened. "So it looks like I need a new disguise," he finished.

"That's easy enough to arrange. We'll drop by Kostume Kult again, pick you out something appropriate."

"So how did your mysterious errand go?" Lorilei asked.

"Quite successful, thank you—the government should be receiving my ransom demands any moment. And while I was out, I heard some *very* interesting things."

"What do you mean?" Dex asked.

"Well, there are two women over at Woonami Village who swear Wade Jickling isn't dead."

"What?" Dex gasped.

"Yeah, but they *also* swear he was a transvestite who was murdered by Christian fundamentalists. They're starting a movement to have him declared a saint."

"Hmmm. St. Wade, patron saint of Dickwads," Lorilei said.

"I've also heard about several Dex sightings. Apparently you're disguising yourself as a woman, a black man, a cop, a cowboy, a *space* cowboy, and Santa Claus. You have attacked several other people, stolen an airplane, been smuggled out of the city in the back of the truck that cleans the Porta-Johns, and been shot dead by the police. Oh, and you're a vegetarian."

Dex looked blank.

"I think he's gonna say 'Ulk' again," said Lorilei.

"What the *hell?*" Dex finally managed.

"Black Rock City generates myth," Fun said. "Every camp, every costume—all of 'em have some kind of story attached, and the best ones take on a life of their own. And a story like yours, it's not just going to grow—it's going to *mutate.*"

"That's true," Lorilei said, "but even so, this one seems like it's going batshit awfully fast."

"Could be 'cause I've been helping."

"Excuse me?" said Dex.

"Classic principle of stage magic—misdirection. The more we muddy the waters, the less likely you are to be found . . . so I've started a few rumors of my own."

"You said I *attacked other people?*"

"No, that one popped up on its own." Fun hesitated, then said, "Remember, our killer is a Burner, too. He might have started some of those rumors himself, to flush you out."

"The more dangerous you seem, the more likely people are to fink on you. So," Lorilei said, handing Fun the flyer, "What do you make of this?"

The Captain scanned it quickly. "Hmmm. Looks weird enough to be real . . . the last thing the killer wants is support for Dex, and the cops just aren't flexible enough to pull a stunt like this with no lead time. It's probably exactly what it looks like—ordinary BRC strangeness."

"Are you aware," Dex asked, "that you just used the phrase, 'ordinary strangeness'?"

"Yeah," Fun said, "but I stuck *Black Rock City* in the middle of it. You do that, you can bring *any* two concepts together. . . ."

Dex's new wardrobe consisted of a white robe with a hood. It could be belted closed, hiding his T-shirt, or left open to reveal it. "Not very swashbuckling," Lorilei said, "but it'll keep the sun off your head."

In return, Captain Fun gifted Kostume Kult with an idea, claiming he could show anyone how to make a sex toy in under thirty seconds using two items commonly found in Black Rock City.

He pulled from his bag a roll of duct tape and a dead glow-rope, the kind made out of thin, flexible plastic tubing around two feet in length. He tore off a strip of tape around four inches long, laid it flat with the sticky side up, and placed the glow-rope on top with its tip centered. He folded the tape back on itself, forming a square at the end of the glow rope, then picked it up and slapped the square against the palm of his hand. "Black Rock City riding crop," he said.

Once Dex was again properly disguised, Dex and Fun checked in with the other members of Tribe Urge while Lorilei retrieved his bike. Cromagg was relieving Sundog while he ate lunch; Sigma Jen was following up a lead on the Temple of Atonement priestess. Food sounded like a good idea all round, so they headed back to Aetheria.

On the way there they stopped at a row of Porta-Johns. While standing in line, Dex noticed another, shorter line to one side. At first he assumed it was alternating with the one he was standing in, but that turned out to be untrue; the people in the other line seemed to be waiting to use one Porta-John in particular.

Not quite sure why he was doing so, he switched lines.

When it was finally his turn to step inside, he saw immediately what people had been waiting for. The interior of the tiny bathroom had been decorated from top to bottom, in a desert island theme: there was a leopard-skin mat on the floor, a paper pineapple on top of the toilet paper dispenser, a garland of plastic ivy and bird-of-paradise flowers draped around a pipe. There were Wet Wipes, a small mirror, a battery-operated light, and even tropical-scented air freshener. A newer, bright green seat had been placed on top of the standard plastic one.

A sign was taped on the back wall. It read:

This bathroom oasis brought to you by:
Olaf thc Outlaw Outhouse Outfitter
"OOOO—it's Olaf!"
Please enjoy the amenities provided and sign the Guest
Book

He looked down and noticed a small hardcover notebook and a pen, attached to the base of the pipe with
a length of chain. He flipped it open and read some of
the comments scrawled on its pages: "Olaf Rules!"
"I see a new Playa tradition in the works—thank
Fuckin' God!" "Thank you for this lovely loo/wc/toi-
let/head. It was a shelter in a storm." "To hell with
my tent—I'm moving in here!" "Yes! I could just
KISS you!"

The book was about half full, page after page of
thank-yous and silly poems and little drawings. Dex
hesitated, then picked up the pen and wrote: *Thanks
for making a stranger feel a little more comfortable.*

Captain Fun volunteered to cook when they got
back to camp, and Dex quickly ducked into the pod
so he could take off the dust mask for a while. Lorilei
followed him in.

"How are you holding up, Ulk?" she asked.

"I'm doing all right, I guess. Not sure where this investigation is going, though."

"Well, we have four days to find out. Reminds me of
something a friend of mine used to do. We'd come here,
see all kinds of amazing things, party our faces off.
Then, when we were all having a really good time, he'd
get this intense look and say, 'I have something impor-

tant to tell you. Something *incredible.*' He'd pause, look you right in the eye, lean forward, and whisper, 'It's only *Wednesday.*' "

Dex began refilling his canteen from a water jug. "Yeah. Hard to believe it's only been three days . . ."

"Time gets kinda strange here. Most people just give up, stop wearing a watch."

"Most people aren't wanted for murder."

"Most people speak Northern Mandarin."

He glanced at her, confused. "What does that—"

"In global terms. More people speak Northern Mandarin than any other language, including English."

"I suppose that makes sense—"

"But is completely irrelevant?"

"Well—"

"I *do* have a point. Two, in fact. See?"

"I *wish* you wouldn't do that."

"Liar. I've always found there's nothing like a little mindless exhibitionism to take your mind off your troubles."

"What does this have to do with the Chinese?"

"The Chinese what?"

"*I* don't know—*you* brought it up."

"I did?" She grinned. "How *far* up?"

"Lorilei, leave the poor boy alone," Fun said from the doorway. "Try eating some lunch instead of him."

"Spoilsport . . ."

Lunch was stir-fried veggies and noodles, with a spicy peanut sauce; it was delicious, but Dex didn't have much of an appetite. He wound up giving most of his to Lorilei, who gladly wolfed it down.

Afterward, Fun suggested a short nap. "A little siesta to recharge our batteries," was how he put it.

Dex agreed—he wanted to do some thinking before he headed out again.

Dex helped Lorilei clean up the dishes, then made another trip to the Porta-Johns. Discovering that he was, in fact, pissing clear did little to cheer him up.

"Where's the Captain?" he asked when he returned.

"He decided to crash in his trailer," Lorilei said. "Looks like you're stuck in here with me . . . oh, don't give me that look. I'll behave, okay?"

"Sure you will," Dex said awkwardly.

The problem was, he was no longer sure *what* he wanted.

He sneezed. "You, uh, don't have a tissue, do you?" he asked. "My sinuses are all blocked up."

"I can do better than that," she said. She rummaged in her pack and pulled out a small squeeze bottle and a roll of toilet paper. She tore off a long strip and handed it and the bottle to him. "You've got playa nose. The aridity makes the blood vessels in your nose swell up, and the dust mixes with mucus to make a kind of cement."

"Wonderful."

"That's saline solution. Squirt some up your nose, it'll clean things out."

Cautiously, he did so. It was messy and stung a little, but seemed to help; after blowing his nose a few times, he could actually breathe again.

"Thanks," he said.

"You're welcome."

He took his robe and shoes off and lay down on top of his sleeping bag. Lorilei lay down on hers. Neither of them spoke for a few minutes, and Dex wondered if she'd fallen asleep; he felt wide awake, himself.

Like many men, Dex had a fantasy of an ideal girl in his head. His was short, blonde, and cute; she had big eyes, lots of dimples, and a smile with a slight overbite. The height and hair color sometimes varied, and even the dimples were optional—but the *kind* of girl she was stayed the same. She was kind, quiet, liked to laugh, and most importantly was fiercely loyal. He didn't know why that last point mattered to him so much, but it did.

He knew he should be thinking about the case—*the case? when did my life become a* case?—but he couldn't get his thoughts away from Lorilei. She was nothing like his ideal; she was outspoken, took a perverse pleasure in torturing him, and—

And she was helping him when he needed it.

Wasn't that the definition of loyalty? Sticking by someone when things got tough? Why *was* she sticking by him, when it could get her arrested or worse?

Because it's an adventure. Because it's just more craziness in a place full *of craziness.*

He considered that bleakly for a moment, then rejected it. If she was looking for adventure, there was plenty of opportunity here that didn't involve taking risks for strangers. And, if he was being honest with himself, it had little to do with loyalty, either; only an idiot would be loyal to someone they'd just met, and Lorilei was definitely not that.

What she was, was kind.

And that, Dex thought, was why she was helping him. She'd sized him up, decided he was *worth* helping, and committed herself to it. She wasn't being loyal to *him*, he realized; she was being loyal to *herself*, to who she was. That's why she wouldn't back off when she made him uncomfortable, and why her teasing bothered him so much; because, on some level, she meant every word.

Every single word.

"Dex?"

He almost jumped. "Uh, yes?" he managed.

"Do you dance?"

The question caught him off guard; the last person that had asked him that was Wade. "Not very well."

"Once we get all this cleared up, we should go dancing. Lots of great places to dance here."

He didn't say anything.

"Dex?"

"Sure," he said at last. "I'd like that."

A minute later her breathing changed, and he realized she was asleep.

He managed to drift off himself, eventually, but he slept fitfully; worry and the heat combined to give him strange, disjointed dreams that jarred him awake more than once. He was grateful when Fun came to the door and announced it was time to get up.

"Cocktail hour," he said. "Let's saddle up. . . ."

"I'm seeing John Wayne in a tuxedo," Lorilei said sleepily. "Is anybody else seeing John Wayne in a tuxedo?"

Sigma Jen and Cromagg had both returned to the camp. Jen reported she'd been following a false lead—apparently the woman from the Temple of Atonement wasn't actually attending the festival this year.

"At least that's one eliminated," Dex said. "How about Sundog?"

"He's still up on the platform," Cromagg said. "He said he'd stay until it got dark."

They looked over the list of remaining suspects. Cromagg and Jen would try to find a technician named Electrolush, while Dex, Lorilei, and Fun looked up Santa Crusty. Dex asked if he could borrow some alcohol to give away, and Fun supplied him with a bottle of vodka.

"I think it's time to upgrade from gift-giving to out-and-out bribes," Fun said. "In which case, I'm gonna have to pull out the Fun Gun." He went into the tent-trailer.

"I thought it was called the Skullbuster," Lorilei said.

"That was last year's model," Fun called out from inside. "This is the new, improved version."

He appeared at the doorway cradling a weapon of Schwartzeneggerian proportions. It had a shotgun-style stock, a Gatling gun barrel, and a large canister strapped to the side of the body. The canister was metal, the rest of the thing blue plastic. Surgical tubing led from the canister to the barrel, with a knob at the base.

"What," Dex said, "is that?"

"Come inside," Fun said with a grin, "and I'll demonstrate."

Lorilei and Dex stepped in. Fun slid behind the small table and put the device down, then pulled out a small plastic bag and a cardboard box about the size of a pack of cigarettes. There was a small metal bowl on the barrel of the gun; Fun dropped a pinch of something green from the bag into it.

"I, uh, don't smoke," Dex said.

"That's okay," Fun said. "You can appreciate this from a purely aesthetic point of view."

"He just wants to show off," Lorilei said.

"Nothing wrong with pride in one's achievements," Fun said. "Are you familiar with nitrous oxide?"

"Laughing gas, right?"

"Correct. Used by dentists everywhere. Also given to women in labor, which I think speaks to the relative harmlessness of the drug."

He opened the box and took out a small metal canister; it was identical to the one Dex had found in his trench coat's pocket earlier.

"On the other hand," Fun said cheerfully, "it's so flammable it's used to supercharge the fuel in race cars. Naturally, I had to find a way to combine it with burning marijuana."

"Nothing your brain produces is natural," Lorilei said. "And I do mean *your* brain, Captain."

Fun lit the bowl, inhaling through a length of the surgical tubing. After a few seconds, he blew out a small amount of smoke and fiddled with a knob on the apparatus. "And now we're ready for the interesting part . . ."

Fun unscrewed a black plastic piece jutting out from the side of the gun. He fitted the cylinder inside it, then screwed it back on. After a few turns, there was a hollow-sounding *fwooosh!* noise.

"Look," Fun said. There was a gap in the plastic structure holding the canister in place; a thin rime of frost had formed on the metal. Dex reached out and touched it with his finger. Ice-cold.

"Using liquids to cool off smoke has been around for centuries," Fun said. "I thought, why not use a gas? The main difference between this and your basic water bong is that this has to be pressurized."

"Are you gonna use that thing," Lorilei asked, "or just talk about it?"

"Patience, dear girl, patience. Half the pleasure of gigglesmoke is in the enjoyment of the ritual. Charging the reservoir, tightening the valves—"

" 'Gigglesmoke'?" Dex said.

"That's what he calls it," Lorilei said.

"—the distinctive sound as the nitrous rushes in to mix with the smoke—"

"Yeah, yeah. Give me that." Lorilei grabbed the tube away from him and put it to her own lips. She put her thumb on a silver lever that stuck out from the side of the gun, and pressed it down slowly. Dex could hear the hiss of escaping gas as she inhaled.

"I call it gigglesmoke because the weed and the nitrous combine to form a new drug," Fun said. He was watching Lorilei intently. "Nitrous by itself produces an intense head rush that only lasts a few minutes. THC hits the bloodstream a little slower, but lasts a lot longer. The combination is less intense than the gas alone but *deeper*. When the nitrous part of the high fades, it leaves the dope stone behind."

While Fun talked, Lorilei finished her hit. She closed her eyes, and the smile on her face grew wider and wider.

"Oh, yeah," she said. Her voice had deepened; it sounded like a record that had been slowed down.

"Is that normal?" Dex asked nervously. "Her lips are turning blue."

"Sure. We call nitrous the anti-helium, because it makes your voice deeper instead of higher. And don't worry about the lips, that's just a touch of hypoxia."

"Hypoxia," Lorilei said, and giggled. Her voice had returned to its normal pitch. "Sounds like a city in a Jewish fantasy novel . . ."

"I am *Cohen,* of Hypoxia!" Fun declared. "Wielder of the Chuckling Sword! Master of the *Bagel of Doom!*"

Lorilei burst out laughing. Dex grinned despite himself; her laughter was so open and unrestrained it was contagious. "Where do you get the canisters?" Dex asked. "They can't be legal."

"Oh, but they are," Fun said, grinning. "They're for use in whipped cream dispensers. The gas aerates the cream, just like carbon dioxide produces the bubbles in soda pop." He refilled the bowl and lit it. Lorilei grinned at Dex, her eyes glassy.

"Why don't they use carbon dioxide for whipped cream, then?"

"Can't. It's acidic, so it makes the cream curdle." Fun took the box, and swapped the empty canister for a fresh one. "They do make canisters of carbon dioxide, though, for use in things like seltzer bottles. You have to be careful, because they look exactly like nitrous canisters. You get a lungful of the wrong stuff, it's extremely unpleasant; it's poisonous as well as acidic."

"So, you're inhaling racing car fuel next to an open flame," Dex said, "which comes in containers that look exactly like something poisonous."

"More or less," Fun agreed. He finished his preparations and took a hit himself.

"What's it like?" Dex asked Lorilei as Fun inhaled.

She blinked. "Hmmm. Well, it's extremely auditory.

Music sounds either profound or flat. You hear this sound—"

"The Universal Dial Tone," Fun said. His voice had dropped several octaves.

"I prefer to think of it as the Crystal Gong," Lorilei said. "It's this kind of high-pitched, resonating hum. Sometimes you get flashes of really intense imagery, sometimes not. Sometimes everything suddenly seems really, really funny."

"And sometimes not," Fun said solemnly.

"And sometimes not," Lorilei agreed. "Either way, it's a nice little trip."

"I'll never look at dentists or whipped cream the same way again," Dex said.

"Mmmm," Fun said dreamily. "Dentists and whipped cream . . ."

"Like I said," Lorilei sighed, "nothing natural comes out of that brain. . . ."

Fun told them he'd see them at Santa Crusty's camp; he had another mysterious errand to run, and just smiled when Lorilei teased him about it.

On their way there, Dex noticed a police cruiser parked next to a camp. There were two officers standing outside, talking to a young guy in a tie-dyed T-shirt and shorts.

As they rode past, Dex recognized Green Grover.

Dex looked away quickly, then realized he looked completely different from the last time they'd met; in any case, Grover seemed too intent on his conversation to notice.

But what, Dex thought nervously, *is he telling them?*

He pulled over at the end of the block next to a stand giving away Popsicles, Lorilei right behind him.

"You saw him, too, huh?" Lorilei said.

"Yeah. What do you think they're talking to him about?"

"Might be anything, but it's probably about you. I recognize those two, saw them hanging around Center Camp earlier; that's Sheriff Tremayne and one of his deputies."

"And if Grover went to them, then he's the killer."

"Could be. Maybe I should do a little eavesdropping," Lorilei suggested. "I could hang out next door by that giant seesaw, look inconspicuous. You stay here and—"

But Dex had already wheeled his bike around and was heading back toward the police.

Lorilei pulled up beside him. "What are you *doing*?" she hissed.

"Participating," Dex said.

In truth, he wasn't sure *why* he hadn't let Lorilei handle the snooping; there was nothing he could do she couldn't do just as well, and it would certainly have been safer. He thought it had something to do with taking control instead of just being a passive observer, but a tiny part of him disagreed with that assessment. A tiny part, he reluctantly admitted to himself, that didn't want to be left out while others had all the fun.

I should leave this kind of fun to the Captain, Dex thought as they rolled up behind the cruiser and stopped. *Playing spy isn't a game I'm likely to enjoy—*

not when the penalty for getting caught is a murder charge.

But it did have, he discovered as he got off his bike and his pulse quickened, a certain thrill to it. Unfortunately, it was a little too close to terror to be enjoyable.

There were four other people waiting to try the seesaw, which gave Dex and Lorilei the perfect excuse to hang around. "That's one honkin' piece of playground equipment," Lorilei observed.

Dex studied the police a few feet away while pretending to admire the seesaw—though it was, he had to admit, a pretty impressive toy. It was made of metal, measured at least forty feet from end to end and had a swivel at the fulcrum that allowed it to spin as well as go up and down.

"—said he was doing some kind of investigation," Green Grover said. "For an insurance company, I think."

Dex froze.

The deputy, a stocky Latino with a thin mustache and mirrored sunglasses, was nodding and taking notes. Tremayne himself had curly gray hair and aviator-style shades tinted brown. He wore a big, friendly grin, his body language relaxed and casual. "Really? I don't suppose—"

Just then the wind picked up, obscuring part of his reply.

"—any kind of ID?"

Dex strained to hear, but could only pick out bits. "Nope," Grover admitted cheerfully. "But he wasn't—" *Ssshhh.* "—power trip or anything. He just wanted—" *Woooo.* "—happened to me last year."

"And what would that be?" Tremayne asked amiably.

Lorilei tugged on Dex's arm. "C'mon, it's our turn," she said.

Dex hesitated, then realized that once he was on the thing, he could use the swivel to actually get closer to the two officers. Of course, this meant they would also be closer to him . . .

Getting on was a little tricky. He let Lorilei straddle the padded seat on her end first, then had one of the previous users help him get his end down so he could climb aboard. After that, it was as simple as he remembered; whoever was closer to the ground pushed off, sending them up and the other person down.

Of course, this version sent you a good fifteen feet or so into the air, while moving sideways as well—it was considerably more vertigo-inducing than he'd suspected. It took several spinning up-and-down cycles before Lorilei and Dex managed to get him properly oriented to eavesdrop, though they had to keep the thing moving to look natural.

"—well, there was one strange thing about him," Grover was saying. "He kept his dust mask on the entire time we were talking."

"Lots of people here seem to wear masks," Tremayne said.

"Yeah, but unless it's part of their costume, most people take theirs off unless there's an actual storm and they're out on the playa. It just seemed a little strange."

Dex was glad his back was to the cops. They couldn't see the mask he was wearing right now—

And then a man wearing sandals, a horned helmet, and nothing else grabbed Lorilei's end, said, "Hey! You should get this thing *moving!*" and gave it a sideways shove. Dex found himself swapping sides—

And meeting the flat glance of the deputy as he looked up from his pad.

It lasted only a second, but the deputy's eyes tracked him as Dex rotated back to his original position and Lorilei managed to get her feet on the ground to stop them. Dex had his back to the cops once again—but he could almost *feel* the deputy's stare.

He's not looking at you, Dex told himself desperately. *You're just another Burner enjoying himself—*

"Yee-*ha!*" Lorilei yelled, and kicked herself up and to the right. Dex found himself angling through the air much faster than before; he hit the ground with a jarring thud and rebounded back up.

"Come on!" Lorilei said. "Let's get *going!*"

Dex caught on. The next time he went down, he kicked up and to the side as hard as he could.

As he whirled past, he saw that both Tremayne and the deputy were watching them. "Yeah!" Dex shouted. "Ride 'em *cowboy!*" He threw one hand in the air and pretended he was riding a bucking bronco. His stomach lurched, and he prayed he wasn't going to throw up.

The next time the officers spun through his field of vision, they were no longer looking his way. Burning Man's inversion of the status quo had worked in his favor; by literally jumping up and down, they had disappeared into the background.

The officers left a minute later. Getting off the seesaw was almost as tricky as getting on, but they managed. Dex picked up his bike, then decided to walk instead. He didn't trust his sense of balance.

"Well, *that* was exciting," Lorilei said. "Learn anything useful?"

"Grover isn't the killer," Dex said. "He would have pointed the cops straight at me instead of being vaguely suspicious."

"Anything else?"

"Yeah," Dex said. "Childhood should come with Dramamine."

CHAPTER 10:

SUBLIME GOSPEL

File K (Desert Vixen): What does Burning Man mean to me?

Touching.

Nerve endings being stimulated by a hundred different sensations: hot sun on bare flesh, icy wind biting through cloth, the powdery caress of dust against the soles of your feet. Warm lotion and cool water and other people's hands.

Skin on skin.

Have you ever been given a massage by six—or more—people at the same time? That's what they do at Sunscreen Camp. You bring them the lotion of your choice, and join a table. On the table is a naked form, lying facedown. The body quickly becomes divided into territories, with borders almost as slippery as the hands that patrol them. Whatever area falls to you, you focus upon: the slope of the neck, the plain of the back, the peninsula of a limb. You rub, you squeeze, you knead. Everybody does. And when every territory has been conquered, when every muscle has surrendered, the body is turned and battle resumes on another front.

Everybody does their tour of duty . . . and then, finally, it's your turn.

The most difficult thing about the entire process is getting up once it's finished. You feel both boneless and friction-free; limp and slick as a jellyfish, you ooze away with a dreamy smile on your face.

But you can't just puddle up and idle away the day—you have too much to do, too much to *be*. You slide over to Mysore Ashtanga and do some yoga; a few limbering-up exercises, some stretching, and you almost feel like you have a backbone again. Invigorated, you decide to drop in on a body-painter, and he spends the next hour turning your body into a work of art: constellations now adorn your back, the sun rises from between your hips, a knowing moon winks from your left nipple.

It's *almost* perfect . . . but that unruly thatch of pubic hair is *ruining* the entire effect. No problem; you pop over to the Body Hair Barber Shop and have them trim that bush into a perfect little semicircle. It looks so good you can't resist having a picture taken, so it's off to the Genital Portrait Studio. They not only take a snapshot of your privates, they give you your own laminated Genital Picture ID.

All this running around is hard on your poor bare feet—and so is the desert. Playa dust is highly alkaline, and too much exposure can lead to a condition called playa foot, basically a low-grade chemical burn. You can't have that—how can you go out dancing if your feet are on fire? Fortunately you can drop by the Foot Oasis to get your tootsies spritzed with vinegar, an acid to neutralize the alkali, Black Rock Chemistry 101.

And then you head home, time for lunch, maybe a nice big salad with iceberg lettuce and croutons and cherry tomatoes, something cool and crunchy in the heat of the day, and you're just slicing some cucumber when you hear the cry: *"Water truck!"*

And you drop the cucumber and bolt out the door and run like crazy. As you tear through your camp, you see the other members of your tribe ripping off their clothes, but you have the advantage because you're *already* naked, ha ha so there, and you go sprinting down the street like a maniac. The water truck is a big silver tanker that drives slowly around the city spraying water to damp down street dust, and its appearance is guaranteed to turn any citizen into a squealing ten-year-old chasing an ice-cream van. You catch up to the throng dancing in the truck's wake, and suddenly you're laughing and splashing and shrieking with a bunch of naked strangers.

It lasts as long as you want it to, and finally you drop back, wet and shivering in the hot desert sun with a big, goofy grin on your face. Watching the truck rumble slowly away from you, Pied-Pipering its shiny chrome way down the street.

Ah, but now you've washed away your masterpiece, haven't you? Your beautiful skyscape is a blur, bleeding stars and melting heavenly bodies, so you go back and have your lunch and decide to get yourself properly cleaned up.

The best place for that is the Human Carcass Wash, an experience in many ways the opposite of Sunscreen Camp, though the principle remains the same: a group focusing their attention on a single person, with everybody taking a turn. Here, though, the subject passes through several groups: soapers, scrubbers, sluicers, and rinsers. You participate in each, working the squirt bottles, running soapy hands over skin hairy and smooth, soft and muscular, washing away dust and paint and even liquid latex. It's a slower, more organized version of the water truck, with less running but just as much giddy laughter. Where the sunscreen massage was slow and deep and intimate, this is fast and happy and playful; by the time you've done a shift in each group, you've made friends with everyone there.

And then *you're* up . . . and now it's *your* naked body being squirted and soaped and scrubbed, a dozen hands sliding over and around and between, your new friends teasing and joking and treating you like a big, slippery bath-toy. And if a hand lingers *here*, it's simply making sure you're clean; and if a nipple stiffens *there*, it's only the breeze on wet skin. . . .

You come out the other side pink and flushed and out of breath, and now that you're immaculate, it's time to get dirty all over again. Off to Glitter Camp to roll in wading pools of the stuff, until your body sparkles in the midday sun like a disco ball come to life. You've been a work of art, a screaming child and a naked plaything—but now you're *magic*, survivor of a fairy-dust blizzard, a fey creature of shiny impulse. You hop on your bike and ride, without destination or purpose, letting pure instinct guide you. The wind gusts past like an indifferent lover, trailing dusty fingertips across your body, making you shiver; you want to reach out and embrace the desert, the city, and everyone in it. . . .

That's what Burning Man means to me.

CHAPTER 11:

PARADOX PROMENADE

They met Captain Fun at Santa's Off-Season, a five-thousand-square-foot air-conditioned theme camp that featured a stage and multiple levels. Santa Crusty was more than willing to talk to Dex, but it turned out he'd been delayed by a family emergency and had arrived only the day before. Besides, he seemed a little portly to be Darth Bunny.

Dex went outside and told Fun and Lorilei. "Well, if he's not a suspect, I'm going in," Lorilei said. "I could use a little air-conditioning . . . besides, look! Extreme Elvis is going to perform in a few minutes!"

She dragged Dex back inside just as Cromagg paged them on the walkie-talkie. He and Sigma Jen had located Electrolush, or at least managed to pinpoint where he was going to be. "There's a parade tonight," Cromagg said. "He's doing support for one of the vehicles."

"Which one?" Dex asked.

"The Laser Orgasmatron. Look for beams shooting out of nipples."

"That'll narrow it down . . . when and where?"

"Vehicles are meeting at Center Camp shortly after dark."

"Got it. Thanks."

"Well, we've got a little time to kill," Lorilei said. She stretched out on the shag carpeting covering the floor and patted a spot next to her. "Come on, guys. Let's take a little break."

Dex sat on one side, Captain Fun on the other. There had been three or four people in the tent when they got there, but more kept coming; another dozen or so showed up in the next ten minutes. They were the usual eclectic mix of Burners, dressed in everything from shorts and T-shirts to elaborate fetish gear.

And then the Santas began to arrive.

They came through the door in a loud, red-and-white pack. There were almost as many female Santas as male, and lots of variation in costume; there were Santas in leather and Santas in sequins, Santas in fur-trimmed miniskirts and fishnet stockings. There were Santas with beards and Santas that had none, traditional Santas with big bellies and nontraditional ones in crimson tuxedos. At least thirty of them poured into the tent, ho-ho-hoing and handing out candy canes.

"Wow," Captain Fun said. "That's a whole lotta jolly."

The Santas milled about, laughing and drinking and wishing everyone a merry Christmas. Dex noted, somewhat nervously, that a few of the Santas carried paddles, but they seemed happy to restrict their spankings to people who admitted being naughty . . . of which there were several.

"Bet you've never seen Santa wear his beard as a thong," Lorilei said.

"That's true," Dex admitted. "And the idea of Santa as a transvestite would never have occurred to me, either."

"Well, Burning Man *did* start in San Francisco . . . lots of people dress in drag out here. Does it bother you?"

"Of course not," Dex said hastily. And it didn't, not in a homophobic way—Dex didn't care about other people's sexuality. It was the loud, garish, in-your-face aspect of cross-dressing that made him nervous, especially when it threatened to drag him into the spotlight with it.

And then—with no clear signal Dex could see—the entire group started singing. Dex had never heard a pornographic version of "Rudolph the Red-Nosed Reindeer" before, but he wound up laughing and singing along himself.

"Santa is off-key," one of the Santas said when they were done.

"Santa is *extremely* off-key," another Santa agreed. "Must be eggnog clog."

"Here," said the first Santa, handing the second a flask. "This'll clear up Santa's pipes."

The second one took a drink, then nodded and patted his belly. "Ah. Santa feels a warm glow in his big red sack. . . ."

"Santa wants Elvis!" someone cried, and pretty soon they all were chanting it.

They didn't have long to wait. The stage wasn't large, but it was big enough for a drummer, a keyboardist, and a guitar player, all of whom were greeted with applause—which exploded into cheers when Extreme Elvis appeared.

He was the seventies version of the King, wearing the white outfit with the high collar and the sequins, heavy sideburns underscoring gold-framed sunglasses. He was big, too, with an enormous gut; Dex would have put his weight at somewhere close to three hundred pounds.

"Thank you verra much," he said, in a perfect southern drawl. "Now, why don't all you white-bearded, red-suited sumbitches shut up and lemme sing."

He launched into "Cold Kentucky Rain," and though Dex had never been much of a Presley fan, he had to admit that Extreme Elvis was pretty good. Not as enjoyable was the fact that Elvis's white pants were struggling to stay up and losing the battle; every time the singer turned around, more and more of his pale, bulging behind was visible.

At the end of the song, he paused and took a sip from a plastic cup. He staggered a little, and wiped his mouth with the back of his hand.

"Elvis is *pissed!*" one of the Santas shouted.

Elvis froze. He grabbed the microphone and snarled, "Who said that? Who said that, goddammit?"

"*And* fat!"

He lurched off the stage and into the crowd. He glared at the closest Santa and demanded, "*What* did you say about me?"

Undaunted, the Santa—a classic one, right down to his wide black belt—beamed at Elvis and said, "Ho!"

"Did you say I was *fat,* goddammit?"

They faced off for a second, Elvis scowling and Santa grinning.

"You really hurt my feelings, man," Elvis finally said. "You really did."

"Awww," the other Santas said.

"Santa is sorry. . . ."

"Anyway, *you're* one to talk, reindeer-boy," Elvis snapped. "I don't know how you get airborne, carrying all that blubber around." He turned and stalked back to the stage, shedding his top along the way, and tore into "Jailhouse Rock." By the end of the song, his hairy, distended belly was streaked in sweat and the Santas were dancing up a storm. Beside him, Lorilei started doing the twist.

The pants drooped a little lower.

A few of the songs were real surprises—Dex particularily liked the rap version of "In the Ghetto." Between numbers, Elvis would launch into rants about Burning Man, the unfairness of love, and the general angst of being Elvis. He told the crowd his girlfriend had left him, and was "runnin' around on the playa right now, with some asshole in dreadlocks."

By this point, the pants had fallen off completely; all he wore was a pair of dirty white socks and his shades . . . and Dex could see just why Extreme Elvis was so bitter.

"The poor bastard," Lorilei whispered. "Jesus, my *clit's* longer than that."

Despite his obvious shortcomings, Elvis wasn't shy about sharing. He got everyone to sit down, then jumped off the stage and roamed through the crowd, telling them they didn't have a goddamn clue what the real meaning of Burning Man was. "It's not seein' how much E you can take. It's not about dressin' up like it was Halloween. It's not about dumb-ass theme camps, or tyin' a buncha CDs to poles with fishin' line and callin' it art." He stopped next to a female Santa, his crotch inches away from her head, and said, "It's about one thing—human contact."

He stalked back to the stage and sat down. "You know, there are a few hard truths that nobody wants to hear. Well, I'm here to tell 'em. And one of the things you're gonna have to confront is the fact that you ain't *gonna* get laid tonight. It's gonna be dark, and cold, and you're gonna enter that tent *alone.*"

He looked straight at Dex—and started to sing, "Love Me Tender."

Behind his dust mask, Dex smiled nervously. *It doesn't mean anything. Performers always focus on somebody in the audience.*

And then Extreme Elvis got off the stage, and onto his knees in front of it. His gaze, hidden though it was behind tinted lenses, still seemed to be locked on Dex. He was singing about never letting go.

Elvis got down on all fours. He began to crawl toward Dex, still crooning, pushing through the Santas in the front row, going right over one that didn't get out of the way fast enough.

Dex couldn't seem to breathe. He had an overpowering urge to get up and run, but part of him thought if he just pretended nothing was wrong, the large, naked, sweaty man would go away.

He was wrong.

The King got right up close to Dex's face. Closer and closer, while Dex tried to lean back and away . . . and when Dex finally lost his balance and fell onto his back, Elvis followed him all the way down. Leapt, in fact, onto his body, straddling him and pumping his famous pelvis up and down.

This isn't happening, Dex thought. *I am* not *being stage-humped by a three-hundred-pound Elvis impersonator. And he isn't still singing "Love Me Tender."*

But he was. And even after it was over—after Extreme Elvis had rolled off him, after a distant, numb part of Dex had noted his robe was now soaked in the performer's sweat—he had to admit that he'd never missed a note.

"Are you *sure* you're okay?" Lorilei asked.

"Uh-huh."

"You don't *seem* okay."

"I'm fine."

"I think you're in shock. He didn't *break* anything, did he?"

"No."

"How about bruises? Did he *bruise* anything?"

"No."

"Not even your *pride?* Your *dignity?* You were *publicly mounted* by a—*a sperm whale in sideburns,* for God's sake!"

"You seem upset."

"Upset? You sound like a zombie, your eyes are focused on something in another *dimension,* and you won't utter a sentence more than three words long."

"Sorry. Is this better? Oh. I guess not."

"Dex, I am *so sorry.* Captain, I think we broke him."

They were sitting on an old-fashioned porch-glider, the kind that looked like a park bench with an awning over it. The smooth, back-and-forth motion it had been named for had been subverted somewhat by bolting it on top of a schoolyard merry-go-round, though it was still at the moment. Dex had simply gone outside and sat down on the first thing he saw that seemed vaguely appropriate.

"Dex?" Fun said. "He looks like he needs a drink. You want a drink, Dex?"

"No. I . . ." He trailed off.

"What?"

Dex started to shake. Alarmed, Lorilei put an arm around him, while Captain Fun looked even more worried.

"He—he—" Dex forced out.

"It's okay. It's all right, man."

"Oh, God. He was . . ." Dex leaned forward, covered his face in his hands.

"Let it out," Lorilei said softly.

Dex straightened up, threw his arms out and howled, *"He was a hunka hunka burnin' love!"*

Lorilei and Fun gaped at him.

Dex stood up. "You know," he said quietly, "that was almost worth it, just to see the looks on your faces." He paused. "Almost."

"You *bastard*," Lorilei said. She shook her head, laughed, and jumped off the glider. "Oooh, I am gonna make you *pay* for that one."

"Looking forward to it," Dex said. "Now. Can we get back to work?"

"Yes, *sir*," Fun said with a grin. "Lead the way, boss. . . ."

It was strange, Dex thought as they got on their bikes. What made it possible for him to deal with the experience, even to joke about it, was one simple fact: he was wearing a disguise. It hadn't been *him* that Extreme Elvis was grinding away on, it had been Curious Urge.

And Curious Urge, Dex was starting to discover, was a very different person from Dexter Edden. Curious Urge jumped from cherry pickers to moving trucks and off again; Curious Urge went windsurfing in dust storms. Curious Urge wore a mask and hung out with beautiful, naked, hula-hooping women. Being sexually assaulted by a naked overweight Elvis while surrounded by Santa clones was all in a day's work to him.

It's a shame, Dex thought, *that the guy's wanted for murder.*

Twilight was deepening into dark as they rode into Center Camp. He'd been there often enough that the place was almost becoming familiar; it was an odd feeling. He recognized the gigantic, rotating Kaleidosphere, the BRC Post Office, the bike repair place and Recycle Camp . . . and, of course, the huge circus tent of the café, right in the middle.

Not that he'd seen everything—every time he turned around there was something new and highly unusual. The two-story-tall inflatable Mr. T on wheels, for instance, or the pack of men and women all dressed in gold lamé cocktail dresses. Over there was a puppet booth, with a show featuring George W. Bush and a monkey; towering above it were a pair of naked stilters doing the tango. The set of the puppet booth featured a mushroom cloud made of dozens of small, gray, helium-filled balloons, and the monkey was in the process of throwing a noose around Bush's neck. The mushroom cloud suddenly rose into the air, pulling the Bush puppet with it, and drifted up past the stilters at the exact second one of them dipped the other.

It wasn't just the overall weirdness, Dex thought. It was the juxtaposition of different kinds of weird that kept you off balance. Just when you adjusted to one, another would pop up, interact with the first and form something entirely new.

They locked their bikes to one of the stands outside the café, and sat down inside near one of the entrances, with a good view into the street. Dex offered to buy coffee, and Lorilei and Fun accepted.

They didn't have long to wait. Vehicles started pulling in almost immediately, of every size, shape, and description: motorcycles tricked out to look like horses, an ATV sporting an enormous phallus, a van that had been transformed into a gigantic orange plush cat. *La Contessa* wasn't there, but many other boats on wheels were—speedboats, tugboats, even a longboat crewed by Vikings. One of the most creative—and comfortable—ones Dex saw was a converted swamp craft, the kind driven by a huge prop in a wire cage mounted at the back. The pilot had rigged a hammock to run the length of the hull, and controls he could work while lying in it; he tooled around in suspended comfort, with the world's biggest fan just behind his head.

And then the dragon arrived.

It was part giant lizard, part freight train; Dex counted six linked sections, each the length of a car and with a hide of rusty scrap iron. When it raised its armored head, fire erupted from between jagged metal jaws.

"Draka," Lorilei said. "Nice to see her running again—they were having problems for a while."

"Engine trouble?" Dex asked.

"Nah. Indigestion from eating too many Volkswagens," Lorilei said.

"German food *is* kinda heavy. . . ." Fun mused.

One of the things Dex had noticed, on many vehicles and costumes, was what looked like a cross between neon and glow-ropes—it seemed to be as thin and flexible as wire, and blinked off and on like a sign would. He asked Fun about it.

"Electroluminescent—or EL, for short—wire," Fun told him. "It's cheap, and you can run it off a nine-volt battery for hours as long as you have a device called a driver to change the amperage. People make really amazing things out of it, too—check that out." He pointed to a woman wearing three staggered sets of fairy wings outlined in bright pink wire; they flashed in sequence, making it appear that the wings were flapping.

"That's a pretty simple animation, but they can get really complex, too," Fun said. "There's an EL cheetah here, mounted on a little mobile billboard that gets towed behind a bike. At night, all you see is a big cat made out of light, loping across the playa."

"I think I just spotted our target," Lorilei said. "Look."

One of the vehicles just arriving featured a trio of female mannequins. The vehicle itself resembled a dune buggy, a stripped-down metal frame with an exposed motor at the front. A long platform was attached to the roof, and the mannequins—womannequins?—were posed atop it. Silver-skinned with fire-red wigs, they featured the latest in breast-mounted technology; nipple lasers razored the dusty air with bright green beams in three different directions.

"Perky," Lorilei said.

There were two people in the buggy. The driver was heavyset with a walrus mustache, the passenger a thin man with blond hair. "Any idea which one is Electrolush?" Dex asked.

"Hang on, I'll see if I can find out," Fun said. He pulled out his walkie-talkie.

The driver headed for the café, while the thin man jumped on the roof of the buggy and started fiddling with the equipment. "Never mind," Dex said. "I think I got him."

Dex studied the man as he walked toward him. He was dressed conservatively in baggy khaki shorts, a multipocketed vest over a T-shirt, and hiking boots. He was the right general size to be Rafe, but that didn't mean much.

"Hi," Dex said.

The man glanced down, but didn't stop working. "Hey."

"I was wondering if I could ask you a few questions."

"Delilah, Jezebel, and the Black Widow," the man said.

"Excuse me?"

"That's their names," he said, gesturing to the mannequins. "I call 'em that 'cause just when you start to love 'em, they'll fuck you over. 'Bout as reliable as a wheelchair made of cream cheese."

"Sorry to hear that. Must be tricky to run something that high-tech out here."

"Aw, these are just toys. *Serious* tech is something like Beaming Man. You catch it, back in 2000?"

Dex shook his head.

"Now *that* was somethin'. Three green lasers—two five watts and a three—and ten thirty-foot antennae towers. Used mirrors to create a gigantic outline of the Man over the playa, four thousand feet long and two thousand feet wide. Biggest human figure ever created."

"Wow," Dex said, impressed. The technophile in him wanted to ask for more details, but he forced himself to focus. "Uh—do you go by the name Electrolush, by any chance?"

"Long as you ain't workin' for my ex-wife, the cops or the IRS I do. What can I do you for?"

"I was wondering about something that happened last year. Somebody damaged a machine you'd built?"

Electrolush looked down and scowled. His face was like the rest of him, long and bony, with a chin and a nose that jutted out and a three-day growth of beard. "Y'mean that Wade guy?"

He was the first person Dex had talked to that actually knew Wade's name, Dex realized. *Or at least the first to admit it.*

"Yes. I'm doing a story for the *Black Rock Gazette*—"

"He was a *ballsy* motherfucker, I'll give him that. After all the work I put into that piece . . . it *still* pisses me off."

"How do you know his name?"

"Well, he spray-painted it all over the front, didn't he? Y'know, you go to all the trouble of building a thirty-seven-foot working penis, the last thing you expect is for someone to fuckin' *tag* it."

"I guess not. . . . Did you say *working* penis?"

"Sure. Anybody can build a gigantic phallus—hell, that's half of modern architecture. You can even cheat and do it the easy way by makin' the whole thing inflatable. But did I? No goddamn way. I used half a ton of latex, hydraulics, collapsible aluminum scaffolding . . . not to mention all the internal plumbing."

"Really." Dex could tell the man was genuinely upset . . . but he kept hearing Lorilei's voice in his head, making inappropriate comments: *Aww . . . sounds like you really got shafted.* "So it was . . . fully functional?"

"Damn right it was. When it was flaccid, water would shoot from the top every thirty minutes or so, in a real high, tight arc—it'd come down on the other side of the Esplanade, in a big toilet bowl with a bull's-eye painted on it. But that wasn't *nothin'* compared to when it blew its load."

"I'm sure it was—" *A real climax of your career.* "—impressive."

"That it was. The whole thing would start to shake, the veins on the outside would bulge, and then SPLOOSH! I injected a lot of air into the main line to make it foam, so's the liquid would read as white, and some really bright spotlights focused on the ejaculate. Had to keep to strictly nocturnal emissions for best effect. . . ."

"I'm sorry I missed it," Dex said. *That's what you get for being cocky . . . What is this world coming to?* He was glad Electrolush couldn't see his face; he was having a hard time not bursting into laughter.

" 'Wade's World' right across the scrotum," the man said mournfully. "It was a fuckin' *travesty.*"

"It . . . it certainly . . . excuse me." He turned away, and managed to fake a reasonably convincing coughing fit. When he'd gotten himself under control, he turned back, wiping his eyes. "Sorry," he said. "The dust really gets to my throat."

"Anyway, that wasn't the worst part. I managed to get most of the paint off, but the next day somebody came in and sabotaged the pumps, which basically shut the whole thing down. I don't know if it was the same guy, but who *else* would fuck with it?"

"I really can't imagine . . ."

Electrolush suddenly grinned and pointed. "Hey, awright! It's Dr. Megavolt!"

A flatbed truck rolled into Center Camp. What looked like two nine-foot mushrooms with thick metal stems and white ceramic caps stood on the back, with a man between them wearing a shiny foil suit with a wire-cage helmet. He lifted his arms up as if he were about to start preaching—and an immense, dazzling bolt of electricity arced from one of the columns to his outstretched hand. Dex could smell the ozone being released; the sharp, buzzing crackle sounded like the world's biggest bug-zapper.

A crowd of about twenty people were chasing the truck; they were chanting, "Megavolt! Megavolt!"

"Fuckin' amazing, isn't it?" Electrolush said. "Dual Tesla coils, twenty-five thousand volts apiece. They pull about two hundred amps when they're both goin' at once, and they say he can generate a million volts off the top."

"How? I mean, why isn't he—"

"Extra crispy? That suit he's wearin' is a Faraday cage—voltage travels over the surface, but not inside."

The truck rolled to a stop. Dr. Megavolt gestured again, and lightning leapt through the air, writhing and spitting light like some kind of demon on a leash. It was both beautiful and terrifying; for the first time, Dex felt he really understood the term, 'mad scientist.' If he'd seen such a thing three days ago, he would have muttered, "But isn't that dangerous?"

Now, he already knew the answer. The man was playing with one of the elemental forces of nature . . . and even though it could kill him, he was in control.

For the moment, at least . . .

Electrolush clambered down from the platform. Dex's robe had been open the whole time so the techie could get a good look at his T-shirt—but then Dex noticed what Electrolush was wearing. His shirt had the *Star Wars* logo across the chest, along with a depiction of Luke Skywalker and Darth Vader dueling with lightsabers. Dex heard that nauseating *crunch!* in his head once more . . . but this time, he didn't let the surge of emotion overcome him.

He swallowed and said, "Nice shirt. You a fan?"

"Hell, who isn't? I'm wearin' this one for a reason, though—supportin' the Rogue-Runner."

That came as even a bigger shock, but Dex kept his voice neutral. "You think he's innocent?"

"Who knows? But I figure there must be somethin' to his story, 'cause it's just so fuckin' *weird*—and out here, weird is the natural state of affairs. I'd be a whole lot more suspicious if he'd said it was self-defense or somethin' normal."

"I suppose—"

"Hey, I just realized—the guy who got killed, his

name was Wade, too, wasn't it? Wouldn't it be wild if it were the same guy?"

"I thought his name was Wayne," Dex said, pretending to be uncertain. "Wasn't it?"

"No, I'm pretty sure it was Wade . . . funny how I didn't put the two together right away." He gave Dex a longer, more careful look. "Guess you don't always notice what's right under your nose."

"Thank you for your time," Dex said quickly. He gave him the name of the decoy camp, and told him when he'd be there if he remembered any other details. Electrolush nodded, but the look on his face was hard to read.

Dex didn't go straight back to Fun and Lorilei—instead, he walked around the curve of the café, went in another entrance, and cut back to where they were sitting.

"And the verdict is?" Fun asked as Dex sat down.

"Hard to say. Wade vandalized an art installation the man . . . *constructed,* but I don't know if that would drive him to murder."

"Don't you mean *erected?*" Lorilei said sweetly. "Remember, we've read those files, too."

"Yeah," said Fun. "And you have to remember how much some of these installations are worth. Artists get grants to build them in the first place, but they can sell for six figures or more. If Wade screwed up the chance for Electrolush to make a sale, it could have cost him big-time."

"I thought Burning Man was a commerce-free zone," Dex said.

Fun shrugged. "Hey, when the week's over, people still have to go back to the real world. Nothing gets bought or sold here, not officially . . . but there's plenty of networking."

"Networking?" Dex said. "No offense, but—the words *Captain Fun* and *networking* don't sound like they belong in the same sentence."

Lorilei rolled her eyes. "Oh, come on, Curious. *Fairy wings* and *flamethrowers* don't sound like they belong together either, but you get plenty of both here. Just because someone creates a theme camp based on hillbillies from outer space doesn't mean they don't go back to work in a bank next week."

She was right, of course. Captain Fun and Lorilei had real jobs and real lives to return to, just like everybody else . . . but right now, sitting in the desert while surrounded by strangeness, it was hard for Dex to picture them in a mundane setting. The festival was just so big, his experiences here so intense, that the outside world seemed like a foreign country he had visited once, a long time ago.

The vehicles had begun to move. With Dr. Megavolt in the lead, they headed out onto the Esplanade, onlookers cheering them on. Dex, Lorilei and Fun sipped their coffee and watched them roll past. Most of the vehicles were loaded with Burners, sitting on roofs or hoods, perched on wings or masts or anything else they could cling to. A fire engine went by with its lights flashing and siren blaring, carrying at least two dozen people; a backhoe trundled past with a crowded couch held aloft in its bucket. There were trucks of every size, ranging from pickups to eighteen-wheelers. There were flying saucers on wheels, finned rocket ships straight out of a fifties sci-fi epic . . . and a perfect replica of a *Star Wars* landspeeder.

Lorilei noticed him staring at it. "Yeah, there's a lot of *Star Wars* stuff out here," she said. "Including a Tatooine Camp and a Mos Eisley Cantina. The whole desert-planet full-of-alien-desperados is kind of a natural fit."

"Haven't seen any Vaders, though," Fun said. "Not the pink kind, anyway."

When the last vehicle was gone, Lorilei suggested they head out to the Man for the Rogue-Runner rally.

"I don't know if that's such a good idea," Dex said.

"Actually, it might be," said Fun. "You could get an idea of how the city feels about you."

"It's not like someone's going to shout, 'It's him!' " Lorilei said. "You're in disguise—you should be perfectly safe."

"No such thing," Dex said, finishing his coffee. "Not in Black Rock City, anyway—but you know what? I don't care. The hell with it, let's go. Maybe we'll find out something interesting."

"Curious Urge is starting to live up to his name," Captain Fun observed.

"I still liked him better in the trench coat," Lorilei said.

They hopped on their bikes and rode out of Center Camp, heading straight up Paradox Promenade. Traffic was fairly heavy; it seemed they weren't the only curious ones.

By the time they got to the base of the Man, Dex was sure the crowd had gathered for some other reason. "There are at least a thousand people here," he said, amazed.

"And still growing," said Fun. "I think you're a hit."

They locked their bikes to a lamppost and walked

up to the edge of the crowd. It felt more like a rock concert than a rally, Dex thought. People were milling about, laughing, talking, and drinking; the breeze carried the aroma of burning ganja undercut with the occasional spike of gasoline or kerosene. Competing boom boxes dueled for the soundtrack, spacey melodic ambient versus upbeat reggae. A drum circle had set up at the perimeter, providing a rhythmic backbeat to the susurrus of voices and music. Several fire-spinners were doing their thing, one of them with a flaming staff.

And still people kept arriving. They came on bikes, on foot, in art cars; they came in groups, or in couples, or by themselves. Some carried signs that said things like, "GO ROGUE-RUNNER GO!" or "DARTH BUNNY AIN'T FUNNY." Somebody had actually mocked up a stuffed-toy version of the Road Runner and was waving it around at the end of a long pole. Dex wasn't sure if it was supposed to be an expression of support or condemnation—the pole went right up the bird's behind.

The temple the Man stood on was designed like a ziggurat, with a series of ascending levels and a staircase that ran all the way to the top. Up close, the Man himself was impressive; he towered at least eighty feet above the playa, his skeletal frame outlined in bright blue neon. His arms were down at his sides, his diamond-shaped head blank and featureless.

The top of the ziggurat's first level was a good thirty feet above the ground, and there was a figure on it holding a megaphone. From the waist up he resembled the Michelin Man; his jacket looked like it was made out of bubble wrap, except the bubbles were the size of baseballs. The collar was a large white circle behind his head, outlined in blue EL wire that haloed his frizzy black hair. White spandex shorts and white PVC boots finished the outfit. He held up the megaphone and addressed the crowd.

"Citizens of Black Rock City!"

A roar of greeting rose up.

"Thank you for coming out to show your support. My name is Moonman . . . and I believe that Dexter Edden is *innocent*."

This time the roar was deafening, almost frightening in its intensity. *Me,* Dex thought, stunned. *They're shouting for* me. *How many—fifteen hundred? Two thousand? More?*

Moonman's voice was strong and resonant; he was a natural orator. "Like most of you, I learned about Dexter's situation through the media. I read about it in the newspaper, I heard about it on the radio. And I probably went through the same stages many of you did; at first I was horrified that a murder had taken place, then I was intensely curious about the details. I wanted justice to be done—but I wasn't sure what justice *was*."

He strode the length of the platform, reached the end and stopped. "Well, I have to thank both the *Gazette* and *Piss Clear* for helping me make up my mind. Both of them made eloquent cases in their own way, but both pointed out the same thing: this is *our* city, and we do things *our way*."

He paused, and the crowd didn't let him down; they cheered in affirmation.

He turned and paced to the other end of his stage. "Well, I guess we don't have anything to worry about, because *the police* are on the job. We *trust* the police, right?"

A loud chorus of boos.

"Remember a few years ago, when the festival moved from one spot in the desert to another? Suddenly it was in another county, with a different sheriff. Suddenly, the cops were arresting anyone that smelled like pot . . . and why? Was it because they were causing *problems?*"

He paused again, and people responded with shouts of, "NO!"

"Was it because there were smugglers moving huge amounts of drugs through Black Rock City?"

More yelling, more denials.

"No . . . it was because the new sheriff had to show everybody how big his *dick* was, and he did it by *fucking* anyone he could. *No* justice, *no* protection of the public, just another *asshole in power* making sure everybody knew who was *in charge.*"

Moonman was getting worked up now, and he was taking the crowd with him. Dex could feel it in the air, could almost smell the rising tension.

"Are we really going to *trust* these fuckers to run a *murder investigation?*"

This time, the outpouring of noise actually hurt Dex's ears. He understood, suddenly, why there were so many people here and why they were so passionate. The people that surrounded Dex had reactions to authority that ranged from distrust to outright hatred— he had simply provided them with a convenient focal point. This wasn't about him . . . it was about the people trying to *catch* him.

But who knew what they'd do in his name?

The realization produced a cold knot in his stomach, and the fragile feeling of control he'd slowly been building vanished in an instant.

Moonman lowered the megaphone for a second, catching his breath and surveying his audience. He was in his late twenties to early thirties, tanned, with thick eyebrows that matched his bushy black hair. He was good-looking in a rock star/revolutionary kind of way, with high cheekbones and a strong chin; Dex could imagine him with either an electric guitar or a rocket launcher in his hands.

"We can *not* allow Dexter Edden to be railroaded! We can *not* allow the police to turn this into a witch hunt! If we let them, they'll search every tent, dome, and structure in this city, all on the pretext of looking for a killer. And if a few civil rights get trampled, who cares? As far as they're concerned, we're just *tourists*. They can fuck us over and get away with it, because we don't actually *live* here. They don't get it, people; they don't understand. They don't know what it means to be a citizen of Black Rock City—but *you do.*"

He pointed into the crowd. "*You* built this place. You *sweated* for it, you *froze* for it, you broke your fucking *back* for it. Maybe we're only physically here on the playa for a week, but our hearts are here *every day. This is our home.*"

He stopped, lowered the megaphone. Lowered his head, as if exhausted by the truth. People screamed for him to keep going. Someone started chanting, "Rogue-Runner! Rogue-Runner!" and it spread throughout the whole crowd in seconds. Dex almost joined in himself.

"Yeah," he continued. "The Rogue-Runner. We got

to support him, people, because out here it's just us and them. That's why I'm organizing the Acme Rogue-Runner Guardians, to provide any help we can. I know, it sounds like a joke, but I'm serious. If anybody knows anything that might help Dexter, or just wants to express their support, come and see me—I'm camped at Vision and two-thirty. For now, we can all light a candle to show him he's not alone."

Moonman put down the megaphone, pulled a lighter from his pocket, and knelt on the platform. It looked like he was trying to set fire to a small paper bag, but when he straightened up, the bag glowed with light. *Must be a candle inside,* Dex thought.

Moonman descended the steps, and others began to come up with candles of their own. Some were in paper bags, some were in little glass jars or wax cups, some were just naked flame.

Within a few minutes, there were dozens. *If they keep going at this rate,* Dex thought numbly, *there'll be hundreds. Maybe even thousands.*

"Wow," said Captain Fun. "This is *amazing*. What do *you* think, Mr. Urge?"

"I think," Dex said, "I want to go home."

CHAPTER 12:

ESPLANADE!

File D (Queen of Denial): Some queens love drama; some queens love jewelry; some queens love Christmas or Abba or running up the plastic at the Mary Kay counter. Some queens love *arias*, period costumes and wigs a mile high; some love sequins and miniskirts and heels even higher. Some love soap operas and little dogs; some love leather and Harley-Davidson hogs . . . and then there's *me*.

I love it *all*.

Everybody has their addictions, darling, and *moi* is no exception. I'm addicted to a big, woody male, a rough-hewn guy who really stands out; I'm talking about that huge flamer, the Enormous Erection of the Desert: Burning Man.

And having a jones for the Man is like having all those addictions rolled into one and sprinkled with Magic Playa Dust. Forget about the drugs and the sex and the nudity—I'm talking about serious *spectacle* here. This is Wigstock and Mardi Gras and the world's biggest sci-fi convention in a threeway title match for Biggest, Bizarrest, and Bad-Ass Craziest.

Personally, I don't do drugs when I'm in BRC. It just seems *redundant*. If I really want to alter my consciousness—alter it *further*, I mean—I'll just give up sleeping for a few days, which is easy to do in the City that Never Slows Fucking Down. You can dance until the sun comes up, spend the day playing in the theme camps, then do it all over again—and never hit the same place twice. Black Rock is like Vegas's bastard child—you know, the one with A.D.D. that hates his dad, breaks into the liquor cabinet and steals his car?

But I'm not really that kind of party animal. The orifices I come to fill are my eyes and ears, not my lungs and liver; anything in between is negotiable. And believe me, there's plenty to choose from.

For instance, there's the annual topless parade known as Critical Tits. Now, you'd think that since I have neither the proper equipment nor a carnal interest therein that the sight of hundreds of bare-breasted beauties biking and bouncing across the playa would hold no interest . . . but you'd be wrong. It's quite a sight, actually, and the fact that nobody can pin down whether this is a powerful pro-feminist statement or a gleeful attempt to outdo *Girls Gone Wild* is what makes it so interesting.

Something a little more inclusive—and revealing—is the nude shoot they've done a few times. They get hundreds of people, make sure they're all starkers, then arrange them in various ways on the playa and take pictures. Now that's what I call a photo spread . . . Gigantic Naked Art! Penii and Pussies and Nipples, Oh My!

If a race of aliens landed in Black Rock City and decided that the biggest attention-grabber was obviously the dominant species, it's hard to say exactly who or what they'd be asking to take them to their leader. On one tentacle, the big art installations are always amazing. You're wandering across the desert, wearing a giant sombrero and nothing else, when suddenly you see a large shape in the distance. Is it a mirage, brought on by dehydration and half a bottle of tequila? No, it's the HMS *Love*, a thirty-foot submarine surfacing through the dust of the playa like a land shark coming up to gobble a buzzard. Or maybe it just wants to gnaw on the Bone Tree, a gigantic mobile sculpture made entirely out of cattle skeletons that roams around like Halloween on wheels.

But then there are the staged events—like Pepe's Opera. My God. The first time I saw it, I felt like I'd fallen in love with an insane asylum. Not in—*with*. Pepe is this artist from Argentina, and he comes out to the desert and stages these amazing productions; they're like *Aida* on acid. For the set, he builds these immense wire-frame *faux* genitalia—male and female—and coats them in mud from a local hot spring. He brings in hundreds of people for the performance, dancers and singers and fire-breathers, and the costumes are just *astounding*. The first one he did was called *The Arrival of Empress Zoe* back in '97, and it was *twisted*. The plot featured a hermaphrodite empress, the Catholic Church, High Priests of Hell, and a goat. At the height of the performance they set the phallic towers—called lingams—on fire from the inside, which turned them into giant chimneys belching smoke and flame. A woman wearing elaborate body-paint and a mask belted out an *aria* while standing framed by a giant adobe vulva and several flaming penises, while men dressed like geishas did an intricate and surreal dance on stilts . . . at least, that's the way I remember it. I've been going to Pepe's Opera for years, and all the insanity kind of bleeds together after a while.

The Black Rock Desert is the perfect place for things on this scale, of course. You can't really get a sense of just how big and empty the place is until you're actually here; it's like God's auditorium. I hear non-Burners wonder about the size of the festival, and say things like "Don't you think it's getting too big?"

Honey, you could add a million people to our population and we'd still be an anthill on Everest.

I like to remind myself of that fact every so often; I walk out to the edge of the city at night, stroll a few hundred feet into the desert, and lie down. Look up at the stars, look around at the emptiness and realize how vast and still and ancient the playa is. It's like the world's biggest piece of blank paper . . . and we hairless apes just can't resist the urge to *scribble,* can we?

CHAPTER 13:

WHOLLY OTHER

Dex had never felt so vulnerable in his life.

When Jimmy had told him he was going to be famous, it hadn't really sunk in. Being famous in a place like Black Rock City, it had seemed to him, didn't really mean much; it was like being a single sparkler on a birthday cake for a thousand-year-old man. There were so many things happening here, so much variety and razzle-dazzle and sheer oddity, that he had just assumed he wouldn't really stand out. He never had before.

But where Dexter Edden, mild-mannered computer geek, barely registered on the radar of Freakdom, the Rogue-Runner showed up as a genuine phenomenon. They'd turned him into a symbol, an icon of rebellion against repression.

Which was ridiculous, of course. If Dex symbolized anything, it was being in the wrong place at the wrong time. He wasn't fighting the establishment, he was just trying to stay alive and out of jail. He felt a lot more like the Coyote than the Road Runner, continually falling off cliffs but somehow managing to survive.

"Hey," Captain Fun said. He was on one side of Dex, Lorilei on the other, as they biked home. "I just noticed something. When we head back to Aetheria from Center Camp, we usually take the same street."

"So?" Lorilei said.

"We don't cut across the playa because it's too empty—we're afraid we might miss something cool. We don't take the Esplanade because it's too crowded. So we go one street up instead."

"And?" Dex asked.

"The next street up is Authority. Authority turns out to be the easiest route—the one we take without even thinking about it."

"Absurd."

"No, I think they actually planned it that way—"

"No, I mean we just passed Absurd. We're almost home."

When they got to Aetheria, Dex parked his bike and went straight to Captain Fun's tent-trailer. He went inside without a word, and closed the door behind him.

Dex lay on the bed in the tent-trailer and stared up at the canvas slanting above his head. He was trying to remember the last time he'd been the center of attention.

He was fairly certain it had been a birthday, but that hardly counted; no matter *who* you were, you were pretty much guaranteed to be the focus at an event celebrating your arrival into the world. Of course, he was hazy on the last time he'd actually *had* a birthday party; he thought it might have been his twenty-fifth.

On a hunch, he got up and checked the map of Black Rock City, the one that listed the theme camps on the back. Sure enough, there was a Birthday Camp. He could imagine how it was decorated, knew they'd be giving out little cone-shaped hats, could guess they'd probably know a dozen versions of "Happy Birthday" that ranged from the silly to the obscene. He didn't have to go there.

He didn't have to go anywhere.

He lay down again. Maybe this whole Rogue-Runner thing might work for him, after all. He could get Fun and Lorilei to coordinate with the Acme Rogue-Runner Guardians; they could be his eyes and ears, and he would direct things from here. He was sure he'd seen a sign on a theme camp proclaiming they could put the Man on any T-shirt—they could probably duplicate the logo on Dex's easily enough. Put those shirts on volunteers of the same general description as himself, slap dust masks on them, let them read the suspect files, and send them out to do interviews. Recruit more people to sit in towers and do surveillance, set up another ring of decoy camps to direct suspects to . . .

Sure. I'll put together a crack team of detectives disguised as me, drawn from a pool of crazed party animals and anarchists. I'll send them out on a scavenger hunt with my life at stake, and trust that none of them screws up. And I'll do it all in the next four days.

He hadn't come up with a strategy. He'd designed a theme camp.

And not a very good one, either. The costumes were

hardly sexy, the activities were interactive but somewhat dull. He had nothing to give away, and there was
no dancing, drinking, or drugs involved. It was more
performance art than anything, and even then, nothing caught on fire and nobody took their clothes off.

He was sure the members of the ARG would come
up with much better stuff on their own. They'd design
some weird version of Clue, with people running
around trading shots of Jägermeister in return for evidence, the whole thing climaxing in a drunken orgy
where everybody wore strap-on beaks. Captain Fun
would probably wind up being Master of Ceremonies,
and Lorilei would finally see how boring Dex really
was and run off with somebody dressed as a parody of
him . . .

A knock at the door interrupted his self-pity in mid-
wallow.

"Mr. Urge?" Lorilei called out.

"What?"

"Captain Fun and I are going out for a while. Are
you going to be okay while we're gone?"

"Sure."

"All right, then. We'll see you later."

Well, that *didn't take long. . . .* His depression deepened. *And why shouldn't they go out and enjoy themselves? You think somebody who calls himself Captain
Fun comes to Burning Man to spend all his time babysit-
ting a clueless loser? They don't owe me a thing.*

*And what about all those other people out there?
Thirty thousand of them, all here to—how did Wade put
it?* "Get wasted, dance naked and set shit on fire." *What
am I to them, except a glorified party game?*

Except that wasn't strictly true, and despite how

sorry for himself Dex was feeling, his innate sense of fairness wouldn't let him get away with such a cynical definition. He'd seen a lot more than just people carousing; he'd seen things it had taken tremendous effort and dedication to create. He'd talked to people to whom the festival obviously meant something much deeper, even if no two of them seemed to agree on exactly what that was.

Which meant that some of the people at that rally had not only taken it seriously, they were going to *do* something.

The more he thought about it, the more his stomach churned. If only five percent of the crowd—which was at least two thousand strong by the time Dex had left—joined in, that was a hundred people. A hundred people who were going to do . . . what?

He had no idea.

He fought down his rising panic and tried to think analytically. They wanted to show their support, Moonman had said. In the normal world, that would have meant signing a petition, maybe holding a rally. Here, that was only a starting point—they'd wind up doing something a lot more radical.

Maybe his earlier idea about an army of Dex clones wasn't so far off. Captain Fun had already tried to confuse his trail by spreading false rumors—what if the ARG took the same approach? There could be a hundred people claiming to be him, roaming through the city and doing God knows what: having sex, setting things on fire, telling outrageous lies. . . .

Sort of like Wade.

He closed his eyes, listened to the sounds of the city, felt a stab of loneliness. He thought about his ex-boss, wondered again exactly why Wade had collected all those files on people he'd abused. Why had he asked each one of them what Burning Man had meant to them?

Wade's original behavior was easier to understand. Although his conduct had been more extreme than Dex had personally witnessed before, Black Rock City was a more extreme environment; he couldn't say he viewed any of Wade's depredations as out of character. He was simply being himself—and for all Wade's faults, at least he'd been consistent. He'd tried—in his own self-centered, crude way—to participate; he just hadn't been very good at it. He reminded Dex of a feral child, trying desperately to join in the games of civilized children but failing to grasp the rules. The whole punk-rock ethic of antiestablishment anarchy just didn't work here—Black Rock wasn't about tearing down society, it was about *replacing* it.

So why had Wade come back?

It must have been immensely frustrating—here was something that looked like a wild, out-of-control riot, but every time Wade tried to cut loose, he ran into an unseen wall of rules. So either Rafe had offered him an irresistable reason to return . . . or, despite all the problems he ran into, Wade had found something here that was worth all the trouble. Something he desperately needed to understand.

What was it he'd said to Dex, when they first arrived? "Just because something is new and scary, that doesn't make it bad"? It almost sounded as if he'd been trying to convince himself, not Dex . . . and even if he *had* been scared, Wade hadn't given up.

Yeah, Dex thought. *And look what it got him.*

For that matter, why had Wade brought Dex? Bringing another person along for insurance made sense, but why *him?* There were plenty of friends Wade could have brought, fellow party animals that would have accepted gleefully, and probably been a lot more useful as a deterrent to violence. Dex didn't really belong here.

And neither did Wade, Dex thought. *No matter how hard he tried, he couldn't quite fit in. Maybe he didn't want someone along to party with; maybe he just wanted someone to talk to. Someone who felt as out of place and awkward as he did. . . .*

The thought made him feel more isolated than ever.

Hours went by. Sleep was out of the question. He could have gone out—he knew how to navigate the streets now, and with his disguise he should be safe—but he just couldn't face the chaos of the city. The confines of the tent-trailer, at least, were predictable; naked people weren't going to burst out of the sink, waving flaming polo mallets and demanding he join them in a game of Whack the Invisible Gopher. He knew it was only the illusion of control, but it was one he needed at the moment.

He passed the time making lists in his head: lists of movies he'd seen, books he'd read, teachers he'd had. It was completely pointless, and therefore completely safe. He managed to avoid thinking about his situation for whole minutes at a time.

He was trying to remember the names of all the dogs he'd known when he finally drifted off.

• • •

A rap at the door woke him. He jerked awake, blinked groggily, and said, "Who is it?"

"It's me," Lorilei said. "Can I come in?"

"Go ahead."

She poked her head inside. "How are you doing?"

"I'm—I don't know. What time is it?"

"Half-past coffee. Want some?"

"I guess." He squinted in her direction, feeling disoriented and resentful, but she was already gone. She reappeared a minute later bearing two mugs, one of which she handed to him before sitting down on the edge of the bed.

He propped himself up on one elbow and took a grudging sip. "Thanks."

She was dressed almost conservatively today, in some kind of long, flowing see-through robe, with a white bra and panties beneath it. Big black army boots made her look like a soldier for Victoria's Secret.

"Did you have fun last night?" he asked. It came out a little more petulant than he'd intended.

"No, but he disappeared with a lovely couple from Palo Alto and a bottle of massage oil, so I imagine *somebody* had him."

"I'm glad someone's enjoying themselves."

"Actually, I'm pretty sure *most* of the people here are—though I admit the possibility that they're simply doing splendid impersonations of people so engaged. You, on the other hand, are doing an eerily acurate portrayal of a wanted fugitive hiding from a crazed mob."

"It's not a portrayal," he said, refusing to go along with her playful tone. "It's what's happening, and there's nothing funny about it."

"Hey, I take it seriously, too. I just don't see the point in getting all negative—"

"Negative? No. Thinking it's going to rain is negative. Thinking that the glass is half-empty is negative. *Knowing* that you're being framed for murder *and* you're trapped in a city full of maniacs isn't negative—it's the cold, hard truth."

"Drink your coffee."

"Stop *humoring* me!" He pulled himself to a sitting position, the sleeping bag pooled around his waist, and glared at her. "You know what the punch line is here? *I go to jail.* Hell, this being Nevada, I might even be *executed.* You and Captain Fun and Sundog and everybody else goes home, to whatever you call a life, while one way or the other mine *ends.*"

She looked at him very seriously, and didn't say a word.

"What, you aren't going to make a joke? You aren't going to flash me or make a clever pun or mention some obscure bit of trivia? Because, hey, that's what I really *need* right now, and you seem to be an expert in that area."

"I'm on your side—"

"I know, I know—everybody in Tribe Urge is on my side, and all those people Moonman whipped into a frenzy, too. You're all so concerned with my welfare you had to go out last night and party your half-naked *brains* out." He hadn't realized how angry he was; it was like he'd struck a match without realizing he was standing in a puddle of gasoline. "I keep hearing all this talk about consequences, but nobody seems to be thinking past the end of this week."

She stood up. "That's not true. But it sounds like

the only truth you want to hear right now is the 'cold, hard' kind; unfortunately, I'm a little short on that. So I think I'll come back when you're a little more open-minded." She opened the door and stepped outside.

"Have a good time," he muttered as the door closed.

When he finally stuck his head out, the camp was deserted. Everybody, it seemed, was somewhere doing something. He found a note stuck to a cooler, telling him to help himself to whatever food he wanted; he had a banana, a nectarine, and two granola bars, washed down with Gatorade. He made a quick pilgrimage to the local Porta-Johns, and returned to the tent-trailer.

He stayed inside for the rest of the day.

He drank water, and even found a bucket with a lid to use as a urinal so he didn't have to keep leaving to use the bathroom. There was a tarp stretched over the top of the trailer that kept the sun off, and there were big screened windows on every side; he half-unzipped the flaps that covered them to let air blow through. It got warm, but not unbearable.

Then he started organizing.

Stuff on the small table went first, followed by the pile of costumes on the other bed. He sorted, straightened, divided into categories: he found boxes of nitrous canisters that clinked when he picked them up, plastic bags full of temporary tattoos, an entire crate of vodka. Drug paraphernalia went in one pile, sex toys in another, costuming accessories to one side. Next he went through the cupboards and drawers in the trailer, finding mainly camping gear and supplies; all the stuff other people would keep safely hidden was already out in the open.

When he had a good idea of both inventory and storage space, he started rearranging. Costumes were neatly folded and stacked; props were collected into a single drawer. Miscellaneous tools and kitchen gear were put away, and garbage was collected and bagged. After that he wiped down all the surfaces he could with a damp cloth, even though a layer of dust seemed to grow on them as soon as he turned his back.

He sat at the small table and surveyed his work. "A little order," he said out loud. "That's all I need. A little order."

A sudden thought struck, popping his tiny bubble of satisfaction. If what he truly wanted was a controlled, orderly environment, there was one already waiting for him . . .

A prison cell.

It was late afternoon by the time Lorilei came back.

"Hello?" she called out. "Anyone home?"

"Just us fugitives," he said.

"Can I come in?"

"Okay."

She entered, and he looked up from the laptop. He'd been going over the files again, trying to see if there was some clue he had missed, something that might jump out at him now that he had a context to put them in. So far, nothing had.

She sat down on the seat across from him. "I see you've been keeping busy." Her tone was neutral.

"I cleaned up a little, yeah," he said.

"Find out anything new?" she asked, gesturing to the laptop.

"Not really. Whatever Rafe's true identity is, it doesn't seem to be in here."

"Maybe not. But it *is* out *there* . . . which is where you should be, too."

"I don't know . . ."

"Well, I do. I know a lot of things, actually—for instance, I know that neither Ann Atomic nor Electrolush are our killer."

He frowned. "How do you know that?"

"Because the members of your tribe spent all of last night and most of today tracking down and verifying alibis. You know, while we weren't busy partying our half-naked brains out."

He blinked. "Uh—"

She held up a hand. "Dex—it's okay. You just hit the wall. You didn't choose to come here; you didn't choose to have your life fucked over. You have every right to be pissed off. But now that you've had a little time to cool off, there's a few things you should really understand, all right?"

He nodded.

"All right. The people that come here—this is *important* to them. Whether it's their first time or their fifteenth, this is a big deal. Some people plan all year long for this week; some people spend tens of thousands of dollars. A week might seem like a long time, but when you look at all there is to see and do, it really isn't. Time is a very precious commodity here. These people have every right to spend it however they choose—and you should feel honored that some of them are choosing to spend it helping you."

Suddenly Dex felt foolish and ashamed. "I know. I'm sorry," he said. "It's just that every time I think I have a handle on the situation, everything changes. I need some solid ground to stand on."

She smiled and took his hand. "I know. That's what your tribe is for."

"But—I don't even know who the members of my tribe *are*. You all know each other, but I don't know anyone—not even you."

For the first time, he saw something like embarrassment cross her face. "Yeah. That's my fault. See, Dex, when I come to Burning Man, I try to leave a lot of my other life behind. It's not that I'm unhappy in it; it's just that I feel more like *me* when I'm here than when I'm anywhere else. I don't have to pretend to be interested in things that I'm not, I don't have to talk or act in a particular way, I don't have to worry about what other people think. But sometimes I get so . . . *enraptured* in being myself that I get a little selfish." She paused. "And you . . . you make it worse."

"Me?" he asked, bewildered. "What did *I* do?"

"Nothing. You're just being who you are, plain old Dexter Edden. But in some ways, that makes you the most exotic creature on the playa." She smiled at the look on his face. "Don't you see? Everybody here has some idea of what's going on. Even the first-timers are here because they want to be. But you—you're like a priest who's parachuted into an orgy. You're this little speck of innocence surrounded by debauchery. It makes me . . . well. You know."

"Blush hungry," he offered.

She laughed. "Yes, but it's more than just that. You can't have a counterculture without a culture to rebel against. You can't be an extrovert without an audience. Every time I come out here, even while I'm reveling in the fact that I'm free and surrounded by people who won't judge me, a small, childish part of me is sticking her tongue out at the rest of the world and saying, 'Bleah! Take that! Look at what *I'm* doing, and you can't stop me, nyah, nyah, nyah!' "

"So when you see me," Dex said, "you see everything you hate."

"No!" She looked stricken. "No, Dex, that's not it. When I see you, I see where I came from. I see someone I have to prove myself to, so I come on a little strong. I don't hate you, any more than I hate the world."

"You just wish it were a little more like here, out there?"

"Yes! That's it, exactly. I usually try to bring some of the energy of Black Rock City out into the world with me . . . but since your situation seems kinda inside out, I'm going to do the opposite and try to bring a little mundane reality in here."

"How?"

Lorilei rolled her eyes. "The name on my birth certificate—I refuse to say my 'real' name—is Laura May Wilson. I work at a photocopy place in Oakland. I watch *The Simpsons* and eat at Taco Bell and have a cat."

He stared at her for a second. "All at the same time?"

"No, I leave the cat at home when I go to work."

"I see. And is *Simpsons*-watching prevalent there as well?"

"Not so much."

"Because I could see the combination of Homer-related distractions and cheap Mexican cuisine being the cause of many horrendous photocopier mishaps."

"That could certainly happen."

"Aren't you going to ask me if I'm enjoying this?"

"Are you enjoying this?"

"More than I expected. Tell me about your cat."

"What would you like to know?"

"You can start with a list of his cat toys," Dex said judiciously, "and then we'll move on to the more *mundane* details."

And so they did.

She told him about where she lived and what she did and all the tiny boring details of her life. Dex felt like an expatriate getting a gift package from his homeland; every trivial fact, every bit of day-to-day minutia brought a swell of nostalgia to his heart.

In return, he made irrelevant observations, injected absurd comments, and even made the occasional off-color remark. Lorilei bore all of this with stoic grace, laughing now and then, wincing often. Dex could see her gritting her mental teeth, but she refused to meet his wit with anything but the blandest of replies.

It was, he discovered, exactly what he needed. The more ordinary the subject, the more relaxed he felt; he could almost close his eyes and imagine they were two coworkers sharing a coffee break, filling the silence with the most banal of conversations. And in some sort of reverse chameleon kung-fu, he found his own skill at verbal banter increasing as she suppressed her own; it was almost as if there were some kind of metaphysical balance that needed to be maintained.

The talk turned from her everyday existence to her past; she told Dex about where she grew up and what it was like, and slowly the natural order of things returned. Dex found himself joking less and listening more as Lorilei's personality crept back into her voice, as she told him about her childhood and what she'd gone through: she'd been given up for adoption as a baby, been taken away from her first home by the state and raised in a succession of foster homes after that. She'd had a total of thirteen parents at one time or another, some of whom she still kept in touch with, others she never wanted to see again. She had been raped once, by a foster sibling.

Despite the darkness of her early life, she didn't refer to it with bitterness or anger. It was simply her history, where she'd come from; Dex understood that without an explanation, though he'd never met anyone like her in his life. She made sense to him on some level he couldn't identify—it was as if the joy she took in life was the only possible response, the only sane choice. It was bewildering and deeply comforting at the same time.

He found himself wanting to share details of his own life, his own history . . . but couldn't. Somehow, the flow of information wouldn't allow it. He felt as if Lorilei and he were equals for the first time, but it was his position as an unknown quantity that balanced her confessions; if Dex had responded in kind, he would have become simply another mundane person, diminished in comparison to her far more interesting life and personality despite her best efforts to make them seem less so.

"So, I guess I came out here the first time because I

was looking for something," she said. "I'm not sure what."

"Did you find it?"

"Yes and no. It's hard to explain—actually, I don't think I should even try." She paused, seemed to come to some kind of decision. "There's a few things I'd like to show you, but you're going to have to trust me. Think you can do that?"

He thought about it for a moment. "I guess I have to," he said slowly.

"Well, you *could* just stay in here until Fun packs up and goes home," she said. "But my way gives you a lot more choices."

He looked around at the sparse little cage he'd created for himself. "Good," he said. "I think I've just about exhausted those in here."

"Oh, I don't know. You could always make little castles out of the dust . . . now get dressed. We're going out."

He pulled on his disguise while she told him what had happened during his self-imposed exile. "The ARG has been talking to anyone who might have seen Rafe in his Darth Bunny outfit. So far, they have five people who remember seeing someone wearing a costume like that on Monday night."

"Five? That's great," Dex said, grabbing his dust mask.

"Yeah, but it doesn't prove anything—just that someone here is wearing an outfit like the one you described. And nobody knows which camp he came from, just that he was seen walking along Reality between Certain and Dubious after dark."

"He probably made sure nobody saw him leave—

maybe even changed in a Porta-John," Dex said thoughtfully. "And I bet he changed again, after the murder."

"What we need is somebody who saw him leaving the RV. So far, a couple of people remember seeing *you* tear past, but that's it. Moonman has people looking, though."

Dex pulled the hood of the robe over his head. "Moonman. You know, I'm still not sure how I feel about that speech he gave—I mean, I don't know if becoming some sort of underground symbol is really the best move."

She yawned and stood up. "Excuse me. Get used to it, Rogue-Runner—Black Rock sprouts minicultures like mushrooms on a wet lawn, and the ARG is the fastest-growing one I've seen since Critical Tits. Besides, the amount of help we've been getting from them is amazing—Captain Fun is over there right now, helping coordinate a tip network."

"Is that where we're going?"

"What? Come on, Dex—it's way too easy to compromise a volunteer organization. Rafe's probably already a member, just so he can keep an eye on what's going on. No, we keep you as far away from them as possible—Fun and I will act as go-betweens. We're not *complete* idiots, you know."

When Dex stepped outside, he was amazed to see how low the sun was in the sky; he'd spent the entire day in the tent-trailer. "Where are we going?" he asked as they got on their bikes.

"Just follow me," Lorilei said.

•   •   •

If only they hadn't stopped to admire the mermaid, Dex would think later, things would have been a lot easier.

She was floating, nude, in the middle of a large plastic bag filled with water beside the Esplanade. The bag was transparent, suspended in an open wooden frame around eight feet high. Her long, black hair swirled around her head like seaweed as she did slow-motion somersaults, sunlight making her pale skin gleam like a pearl.

Dex and Lorilei got off their bikes and joined the small throng of people clustered around the tank. Several of them were taking pictures, and the mermaid paused in her acrobatics to come up for air and spew a mouthful of water at the cameras. As the photographers yelped and jumped back, the rest of the crowd laughed and applauded. "Thank you for participating!" one of them called out.

And then the police cars pulled up.

There were two of them, and they parked at an angle that trapped Dex and Lorilei between them and the mermaid's tank. Two officers got out of each car, and one of them was Sheriff Tremayne.

"Hello, folks," he said cheerfully. "I don't want to ruin anyone's day, but it would *really* help me out if I could ask a few questions."

"You can *ask*," a man with a bushy blond beard said, and there were a few chuckles. Dex tried to laugh too, but it came out more like a dry cough. There were only eight or so people in their group—but why had they picked *this* little cluster to question? As far as he could tell, they were just a random knot of Burners standing around—

—And he was the only one wearing a mask.

There's almost no wind, no dust to keep out. Tremayne's been keeping an eye out for someone like me, and all he has to do now is ask me to pull down the mask.

"Dex," Lorilei said quietly. "Get ready to run. It's your only chance." She moved away before he had a chance to reply, and he realized she was about to do something stupid.

"Hey, is it true you guys arrest people for having sex in public?" she said brightly to one of the officers, the same Latino deputy Dex had seen before.

"Public sex is illegal, yes," the deputy said flatly.

"Well, how far can you go before it's actually sex?" Lorilei said, undoing her robe and letting it drop; she pulled off her bra and panties as she talked. "I mean, what about *this*?"

"Nudity is fine—oh. Ah, ma'am, I'm not sure if that's a proper use of your water bottle. . . ."

Dex walked past the water tank, moving quickly but not running. He'd gotten four steps before he heard a voice call out, "Sir? *Sir!* Please stop!"

Dex broke into a run. There was only one place to go, right ahead of him, a large wooden structure made of rough plywood. The sign over the door identified it as The MysTickal Maze; Dex took a sharp right as soon as he was inside, darted down a narrow corridor, then started taking corners at random.

When he was sure there was no one right behind him, he stopped, listening hard and trying not to breathe too loudly. He seemed to be right next to an exterior wall; he could hear Tremayne's voice only a few feet away. "All right, spread out around it," the sheriff said. "There's only four sides to the thing. Jackson, you come with me; we'll go in and flush him out."

Dex kept moving. He didn't know where he was going or what he was going to do, but the deeper he went into the maze the further he'd be from the law . . . he hoped. It was just as possible he'd turn a corner and run straight into Tremayne himself.

The maze was covered on top with blue fabric of some kind, giving everything a kind of swimming-pool glow. The walls were painted with cryptic messages: "ROOF-PIG, MOST UNEXPECTED" was one, and "IF YOU'RE REALLY EVIL, EAT THIS KITTEN"; perhaps strangest of all was "YOU CAN'T FIGHT CRIME WITH A MACARONI DUCK." There were wall hangings too, large pieces of brightly colored cloth in psychedelic patterns; on a hunch, he started looking behind them.

The third one concealed an entrance to a small room. Dex ducked inside—then noticed he wasn't the only one there. A man in a bathrobe was sitting on a beanbag chair, smoking dope from a corncob pipe. He had a large pair of black horns jutting from his head.

"Hey," the man said. "Congratulations, you have found the Lungs of the Beast. Care for a hit?"

"Uh, no, thanks," Dex said. "Look, I've kind of got a problem. . . ."

"If the Lungs of the Beast can help," the man said, blowing a smoke ring, "they will."

"Okay. I don't suppose you've heard of a group called the ARG?"

"Are you kidding?" the man said. "Go, Rogue-Runner."

"I was hoping you'd say that . . ."

• • •

Surrendering to the police, Dex thought later, was really his only choice. Apparently the police thought so, too; when Dex strolled out of the exit with his hands up, it didn't seem to come as much of a surprise.

What was unexpected—at least to Lorilei—was when "Dex" pulled down his dust mask, gave the cops a stoned smile, and said, "Tag. You're it."

"This isn't Edden," one of the deputies said.

"No kidding," the other replied. "And from the reek, I'd say he just took off to ditch his stash."

"Any dope you find in there," the man said, "isn't mine. Or maybe it isn't even *dope*. . . ."

Dex sighed, and swiveled the periscope, looking for Lorilei. The man that had switched clothes with him had sworn the scope was disguised on the outside—"Don't worry, man," he'd said. "This place is totally *Hogan's Heroized*. Just hang out until the coast is clear." And then he'd taken one last toke, pulled up the dust mask, and slipped out of the hidden room.

But Treymayne hadn't come out the exit yet—and suddenly, Dex could hear his voice right outside the hidden door.

"Mr. Edden? If you can hear me, it's in your own best interest to come on out. You know you can't stay in here forever. All I really have to do is wait . . ."

Dex swallowed.

"We *are* going to find you," Treymayne went on. "Now or later, it's up to you. Sooner would be better, in my opinion. . . ."

And then one of the deputies outside shouted, "Sheriff! We've got him!"

"Guess he got smart," Tremayne muttered. "Now, how do I get out of this damn thing. . . ."

When the police finally left, Lorilei came in and found him, calling softly, "Inspector?" until he could direct her to his hiding place. She brought him a scarf to tie around his face and a floppy-brimmed hat with flowers on it.

"I can't believe you got away with that," she said.

"I guess being a celebrity has its advantages," Dex said. "Now, can we get out of here, please?"

"Sure."

They got on their bikes and pedaled away, Dex nervously glancing around for cops. Nobody seemed to notice them. Once they were onto the open playa, Dex breathed a little easier.

"Look," Lorilei said suddenly.

She stopped her bike and pointed up. High above, brightly colored arcs of fabrics were slowly spiraling downward as the plane that had released them inched toward the horizon.

"Sky-dive into Burning Man, you get in for free," Lorilei said. "Or so I've been told. Personally, I hope it's true—it feels appropriate, somehow. Like being rewarded for making a leap of faith."

"And if you were pushed, instead of jumping?"

She grinned. "Then it's a reward for surviving."

They watched the chutes get closer and closer; there were six of them, in various bright colors. Three of the dangling figures seemed to have something strapped to their backs.

"Parahawks," Lorilei said. "Man, that must be sweet."

As they neared, Dex could make out the shape of what looked like oversize fans jutting out behind them. They swooped overhead, engines buzzing, no longer dropping but soaring.

"Now that's something I'd like to try," Dex said.

"Really? Well, I don't have an airplane handy, but I can give you the next best thing," Lorilei said. "But like I said—you'll have to trust me. . . ."

She took off on her bike, Dex following. When they were going at a good clip, she held her arms out to her sides. "Can you do this?" she called out.

"Ride no hands? Sure," Dex said. He probably hadn't tried to do so since he was a kid, but he didn't remember it being that hard. After a second's nervous hesitation, he let go of the handlebars and stretched his arms out to the side.

"Good. Now close your eyes."

"What?"

"Look around you; there's nothing but flat playa for hundreds of yards. Trust, remember?"

Dex had to admit she was right. He swallowed, then shut his eyes.

It was scary, but he didn't crash—it just *felt* like he would at any second. The longer he kept his eyes closed, the more intense the feeling got; but there was something else, just as strong, compounded of the air rushing past him and the sensation of movement in his belly. A feeling of freedom.

He went over a bump, opened his eyes with a gasp

and grabbed for the handlebars. He looked over at Lorilei; she was still sailing along, arms outstretched, eyes closed, a serene smile on her face.

Not sailing, Dex thought. *Flying.*

She finally opened them and coasted to a halt. Dex stopped beside her.

"See what I mean?" she asked.

"Very cool," Dex admitted. "Is that what you wanted to show me?"

"Nope, that was a bonus. C'mon."

She took him all the way to the other side of the city, then darted up and down streets as if she were searching for something. He followed her, trying to not get his robe caught in the bike's chain, trusting that wherever they were going was important.

When a gong sounded in the distance, she veered toward it immediately. A block later she slowed, then stopped and set down her bike. Dex joined her.

"Look," she said, and pointed.

A parade was coming toward them. *No, not a parade,* Dex thought. *A procession.*

It was the Lamplighters, row after row, each dressed in a long, hooded white robe with a flame motif reaching up from the hem. Each of them carried a long pole across his or her shoulders, with six lit lanterns suspended from hooks on either side. A large metal gong suspended from a wooden frame on wheels led the procession; a woman sounded it every few moments, letting its deep, sonorous voice fade before striking it again. Lamplighters with even longer hooked poles used them to hoist lanterns to their proper place on lampposts.

Giant puppets on sticks danced around the edges,

nearby people toasted them with raised bottles and cheers—but even so, there was a quality of solemnity to the whole process that Dex hadn't seen since he arrived in Black Rock City. Two drummers with handheld tom-toms kept pace, thumping out a slow, steady rhythm that was more like the beating of a giant heart than something to dance to. The sun had set only minutes ago, and in the rich desert twilight the dusty robes of the Lamplighters seemed to imply they had come a long, long way; that their slow, measured footsteps had surely started at the break of day in another land, that they had trudged their stately way across some vast, hostile gulf to get here.

"I thought you should see this," Lorilei said, her voice soft. "I always find the Lamplighter procession *reassuring,* you know? I look at them and it feels like they've been doing this for a thousand years."

Dex remembered filling lanterns the day before. He felt no pride, though—just a small surge of guilt. His contribution didn't seem like much compared to miles of walking with a dozen full lanterns on your shoulders. Suddenly, Glow Shtick's comparison of vandalism to sacrilege made a lot more sense.

"Thank you," Dex said. "This is . . . nice."

She grinned at him. "Don't thank me yet. I showed you this first because it's the right time of day for it. But this is a city of extremes, and the other thing I want you to see is—well, I wouldn't use the term *nice.* Not out loud, anyway."

"Does it involve Ping-Pong paddles?"

She laughed. "Definitely not."

"Then lead on."

• • •

As they rode, she called out over her shoulder, "You like sports?"

"I watch a little baseball."

"Ah. Go to any games?"

"Sure. I've seen the Mariners play a few times."

"So you've experienced the roar of the crowd, the crack of the bat. . . ."

The nervous feeling in the pit of Dex's stomach woke up and he started looking around anxiously. "You're *not* taking me to a baseball game. Are you?"

"Despite how much we love to play *anything,* there's no baseball here that I'm aware of. I've seen tennis, pyro-badminton—you play that one with a kerosene-soaked tampon for the birdie—even a full-sized iceless hockey rink. But you know, every world-class city needs their own sports franchise, and Black Rock is no exception. We don't really go in for teams or corporate logos or merchandising—but we *do* like our big-scale spectacle."

They'd been heading toward the Esplanade, and now Lorilei turned onto it. Across the street, a crowd was gathered around the base of a large geodesic dome, one with its aluminum-frame skeleton exposed. Dex had ridden past it before and always assumed the structure was just incomplete; now he saw people climbing the exterior and using the frame as a convenient perch to observe whatever was happening inside. It seemed eerily familiar, though he couldn't put his finger on why—and then he read the big rectangular sign on the very top of the structure. He couldn't believe he hadn't noticed it before.

There were a few cars parked at haphazard angles around the dome; they looked like they'd been spit out by the same factory in Hell as the deathmobile that had chased Dex through the dust storm. Lorilei brought her bike to a halt, and Dex stopped beside her. "Other cities have baseball, basketball, football," she said. "Well, *fuck* that—we've got a sport that takes *real* balls. Welcome to Thunderdome."

"You've *got* to be kidding. . . . Thunderdome like in the *Mad Max* movie? 'Two go in, one come out'? With chainsaws and bungee cords and people doing back-flips and trying to kill each other?"

"Pretty close. C'mon, let's grab a seat."

"Uh—I don't know if that's such a good idea."

Lorilei was already locking up her bike. "Why not? Afraid you're going to be hit by a severed limb?"

"No, afraid that the guy that tried to run me down is probably here. And going out to see a procession is one thing, but this is—"

"This is a crowd," she said patiently. "And you are exactly as anonymous here as you would be anywhere else in the city. Don't worry about Scorpion-face; there's no way he's going to spot you in that disguise."

"Well, maybe not. But—" He lowered his voice and glanced around. "There are a lot more factors involved now."

She raised an eyebrow. "Oh, please. Unless somebody rips off your scarf, you're perfectly safe. And I thought you said you were going to trust me?"

"But—"

She put her hands on her hips, and waited.

"All right, all right," he grumbled. "Just keep me away from anything with wheels and a flamethrower."

"Getting a seat" meant finding a spot to clamber up the side of the dome. A minute later, Dex found himself standing on a metal strut thirty feet above the ground, with an excellent view of the arena below. It was as high as they could go; the very top of the dome, where the sign was mounted, was off-limits.

On the dusty floor below, two women were being buckled into harnesses. Each harness was suspended from twin elastic cords, clipped on at waist level. The cords went up around ten feet, where they were attached to either end of a three-foot-long rod; a rope ran from the center of each rod to the roof. The whole thing reminded Dex of an oversized set of Jolly Jumpers.

The combatants were a tall, rangy redhead and a statuesque brunette. Both were dressed in skintight, dusty leather outfits that managed to give the impression they'd killed and skinned the animals themselves. The two men strapping them in were dressed in the same postapocalyptic fashion, chain-draped and leather-bound, dirty chrome glinting sullenly beside sunburnt tattoos.

No chainsaws, though; the women each held a long padded club, covered in gray duct tape. Loud, throbbing music blared out suddenly, the kind of headbanging metal you could imagine staging a riot to. The men, two per fighter, hauled the combatants to opposite sides of the arena, holding them ready with the bungee cords stretched tight and the women's feet dangling off the ground. A scarlet-robed figure holding a long staff tipped with a skull stepped to the middle of the arena; he held the staff aloft, glanced to either side to make sure both fighters were set. The women's faces were grim, their weapons held at the ready.

The staff slashed down. The crowd roared as the women flew at each other.

The robed figure—Dex assumed he was some sort of official—was safely out of the way by the time the women came together. They didn't collide, but passed within inches of each other, both furiously swinging away and landing a flurry of blows for the second they were in range of each other. The crowd howled.

Then they were past, the cords reached their limit, and they snapped back. They came together again, this time from opposite directions, and another flurry was exchanged.

Dex was amazed at the speed and intensity of the attacks. Nor were the clubs the only weapons—both women were flailing about with their legs, though none of the kicks seemed meant to do damage.

The cords' impetus was mostly spent, and at a signal from the man with the staff the opponents were hauled back for another launch. While they seemed evenly matched, Dex thought the brunette had the edge; she seemed to have a little more muscle than the redhead.

On the second launch, he understood what the kicking was about. The redhead managed to hook a foot around the brunette's hip, and suddenly she had both legs locked around her waist.

As the mob screamed in glee, both fighters went all out. There was no parrying or dodging; they just hit each other in the face as hard and fast as they could. It was like watching two cats with their tails tied together slung over a clothesline, a blur of movement that lasted only seconds. The end wasn't as flashy as a knockout, but it was just as decisive: the brunette flinched. Her club moved from offense to defense, and the official stepped in and raised his staff. The match was over.

In that instant, with the crowd going crazy, the redhead dropped her club and threw her arms around her opponent in a fierce hug. The pure, open emotion of the act caught Dex off guard; it seemed both deeply intimate and defiantly proud at the same time.

She's saying thank you, Dex thought. *Thank you for sharing something with me. Something powerful and scary and unique.*

He thought of Wade, and suddenly realized that *this* was the reason he'd brought Dex along; that this was the kind of feeling he'd been talking about when he'd gotten nostalgic for his punk-rock past, and that he'd wanted to give that feeling to Dex.

He looked over at Lorilei. She was staring downward, a wide smile on her face—and then, perched on a strut on the other side of the dome, he saw a familiar visage. The man with the scorpion tattoo was looking right at him.

Dex froze—but a second later the man looked away, and so did Dex. He hadn't recognized Dex . . . had he?

Should I tell Lorilei? No—I can't react. Can't risk letting him know I noticed him. But did he even notice me?

He wasn't sure. That might have been a suspicious look on Scorpion-face's features . . . but it could just as easily have been Dex's imagination. And now he *couldn't* look back, couldn't show any interest at all.

You're being ridiculous. You're just another face in the crowd—a masked face. There are far more interesting things to watch here than you.

He tried to concentrate on what was going on down below. The women had been unharnessed and two men were taking their place . . . but their replacements were hardly cut from the same cloth. One wore clown makeup, a huge purple wig, and gold lamé shorts; the other was dressed as the pope.

"His Holiness is going to have to lose the hat," Dex said. Lorilei didn't reply—Dex had been so busy trying to not look at Scorpion-face he hadn't noticed she was on her walkie-talkie. She signaled for him to wait.

"Okay, thanks," she said. She looked at Dex and said, "Interesting news."

"What?"

"Captain Fun says he needs to talk to you in person. Doesn't want to risk saying anything over the airwaves."

"So we go back to camp?"

"No, we set up a central rendezvous point this afternoon—made more sense than always running back to one end of the city. The 'Justice League Watchtower,' Fun calls it. He is *such* a comic-book geek."

"Then let's get out of here," Dex said. "Uh—not that I didn't enjoy myself. It was incredible, really." He told her about spotting Scorpion-face.

"Is he still there?"

"I'll point him out once we're on the ground."

But by the time they'd climbed down, the man had disappeared. Dex looked around, trying to look nonchalant but feeling nervous and exposed. "I don't see him," he said.

"We'll take a roundabout route just in case," Lorilei said. "No way he'll be able to follow us without being seen."

They took off across the playa on their bikes. It was almost full dark, but not quite; traces of light peeked out from behind the mountains. Dex kept glancing behind him, but if they were being shadowed it wasn't by the deathmobile—though a living room on wheels did keep pace with them for a while. They rode up to the Man, then did a big loop and wound up at Center Camp. By that time, Dex was slightly less worried—but only slightly.

The 'Justice League Watchtower' turned out to be a watering hole called the Starlust Lounge. It was right beside Arctica, the big tent where they sold ice, with a flying saucer the size of a Buick that appeared to have crashed next to a sign proclaiming, "Open Dusk to Dawn." The bar was shaped like a large, square doughnut, with the bartenders on the inside and the patrons around the perimeter. Lights were strung from a tall central pole to an open-air framework above the bar, providing illumination without obscuring the night sky. Barstools were saddle-shaped chunks of duct-taped foam atop pieces of rebar sunk deep into the playa; they were quite comfortable, despite their disturbing tendency to sway back and forth if your feet weren't planted firmly on the ground. A good way to test your level of inebriation, Dex supposed—if you couldn't stay on your stool, you'd had enough.

Fun was already there, waiting for them. "Welcome to my favorite neighborhood bar," he said. "This is Sheriff Marty, the best bartender on the playa."

The man behind the bar gave them a roguish grin. His head was clean-shaven, his beard short and neatly trimmed. He sported a pair of extremely dark sunglasses, a priest's collar, and a flowing purple robe.

"Welcome to the Starlust," he said. "Don't worry, my affiliation with the law is strictly imaginary."

"Marty, this is Curious Urge," Lorilei said.

"Uh, hi," Dex said.

"Nice to meetcha," Marty said. "Have a seat, shake off a little of the dust you've picked up and try some of ours instead."

Dex eased himself onto one of the stools. "What's the difference?"

"We cut ours with alcohol. Makes it easier to swallow and kills most of the germs."

Lorilei had told him how barter bars functioned; Dex reached into his bag and brought out his vodka. "Would this help?"

Marty accepted the bottle graciously. "Well, it'll certainly broaden our choices. Up until a second ago, all I could offer you was tequila, tequila, tequila, or Mexican vodka."

"Mexican vodka?"

"Well, *technically* it's tequila, but I put a fur hat on when I pour it and talk in a Russian accent. Or you could try the Wheel of Destiny." He motioned with his thumb toward the back of the bar, where a large wooden dial was mounted on a post. It was divided into different sections, each marked with a choice: they ranged from "Hug For A Chug" to "Whip For A Sip."

"I'll stick with the tequila," Dex said.

"Me, too," Lorilei said.

While Marty poured, Captain Fun told them why he'd contacted them. "There's been an intriguing development. Moonman's been talking with the cops, and apparently they've started taking the whole Darth

Bunny thing seriously. The initial findings of the CSI team seem to support the fact that there were three people in the motor home at the time of the murder."

"That's great," Lorilei said.

"Yeah—as long as they're telling the truth," Fun said. "They're pressuring Moonman pretty hard to have Dex come in."

Marty set their drinks—shots in plastic tumblers—down in front of them with a smile, then moved off to the other side of the bar to welcome some newcomers. Dex took a plastic straw out of his bag—Lorilei had found one for him, somewhere—and stuck it in his cup. Fun waited until the bartender was out of earshot again, then continued. "Moonman made me promise to talk to you, but even he says the cops could just be bullshitting. From what *I've* heard, they're still concentrating on finding you as opposed to Rafe."

"I don't know," Dex said. "I just don't know. Are *we* any closer to finding him?"

"Well, we've talked to all the suspects," Fun said. "At least, all the ones that we know for sure are here."

"Really?" Dex said, surprised.

"Yeah. Some of the ARGers are just in it for laughs, but we've got some real eager beavers, too. A few of the suspects have really solid alibis, and we've eliminated a few more for other reasons, but the number of possibles is still pretty high—three, maybe four."

"Who are they?"

"Playa Fiya, Glow Shtick, and a couple of fratboys named JD and Cody. They're all here, they all have a motive, and none of 'em have an alibi."

"That's still better than before," Lorilei said. "And by now, Rafe has got to be feeling the pressure, too."

"I think I know a way to ratchet it up even higher," Fun said. "We should turn a copy of the computer files over to the cops."

"I don't know. . . ."

"Well, we've gone about as far as we can go," Fun said with a shrug. "We've got people keeping an eye on the prime suspects, but there's not much else we can do. Cops could at least get search warrants—which, frankly, is better than the alternative."

"What do you mean?" Dex asked.

"He means," Lorilei said, "that it's awfully hard to lock a tent, and some of the ARGers are a little more enthusiastic than others."

"Of course," Dex sighed. He had visions of crazed amateur detectives rooting through some innocent person's belongings, looking for a nonexistent clue— all in his name. "You're right. Maybe the authorities can find something we can't. Uh—you're not going to get in trouble for this, are you? I mean, we did tamper with evidence."

Fun dismissed the objection with a wave of his tequila. "Don't worry—it'll be delivered anonymously. So far the cops don't even know the files exist, but I'll tip them off before they show up—if I play it right, it'll give me some added credibility."

"Yeah," Lorilei said, "or they'll think we cooked them up ourselves to throw them off."

"Maybe I should just give myself up," Dex said.

"You don't mean that," Lorilei said. "Come on—it's only Thursday."

"Yeah, I'm sure something will shake loose in the next few days," Fun said. "You know what you need right now? You need to blow off a little steam."

"What do you mean?"

"I mean you've been under a huge amount of pressure, and it's starting to make you go a little bugfuck," Fun said. "Look, we let you have your space today, because that's what you needed. But you can't keep on hiding and worrying, waiting for the ax to drop—that'll just make you crazy."

"Well, I'm all for doing *something*," Dex said. "I just don't know *what*."

"Honestly, at this point there isn't much you *can* do," Fun said. "But speaking as a semiqualified expert in the field of hedonistic expression, I highly recommend a short mental vacation." He raised his drink.

"You think I should get *drunk*? Well, *there's* a productive use of my time—"

"Hang on," Lorilei interjected. "I don't think that's what he means."

"Actually, it is—"

"Yes, but you don't mean he should just dive into a bottle and give up, right?"

"No, of course not. I just meant that in extended stressful situations it can be helpful to stop bashing your head against a wall for a while and relax. Loosen up. Plus, getting a little emotional distance from a problem can give you a whole new perspective."

Dex thought about it. It ran counter to all his normal modes of behavior, but he'd faced that so many times in the past few days he was almost used to it. In Black Rock City, everything seemed inside out: you took your clothes off to go outside, money was something to be avoided, and weirdness was mundane. Responding to the most serious trouble he'd ever been in by getting sloshed seemed perfectly consistent.

Lorilei leaned over and said, "Hey. Don't worry. We're not saying you should go on a bender or anything. But if you'd like to just cut loose and enjoy yourself for a while, I promise we'll take care of you."

Dex raised his drink, looked her in the eye. "I trust you," he said.

She smiled and raised her own, and so did Fun.

"To Tribe Urge," Fun said, and they all drank.

"Nonlinear thinking," Fun said. *"That's* what I'm talking about."

Dex sucked the last of his tequila through his straw and considered. He'd had several so far, and while far from drunk, he was equally distant from the shores of sobriety. He felt, in the words of the late, great Jimmy Stewart, "squiffed."

"The problem with nonlinear thinking," Dex said, "is that it's unreliable."

"Life is unreliable."

"Exactly. So why add to it?"

"Because that's how you *deal* with it. You know, I really hate to fall back on the Southern California surfer-Zen stereotype, but the whole riding-the-wave-thing does work as an analogy. Chaos isn't something you control; it's something you go with. There's an entirely different mind-set you have to use when dealing with large numbers of variables—it's no longer about rigidly controlling the situation by eliminating chance, it's about guiding your direction by making choices."

"Sure. That woman has *amazing* breasts."

"Which one?"

"The blue one."

"With the feathers?'

"No, with the horns."

"Oh. Yeah, she sure does. Speaking of which, where's Lorilei?"

"Gone to the john."

"Well, that's how things go here. It's not that we have short attention spans, just full bladders. Speaking of which, excuse me." Fun got up and left.

Dex looked around. There were several clusters of people at the bar, all of them laughing and talking. The situation wasn't exactly new to him; he'd been to parties more than once where he'd found himself standing in the corner with no one to talk to. He'd be eavesdropping—more out of boredom than anything else—and an overheard statement, taken out of context, would suddenly stand out as bizarre. Now, though, he was listening to three such conversations at the same time.

"I am John Monkeypants!"

"—so we were looking for Pinky's Pirate Bar, but we're hopelessly lost—"

"You know that eye shape on peacock feathers? These wings had that pattern, but made out of *fire*— blue in the center, yellow and orange at the edges. . . ."

"The Cult of the Red Lectroid follows the mighty John Worphin! Welcome John Fuckfuck! Welcome John Boysenberry!"

"—and he says he thinks it's on Certain, but he's not sure—"

"Two women on stilts wearing these amazing pairs of flaming wings, striding across the playa . . ."

"Membership entitles you to speak in a bad Spanish accent and blame everything on Monkeyboys!"

"—so we start singing the theme song from *Pinky and the Brain*—"

"In the darkness, you could hardly see the stilts. As if they were walking on air . . ."

"Where are we going? *Planet Ten!*"

"—and we start dancing down the street, singing at the top of our lungs—"

"It was like looking at two fallen angels. . . ."

"When are we going? *Real soon!*"

"—*One is a genius, the other's insane*—"

"Like their wings had caught on fire from sheer velocity . . ."

"—and we both scream NARF! at the end of the song, and at the exact same moment we see this little pink light on top of a pole off in the distance. And I say, hey, ritual magic doesn't *have* to be serious, and he says, good, 'cause we're a looong way from Serious. . . ."

Sheriff Marty came over and poured him another drink. "How you doing, Inspector?"

"You know what I find astounding?" Dex asked. He tried to take a drink, but stabbed the straw into his scarf instead. "You can be walking down the street here, and somebody will say, 'Holy shit! Look at that!' and the proper response isn't, 'Wow!' or 'Oh my God, I've never seen *that* before,'; no, the proper response is, 'Could you please be more *specific.*'"

Marty laughed. "Right. Are you referring to the jaw-dropping spectacle over *here,* over *there,* or directly over*head?*"

Lorilei bounded up. "Over here, obviously!" She spread her arms and spun around once, coming to a stop with a dusty stomp of her right foot.

Dex smiled, and wished she could see it. He

scratched at the three-day growth of beard chafing under his scarf.

Lorilei sat down beside him. "I miss anything?"

"Third coming of Christ, a life-size replica of the *Hindenburg* on fire, and a naked Abraham Lincoln. Not much, really."

She giggled. "And how are you doing?"

"Actually," he admitted, "I'm having a pretty good time. As long as I don't think about the recent past or the immediate future, I'm almost happy."

"Good. You have to grab happiness where you can, you know."

"I'm not sure I did. Know that, I mean."

"Well, where do you *get* your happiness?"

He didn't know what to reply. Happiness for him was largely a negative, composed of things he didn't have as opposed to things he did; happiness was not having to worry about money, not being sick, not feeling frustrated or anxious or lost. He liked being comfortable, he supposed—but comfort was not the same as happiness.

"I'm not sure," he said at last. "I guess I get my happiness from security."

"You feel secure right now?" She poked him in the ribs with a finger.

"Not particularily."

"But you *are* enjoying yourself?"

"Yes."

"Why?"

He looked at her, then looked away. An art car shaped like a gigantic brain trundled slowly past, neurons blinking red-yellow-green. *Because you're here,* he wanted to say.

"Because it's all *new*," he said. "And it's exciting in that way only new things are. I feel like I'm falling, and even though I'm terrified of hitting the ground, part of me is starting to think maybe I can fly."

Her eyes widened. The smart-ass grin on her face softened into a smile. "Yeah. You want to know the secret to striking up a conversation in Black Rock City?"

"Shoot."

"Just ask, 'Is this your first time here?' Doesn't matter what the answer is; virgin or veteran, you can compare experiences."

"Huh. Maybe that's what Wade should have asked, instead of 'What does Burning Man mean to you?' "

She shook her head. "If he was looking for some kind of defining answer, he never had a chance. You ask a thousand people here that question, you get a thousand different answers. Burning Man isn't about any one concept or idea."

"Yeah. If it's about anything, it's the unexpected—"

She pulled his scarf down and kissed him.

Some kisses were questions; this one wasn't. It went on for a long time, and when it was over she slipped his scarf back into place, took his hand, and tugged him gently toward their bikes.

Somewhere in the distance, he could hear somebody setting off fireworks.

CHAPTER 14:

SOMEWHERE BETWEEN SACRED AND PROFANE

File X (Pansexual): I guess the thing I associate most with Burning Man is sex.

There's this whole Sodom and Gomorrah vibe that's really hard to get away from. Everyone's running around naked, or in drag, or wearing some kind of costume that goes right past *revealing* and into the downtown core of *displaying*. People paint their asses red, beat their chests, and generally act like horny baboons.

Not that I have anything against that. Frankly, I spend most of my time in Black Rock City on my back or my knees, and I don't care who knows. Somebody told me once I had the kind of sex drive that could power an eighteen-wheel truck, and I just laughed and said eighteen was almost enough.

But that's just me, and I'm like that all the time. Burning Man gives me the opportunity to meet new and interesting people in a unique and stimulating environment—I like to say it's as if Disneyland opened a theme park in Amsterdam, but that's not really accurate—and fuck them.

But here's the thing; I'm at the very end of the spectrum. I'm an uninhibited polyamorous bisexual, and an exhibitionist to boot. You want to do it Greek style in an art installation called the Anus of the Goat? I'll bend over and bleat. You want me to blow two guys at the same time while their girlfriends watch? Just let me get my kneepads.

I could go on and on—and as you can probably tell by now, I usually do—but as entertaining as that might be, I'd never be able to list every sexual curve and kink available in Black Rock City. The general consensus among the population seems to be that there's nothing wrong with enjoying physical pleasure, goddammit, so why shouldn't we play with sexuality the same way we play with everything else?

So we do. And I don't know about you, but nothing—and I mean nothing, not a hot tub full of greased strippers, not a transsexual with a twelve-inch tongue and an oral fixation, not being locked overnight in a sex shop with twin porn stars, a dozen hits of Ecstasy and a crate of batteries—gets my motor running like a playful attitude. Romance is sweet and S and M is savory, and there's all kinds of flavors in between; but show me someone who's invented a game that combines spanking, blow jobs, and hopscotch, and I'll jump their bones just to say thanks.

Everybody has little games they make up around sex. Problem is, most of those games stay very private; sometimes, they're played exclusively in one person's mind. Personally, I don't think that's very healthy. Much better to haul those perversions out on the playa and let *everyone* share in your reindeer games—or whatever large, horned animal you prefer.

And Burners will do all sorts of things to you if you ask: paint on a second, shiny skin of liquid latex; immortalize your erection in plaster of paris; take gorgeous, artistic photos of you astride a twenty-foot-long penis, wearing nothing but fairy wings and a smile. The Canadian contingent, clever boys and girls that they are, have combined national pride with perversity to stage an Annual Beaver-Eating Contest—and of course, there's always the Kama Sutra Wheel of Fortune.

There are camps with names like Arousal, the Smoochdome, Camp Cock Ring, Penetration Village and Casa de Slutmonkey. There are camps dedicated to tickling, to polyamory, and to tea-bagging (don't ask). Or you can just go down to Bianca's Smut Shack and enjoy a grilled cheese sandwich while watching people shag on one of their umpteen dusty couches.

Now, even if you're not a slut like myself, there are two factors that make this whole circus even more arousing. First is contrast; right next door to that couple trying out the Chinese basket swing is another couple giggling and playing with little Hot Wheels cars. Decadence seems *so* much more depraved when it's dancing cheek to cheek with innocence, no?

The second factor is the appeal of the new, which sort of combines the uniqueness of perversion with the exciting potential of novelty. Burners put as much imagination into sex as they do art, which is only fitting; after all, a new relationship is just as much an act of creation as a sculpture or a song is. When you create a setting where people can come together for the first time—or come separately, for that matter—it's not just an act of coitus but collaboration. Art, especially temporary art, relies heavily on that moment of

"Wow, I've never seen that before"; and new relationships—especially temporary ones—rely on the same kind of energy. Infatuation and inspiration are not so far apart.

But burning love, like Burning Man, is built on myth. It's a wonderful fairy tale that we tell ourselves, where everything is perfect and the stars live in our lover's eyes. People come here and fall in love with the event itself, and when they're surrounded by beautiful, scantily clad people consuming outrageous substances and doing outrageous things, nothing seems impossible—least of all, getting laid. And when they don't, when they wake up in their tent cold and alone, they wind up thinking there must be something wrong with them.

Well, maybe there is—I don't know. If you can't find someone to fuck you in the mundane world, there's probably a reason, and that reason isn't going to just evaporate in the desert sun. Getting an invite to the ball doesn't mean you're no longer a frog, or even that you're going to find a princess with an amphibian fetish. If you're not already kinky, I think getting laid in Black Rock City is actually *harder* than normal; sure, you're surrounded by like-minded people, but the ones that aren't too wasted on margaritas or 'shrooms are so dazzled by their surroundings that sex just seems like a distraction. And no matter where you go, people find their own level; that astonishingly good looking girl wearing nothing but a cowboy hat is probably going to hit the mattress with someone just as stunning. Painting yourself red and running around on stilts might get her attention, but keeping it is another matter altogether.

So, what I'm saying is this: Don't go to Burning Man with false hopes. All the games and costumes and role-playing are really just flirtation, and you can't count on a flirt. Consider yourself lucky if you get a kiss or a spanking or the chance to watch somebody else getting their rocks off, and don't feel bad if that's all there is. If nothing else, "Hey, did I ever tell you about the time I saw a couple making it on a trampoline?" is a great conversation starter . . . and if that doesn't work, you can always look *me* up.

Just don't be surprised if there's a line.

CHAPTER 15:

HALF-PAST REAL

Right up until the moment of truth, Dex wasn't sure if she was serious. He kept expecting her to start laughing, or to yank aside some previously unnoticed curtain to reveal it was all an elaborate practical joke. She'd been teasing him ever since they met, and the only reason he'd been able to handle it was that, deep down, he hadn't believed she could possibly mean all those things she'd said.

Different people had different styles—dealing with Lorilei really wasn't all that different from dealing with Wade, when Dex thought about it. In his own way, Wade had been just as expressive and self-assured; like Lorilei, he didn't believe in censoring himself and enjoyed provoking a reaction.

But then Dex and Lorilei had gotten back to Aetheria, and they'd locked up their bikes, and they'd gone into the tent-trailer, and she still had that look on her face. And suddenly Dex was terrified, in a way completely new to him; he felt as if he were being offered something priceless only because he wouldn't be allowed to keep it, and that losing it would be more than he could bear. He felt like a man trapped in a burning building who's just found a winning lottery ticket in his pocket.

"Dex, there's something I have to tell you," Lorilei said. She sat down on the bed.

I knew it, he thought. He had absolutely no idea what she was going to say next, but the sudden feeling of doom was overpowering.

"I haven't been completely honest with you since we met."

"Oh?" he said faintly.

"All that teasing wasn't what you think."

"So . . . what was it?" he asked, dreading the answer.

She made a long arm, grabbed him by the robe, and pulled him onto the bed.

"Foreplay," she said.

It wasn't as if Dex had never made love before. His experience, while not extensive, had nonetheless covered most of the bases and even included the occasional flashy home-run.

Lorilei, he quickly found out, was a whole 'nother ball game.

No orderly progression of swings, hits, and misses for her; before he'd even figured out who was pitching, she'd grabbed his bat, kissed the umpire, and run around the bases backward, stopping briefly to tickle his shortstop and form a conga line with his outfielders.

It was the most amazing sex he'd ever had—not to

mention the dirtiest. Not just in the highly descriptive things she whispered in his ear, but in the literal sense of the word: after four days in the desert, they were both less than pristine. Normally, Dex would have found that off-putting, but now it charged everything with a primal, intoxicating energy. There was a raw purity in the taste and smell of her sweat; there was a profound honesty in the dustiness of her hair.

And then, as their rhythm got faster and more urgent, she moaned, "Don't laugh or I'll come . . ."

"What?" he gasped in midstroke.

She crossed her eyes and hooted like a chimpanzee, and he burst into helpless laughter at the same moment he reached the point of no return. She joined him an instant later in a series of orgasmic, squealing giggles, managing to sound simultaneously ludicrous and pornographic, and they came together for the first time.

It had been a long while since Dex had laughed so hard his sides were sore, and he'd *never* had sex so intense his balls hurt. *Who would have imagined,* he thought dazedly, *that you could do both at once?*

"That," he said when he could breathe again, "was . . ."

"Spectacular?"

"No . . ."

"Earth-shatttering?"

"Uh-uh . . ."

"Mind-boggling?"

"Goofy," he said. "Deeply, intensely, *profoundly* goofy. I feel like I just slept with an amusement park."

"Oh, *that* was just the kiddie ride. You haven't even *seen* the grown-up stuff."

"Such as?"

"Well, I don't know if you're ready for that yet. You have to be *this* tall to ride the roller coaster."

"How tall?"

"*This*—hmmm. How about that . . ."

Talking about it later, they both agreed that the tunnel of love was their favorite.

Dex had slept with girls that wanted to cuddle between lovemaking, or fix a midnight snack, or even watch TV. At three AM, Lorilei took him outside and taught him how to play with fire.

"It's not that hard," she said. "It just *looks* scary."

"Right. The whole going-up-in-flames, scarred-for-life thing is just an illusion."

It was cold out; Dex shivered and wrapped his bathrobe tightly around himself as she laid out her equipment. The Coleman lantern they were using for light hissed softly beside him.

"All right. These are called fire poi." She pointed to two short lengths of wire with white cloth balls at the ends.

He examined the poi curiously. There was a metal swivel at one end that looked like it was from a fishing lure, and the cloth ball was actually an intricate knot of thick, pale yellow cables.

"That's called a monkey's fist," Lorilei said. "There are different kinds of wicks for different effects. That one's made of a Kevlar-cotton weave."

"Really? You mean the stuff they use for bulletproof vests?"

"Yeah. It's really durable and absorbs fuel well. The

cotton has a high absorption too, but it's basically there because pure Kevlar would be way too expensive."

She took the cap off a metal can and poured a small amount of liquid into a jar. "There are a lot of different fuel mixes you can use, but kerosene is pretty much the standard. It's the safest—least likely to blow up, anyway." She recapped the can and set it aside. "I use unscented lamp oil, which is kerosene with additives that make it burn with less smoke and stink. Unfortunately, this also makes it more toxic—and believe me, you don't want stuff like benzene getting into your system. Pure kerosene is relatively harmless—you get it on your skin, it'll only give you a rash—but it's used mainly in aviation fuel and is hard to find. Plus it tastes terrible."

"You've *drunk* the stuff?"

She laughed. "Not on purpose. But I've done fire-breathing before, so I've had it in my mouth. Small amounts won't give you anything more than indigestion, though it is carcinogenic."

"That explains some of the coffee I've been served. . . ." He slipped the ring at the end of the poi over his fingers and let the wick dangle over the jar.

"Hold on there, Speedy," she said. "First of all, you're not dressed for fire-spinning. Loose, baggy clothing, especially a loose weave like cotton, is a hazard; spinners don't just wear those tight-fitting outfits for show. Second, when you're starting off you don't use fire at all; beginners *always* whack themselves, usually in the spot it hurts most, and if I'm gonna be responsible for bruising or burning your groin I'd rather be a little more personally involved." She took the poi from him and set it down, then picked up a small cloth bag and shook the contents out. It was another set of poi, but these had translucent plastic balls at their ends. She fiddled with one, and a scarlet LED inside the ball came on, blinking rapidly. "Some twirlers don't even do fire," she said. "They use these, or ones that are black-light reactive." She got the second one turned on and handed them to him.

It was, he discovered, not as hard as he'd thought. She showed him the proper way to hold the looped ends, and how to hold his hands once the poi were moving. She showed him how to swing forward, then backward. Sure enough, he smacked himself several times in the shoulder, thigh, and head, but before too long he had the basics mastered. The whirling LEDs had a beauty of their own, strobing through the darkness; the scarlet tracers they left behind seemed almost solid, curving neon hanging unsupported in the air.

"I think you're ready for the real thing," she told him. "Take off the robe."

It was brisk wearing only a T-shirt and shorts, but the exercise had warmed him up a little. She gave him her poi, then showed him how to dip the wicks and shake off the excess fuel. "Don't be nervous," she said, pulling out a lighter. "Just take it easy. Remember, I've got a fire extinguisher right here."

"Right," he said. "No problem."

He held the poi as far away from his body as possible, and she lit the wicks. The smell of the burning kerosene and the heat licking at his hands ignited a flare of panic in his gut, but he fought it down and started swinging the poi back and forth in short arcs like she'd shown him.

She didn't rush him, just watched calmly and alertly. *She really thinks I can do this,* Dex thought.

He took a deep breath, concentrated on the motion of the poi, tried to forget that they were on fire. Tried to stop thinking altogether, and just do it. *Just add a little more power to the swing, push them up and over, around and around, just like that . . .*

"Dex," she said. "Open your eyes."

He did. Twin circles of flame spun on either side of him, making a noise like a soft roar, the sound of a dragon trying to purr. For a second he feared that his awareness of the act was going to end it, like a centipede looking down and tripping over its own legs, but he found that simply closing his eyes again helped him lock onto the rhythm.

When he opened them again, he looked straight ahead instead of at his hands. "I'm doing it," he said. "So far . . ."

"How's it feel?"

"Like I'm afraid to stop . . ."

"Is that all?" she asked.

And, he had to admit, it wasn't. Underneath his nervousness was another feeling, one he couldn't quite define. It was connected in some way to how he felt about computers, which didn't make any sense at first.

But as the fire swirled around him, as his confidence grew and his fear faded, he finally recognized the feeling for what it was: control. He was intimately connected to a powerful elemental force, a force of both destruction and creation, and it was doing what he wanted. Centrifugal force and momentum had replaced electricity as the conduit of his will, and the intricacies of data had been swapped for one of mankind's oldest tools.

It was glorious.

He wondered if this was how Prometheus felt, holding the stolen fire of the gods . . . and then remembered what the gods had done in return. Chained him to the side of a mountain, where vultures would devour his liver.

The vultures are already circling, he thought. *Well, let them come. They'll never be able to touch me, not as long as I've got fire in my hands.* It was a wild, irrational thought, completely out of character, but Dex didn't care. *Let them come,* he thought fiercely. *I'm tired of being afraid.*

And when the flames had spent themselves, he took his new lover back to bed and showed her his appreciation.

When he woke up, she was already gone. She'd left him another note, scrawled on a scrap of paper bag.

It read: Gone to do some yoga. Couldn't bear to wake you—thought I'd already robbed you of enough sleep. Be back before noon.

He yawned, smiled, then put on a paper dust mask and shorts and went outside to forage for breakfast and coffee. He found Sigma Jen and Cromagg already up, eating scrambled eggs; they told him to help himself, and he did. He had to take his dust mask off to eat, but he sat where he couldn't be seen from the street.

"How's the investigation going?" Sigma Jen asked. She was wearing a minidress made out of a green plastic garbage bag and duct tape.

"You tell me," Dex said around a mouthful of food. "The ARG has more or less taken over. At this point I think I'm too high-profile to go around asking questions, anyway."

"Yeah, you're probably right," Cromagg said. He scratched his beard absently. "But don't count out Tribe Urge, either. Jen, Sundog, and I have been doing a little metasnooping."

" 'Metasnooping'?"

"Investigating the investigators," Cromagg said. "It occurred to us early on that Rafe would probably join the ARG just to keep an eye on things, so I convinced Moonman to keep a list of volunteers and where they're camping."

"I don't know," Sigma Jen said with a sigh. "Now we're keeping tabs on people who are trying to help? This whole thing is turning into an exercise in paranoia."

Dex felt a stab of guilt. He remembered what Lorilei had told him about how important this event was to some people, and thought, *I'm like some sort of foreign germ. I don't really belong here, and my presence is making them sick.*

It almost worked as an analogy, except for two things: First, antibodies didn't usually change sides to defend an invading organism. Second, he no longer felt quite as out of place as he once had. The sun was warm on his face, he could hear people laughing in the distance, and the eggs he was finishing off were pretty damn good, too.

"Who is this Moonman, anyway?" Dex asked. "I was at the rally he held, and I couldn't tell if he was a lunatic or a politician."

"Yeah, he's a bit of both," Cromagg said with a chuckle. "Real Rasputin type, lots of charisma and wild-eyed fervor. Not really that uncommon here."

"You should know," Sigma Jen said pointedly.

"Who, me?" Cromagg said. "I'm way too intellectual. I like to read about revolutions, not lead them."

"What kind of intellectual spends a year living in a tree house?"

"A student trying to save money on rent?"

"Ha!" Jen snorted. "Come on, admit it—you loved being the wild man of the woods. You spent half your time banging beautiful women and the other half pretending you were Tarzan."

Cromagg glared at her in mock indignation. "I prefer," he said haughtily, "to be referred to as Lord Greystoke."

"Have, uh, either of you seen Lorilei today?" Dex asked. He took a last swallow of coffee and slipped on his dust mask.

"Well, I saw *someone* bounce out of camp this morning," Sigma Jen said. "Looked like her, but she was giving off such a bright glow it was really hard to tell."

"Yeah," Cromagg added. "Plus, the fog of hormones around her kinda blurred her features."

"Okay, okay," Dex said. He felt embarrassed and absurdly proud at the same time, but he'd encountered so much strange emotional alchemy in the last week that the mix didn't seem that odd. "How about Captain Fun?"

"He didn't come home last night, but that's hardly unusual," Cromagg said. "Last I saw him, he was—right behind you."

Fun rolled up on his bike. "Morning, folks. Ah, Inspector Urge—just the man I want to see."

"What's up?" Dex asked.

"I could ask you the same question—but I just talked to Lorilei, so I don't have to." Fun grinned. "Anyway, she told me to tell you she's going to be a while—she ran into an old friend at yoga and got dragged off to some kind of craft workshop. They're either making space helmets or vodka—it was a little unclear."

"Oh," Dex said.

"But—and she was *very* clear about this—she said I was supposed to take care of you in the meantime, so you won't feel abandoned or unloved or that last night wasn't absolutely fantastic and she can't wait to do it again. She also told me to hoot like a monkey, but I'm not going to do that."

"Oh," Dex said again, but this time there was a lot more relief in his voice.

"Yeah, she said she'd meet up with us in a couple hours. In the meantime, what do you say we tour around and look at some art? I'll fill you in on the latest."

"Sure. Just let me refill my canteen and put on some sunscreen."

Dex was tired of wearing the bathrobe—it got in the way when he was riding his bike, and since he wasn't questioning suspects there was no reason to wear his identifying T-shirt, either. He stripped down to shorts, shoes, sunglasses and a dust mask, and added the hat he was wearing earlier. It felt a lot better.

"All right, I'm ready," he told Fun.

Fun looked him up and down. "Amazing. Three

days with me turns you into a hermit—one night with her and you're a Chippendale dancer."

"That's right. I even have my own pole. . . ."

Fun's eyebrows went up. "Okay, who are you and what have you done with Curious Urge?"

"That's *Inspector* to you," Dex said. "And I guess Urge has had his curiosity satisfied."

"Come on, Inspector," Fun said, laughing. "Let's go have our flabbers gasted."

They rode down to the Esplanade, across it and onto the open playa. In the sky above them, a hot-air balloon painted like an enormous globe floated, like some parallel Earth on a collision course with the city.

"I got the files to the cops," Fun said. "Don't know if they're going to take them seriously or not, but at least we're doing something."

"It's not enough," Dex said. "I think we should be more proactive."

"How?"

"I was thinking about how information moves out here. If we plant the right kind of rumor, we might be able to get Rafe to panic, do something stupid."

"That could work," Fun admitted. "Between the papers, the radio, and the ARG, we could spread it pretty fast. But what would we say?"

"I don't know yet. Give me a little time to work on it."

"All right, but remember—the Man burns tomorrow night. I don't know if Rafe'll stay much longer than that."

"He might already be gone," Dex said. "But I think you're right—he'll stay until at least Sunday."

"How do you know?"

Dex hesitated before answering. "Because he won't want to leave," he said finally. "It would be too easy. And if there's one thing I've learned, it's that Burners never do things the easy way. . . ."

The first art installation Fun took him to was called the Temple of Gravity. It was about the same size and shape as the Thunderdome, but instead of a geodesic structure, it had five thick, curving steel poles that met at the apex; each was embedded in a heavy chunk of raw stone at the base. Suspended from each pole was another granite wedge, big enough to park a car on, hanging from two long chains. The upper ends of the wedges were about twenty feet off the ground, the bases at head level. At the Temple's center was an iron brazier, dangling from another chain attached to the very top of the structure.

"Pretty amazing, huh?" Fun said as they got off their bikes. He led Dex inside, where several other people were standing. "Those chunks of rock weigh eighteen thousand pounds apiece. Kind of makes you feel like you're in the middle of Stonehenge during an earthquake."

Dex eyed the slabs overhead; they seemed poised to fall at any moment. "It's . . . impressive," he said. "But a little too close to my own situation at the moment."

"You should have seen it last night. They had a fire going, music playing, people dancing. Not just inside the Temple, but *on* it—those slabs will fit a dozen people each, and you can really get them swinging if you try. And down here, people were trance-dancing with their eyes closed, with these gigantic, swaying tombstones at the same level as their skulls." Fun shook his head. "It was like watching one of those old cartoons, where someone keeps walking under a pile driver that just misses them."

Dex put out a hand, felt the rough grain of the rock. It felt as solid and immovable as the side of a building, but that was an illusion. *It's hard to know what's real here,* he thought. He wondered where Lorilei was.

"It always astounds me what people are willing to haul out to the desert," Fun said. "And in a week it'll all be gone. No matter how big and impressive it all looks, it's just temporary." He glanced at Dex, then looked away.

"Ah," Dex said. "You're not talking about the art."

"I've had my share of desert romance," Fun said. "Lorilei's great, but I don't want you getting in over your head. Black Rock City is its own reality; relationships that start here don't necessarily work in the outside world."

Dex smiled despite himself. "Getting in over my head? I think I passed that point a few crises ago . . . Look, I appreciate your concern, but I think I'm getting the hang of this place. It's—it's like when I was on the Windsurfer in that dust storm. No brakes, no visibility, dangerous as all hell . . . but I managed to make it out in one piece by making a last-second, crazy choice. I just went with the moment. Now, I have zero experience in doing that kind of thing, but I'm a fast learner—and while I have no idea where Lorilei and I might wind up, for now it just *feels* right."

Fun studied him, then nodded slowly. "Fair enough. Go with your instincts—just make sure you know what the consequences are. You're not the only one who could get their heart broken."

Dex didn't know what to say to that. Somehow, the

idea that Lorilei—wonderful, crazy, self-assured Lorilei—could wind up being the one who got hurt had
never occurred to him.

But he was the one who might be going away for a
long, long time.

"I'll keep that in mind," Dex said. "Along with
everything else I have to worry about."

"Ah, I'm sorry," Fun said. "You finally manage to
find something good in a crappy situation and I piss all
over it. Look, forget I said anything—you're both
adults and it's none of my business anyway."

"You're just looking out for your friends," Dex said.
"Nothing to apologize for. And you're right." Dex
paused. "I mean, what do Lorilei and I have in common, really? She's this outgoing free spirit, and I'm—
well, I'm *boring.*"

Fun frowned. "No, you're not. You're just inexperi-
enced—or at least you were, a week ago. It's my firm
belief that everyone has a little bit of freak inside
them; you just need the right stimulus to bring it to the
surface. And you, my friend, are standing in the middle of a whole lot of stimuli."

"So what has it brought to the surface?" Dex said.

"Are you kidding? You've turned into a—a *swash-
buckler,* man. You've turned leaping to, from, and off of
moving vehicles into your own personal hobby. You've
become a celebrity and inspired a movement."

Dex considered this while he uncapped his canteen and took a long drink. When he was done, he
said, "Yeah, but all that was reactive. I mean, you put
anyone in a corner and stress them out, they'll fight
back out of sheer desperation. But you and Lorilei—
all the other Burners—they do that kind of thing by

choice. They take chances, they express themselves, they create."

"So what?" Fun asked cheerfully. "Most of these people have taken a lifetime to get to this point—you were thrown in without warning. Consider what you've gone through as Freakdom 101; as one of your professors, I give you high marks for adaptability and stamina."

"I just wish I could *do* something," Dex said. "Something . . . unconventional. Something that uses *my* imagination."

"Well, there's always magic mushrooms."

Dex smiled wryly. "Sure. My situation isn't surreal enough—let's add some psychedelic drugs to the equation. That makes *perfect* sense. . . ."

Perfect. Sense.

The grin on Dex's face felt like it was two miles wide. Butterflies were dancing in his stomach, everything looked cartoony and two-dimensional, and he was pretty sure gravity was now optional. He was in the middle of a desert, he was very stoned, and he was riding a camel.

He glanced over at Captain Fun, who was on another camel beside him, and giggled.

It wouldn't make sense in the outside world, of course, with its rigid, stratified rules and hierarchies. There, it would have been lunacy. But Burning Man rules were different; they were inside-out, upside-down, back-to-front. Taking something that made you hallucinate was the only logical course of action.

Of course, Captain Fun had taken some convincing.

But the more questions Dex had asked him about the drug (psilocybin), its duration (four or five hours), and its effects (which he was experiencing now), the more he thought it was something he should try. It was, according to the Captain, a relatively mild high; it was neither as intense nor as long-lasting as LSD, rarely produced hallucinations beyond a distorted visual sense, and could usually be counted on for a euphoric trip. "It's a good party drug," Fun had told him. "You see a lot of it out here. It's largely a body-stone, but it doesn't dehydrate you the way Ecstasy does."

When it turned out that Fun had planned to do some that very afternoon, that he in fact had enough for two in his pack, Dex had made a decision.

"Remember what you said about nonlinear thinking?" Dex said. "Well, maybe this will jar something loose."

At least, that's how he'd justified it. Now, with the strangely random focus of the drug, he knew the truth. He wasn't doing this to get a new perspective on his problems, or even to forget about them for a while. He was doing it to impress Lorilei.

Gotta show her I can be as spontaneous as she is. Do something wild, unpredictable. Damn, this camel is uncomfortable.

As if it could hear his thoughts, the camel stopped and looked back at him. It made a noise he'd previously only heard in science fiction movies, and its breath smelt like it had been eating sewage. He vaguely remembered reading once that a camel's bite was poisonous—not due to any actual venom, but because its mouth was such a filthy environment that almost any type of bacteria might be present. *Like being bitten by an ecosystem,* he thought, and had a sudden flash of a rich, verdant microcosm behind the beast's lips: vertical fields of fungus on the cracked yellow cliffs of its teeth; rolling forests of mold on the foothills of its gums; oceans of plankton in the thick fluid of its saliva. Herds of thundering amoebas rolling down the majestic, rippling plains of its tongue . . .

"Okay, end of the ride," the man leading his mount said. He was dressed as a Bedouin, with only the sneakers he was wearing spoiling the illusion. "Here, I'll give you a hand getting down."

When they were both on solid ground again, Fun said, "How are you doing?"

"That," Dex said, "was a great idea. Desert. Camels. Psychadollics. Dilliks. Daleks."

"Aren't Daleks killer robots?" Fun asked.

"Well, *that's* kind of judgmental, don't you think? Maybe they were *framed.* I mean, something goes wrong, why is it always the *robot* that gets the blame? You run out of mustard, who's fault is it? The robot. Global warming? Too many robots. You got the flu? That damn *robot* must have given it to me. And just because you're named 'the Terminator,' everybody thinks you're a mass murderer."

Fun stared at him. "That," he said solemnly, "was a world-class, drug-induced rant. Congratulations, you are now a full-fledged freak. There is no turning back."

"Then let's go forward. Or maybe sideways . . ."

"Hey. Where'd we leave the bikes?"

"They're back at the Camel tent. I think."

"Let's walk for a while. Bikes are too . . . wheely."

"Oh, yeah."

Dex glanced down at his feet. The surface of the

playa, where it wasn't worn down by traffic, was covered with a maze of intricate cracks; it reminded him of the bottom of an old teacup. At the edges of his vision the cracks seemed to move, to twist together like some vast knotted network that untangled at his approach and retied itself at his departure, a weedy sea of chaos surrounding the tiny, ordered island of his immediate vision.

"Hey," Fun said. "Hey, we should go on *that.*"

Dex looked up. Across the Esplanade was a steel *U* three stories tall, with a tower of scaffolding attached to one side; a sign declared it THE ROASTER COASTER. A metal cage on the scaffolding's top held a woman in a white cowboy hat and a floral print dress, hanging on to the bars of her prison and doing a hip-grinding dance to the raunchy Texas boogie the camp's sound system was blasting out. She weighed at least three hundred pounds, and the entire structure shimmied when she did.

The *U*, Dex saw, was a track; an enclosed car on gimbals sat atop one end. As he watched, it hurtled downward, going into an intense spin as it whipped around the curve and up the other side, then back again. When it finally stopped, three people in white coveralls and armed with rolls of paper towels unlocked the door and helped the occupant out. They had *CLEANUP CREW* stenciled on their outfits.

"Let's not," Dex said.

"Yeah, that might be a little too intense. . . . Hey, how about *that?*"

"Magic Glasses Camp? Yeah, okay . . ."

The camp was a simple open-framework tunnel, tall enough to walk through. Its interior had been festooned with strings of multicolored lights. The Magic Glasses were made of cardboard, with some kind of plastic film for lenses; there was a person at one end of the tunnel handing them out, and one at the other end collecting them.

Dex put his on and stepped inside. The glasses turned the lights into a prismatic, shattered rainbow; everything else seemed out of focus. He walked forward slowly, feeling like he'd entered another dimension.

"Whoa," Fun said. "I knew I shouldn't have eaten that second kaleidoscope."

"It's beautiful," Dex murmured. "Like—like a rainbow in a blizzard . . ."

He gave the glasses back reluctantly when they reached the end.

"Tourist," Captain Fun announced.

Dex glanced around. "Tourist" was another term for "spectator"; according to Fun, they were the ones that came to Burning Man and acted like it was Disneyland. "I don't mind the ones that just gawk," Fun had told him. "They're clueless, but they can be taught. The ones that really piss me off are the video voyeurs. All they care about is taking pictures of naked women—which is okay, as long as you ask permission. Most of them don't, just shoot away and then stick the photos up on their website. Some even sell 'em."

The man Fun pointed out seemed to fit Fun's description: middle-aged, scruffy beard, potbelly, wearing a baseball cap, T-shirt, khaki shorts, and sandals with socks—black ones. He stood in the shadow of a tent, holding a small digital camera in his hand that was obviously focused on a nude girl a short distance away.

"I hate those fuckers," Fun said. "Goddamn Peeping Toms."

Another man strolled up to the tourist. He also had a camera in his hand and was dressed much the same, except for his loud tropical shirt. He starting taking pictures, too.

"That's it," Fun said. "Let's go over there and steal their clothes. *That'll* show 'em." He stalked toward the two men, Dex in tow.

Before he got there, someone else did. A Burner carrying a knapsack, wearing bug-goggles, silver-and-black checked shorts and nothing else tapped the second tourist on the shoulder as Fun and Dex walked up.

"Yeah?" the tourist asked.

The bug-eyed man smiled, and pulled out a plastic bag. He mimed putting something into it, pointed to the man's camera, then picked up a pinch of playa dust and shook his head.

"Oh, I should keep my camera in a plastic bag? Because of the dust?" the man said.

Bug-eyes nodded. He held out his hand, smiled, and nodded. The man hesitated, then gave him the camera. Bug-eyes carefully put it into the bag, sealed it, then held up a hand—*wait*. He lay the bag on the ground and rummaged in his knapsack.

And brought out a large wooden mallet.

Before anyone could stop him, he'd smashed the bagged camera into smithereens. Grinning hugely, he picked it up and presented it back to the tourist, who stood there dumbstruck.

"Pretty girls like to be *asked* if you can take their picture, yes?" Bug-eyes said. Mallet in hand, he turned to the other tourist. "Don't you agree?"

The first tourist had gone a sickly shade of white. "Stay away from me," he said. He backed away, almost tripped over somebody's bike, then turned around and walked off at a rapid pace, glancing behind him every few steps.

Dex couldn't take his eyes off the tourist with the smashed camera. He seemed to be in shock; his eyes and mouth competed to see which one could open wider and stay that way. Dex wondered if there was going to be violence—Bug-eyes, despite having made his point, was just standing there with a crazed smile on his face and his mallet in hand.

"Your own damn fault," Fun said cheerfully.

"Do—do you know what that camera *cost?*" the tourist managed.

"How much?" Bug-eyes asked.

The tourist studied the bag of shattered components in his hand. "Almost a dollar," he said mournfully.

"So? It was *my* dollar," Bug-eyes said.

The tourist and the Burner grinned at each other, and then both Dex and Fun whooped with laughter.

"Now, *that,*" Fun said when he'd regained control, "was funny."

"The old Shatterbug routine," the man with the mallet said. "You think he'll think twice about taking pictures without permission?"

"At least," Dex said. "Possibly three or four times."

The pair introduced themselves. The man playing the tourist was Robin, his partner BJ. The naked girl was in on the gag, too; she called herself Zebragirl. "Yeah, she's the hook, Robin's the shill, and I'm the Hammer of Doom," BJ said. "I pick up junk cameras from thrift shops, usually for less than a buck apiece—'course, the mark never gets a good look until it's in pieces."

"Nice," Fun said.

"Just upholding the grand tradition of pranking," Robin said. "'Putting the practical back in practical jokes,' that's our motto."

"Social engineering at its finest," Fun agreed.

"No, that would be the ARG," Robin said. "The whole murder-investigation thing is *classic.*"

"Wait," Dex said, frowning. "You mean you think the ARG isn't real?"

BJ chuckled and shook his head. "Well, it *exists*—it's just a question of what it's really trying to *do.* I don't think it's so much an investigation as a disruption—you know, generating as much interference as it can while looking like it's helping."

"You really think so?" Fun asked.

"Sure," Robin said. "And I think it's a good idea, too. The cops will use any excuse to clamp down on us—"

"Here we go," BJ said with a sigh.

"I don't think there even *was* a murder," Robin said. "I bet some guy keeled over of heatstroke or a heart attack while heating up his dinner, a fire got started, and then the cops came in and sealed everything off. Takes a couple days before the medical examiner declares it accidental death, and in the meantime they use it as an excuse to start searching tents."

"Dude, you are *so* paranoid," BJ said. "How about

whatshisname, Dexter Edden? The cops just make him up, too?"

"No, they're definitely looking for him," Robin said. "But not because he killed someone. I bet they found a bunch of drugs in that RV, and *that's* why they want him. They're just saying he's a murder suspect because they know Burners wouldn't help catch a drug dealer."

"Interesting theory," Fun said. "You think this Edden guy has any drugs on him?"

"Can I see that mallet?" Dex asked.

" 'Cause if he did," Fun said quickly, "he might be grateful for any help he got. If *I* ran into him, I'd *definitely* help him out."

"What about that whole story in the *Gazette?*" Dex asked. "You know, where the guy told his side of things?"

"See, that's the part *I* think is bogus," BJ said. "I think someone *posing* as Edden gave that interview."

"Why?" Fun asked.

"Because it's a great prank. It's high-visibility, it's entertaining, and it confuses the hell out of the cops. What else could you want?"

"A little truth would be nice," Dex said.

Truth.

It came to Dex while he was in the Porta-John; truth was exactly what he needed, but it kept eluding him. And he knew why.

He was a fake.

"I'm a fake," he whispered. His voice sounded echoey and strange to his ears. He'd always thought of himself as someone who was basically honest, but now he saw that was only when dealing with others. He'd been lying to himself his entire life.

He'd always defined himself by what he did, but he'd never really done anything. He suddenly had a vision of himself as a robot, an extension of his computer—just another peripheral.

"No," he said firmly. He had to break the program, exit the system; he saw, quite clearly, the inevitable crash he was being led to.

What he couldn't visualize was a way out. And he knew, suddenly, that there *was* one; he just couldn't see it. It was invisible to him because he was trapped, trapped by years of sensible, reasoned actions; trapped in a maze he'd built himself, with walls of sturdy logic and a solid, predictable foundation. The only way out was to get above the whole thing somehow, look down at the pattern and find that exit he knew was there. . . .

Fun was waiting for him at a theme camp on Authority, chilling and enjoying a cold beer. Dex left the Porta-John and walked the opposite way; when he reached the Esplanade, he crossed it and kept going.

Out into the desert.

Into the Wholly Other.

CHAPTER 16:

DOWN AT THE END OF CERTAIN

Yes. This feels right.

No bike. No well-meaning friends. No brakes, no safety net. Just the sun, the dust, the wind and some water. And me.

Oh, and that giant inflatable sex doll. And the shark-car. And those purple people on unicycles . . . ah, the purple people. Wonder if they'll get eaten. Wonder if I'll get eaten . . . maybe I've been eaten already. Dessert for the desert? And I'm deserting. . . .

He let his feet and his mind wander, moving forward but with no particular destination. He was intensely aware of his body, not so much the outside but the in; the gurgle of his stomach, the pull and twinge of muscle, the frictionless swivel of joints. He felt like an explorer on an alien planet, protected by the space suit of his skin, receiving data from an array of sensors.

But I'm not. I'm not driving a machine, I'm walking. This is real, dammit. He tried to banish the mechanical imagery from his head, replace it with something more organic. *A tree? A rainstorm? A herd of penguins?*

He was still groping for a better metaphor when he saw the shack.

It looked like it had been there for a hundred years. Tumbleweeds had piled up against one ramshackle wall, which seemed to be made of large, oddly shaped sheets of wood hammered roughly together. As Dex got closer, he saw that the entire structure was built from pieces of old pianos, many of them scarred by fire. Keys of cracked and stained ivory lined the doorway like ancient teeth, flanked by rows of rusted wire like exposed tendons. A square pane of glass mounted above the front door was no ordinary window, but an oversize magnifying glass, the kind they used to mount in front of old televisions to make the screen bigger.

He stopped and looked around. Dust was kicking up in the distance, between him and the city; no one else was in sight. He might as well have been in the middle of the Sahara.

He walked through the front door—and stopped, transfixed. The shack was wedge-shaped, narrowing toward the back, and the interior looked exactly as he would have imagined a hermit's shack to look: an old wooden table stood against one wall, with an equally old wooden chair beside it. There was a single shelf on the opposite wall, with a dusty can of beans sitting on it; the can looked like it had been produced around the time Dex's grandfather was born. Little drifts of dust had collected in the corners of the room.

But it was the quality of light that was astounding. A soft golden glow lay over everything, with brighter sparks of light drifting over that. The far end of the shack was lined with crumpled golden foil and dozens of mirror-balls and suncatchers; they took the light being focused by the screen-magnifier and scattered it around the room like luminous confetti. The effect was wistful, somehow; it seemed to project both the sadness of things long-gone and the bright sheen of nostalgia.

"Beautiful, isn't it?" The voice came from behind him.

Dex spun around. The man standing in the doorway wore khaki pants, a short-sleeved white shirt, aviator-style sunglasses and a white Stetson. He was in his forties or maybe fifties, smoking a Camel cigarette.

"Uh, yes," Dex said. He hadn't seen anybody when he arrived, but he supposed the man could have been on the other side of the shack. "It's very striking."

"The simple ones are always my favorite." The man stepped inside, peered at the can of beans without touching it. "Nice attention to detail."

"Yeah. It feels spooky . . . but comforting, somehow."

"Welcome to the empty heart of America," the man said. He took a small metal tin out of his pocket, opened it, and crushed his cigarette out in it carefully.

"That's kind of cynical." Normally Dex would have just nodded and said something noncommittal; the 'shrooms had their own approach.

"Not at all. Emptiness doesn't have to be a negative thing." The man didn't seem offended; a slight smile played on his lips. "Emptiness is potential. Most of the universe is empty, after all; even on a molecular level, we're mostly just space between particles."

"But an 'empty heart'?" Dex said. "That's a different kind of emptiness, isn't it?" Personal as the question was, it didn't seem strange to be asking it of a complete stranger; the surroundings somehow made it appropriate.

"True," the man admitted. "The empty heart of a human being is either sad or callous, and that's never good. But I was speaking of the heart of something much larger; the heart of a concept, if you like. And that's never empty for long."

"Why not?" Dex asked. "If a person's heart can stay empty, why should a concept be any different?"

"Because Nature abhors a vacuum. And when we're talking about a big enough concept—a concept like America—then there's a huge mass of other concepts swirling around that empty heart. Inevitably, they'll be drawn to it, like galaxies swirling around a black hole."

"Black holes crush everything they swallow," Dex said, then grinned. The remark sounded bleak, but he didn't feel that way at all; actually, he was enjoying the exchange immensely.

"Emptiness is always dangerous," the man replied, smiling back. "As it should be. But no hole is bottomless. You throw enough stars into one, it'll light up like . . . well, like this." He indicated the room they stood in with a wave of his hand.

"And the human heart?"

"Personally, I think it can hold as many as the sky," the man said. "But it only needs two to really light up."

"Two?"

"Absolutely. Some people think a single star is all

they need, but they tend to be a little too focused for their own good."

Dex's smile faded a little. "And what would the second star be?"

"Yourself," the man said. "You have to make space in your heart for your own star, too. If all you do is bask in the light of someone else, you wind up cold and lonely as the moon."

"And as empty," Dex said.

The man walked across the room, stopped at the far end. He reached out, touched one of the mirrored globes gently. "Sometimes, emptiness is good just for its own sake. Makes you appreciate everything else."

Dex felt a sudden wave of dizziness that started in the pit of his stomach and blossomed at the top of his skull. "Whoa," he said, and sank into the wooden chair.

"You all right?" the man asked.

"Fine. Just a little . . . stoned," Dex said. The admission came naturally; lying seemed out of the question. "I guess that's a kind of emptiness, too."

"Depends on the drug, I suppose. And the person."

"My drug was always cyberspace," Dex said. His mouth suddenly felt dry and cottony; he fumbled for his canteen. "This is my first time taking something else."

"Black Rock is a city of first times," the man said. "A city of cyberspace, too, for that matter."

Dex took a long, grateful drink of water. "How so?" he asked when he was done.

"If people are like planets, then most spend their lives in the same solar system. Your community is defined by what's available locally. If you live in a big city, you can probably find other people like your-self—your tribe. If you live in a small town, you're stuck with what's available.

"The Internet changed that. Suddenly, you could visit other planets without actually leaving your own. Even better, there was all this empty space in be-tween."

"And people started building their own planets," Dex said.

"Planets, moons, stars, asteroid belts . . . whatever they wanted. Domains, Web pages, sites of every de-scription. New cultures sprang up overnight, mutated, and bred with other hybrids. But there was still some-thing *missing*. Do you know what that was?"

"It wasn't *real*," Dex said slowly. "You could pre-tend to be anybody, and it didn't matter. You could say anything, and not mean it. There weren't any *conse-quences*."

"There are always consequences," the man said, and now he seemed almost sad. "As it should be. But there are no *immediate* consequences in cyberspace—information leaps ahead of action. And for a commu-nity to grow and thrive, it needs to exchange more than just data. You need the earthy, basic stuff for that—blood and tears, semen and sweat. You can't do that online."

"So they came out here," Dex said. He saw the anal-ogy suddenly, as clear and obvious as a blueprint. "The theme camps—they're like Web pages. Little self-created communities, where people can make their own rules. Black Rock City is like a physical extrusion of cyberspace itself. . . ."

"Yes," the man said. "But once you drag an idea

into the real world, all kinds of rules begin to apply. Basic, primitive, rules."

" 'Piss Clear,' " Dex said.

" 'Leave No Trace,' " the man replied. "And a bunch of others. All of them tribal, because that's what these communities really are—tribes. And when they come out here to actually meet face-to-face, they do all those things that tribes do to bond. They dance, they drink, they play."

"They mate," Dex said.

"Of course. There's lots of mating going on, not just between individuals but between the tribes themselves. A cross-pollination that's sexual, political, emotional, and artistic—"

"Not pollinated," Dex interrupted. *Forged.*

The man's smile grew wider. "Yes. Pounded on the anvil of the playa. Melted in the blaze of the desert sun. Tempered with sweat, and dust, and bitter cold. Bonds made under those conditions have real strength to them."

"Battlefield loyalties," Dex said. "Sure. But what about when the battle's over? Are they strong enough to take the weight of—of *ordinary* life?"

The man regarded him calmly for a second. Then he walked over, hands in his pockets, and said, "You never know until you try. But there's two things you should remember: One, there's really no such thing as 'ordinary life.' And two—there's always next year."

Dex thought about that. Was it possible to have a relationship with someone when you only saw them one week of the year? Even if that week was filled with magic?

He didn't know. He wasn't even sure it was the

right question, or if it was, if he had the right to ask it. He had a sudden, intense craving for a laptop with an Internet connection; he could almost feel the keyboard under his fingers. It was the same blind desire a caveman would have felt for a stone ax when facing a saber-toothed tiger: the simple need for a solid, reliable tool in his hands. Something that would just let him get a handle on the situation . . .

The feeling was followed almost instantly by a mental image: Wade, sitting in the very same chair Dex was right now, staring out at a billowing dust storm with the same desperate hunger in his gut.

And just like that, Dex understood.

A pattern crystalized in his mind, more visceral than cerebral; he could *feel* the connections between certain events and people, though he would have been hard-pressed to describe those connections in words. The pride in Lorilei's face when she showed him the Lamplighters' procession was there, and so was Wade's drunken frustration. There was a sense of the festival as a whole, of the amount of planning and careful social engineering that went into directing this much chaos; for the first time, Dex felt as if he'd glimpsed the mountains hidden behind a swirling wall of dust.

"I've been doing this all wrong," Dex said wonderingly. "I've been talking to rabbits instead of looking in the hat. And I *make* hats."

The man considered this soberly for a second. "Well," he said at last, "I kind of have a fondness for them myself." He touched the brim of his Stetson. "A word of advice, though?"

"What's that?"

"Don't forget your dust mask. Hats only protect you from the sun. . . ."

The man strolled out of the shack. Dex reached down to the dust mask he'd left dangling around his neck ever since he took a drink of water, and slipped it back into place.

When he left the shack, the man was gone.

Dex knew what he had to do.

He strode back toward the city, head buzzing with insight. His conversation with the man in the shack already seemed distant and unclear, eclipsed by the understanding that now burned inside him. *He knew what he had to do.*

It was a long walk; he hadn't realized just how far he'd wandered. By the time he reached the Esplanade, his feet were sore and he was almost out of water. He looked around and realized he was on the eastern edge of the city, near Aetheria.

Captain Fun and Lorilei were both waiting for him when he walked into camp. "And he's back!" Fun said cheerfully. "I knew you'd find your way home."

Lorilei seemed torn between being glad, pissed off, and confused; Dex laughed at the look on her face despite himself.

She finally settled on mild exasperation. "Been adventuring, have we? Or did you just get lost?"

"Not lost," Dex said. "Found. And right now, I need a little help from Tribe Urge." He went straight to a carboy of water and started refilling his canteen.

"Found? What, did you get busted by someone?" Fun asked.

"No, no. I mean I had a revelation. And I need you to find me something, right away."

"What?" Lorilei asked.

"An Internet connection. Wade's laptop doesn't have a network card, or I'd use that."

"Easy enough," Fun said with a shrug. "They've got some public terminals set up down at Playa Info, but if you want something a little more private, I know a guy over on Dogma. He's got a full PC setup."

"Great," Dex said. He topped off the canteen, took a long drink, and capped it. "Let's go."

"Wait," Lorilei said. "Aren't you even going to tell us where you—"

He grabbed her, pulled her close, and kissed her.

A minute passed.

When their lips finally parted, he looked into her eyes and said, "I promise I'll tell you everything—but there's something I have to do, and it's too hard to explain, and I have to do it *now.*"

She grinned. "Can I come with? Or is this a solitary vision-quest kind of thing?"

"Uh, yeah. Sort of."

She sighed, then turned and glared at Fun accusingly. "You had to go and give him mushrooms . . . okay, Don Peyote. Bring me back a few secrets of the universe, okay?"

"We'll see," Dex said.

The camp Fun took him to consisted of a green canvas army tent pitched next to a camperized school bus. The bus was covered in quasi-Egyptian hieroglyphics, and had a huge gold sphinx on top of it with pyramid-shaped breasts. A hand-painted sign proclaimed it to be Camp Titankhamen.

A man in his late forties with a long, salt-and-pepper beard sat in a lawn chair next to the bus. He wore sandals, a gold-trimmed toga and a King Tut headdress. He was very carefully applying eyeliner with the help of a small mirror in his lap.

"Hey, Pharoah," Fun said.

The man looked up. "Aloha, Captain Fun," he said amiably. "Have you come to quaff a cold beverage and discuss the afterlife?"

"Nope. I'm here to quaff a cold beverage and borrow your computer. Actually, he is." Fun jerked a thumb at Dex. "If that's okay."

"Sure. Just give me a sec. . . ." He added a short black line with a curl at the end from the outer edge of his left eye, studied it critically in the mirror, then nodded and got up.

He led them onto the bus, which was swelteringly hot even with all the windows open. Inside, it looked more like a tent than a vehicle; the ceiling and walls were draped with gauzy fabric, and the floor was covered in oversize pillows and two large beanbag chairs. He walked straight through to a door on the far side behind a beaded curtain. On the other side was a small galley and a bathroom; beyond that, a small and tidy office, complete with filing cabinets, a bookshelf that took up one wall, and a desk holding an iMac—one of the apple-green ones.

"You can take the geek out of the city, but you can't take away his computer," the Pharoah said. "I'm already logged on to Playanet. You need any help?"

"No, I can take it from here," Dex said. "Thanks,

this will really help. Uh—I don't have anything to gift you with."

"Don't sweat it," the Pharoah said. "I owe the Captain a few."

Fun and the Pharoah left Dex alone, while they went outside to drink beer and talk metaphysics. "It's a tough job," Fun said as they left, "but somebody's got to step up."

Dex just sat and stared at the screen for a few moments. Suddenly, he felt exhausted; the heat, the walking, the drugs were suddenly taking their toll. The bright blaze of inspiration he'd felt not half an hour ago had dimmed to a guttering flame; everything that had been so clear seemed murky and nebulous.

He took a deep breath, and put his fingers on the keys. It didn't matter how weary he was; it didn't matter if he no longer felt inspired. The central idea that he'd had was still relevant, it wasn't simply a chemical mirage. What came next was just work, the kind of work he was good at, the kind he could do—and had done—when bone-tired and half-conscious.

Not on magic mushrooms, maybe, he thought as he started tapping keys, *but like the man said: this is a city of firsts.*

He'd never been much of a hacker, but he'd learned a few tricks over the years. Because Wade had hired him to set up a website for his new business, Dex already had a certain amount of access; now, he tried to go further. What he needed to do was access Wade's private email accounts.

It took him a while. He had to have Captain Fun run back to camp at one point and grab the laptop—in his excitement he'd forgotten to bring it along—and it finally gave him the clue he needed to crack Wade's password. The fact that the word itself incorporated both an obscenity and a reference to alcohol came as no surprise.

By that time the drugs in his system had faded to a background hum and an overwhelming sense of fatigue; both were forgotten as soon as he read the first email. "This is it," he murmured to himself. "I've got you now, you murdering, long-eared, Lord of the Sith bastard. . . ."

He pored through emails for an hour, and transferred all of it to a disc he'd borrowed from the Pharoah. When he was done, he stood up, stretched, grabbed the laptop and staggered out into the sunlight.

Fun and the Pharoah glanced up from where they sat. "Well?" Fun asked. "Did you crack the case?"

"Yeah, I think I did," Dex said. "Can I tell you about it over dinner? I'm starving."

"Sure thing," Fun said. He stood, thanked the Pharoah for his hospitality, and he and Dex headed back to camp.

Dinner was beef stew, served with soft tortillas on the side. Dex dug in ravenously. Lorilei and Fun eyed him with mounting curiousity, but they let him eat.

"Okay, what gives?" Lorilei finally demanded as Dex was halfway through his second bowl. "You show up wired, you run off to do mysterious computer things, and now Fun says you've solved the mystery. Spill."

Dex leaned back in his chair, still chewing, and closed his eyes. He swallowed, burped, and sighed.

"You know," he said, "that was really excellent stew."

"Yeah, yeah," Fun said. "So who is Rafe?"

Dex paused, looked at Fun, then at Lorilei. "Wade's son," he said quietly.

"What?" Fun said. "I thought he was a Burner."

"He is," Dex said. "But he's not one of the Burners Wade pissed off last year. We were chasing after the wrong suspects the entire time."

"And you found this out how?" Lorilei asked. "You went online and Googled him?"

"No, I broke into Wade's email account. There was a bunch of stuff stored there, including all the correspondence between him and Rafe." Dex yawned. "Excuse me. I got the idea out in the desert—it's kind of hard to explain. I just saw all these patterns below the surface of the city—all the stuff that makes it run, that lets the craziness happen on the surface while still making sure the Porta-Johns get emptied every day. It was almost like seeing an iceberg, except while the polar bears are having this big party on the surface, there are all these industrious little penguins in ice caves below the surface, pecking away at little igloo-shaped computers."

"Penguins," Lorilei said.

"Pecking away at igloo computers," Fun said. "Boy, those were good 'shrooms."

"Anyway," Dex continued, "I suddenly saw all relationships in that light, and realized that Wade and Rafe must have their own iceberg."

"And their own penguins?" Fun asked, sounding confused.

"He means their *history*," Lorilei said. "Right?"

"Yeah. And sure enough, that history was documented." Dex smiled. "Which told me not only who Rafe was, but why he was meeting Wade here."

"I'm guessing they didn't exactly have the same agenda," Fun said.

"Wade thought they did." Dex paused. "He thought his son would be as glad as he was—because they were meeting for the first time."

"You're kidding," Lorilei said.

"Nope. It probably comes as no surprise that Wade has sewn a few wild oats in his time; until a year ago, I doubt he ever gave those oats a second thought. But Burning Man has a way of making you . . . *reevaluate* things. It made Wade think long and hard about himself, and he wound up getting in touch with a few people from his past. That's how he found out he had a son he never knew about, one the mother gave up for adoption at birth."

"Maybe she was afraid he'd turn out like his father," Fun offered.

"Or maybe she just wasn't ready to have a child," Lorilei countered.

"Either way," Dex said, "Rafe didn't know anything about Wade until last year, when the adoption agency put them in touch via email. They started to correspond."

"That must have made for some interesting reading," Fun said.

"It was. I never thought of Wade as the family type—and from what I read, I guess he wasn't. But he was trying." Dex paused. It seemed a little disrespectful to be discussing something as personal and private as the letters between a dead man and his long-lost son . . . but then he seemed to hear Wade, laughing at him. *Get the fuck outta here, Dexter. You think I wouldn't read your diary out loud at your funeral and make fun of it? You know me better'n that. Beside, I'm a stiff—what am I gonna do, haunt your repressed ass?*

"Anyway," Dex continued, "Rafe and Wade found out a lot about each other, but there are two details that stood out for me, one about each of them. First, Rafe is a struggling artist in New York."

"And the second?" Lorilei asked.

"Wade is a rich man with no wife and no other close relatives."

"And until recently, no children," Fun said. "So if he died . . ."

"Rafe would inherit everything," Lorilei finished.

"Right," Dex said. "So he lured Wade out to Burning Man, a place Rafe claimed he'd never been to but had always wanted to visit. He swore Wade to secrecy, said that he needed time to adjust to the whole father-son thing. He was trying to control the situation, get Wade into an isolated environment where he could knock him off. But Wade was a little more paranoid than Rafe thought; he brought me along, and held on to the emails."

"And when Rafe saw you, he panicked and thought he could just eliminate you both," Fun said.

"That's what I think—but I guess we'll have to ask Rafe to know for sure."

"So we know *who* the killer is," Lorilei said. "And we know why he did it. But we still don't know what he looks like or his real name, do we? I assume since Rafe was big on secrecy, he kept everything on a first-name basis."

"That he did," Dex said. "But Wade wasn't a complete idiot. He must have done a little snooping on his own, because when I checked his address book, guess what I found?"

"Rafe's last name?" Fun said.

"And address," Dex said. He fished the disc out of his pack, and held it out to Fun. "It's all right here. You get this to the police, and if he's still here they should be able to find him."

"They haven't found you," Lorilei said.

"True," Dex admitted. "But *I'm* a living legend."

"Like Extreme Elvis?"

Dex shuddered.

Fun left with the disc. Lorilei grabbed Dex and pulled him into the tent-trailer.

"Wow," Dex said afterward, trying to catch his breath. "If I didn't know better, I'd think you missed me."

She looked down at him, grinned, and tweaked his nipple. "I was worried about you, okay? Worry makes me tense—and this is how I deal with tension."

"You must be a lot of fun around tax time."

"I always file early."

"See, now that's the kind of thing that gets *me* hot."

"Sure. You're just a meek little number-cruncher," she said. "Who takes mind-altering drugs and goes for a stroll in the desert. Who do you think you are, anyway, Moses?"

"Moses didn't do drugs. And he left for forty days and forty nights—I was only gone a few hours."

"Well, it felt like forty days and nights. When Fun told me what you'd done I almost throttled him."

"Sorry." Dex hesitated, then added, "No, actually I'm *not* sorry. It was something I needed to do. I can't really justify it in any logical way, but—"

She touched his lips. "You don't have to," she said gently. "You followed your instincts, and they led you to the truth. That's the way it's *supposed* to work."

He smiled, and kissed her fingertips. "I hope so. And I hope you and Fun don't get in any trouble for helping me."

"Don't worry about us. Fun's being careful—he's using the ARG as a go-between."

"I guess. I really owe him—all of you—a lot."

She shrugged, which made her breasts do interesting things. "Well, you've definitely made it worth *my* while," she said. "You'll have to work out your own method of repayment with the Captain."

"How long have you known him, anyway?"

She brushed a loose strand of hair behind her ear. "We met here last year. He was running this superhero theme camp and we hit it off right away. And no, we didn't have sex—he was too busy running around enjoying himself to stay in one spot for more than twenty minutes."

"Any idea what he does in the—" Dex paused. He was going to say, "normal," but that didn't sound right anymore. "—ordinary world?"

"He's a writer. Science fiction novels and comic books."

"Of course."

"Well, some of us are freaks all year round." She shifted her weight, wiggling her hips. "Comfy?"

"Ecstatic. Any idea where he goes when he disappears?"

She raised her eyebrows. "You're starting to take this investigator stuff seriously, huh?"

"Just curious."

She rolled off him and snuggled up to his side. "I don't know. It's kind of hard to imagine Fun hiding anything—he'll gladly list all the illegal drugs he did at the last orgy he attended—but everybody has secrets. I don't pry."

"None of my business, either. He's probably sneaking off to do something mundane, anyway."

"Sure. He's reading to senior citizens over at Rest Home Camp," she murmured into his neck.

"Donating blood to needy alcoholics."

"Manning phones down at the Superhero Crisis Line."

"Volunteering to . . . do something. You win."

"And the crowd goes wild," she whispered.

"That's not a crowd."

"Not yet . . ."

Lorilei made coffee and they sat outside on lawn chairs and drank it while watching the sun set. Dex had to lift his dust mask for every sip, but he was getting used to that. People strolled or rode or drove by. A woman in a sari offered them sliced watermelon from a silver tray, and they took some and thanked her.

"I think I know why he did it," Dex said.

Lorilei nibbled on the rind of her watermelon. "For the inheritance?"

"Not Rafe. I think I know why Wade contacted all the people he'd abused."

"Did it have something to do with his son?"

"Indirectly, maybe. I think he was just trying to understand—I mean, here's this place full of naked people, dancing and drinking and setting things on fire, and at first he must have thought he was in heaven. Wade always hated following rules, and at first glance Burning Man doesn't seem to have any."

"But he found out pretty fast that wasn't the case."

"Yeah. He kept trying to participate, but every time he did, he pissed somebody off. The more frustrated he got, the worse he screwed up. He just couldn't wrap his head around the way the place functions."

A beautiful woman with a shaved skull came by on a bicycle, wearing an elaborate set of white silk wings that arched a foot higher than her head. She smiled as she rode past, and rang a little bell on her handlebars.

"Normally," Dex continued, "he would have just said screw it. But the city got to him. I think . . ." He broke off, and looked over at Lorilei. "I think he fell in love."

She met his eyes. "I can see that," she said. "Sure."

"But it was unrequited. The city didn't love him back. It was this tangle of contradictions that frustrated him at every turn. So he did something he had very little experience in—he sat down and tried to figure out what he did wrong."

"And asked the people he'd wronged for advice?"

"Seems weird, I know—but if you knew Wade, it would make sense. He was so self-centered he had trouble seeing things from any point of view but his own, so he tried collecting other people's opinions. At first, I think he was trying to put together some kind of cohesive overview that would let him fit in."

"At first?"

"This next part is just theory, but . . . well, it feels right. I think Wade came to a major realization about himself and his life. He started thinking about consequences—and that's what led him to get in touch with his son."

"Consequences," she said thoughtfully. "You never know what you'll wind up paying for, do you?"

"Life," Dex said. "And death."

Chapter 17:

Avenues of Belief

Fun came back about an hour past sunset. Both Dex and Lorilei had changed into warmer clothes by then; the temperature was dropping rapidly.

"Okay, I got it to the cops," he said. "The message that came back through the intermediary is that they're going to get in touch with someone in New York, have somebody there check it out. I gather the FBI may have to get involved—conspiracy to commit murder across state lines."

"At least they're taking it seriously," Lorilei said. "Or do you think they're yanking our chain?"

"Moonman thinks the cops are listening to what we have to say," Fun said. "They really don't want to have to search every vehicle leaving the site on Sunday and Monday—it'll be a logistical nightmare."

"True enough," Dex said. "So what'll happen next—they'll get a picture of Rafe and circulate it?"

"I guess," Fun said. "Unless he's been hiding his face all week the way you have, someone will have seen him."

"But will they turn him in?" Dex said.

"They will if we get the word out," Lorilei said. "We should talk to Jimmy, get her to do a follow-up piece. If we do it now, it'll be in tomorrow's paper. Maybe we can even get hold of a picture."

"Good idea," Fun said. "I'll see if I can track her down."

"And I'll hit the radio stations and talk to someone at *Piss Clear,*" Lorilei said. "If we're going to use the media, we might as well use all of it."

"I'm going to take a nap," Dex said.

Fun and Lorilei stared at him.

"I had no idea mushrooms could make you so sleepy," Dex said, stifling a yawn. "No wonder people who do drugs never get anything done."

"Oh, we get plenty done," Fun said. "Lots of it never makes any sense, but it gets done."

"Getting some sleep's a good idea," Lorilei said. "You should rest while you can." Her smile told him he wasn't likely to get much sleep when she got back.

"Okay then," Dex said. "Happy hunting."

He went back to the tent trailer, and was snoring before they rode out of camp.

He slept until midnight. His dreams were strange and fragmented, and he had a hard time remembering them when he finally woke. *Something about a tornado,* he thought groggily. His mouth was dry and scratchy and tasted like overcooked cabbage. *And alligators. Alligators riding bicycles.*

He fumbled for the water bottle beside the bed and drank deeply, feeling the plastic crinkle inward as he sucked it dry. The water cleared his head a little, but he still felt exhausted, like he hadn't slept at all.

He got up, shivering, and turned on the battery-operated lamp on the counter. He put on an extra sweatshirt of Fun's, then rooted through a pile of clothes and added a pair of gray sweatpants as well. His stomach rumbled, so he went outside in search of sustenance.

He found Sundog and Cromagg sitting in lawn chairs, with a chess set on a cooler between them. Cromagg was studying the board intently; Sundog was swigging from a bottle of champagne. Cromagg wore his usual neo-caveman outfit, while Sundog wore a pair of ragged jeans, a buccaneer's coat and a pirate hat. A tattered stuffed parrot hung crookedly from one shoulder.

"Hey," Dex said.

"Arr," Sundog said. He wiped his mouth theatrically with the back of one hand. "Young Master Urge be awake."

"And you be in check," Cromagg said, moving his queen.

Sundog glared down at the board. "Goddammit," he grumbled. "Pirates don't play chess, anyway. Got a backgammon board?"

"What's happening?" Dex said, yawning hugely. "Are Fun and Lorilei around?"

"They sent us to babysit," Cromagg said. "Worried you might gobble a handful of acid and steal a blimp or something."

"Right now I'm more interested in gobbling some food."

"There's some leftover chili in the blue cooler," Cromagg said. "Help yourself."

Dex did. He didn't even bother heating it up, just grabbed a spoon and ate right out of the Tupperware. It was spicier than he remembered; he found a can of beer to help wash it down.

"You guys don't have to stick around here," Dex said. "It's Friday night—shouldn't you be out debauching?"

Sundog took another drink from his champagne bottle. "We *are* debauching. I'm just waiting for the drugs to kick in." He settled back in his chair with a thoughtful look, then beamed. "Ah. There they go now. . . ."

"Personally, I want to stick around to see how things turn out," Cromagg said. "I get the feeling events are building to a head."

"Maybe. Depends on whether or not they find Rafe, and that probably won't happen until Saturday's *Gazette* comes out."

"If he's even still here," Sundog said. "The scurvy swine may have scuppered."

"You don't even know what that means," Cromagg said.

"I'm a pirate, not a thesaurus."

There was a walkie-talkie at Cromagg's feet. It crackled and Fun's voice asked if anyone at Tribe Urge was listening.

Dex picked it up. "Inspector Urge here, Captain. What's up?"

"Got some news for you, Inspector—but it's not good."

Dex's stomach tightened. "What's happened?"

"The FBI paid a visit to Rafe's loft in New York. He was there."

"But—that's good, right? He must have left right after the murder—"

"He's been there all week, and he could prove it. Whoever killed Wade, it wasn't him."

Dex's heart sank. "Thanks, Captain," he said numbly.

"Back to square one," Cromagg said.

Dex sat down on a cooler. "If the real Rafe was in New York," he said, "then who was the guy in the Darth Vader outfit?"

"And what's the *Gazette* going to print now?" Cromagg pointed out.

"Oh, crap," Dex said, rubbing his temples. "That's right. We have to tell Lorilei to tell everyone . . . oh, hell. What *should* we tell everyone? That I've got this great theory that's completely wrong?"

"Arr," Sundog said, stroking his beard. "It's royally fucked-up, that it is."

"I guess we have to tell them the truth," Dex said. "Or we'll lose whatever credibility we have."

"I'll try and raise Lorilei," Cromagg said, holding out his hand for the walkie-talkie. Dex gave it to him. "Maybe she's with Fun or hanging out with the ARG—that's where we ran into her."

But she wasn't. Fun hadn't seen her in hours, and neither had anyone at the *Gazette* or *Piss Clear*.

"She's probably making the rounds at the radio stations," Cromagg said. "There's a bunch of them besides the official one. FCC keeps threatening to come out here and shut them down, but so far it's all talk."

"Talk. Radio. Harrrr," Sundog said.

Whatever he took, Dex thought, *his sentences are get-*

ting shorter and shorter. Pretty soon he'll be down to Aye, Arr, and Ho.

"She would have gone to the papers first," Dex said. "Something's wrong."

"She'll turn up," Cromagg said. "Worse thing you could do is go out looking for her. Just wait here, and she'll come back to camp eventually."

But she didn't.

Dex finally fell asleep around three AM, slumped in a lawn chair with a sleeping bag around him. He woke at dawn, stiff and cold, and looked around blearily. Still no Lorilei. Cromagg and Sundog had finally gone out to look for her, leaving Dex to guard the fort. Captain Fun had rolled in around two, but he'd had no luck, either. "The last time I talked to her she said she was coming back to check on you," Fun told him. "This is kinda weird."

Dex got to his feet, feeling sore and creaky, had some water, then made his way into the tent-trailer, dragging the sleeping bag behind him. He crawled into bed, closed his eyes, and tried to get back to sleep.

Slumber wouldn't come. Worry gnawed at him. The more he thought about it, the more he knew what must have happened: Lorilei had been arrested. She'd been taken off-site in a police car and was sitting in an interrogation room right now. Some hard-ass detective was filling her in on exactly how long she'd be spending in jail for aiding and abetting a fugitive, and trying to persuade her to cut a deal. "All we want to know," the hard-ass would say, "is where he is. That's all. Just tell us where he is, and you can go free."

Tell them, he thought bleakly. *Don't sacrifice yourself for me. Just tell them.*

Somehow, he knew she wouldn't.

He didn't remember falling asleep, but the next time he opened his eyes the trailer was bright and warm. Someone was fumbling with the door latch, and he heard a female voice.

He leapt out of bed and snatched the door open. It wasn't Lorilei standing there but a woman dressed in a furry pink skirt, pink cowboy boots, a pink wig and fairy wings. She had a canvas bag slung over one shoulder. "Good morning," she said, sounding startled but cheerful. "I was just delivering some mail."

She plucked the envelope from where she'd stuck it in the door handle and handed it to him. "Hope it's good news," she said with a smile. "Gotta go."

"Uh, thanks," Dex muttered. He looked at the envelope in his hands, turned it over. It was cream-colored, the size you usually got a birthday card in. On the front was written: "CURIOUS URGE, TENT-TRAILER, AETHERIA."

"Lorilei?" he said out loud, and ripped it open.

Inside was a single sheet of paper. In block lettering it said:

I HAVE LORILEI. MEET ME AT THE TEMPLE OF THE PHOENIX, 9:00 TONIGHT, OR SHE DIES. TELL NO ONE. IF YOU DO, I'LL KNOW—I'M CLOSER THAN YOU THINK.

There was no signature.

"Oh, fuck," Dex whispered.

• • •

His first impulse was to run after the woman who'd delivered the note, to grab her and shake her and make her tell where it came from, even though he knew that was stupid and pointless. She'd gotten it from the Post Office, where it had no doubt been dropped off anonymously.

I shouldn't have taken those mushrooms, he thought. *Then I wouldn't have been sleepy and I could have gone out with her and—*

He stopped himself angrily. He could trace the blame back as far as he wanted, all the way to him choosing computers as a career, and it wouldn't do Lorilei a bit of good. He had to focus.

I'M CLOSER THAN YOU THINK.

That was the phrase that really chilled him. He'd never seen Rafe's face, had never heard him speak more than a few words in what had sounded like a phony voice; he could very well turn out to be almost anyone.

Except for the name, he thought. *Rafael Tomasini.* If the killer wasn't Wade's son, why would he go by his name? How would he even know it?

He realized, with a sudden, shaky awareness, that he really didn't know anyone he'd met in the last week. Of the two people at the festival he had more than a superficial relationship with, one was dead and the other kidnapped. Even Captain Fun, who'd done more for him than anyone, was really just a friendly stranger.

A friendly stranger who sometimes disappeared for no apparent reason.

No, he thought. *That's crazy.* Fun had never done anything but help. Helped him gather evidence, helped him get that evidence to the police . . . except Dex had never *seen* him hand that evidence over, had he? He'd just taken Fun's word for it.

So how do you find someone at Burning Man, someone who's lost and on the run? Someone whose face you'll recognize, but won't recognize yours? Maybe you just sit down in the Center Camp Café and wait for them to come stumbling in, looking for coffee.

But why introduce him to Lorilei and everyone else? It would have made more sense to get him alone somewhere and kill him. Unless Fun was after something else, and needed Dex to find it out for him . . .

Paranoia whirled in his head and churned in his stomach. He had to find Lorilei, and he had to do it on his own. But where to start looking?

He came to a quick decision. He went through the tent-trailer, grabbing supplies: some warmer clothing for later, a flashlight, a map, lip balm, some energy bars and beef jerky. He filled his canteen and two other water bottles and stuck them in a knapsack, then added a bottle of vodka from a crate Fun had stashed under the table. Even though his gut felt jumpy and knotted, he made himself eat some fruit and a can of tuna. Fun was still asleep in one of the pods, or at least his bike was locked up beside it. Dex hoped he wouldn't wake up—he didn't know what he'd say to him if he did.

He put on his sunglasses and dust mask, took a last glance around, and hopped on his bike. He wondered if he'd ever see the camp again.

He rode off into the rising heat of the day.

• • •

He had to think like Rafe.

Okay, so I've lured Wade to Burning Man to kill him. No witnesses. I wear a disguise anyway—extra precaution, just in case. I'm going to use a piece of rebar with a handle, for a good grip. It looks just like part of my costume, and it's a lot quieter than a gun.

A memory tugged at the edge of his attention—something to do with a gun?

And then he remembered.

Quieter than most guns, anyway. The pellet gun Wade used to nail lamppost lanterns was pretty quiet—that Lamplighter said it was CO_2 powered. But how would she know that? Unless maybe she found an empty CO_2 cartridge, or Wade showed her one when he was talking to her?

An empty cartridge that, according to Captain Fun, would look exactly like the canister I found in the pocket of the trench coat he lent me.

He thought about it, but he couldn't make any of the connections work. Even if Fun was somehow involved, Dex couldn't see the significance of the canister. Was Fun planning to shoot Wade with the same kind of gun Wade used for vandalism? A pellet gun was hardly lethal.

It just didn't make sense. He shook his head and tried to refocus.

But then this Edden guy shows up. Gotta get rid of him, too. No problem—I'm a bad-ass Burner, aren't I? I can adapt to anything.

He gets away, but so what? Where's he going to go? I can tell just by the way he talks that he's way out of his el-

*ement. By the time he even finds a cop, I can make it look
like he did it. Yeah, that's brilliant—get his prints on the
weapon; that'll be hard to explain.*

*How about a fire? Wade might have left something
around that would incriminate me, right? Better burn it
down, just in case.*

*Leaving now makes no sense—if I'm found out later,
it'll just look suspicious. So I stick around, keep my ears
open. Can hardly believe it when Mr. Edden goes underground, and then starts spreading his version of events.
Still, the fact that he's a fugitive works in my favor—the
cops aren't as easily swayed as the public.*

*Then he figures out a little too much. He links me to
Wade's son. He doesn't quite understand the significance,
but he knows it's important. He gets the information to
the police.*

I have to shut him up.

*Can't get to him directly, but I find somebody who's
close to him. If I use her, I can get to him. So I grab Lorilei,
stash her away. Of course, eventually I'll have to kill her,
too. . . .*

*But not right away. This time, I'm going to control the
situation completely. I'll pick the one time everybody else
will be occupied, during the burning of the Man. And I'll
make sure Edden gets all the blame, because there's only
room for one villain in this scenario—and it's not me.*

"He's going to kill her right in front of me," Dex
whispered. "Just like Wade . . ."

*Not quite. This time, I'm going to kill you, too. A nice
murder-suicide should fit the bill, right? You killed her
because she found out the truth, and killed yourself because—well, after two murders I guess you just lost it,
didn't you? Probably a little too tightly wrapped in the*

first place. You know what they say about the quiet ones. . . .

The tents and costumes and art cars that blurred past him as he pedaled barely registered. Only one fact gave him any hope at all: if Rafe was going to try to frame him for Lorilei's death, that meant she was still alive. Still alive, and somewhere in the city.

But *where?*

I should check the last place she was seen: the ARG. Which means I might run into Rafe without even knowing it, because he's probably a member.

But so what? He can't turn me in now, because that'll ruin his chances to frame me. He's already gambling that I won't turn myself in, get the cops to search for Lorilei.

That bothered him. Rafe had already proven he was willing to take big risks, but this one seemed wrong, somehow. How did Rafe know he wouldn't surrender? In a way, it was the perfect solution—he could get help for Lorilei at the same time he proved Rafe existed.

Except I wind up in custody—and Lorilei might die anyway.

There was something else, something he was missing. He couldn't quite make it out, but he knew it was there. Until it became clearer, he'd have to struggle along on his own.

The ARG was headquartered out of a beat-up Airstream trailer that had big aluminum fins added to make it look like a rocket ship. A spray-painted sign was lashed to the door with twine, with a stylized Road Runner beneath it. Beneath a striped awning, a card table was set up with two people seated behind it: a pudgy woman with stringy orange hair, wearing a psychedelic-patterned caftan, and a skinny man sporting sideburns, a red fez and a matching kimono. It wasn't exactly the beehive of activity Dex had imagined.

Dex pulled up and got off his bike. "Hey," he said.

"How do," the man with the sideburns answered. He had a pronounced southern drawl.

"I'm looking for a woman named Lorilei," Dex said. He described her. "She was here last night?"

"Yeah, I remember her," the woman said. "Wow, was she hot. Wasn't she hot, Frank?"

"In-ah-gu-ably," Frank said. He turned the single word into an entire sentence.

"Did you see who she was talking to, or where she might have gone?"

"Well, I talked to her," the woman said. "But not for long. I get all tongue-tied around women like that. I can't talk to half the women here without mumbling or making a fool of myself. Isn't that right, Frank?"

"Ab-so-lutely," Frank said.

"It's because of the whole Desert Lesbian thing," the woman said. "Straight girls come out here and suddenly they're necking with their best friend. I think it's got something to do with the alkali—screws with the PH level of female plumbing, that's my theory. I'm not complaining, just confused. Women I'd never dream of making a pass at in the outside world get a little dust in their boots and turn all flirty. Half the time they mean it, the other half they don't. More mixed signals than a traffic light in the Twilight Zone."

"In-ex-cusable," Frank said.

"Uh, yeah," Dex said. "Did she talk to anyone else?"

"She talked to Moonman for a while before she left," the woman said. "Of course, you never see *him* at a loss for words. He could talk the knob off a door and still get it to open."

"Is he around?"

"He went foah walk," Frank said, "but he'll be back forthwith."

Dex nodded. "How's the . . . movement going?"

"Not a lot of movement at present," Frank said, indicating the table with a lazy wave of his hand.

"Folks are resting up for the burn tonight," the woman said. "We still have a lot of support, though. People are behind Dexter Edden one hundred percent, no matter what the *Gazette* says."

"I thought the *Gazette* was behind him, too," Dex said.

"Guess you haven't seen today's edition." She reached down, pulled a folded paper out of an oversize purse at her feet and handed it to him.

Dex read with a growing sense of dismay. The *Gazette* detailed his theory about Wade's son—but it also reported the results. While it didn't come right out and say so, the article hinted that maybe Dex hadn't been entirely truthful.

"Heah comes our lunah leadah now," Frank said.

Dex looked up. Moonman was approaching rapidly down the street—or more accurately, bounding rapidly down the street. Strapped to either foot was a device of curved white plastic, one that bent and sprang back with every step he took, giving him a long, bouncing stride that suggested gravity worked differently in his immediate area. He was dressed in blindingly white, tight shorts, a broad-brimmed white

Panama hat, and white sweatbands on his wrists. His body was lean, tanned, and entirely hairless. He wore sunglasses with thick white plastic frames.

He came to a dusty, thumping stop right in front of them. He had to rock back and forth ever so slightly to keep his balance, but only his legs moved; his upper body was as steady as a rock. The foot-springs made him about seven feet tall.

"Whew," he said. "Jody, can I have some water?"

The woman handed over a large water bottle. He took it, snapped open the nozzle with his teeth, and drank heavily, not stopping until it was empty.

"Thanks," he said, handing it back.

Jody took it and said, "I'll refill it." She stood and went into the Airstream.

"Hot today," Moonman said to Dex. He grinned, showing teeth even whiter than his shorts.

"Sure is," Dex said, scratching at the edge of his dust mask and wishing he could take it off. "I'm a friend of Lorilei's—were you talking with her last night?"

"Yeah, she stopped by," Moonman said. "Why?"

"I've kind of . . . lost her," Dex said. "Any idea where she might have gone?"

Moonman frowned, his heavy eyebrows flexing like muscular caterpillars. "She was supposed to go to the *Gazette,* but I checked there and she never showed," he said. "Guess she got sidetracked by her date."

"Date?"

"Yeah, we went over to the Starlust to talk—she said she was meeting some guy and didn't want to miss him. He showed up and I got the feeling they wanted to be alone, so I left them there."

"What did he look like?"

"Tall, dressed in leather. Looked like a Death Guilder to me, but I could be wrong. Lots of guys go for that look."

"Maybe he was a reporter," Dex said. "She was supposed to drop by *Piss Clear,* too."

Moonman grinned and shook his head. "If he was a reporter, he was doing a story on her tonsils, if you know what I mean."

Dex swallowed. He did his best to sound casual. "Ha! Sure. He didn't have a scorpion-tattoo on his face, did he?"

"Kinda hard to see his face, most of the time," Moonman said. "But he might have. You know him?"

"Not exactly," Dex said. "Look, you have any idea where this guy was camped? She's probably just sleeping in, but it's kind of important I talk to her."

"I think I overheard something about Camp Bayou," Moonman said. "Yeah, I think that was it. Didn't catch his name, though."

"Thanks."

Moonman did a slow squat and started undoing straps on his feet. The muscles in his calves bulged. "Glad to help," he said.

Scorpion-face? It can't be. Moonman didn't sound sure. It must have been somebody else—somebody else Lorilei was kissing....

So what? That kind of thing is normal here. It's not like we had some kind of commitment to each other.

But what if it was more than that? Could Lorilei be involved in some way he didn't understand? Conspiracies sprouted in his mind like flowering vines, endless dire possibilities branching off and twisting back on themselves in tangles of coincidence and bright little blooms of fear.

Fun approaches me. Introduces me to Lorilei and everyone else. Complete strangers, but they're so helpful. A Death Guilder finds me right after I leave Lorilei, and later she's seen snogging with one. She was the one who brought me to Thunderdome. Maybe my whole camp is involved . . . maybe it's not Tribe Urge at all. Maybe it's Tribe Deathtrap.

He realized his breath was coming a little quicker—he was becoming panicky. He made a conscious effort to get himself under control, mumbled another thanks to Moonman and got back on his bike.

A block away he stopped, got out his map, and found Camp Bayou.

Camp Bayou had a whole hillbilly theme going, with a big central tent that featured lots of foliage, rocking chairs, and an indoor waterfall. Some kind of dance music with a lot of banjo in it was playing in the background, and people were bustling around doing morning things. No one had seen Lorilei, and nobody fitting the description of her friend was camped there.

He thought for a moment, then rode off toward Center Camp.

The Starlust Lounge was closed—their sign clearly stated their hours were "Dusk to Dawn"—but he was in luck; Sheriff Marty was lounging on a folding canvas chair next to a camper parked in the back. He was wearing sunglasses, sandals, and a blue silk robe with an oriental dragon done in scarlet curving over one shoulder. He was sipping from a plastic mug full of coffee.

"Howdy," Marty said as Dex got off his bike. "Curious Urge, right?"

"Right. You have a good memory."

"I never forget a drinking straw."

"I was wondering if Lorilei was here last night?"

Marty took a sip of coffee before answering. "Yeah, she was here—for a little while, anyway. I don't know how long she stayed, though—I took off just after she got here."

"Did you see who she was with?"

"Boy, you really live up to your name, huh?"

"It's just—" Dex took a deep breath. "Look, I'm not trying to be the jealous boyfriend. But she never came back to camp last night, and I think something might have happened to her. Seriously."

"Well, if she left with someone, I didn't see it. Last I saw she was hanging out with that ARG guy, whatshisname—"

"Moonman?"

"Yeah, that's him. Come to think of it, she looked kind of wasted."

So maybe she had a few drinks, overdid it a little, and wound up going off with someone on an impulse. Maybe Rafe was hanging around, saw what was happening and decided to capitalize on it. Send me a note, see if he could make me do something stupid.

He realized abruptly that he *was* acting stupid, or at least not thinking straight. There were two separate questions: *what happened to Lorilei?* and *was Lorilei with another guy?* and every time he tried to answer the first, he kept coming up with rationalizations for

the second. *That's not what's important. What's important—the* only *thing that's important—is whether or not
she's safe. And if I'm going to find that out, I'm going to
have to take some risks.*

He sized Sheriff Marty up and came to a decision.
He pulled down his dust mask and said, "Do you recognize me?"

Marty looked at him calmly. "Sure. But I knew who
you were the first time you came into the bar."

"You did?" He felt vaguely let down. "How?"

"Not a lot of people so worried about dust they
spend the night drinking through a straw." Marty
grinned. "Hey, don't worry—I'm not gonna turn you
in. Lorilei and Fun are good people, and if they support you then so do I."

"I hope so," Dex said. "Lorilei's been kidnapped."

Marty raised his eyebrows. "No shit?" he said.

"Deep shit," Dex said grimly. "Moonman says she
was here and left with some guy in leather—might
have a tattoo of a scorpion on his face. Said he looked
like a Death Guilder."

Marty shrugged. "I'll go wake Horse up—he was on
duty last night. Maybe he'll remember who she left
with." He got to his feet and went into the camper.

He came out a minute later with a long-faced, sleepy-
eyed man in boxer shorts. "Morning," he said with a
yawn. "You're looking for that fire-twirler?"

"Lorilei, yes," Dex said. "Did you see who she left
with?"

"Didn't see her leave. Saw her show up with Moonman, but he didn't hang around that long."

"How about a tall guy in leather, scorpion tattoo on
his face?"

Horse considered that, and scratched one stubbly cheek absently. "Real or fake?"

"Real or fake what?"

"The tattoo. Not too many people get the genuine article on their face, but you see temporary ones all the time."

Dex hadn't considered that. *Fun had a whole bunch of those. And didn't he say he got them from Cromagg?*

"I'm not sure," he said.

"Well, I don't recall anyone like that, but the bar was pretty busy last night. I remember she went and sat back here for a bit—she looked kind of looped. Next time I looked around she was gone."

"Look, are you sure this is a real kidnapping?" Marty asked. "I mean, people do that kind of thing as a joke, out here. Animal Control is always locking somebody up."

Dex thought about showing him the note, but it had the location of the meeting on it; what if Marty went to the cops and they screwed everything up?

"I'm sure," Dex said. He glanced around, trying to picture Lorilei sitting in one of chairs, her feet up on a cooler, drink in one hand. And maybe necking with a guy in leather . . .

"Sometimes patrons come back here for a little privacy," Marty said. "That's what this corner is for. Hell, we even have our own massage table."

"Privacy isn't something that Lorilei would worry about," Dex said. "Not if she was making out with someone, anyway. But she might have come back here for a private meeting." He spotted something on the ground, leaned over and picked it up.

"Moop," Marty said.

"What?"

"Matter Out Of Place," Horse explained. "It's the catchall phrase for anything that hits the ground and isn't supposed to. We try to keep an eye out for it."

"Damn straight," Marty said. "We run the cleanest goddamn joint on the playa."

"I believe you," Dex said. "And I bet this hasn't been here for long."

It was a small silver ring with a black stone in the middle, caked with dust and some reddish-brown flecks.

"An earring?" Marty said.

"No. A belly ring," Dex said. "Lorilei's. I—I think it was pulled out. Without being opened."

"Must have hurt like hell," Horse said. "No way somebody could have done that without causing a ruckus. I don't care how busy it was, I would have noticed."

"She did it herself," Dex said.

"Why would she do that?" Marty said.

"Because she was about to pass out," Dex said. "That's why she looked so wrecked. Somebody drugged her—not hard to do with all the free drinks being handed out. When she realized what was happening, she either tried to jolt herself awake, or leave a clue something was wrong."

Dex took a few steps to the edge of the camper. "Lots of dark places to hide and watch. Easy for someone to wait for the right moment, then grab her and carry her away."

"Her mystery man with the tattoo?" Marty asked.

"Maybe."

"That wound would be bleeding," Horse pointed out. "Maybe she left a trail?"

Dex was already checking. "I don't see anything," he said. "Her clothing might have soaked it up."

"Man, this is heavy-duty," Marty said, shaking his head. "We have to get the cops in on this."

"We can't," Dex said. "The only reason he's keeping her alive is to try and frame me. If the cops start a search, he might kill her and run. The last time he got pushed into making a quick decision, he tried to kill *me*."

"How did you know she was kidnapped in the first place?" Marty asked. "You get a note?"

"Yeah," Dex said. "He wants me to meet with him. There's only one reason for that."

"What, so he actually figures you're gonna show up and let him kill you?" Marty shook his head. "He's taking a pretty big gamble."

"If there's a chance he'll let Lorilei go," Dex said, "I have to take it."

He rode to the Temple of the Phoenix to check it out.

It was in a remote region of the Wholly Other, but far enough from the outer edge that anyone patrolling the perimeter wouldn't see much. There was a big central tent structure, with a large wood-and-metal sculpture of a bird with outstretched wings about twenty feet away from the front entrance—the Phoenix, Dex supposed—and the usual cluster of bikes sprawled around. There was also a metal ring about seven feet in diameter between the Phoenix and the tent; a woman was kneeling beside it, fiddling with a small rubber hose that led to a propane tank a few feet away. Fire sprouted around the circumference of the ring, then leapt up to a height of about three feet.

Inside the tent was a kind of foyer, with a small table, some pens, and a box filled with blank slips of red paper. A small sign explained that you were to write down a wish for renewal or rebirth, and place it in the altar. The altar would be burned in a ceremony on Sunday night.

Beyond the foyer was a much larger space. In its center was a large papier-mâché egg, big enough to hatch a full-sized man. It was honeycombed with fist-sized holes; Dex gathered this was the altar.

Soft music was playing in the background. Dex looked around, trying to figure out why Rafe had chosen here for the meeting. It was enclosed, but isolated; it would almost certainly be empty during the burn. It would be easy to keep an eye on from a distance if you had binoculars.

People came and went. Some wrote on the little slips of paper and placed them in the egg; others did not. Dex wondered if any of them were Rafe.

It was cooler in the shade of the tent than outside, so he decided to stay a while—actually, he didn't know where else to go. He walked around the egg a few times, trying to order his thoughts.

A man in a puffy-sleeved white shirt and black, pin-striped pants stood beside the egg for a long time. He sported a goatee, a black leather fedora, frameless glasses, and a thoughtful look. He carried a small bundle in his hands, brown suede wrapped in a brightly colored web of yellow, green, and blue thread. He held it as if there was something inside that might break.

"You believe in fate?" the man asked. He didn't

look at Dex, but at the moment they were the only two people in the tent.

"I'm not sure," Dex said.

"Funny thing happened to me on the way here," the man said. "On the way to Burning Man, I mean. My friends and I were on this little desert road after dark on Sunday night. We'd been driving all day, so we were kind of tired. We were in my little Tercel hatchback, towing this trailer that was way too big for the car. We had to stop on upgrades to let the engine cool down, and stop on downgrades to let the brakes cool off. The trailer was loaded down with water and supplies and probably weighed more than the car did.

"Anyway, all of a sudden this nighthawk flies out of the scrub and right into the windshield. Just commits hari-kari right in front of us. My friend that's driving gives a little start, and we comment on the strangeness of the incident, and all of a sudden there's this big black Cow from Hell in the road. Right in the middle of our lane. Its eyes in the headlights looked like they were glowing bright yellow.

"And then we were past and it was over—Nick managed to swerve around it without losing control. There was no way we could have stopped, and if we had hit the cow the car would have been crushed between it and the trailer. We were incredibly lucky we didn't go off the road or jackknife."

The man turned the package over in his hands. "We realized that if Nick had been just a little less alert, we'd be dead or seriously injured. And he wouldn't have been alert if that bird hadn't woken us up. We all thought that that was pretty spooky . . . but it got a little spookier when we got here. We had our bikes lashed to the top of the trailer, and when I went to get them down I found the bird. It must have been thrown over the roof, hit one of the bikes and dropped onto the trailer."

"Is that it?" Dex asked, nodding at the bundle.

"Yeah. We decided it needed a proper ceremonial send-off. And then we heard about this place and, well, what could be more appropriate than the Temple of the Phoenix?"

"New life rising from the ashes of death."

"Yeah. It gave up its life so we would live. I can't tell you how strange that makes me feel . . . and it wasn't even a straight-across trade, you know? It died just to get our *attention.*"

"After that it was up to you," Dex said. "I guess that's how it always works."

"All I know is, I'm glad I'm not dead," the man said.

"Second chances," Dex said. "We should all be grateful for them."

Somehow, the setup didn't make sense.

He rode around aimlessly in the hot sun, trying to think. *It's the timing that's the problem. Why wait until tonight for the meeting? Sure, it'll be during the Burn, when all the Burners will be distracted—but so what? There are plenty of deserted places he could set up a meet. And now I have all day to come up with a plan of my own.*

For that matter, why arrange a meeting at all? If he knew where to have the note delivered, he knew where Dex was—why not just try to kill him there?

He tried to think it through. *Attacking me in Aethe-*

ria must be too risky—too great a chance of being seen. His plan depends on framing me, so he's got to remain invisible if possible. Even the note isn't hard evidence—I could have written it myself.

In that light, I guess a meeting during the Burn does make sense—during the day, even a remote art installation could get an unexpected visitor at the wrong time. This lets him control the situation . . . except it still gives me time to plan.

Or to panic. Maybe that's what he wants. To actually turn myself over to the police and tell them everything. They'd stake out the Temple of the Phoenix, and of course Rafe would never show. That'd look like I made the whole thing up. . . .

So what would happen to Lorilei?

He hit the brakes and came to a sudden stop. A dust devil whirled past to his left, a scrap of silvery plastic caught in the funnel winking sunlight as it whirled past.

Lorilei would have to be found dead.

And it would have to look like I did it. It would have to look like I knew I was going to get captured when the festival ended anyway, and I was trying to make it look like there was somebody else involved.

But that would be tricky to pull off. If she died at a time I could prove I was somewhere else, with other people around, it wouldn't work. So how would Rafe get around that?

He had a sudden flash of the Egyptian-themed school bus Fun had taken him to, where he'd broken into Wade's email account and discovered Rafe in the first place. *That's not going to help me now,* he thought grimly. *I'm not going to find Lorilei in cyberspace—she's out here in the real world. The one where you can die.*

Still, the image wouldn't go away. It nagged at him. It wasn't so much the computer in it as the school bus itself—that, and kidnapping. There was some sort of connection. . . .

He closed his eyes. Tried to just let go, to let his thoughts swirl around. *There's a pattern. I know there's a pattern. In all this chaos there's a thread of logic, twisting its way through it all. . . .*

And then he saw it.

CHAPTER 18:

ABSURD PLAZA

Dex rode as fast as he could back to the Starlust Lounge.

He half-expected to see a patrol car parked outside, but there wasn't one. There was a line of people next door at Arctica, though, people waiting to buy ice. Dex swerved around them, dumped his bike on the ground and ran up to the camper. He pounded on the door. "Hey! Sheriff Marty!"

Nobody home. Marty was probably out roaming around . . . maybe even talking to the cops right now. Dex had no way of knowing.

"Plan B," he muttered.

He got back on his bike and rode along Authority, all the way up to Absurd Plaza. It was a smaller version of Center Camp, with a fountain instead of a café. What he was looking for was housed in a small rectangular building with a large front porch and two wooden benches flanking a glass front door. A sign on the roof proclaimed it was the headquarters of Radio Free Burning Man, "99.5 FM, Est. 1994."

Dex opened the door and went in. The interior was

only two rooms, one of which was filled by a table loaded with broadcasting equipment. Mikes on spindly metal arms angled over the console, with a young black woman sitting behind it.

"Hi," she said with a smile. "Can I help you?"

"I hope so," Dex said. "I've got a message to get out, and it's got to get out right away." He hesitated, then pulled out his wallet.

"It's okay, we don't charge," she said, grinning.

"I just wanted to show you my ID," Dex said. He pulled down his dust mask as he handed over his driver's licence. "And I hope you'll listen to what I have to say. . . ."

"Hello, all you Burners out there. This is Tiya at Radio Free Burning Man with an update on the Rogue-Runner situation. This one is urgent and affects every one of you, so you better listen up.

"Mr. Dexter Edden himself has just been in to see me. If you haven't been out of your head all week, you know that Dex is the number one suspect in a murder that took place in Black Rock City on Monday night. He's been claiming his innocence in articles in the *Black Rock Gazette*, and says a man in a pink Darth Vader outfit is actually to blame. At Burning Man, as we all know, when you think things can't get any stranger is usually when they do. Dex is now saying that a woman named Lorilei from Aetheria has been kidnapped by the real killer, and according to him, has been drugged and placed inside an art installation to die.

"He believes the killer is doing this to frame him.

He says, and I quote, 'If Lorilei's been stashed inside a piece of art out in the sun and dies as a result of dehydration, it'll be very hard to determine exactly when she was put in there. That makes it hard for me to establish an alibi.'

"When I asked him how he came up with this theory, he told me he'd remembered previous cases of kidnappers imprisoning their victims underground—once in a buried school bus. In those cases the air supply was the important thing; out here, of course, it's water.

"So, here's what he wants you to do. Go out to the Wholly Other and poke around. Is there a hidden room in that maze, with a drugged woman in it? Does that huge wooden duck have a kidnap victim in the beak? No way to tell until you look. He can't search every piece on the playa himself, so he needs your help. This applies to the police, as well—I'm going to be talking to an officer right after this. This is not a gag or hoax, people. Don't go tearing art apart, but keep your eyes open. A woman's life could be at stake."

Then all he could do was wait.

He rode around until he found an open, empty tent with some couches in it, and sank into one of them. What he wanted more than anything was to be out searching for Lorilei himself—but once the police got involved, the chance was too great they'd notice him.

And Rafe was still out there.

Not that Dex was afraid—just the opposite. What he felt was anger. Until now, it had only been *his* neck on the line; now, it was Lorilei's.

He was going to catch the bastard. It was that simple. He was going to catch him, and he was going to pay.

Dex couldn't count on the cops, and that was just fine with him. He *could* count on festivalgoers helping out a fellow Burner, though; if anyone could find Lorilei, they could. He thought long and hard about what they would probably find, and cried a little. He thought about Lorilei, and Rafe's arrogance, and how it was possible that Wade's son was still back in New York.

When he was done thinking, he got back on his bike and went in search of supplies. He picked up another long coat, floppy hat, and scarf at Kostume Kult, then went to Barter Bob's and swapped all his beef jerky for a little battery-powered AM/FM radio with headphones. He grabbed a pen and a piece of paper at Playa Info, and wrote a note. He went to the post office, stood in line for twenty minutes, listened politely to a rant about Mongolian postal rates, and bribed the clerk with some vodka to have the note delivered within the hour. He picked up a few other things, either bartering or just asking if he could have them. Mostly, people said yes.

He was riding down the Esplanade when he heard about Lorilei.

"Well, Burners, it looks like the Rogue-Runner was right," Tiya's voice said in his ear. "A woman was just found, unconscious but alive, in an art installation in a remote corner of the playa. She was spotted by an alert couple who pried the lid off a coffin-shaped wooden box that was part of the installation, apparently after hearing my earlier broadcast. The woman is being airlifted off-site right now; she's quite dehydrated, but she is alive. I was going to send a big thank-you out to Mr. Dexter Edden, but according to the officer I just talked to, things aren't that simple. There is, he says, some indication that Mr. Edden may have been involved in placing her in the box in the first place, possibly to gain sympathy for his cause. They are still very interested in talking to him, and they say they will search each and every vehicle leaving the site until they find him. Some estimates say that will add up to *twenty hours* to the time spent in the exit line. Come on, Dex—you're going to have to talk to them sooner or later. Make it sooner and give everybody else a break."

She was alive.

That was what mattered. It didn't matter that the city would now turn against him; it didn't matter that his time was running out. He hoped fervently that she would be all right, that she hadn't suffered brain damage or liver failure or whatever happened to people with severe dehydration—he didn't know what the possibilities were. He just knew that she had a chance, now, and before she hadn't.

That would have to do.

He was on his own. No friends, no allies, no resources but what he had with him. He couldn't risk going back to the tent-trailer, couldn't even talk to anyone he knew. He thought he'd prepared himself as best he could, but it still caught him by surprise when it happened.

He started to enjoy himself.

It was crazy. He was a fugitive, trapped in a hostile environment. He was being hunted by the police, a killer, and probably most of the city. A woman he had just fallen in love with was badly hurt. His boss was dead, leaving him technically unemployed—a fact so far down on his list of priorities that he hadn't even considered it until now, which said volumes about his situation by itself.

So why couldn't he get this big, loopy grin off his face?

He rode aimlessly, just killing time. He stopped for a while and watched some acrobats with a full trapeze setup somersault at each other thirty feet above the ground. He followed the smell of cooking fish and found a camp that was grilling fresh tuna steaks and giving them away; he had one and poured shots of vodka for each of the cooks.

He had never felt so free in his life.

Everything seemed brighter, more intense. The grilled tuna was the best thing he'd ever tasted. He felt completely focused on the moment, on every sight and sound and smell around him. It was all so *alive* . . .

And so was he.

People started to gather at the Man soon after the sun went down. By the time he rode out to the Temple of the Phoenix, the crowd was immense, twenty thousand people or more. When the Man went up, ninety-nine percent of the city's population would probably be there. He could see some sort of huge parade making its way up the Promenade, and felt a brief pang at the thought that, after all he'd been through, he was going to miss the one thing everybody came here for.

He stopped, standing with his bike between his legs, and looked at the Man. Dex was on Real Promenade, one of the avenues that led to the Man from the side, and he suddenly recognized what he was looking at; the neon structure that had reminded him of a pineapple on a pole the night he'd gone on the run was the head of the Man, seen in profile.

When he got to the Temple of the Phoenix, his was the only bicycle there. The metal ring out front was burning with a low, bluish flame, like a circular campfire. Dex set his bike down, not bothering to lock it. *What's he going to do?* he thought. *Kill me, then steal my ride?*

There was no one inside. A string of electric lights around the perimeter of the ceiling—battery-powered, Dex supposed—lit the tent. Dex looked around cautiously, but he and the egg were the only residents. *Does that make me the chicken? After all, I came first.* He had the insane urge to giggle, but fought it down.

There was a folding chair in one corner. He sat down, water bottle in one hand, and waited. Even this far away, he could hear the noise of the crowd as it grew. *Lorilei's going to hate that she's missing this. . . .*

Almost an hour passed before anything happened. Finally, a figure walked through the entrance. Like Dex, he was dressed in an outfit that covered him from head-to-foot: it was sort of a ninja/space-pirate getup, with baggy black trousers, a black shirt with puffy sleeves, black gloves, a black hood, and a mask that covered everything but his eyes. Silver wire was wound in elaborate patterns at his wrists and ankles, and he wore a belt at least two feet wide that seemed to be made of chain mail. A navy blue knapsack was slung over one shoulder.

He wandered in, glanced at Dex, then took a slow stroll around the egg without saying a word. Dex watched him steadily. The ninja stopped a few feet away and studied the egg calmly.

Dex got to his feet and pulled down his dust mask, exposing his face. "If you're looking for a trap, there isn't one," he said.

"In my profession," the ninja said, "one must be careful." His voice had a pronounced, obviously phony British accent. "Nice Walkman you have there."

Dex realized the headphones from the little AM/FM unit were still around his neck. He shrugged, pulled the radio out of his pocket and dropped it on the ground. He stomped on it, smashing the case. "It's not a wire," he said. "I said I wouldn't go to the police, and I didn't. They wouldn't believe me and you know it. Whatever you put in that coffin with Lorilei must have been pretty convincing."

The ninja glanced down at the wrecked radio, and nudged it with one black-booted foot. "If you're referring to the girl they found in the art installation," he said carefully, "I did hear they discovered a fingerprint on the duct tape she was tied up with."

"I bet they did," Dex said grimly. "Saved a little from the handle of the lightsaber, did you?"

"Someone told me this egg is supposed to be like a giant fortune cookie," the ninja said. He reached into one of the holes and pulled out a small slip of paper. "You choose for a friend, and whatever the paper says, they're supposed to do." He handed the slip to Dex.

It read: "TAKE OFF ALL YOUR CLOTHES AND GO OUTSIDE."

"Good advice, don't you think?" the ninja said.

"If that's what you want," Dex said. He didn't know if the paper had been planted earlier or if the ninja had just palmed it and pretended to take it out of the egg; it really made no difference. He put his water bottle down on the chair, pulled off the coat, and shucked out of his T-shirt and shorts, leaving only his shoes on. He'd never been comfortable with public nudity, even in locker rooms, and this was worse by far. He picked up his water bottle and tried to use it to give himself a little coverage while backing out of the tent slowly. The ninja followed a few steps behind.

Once they were outside, the ninja said, "Stop." He glanced around, then motioned Dex to go to the right. Dex did. Now the bulk of the tent was between them and the crowd at the Man; there was nothing but open playa all around them. The ninja took a pair of binoculars out and scanned the horizon; he seemed satisfied with what he saw.

"Well?" Dex said. "No bugs, no surveillance, nobody waiting to ambush you. Happy?" He took a long pull from the water bottle.

"Quite," the ninja said. "You know, I really didn't think you'd show. At the very least, I thought you'd send a decoy."

"And give you the chance to hurt someone else?" Dex said. "No."

"I don't suppose you have many allies left, anyway. You must be desperate to want to make a deal with *me*."

"I don't have any choice. You've won. I know who you are, but I can't prove anything. If I go to the cops, it'll be my word against yours, and the evidence points to me. I'm sure you've already burned anything incriminating."

"Yeah, you're pretty well screwed," the ninja said. His accent had vanished. "Even my being here doesn't mean a thing. I got a note and was curious; that's all."

"Not curious," Dex said. "Arrogant."

"An arrogant person wouldn't have a backup plan."

"And you do, of course." A chilly wind blew past, but Dex could hardly feel it; he wasn't cold at all. "Like any good Burner, you're well prepared for any eventuality. That box you stuck Lorilei in, for instance—you brought that out here for Wade, didn't you? Drug him, stick him in that and make it look like he crawled in there himself."

"Interesting theory. Almost as interesting as your proposition."

"It makes perfect sense. Maybe not in the outside world, but here it does. Me loose and on the run is better for both of us than me in custody. Maybe I can't prove you did anything, but I *can* drag you into the investigation. Better if you stay invisible, at least until you leave the festival—then you can vanish. Besides, if I get caught later, who'll believe the killer helped me escape?"

"What makes you think I can smuggle you off-site?"

"Like you said—you have a backup plan. You planned this too well not to. Use it to get me out instead."

The ninja laughed. "You know, I misjudged you. You looked like a complete corporate dweeb when I first met you, and I figured you wouldn't last twenty-four hours on the playa. But you did. You not only survived, you *thrived*. You made friends, you even scored yourself a dustbunny. And this plan of yours—damn, it's the kind of thing I'd come up with. It's a *Burner's* plan, you know?"

"I *do* know," Dex said. "It's half pragmatism, half imagination, and mostly crazy." He took another long drink from his bottle, lowered it—then sprayed the contents of his mouth all over the ninja.

"What the *fuck?*" the ninja said, taking a startled step backward. The front of his outfit was soaked. Dex brought his right foot up and plucked the lighter from where it was tucked in his shoe.

"I'm sure you recognize the smell," Dex said. He held up the Zippo, flicked the top open with his thumb and lit it with his other hand. The flame guttered in the wind, but didn't blow out. "You're now a large road-flare. Don't make me light you."

"Aw, man," the ninja said. "You got it all over my face." He reached up and pulled off his mask. "The fumes stink, but if you were trying to knock me out," Moonman said, "you should have used chloroform, not kerosene."

"A Burner uses what's available, right? This was the best I could do."

"It's not bad," Moonman admitted. "But it's gonna be pretty hard to keep that lighter going . . . and *this* isn't going to go out."

Suddenly, there was a knife in his hand.

"Oh, good," Dex said. "I was worried you might have a gun."

"What's the plan, Dex? Gonna set me on fire?" Moonman had gone into a crouch, holding the knife in front of him at belly height. He started to weave the blade slowly back and forth. "That'll just make you look worse. No way I'm going down for this."

Dex had thought he couldn't feel any more vulnerable; he was wrong. The sight of the steel blade made him suddenly, acutely aware of every inch of bare, exposed skin on his body. His genitals were doing their best to retract into his groin.

"Put the knife down," Dex said. He tried to protect the Zippo's flame with one hand while holding it ready to thrust forward with the other. "You can't use it, and you know it. You think people will believe I stabbed *myself*?"

Moonman edged forward, and made a tentative swipe with the knife. Dex took a step back, and Moonman grinned and got a little closer. "Self-defense," he said. "I came out here for a little quiet meditation, and you jumped me."

Dex's stomach felt as if it had contracted to the size of a golf ball. "Who *are* you, anyway?" he said. "Some friend of the real Rafe?"

"Something like that," Moonman said. "Far as Wade knew, though, I was his long-lost baby boy."

"So Rafe gets an alibi and you get—what?"

"Let's just say that when Rafe inherits all that money, he's gonna be real grateful to the person who helped him get it."

"Good, he can pay for your skin grafts," Dex said. He tried to keep the quaver out of his voice. "I'm not kidding—I'll set you on fire."

"You think I'm afraid of *fire*?" Moonman laughed. "Oh, man. You have made a *serious* error in judgment. You can't bluff a Burner with flame. . . ."

He made a sudden lunge, slashing at Dex's hand. Dex pulled his arm back, closer to his chest. Moonman compensated on his backswing, and Dex felt the sharp bite of the knife in a long gash along his forearm. He jumped backward out of range, but didn't drop the lighter.

"That's a pretty deep cut," Moonman said. He voice sounded almost casual. "I could just wait until you bleed enough to pass out. Hey, maybe you're one of those people who faints at the sight of blood. Are you?"

"No," Dex said, and lunged forward with the Zippo. Moonman tried to slash it out of his hand again, but Dex used his other arm to block. Then they were grappling, Dex trying desperately to keep the blade away with one hand while thrusting the Zippo at Moonman's chest with the other. Moonman had at least twenty pounds on Dex, and his weapon wasn't limited to one target area; Dex took another cut on his arm before he latched onto Moonman's wrist. Blood flowed down Dex's arm, hot spatters hitting the bare skin of his legs and torso.

Moonman had gotten hold of a wrist too, keeping the Zippo at bay. He tried to knee Dex in the groin, but Dex turned sideways and took it on the hip bone instead. It hurt almost as much.

Moonman suddenly stopped fighting to keep the lighter away, though he still had a good grip on Dex's wrist. Dex got the Zippo within six inches of the kerosene-soaked patch on Moonman's chest before his opponent locked his arm and stopped him.

And then, with a feral smile on his face, Moonman leaned forward and blew out the flame.

Dex didn't waste time trying to relight it. He jerked his own head forward and down as hard as he could, smashing his forehead into Moonman's nose. The Burner roared in pain and let go of Dex's wrist, staggering backward a step. Dex released his hold on Moonman's knife hand and took a step back himself.

He flicked the wheel of the Zippo without looking at it, and tossed it at Moonman's chest. He knew Moonman would bat it out of the air before it hit its target.

He had a split second to see that the wick had caught as the silver lighter spun through the air, and then Dex's head was down and he was charging. If Moonman knocked the Zippo away with his knife hand, Dex could get inside his range, maybe keep him from using it again; if Moonman used his other hand, the blade would be waiting.

He slammed into Moonman's belly skull-first, his head still ringing from the last impact. An instant later, a deep and terrible pain lanced into his own stomach, and he had his answer.

Momentum carried both of them backward. Moonman's ankle hit something and he went over, Dex on top of him. The knife twisted as they fell, and there was a horrible ripping sensation that almost made Dex black out. A surge of intense pain at his ankles brought him back like a slap in the face; they'd fallen over the metal fire-ring, were now lying inside its boundary with their lower legs across it. Dex bent his legs at the knee, getting them out of the way of the flame.

The knife pulled out of his body, then slammed back in a few inches away. The pain wasn't as bad this time; he supposed he was going into shock. His limbs suddenly felt shaky and weak.

"*Fuck* that," he said out loud, grabbed the front of Moonman's outfit, and heaved to the right as hard as he could, throwing the entire weight of his body with it and ignoring the burst of pain in his gut. They rolled, Moonman landing on top. He yanked out the knife for another strike, trying to get his forearm under Dex's chin to force his head back, and for a second Dex's eyes locked onto his.

"And fuck *you*," Dex hissed, and used every ounce of remaining strength he had to keep the roll going. They flipped once again, and this time Moonman landed on his back, square on the fire-ring.

The loose, blousy fabric of his costume caught immediately. The kerosene must have soaked into more of the fabric than Dex had realized, because Moonman's torso went up like a fireball. His pants were already on fire, had caught when they tripped over the edge of the ring; now his whole outfit was ablaze. He screamed, dropping the knife and throwing Dex off him in an adrenaline-fueled burst of terror, and sprang to his feet. He tore at his clothes, but the wire at his wrists and ankles and the wide chain-mail belt made it impossible to remove them quickly. The hood was burning now, wreathing his horrified face in fire, and instead of dropping to the ground and rolling, he did the worst thing possible; he ran. He made it about thirty feet before he collapsed.

Dex lay on his side, panting. It hurt to breathe. It felt like he'd swallowed long shards of broken glass. His ankle was starting to throb the way a bad burn does, and his arm stung where playa dust had gotten into the wound. The low flame of the fire ring surrounded him, but he still felt cold. The pyre of Moonman's body was just a slightly higher tongue of distant flame; as it burned down, it seemed to merge with the fire that encircled Dex.

In the shimmer at the top of the flames, bizarre shapes danced in the heat haze: a white tree, a golden bull, an immense wheel. Huge mobile art installations, parked around the Man. The fire blocked his view of the crowd, but he could hear it, a noise like the ocean. Were those drums in the background, or his own heart?

He struggled to sit up, managed to make it to his knees. His head swam and the night suddenly got darker, as if someone had turned out the stars. He waited, holding his hand over his stomach, hoping nothing was going to fall out.

The crowd roared. He looked up, and saw that the Man had raised its neon-lined arms over its head. Fireworks erupted from its skull in brilliant streamers of gold, and flames began to flicker at its base. Strangely, the sound of the crowd got fainter, diminishing as if it were getting farther and farther away. . . .

He came back to himself with his cheek pressed against the cold ground, grit in his mouth. *Can't let that happen again. Have to get out of here. Get help.*

The Man was a blazing tower in the distance. He could see what looked like whirlwinds of fire spinning around the edges, fire tornadoes that formed and dispersed from second to second. A distant part of him was very glad he'd gotten to see them. Music and cheering and drums. He got to his knees again, saw how much blood had soaked into the ground, felt a wave of dizziness wash over him. He clenched his teeth, refused to be dragged under. When it had passed, he very slowly got to his feet. Again, the world tried to go sideways; he stood there, breathing shallowly, until it passed.

He took a slow, shuffling step to the edge of the fire ring, then stepped carefully over it. It singed the sole of his foot anyway, and the inside of his calf. The pain hardly seemed worth noticing.

Moving like an old man, he made his way around the side of the tent. Moonman's ride was there, a homemade three-wheeled bike with a big plastic bin between the two back wheels. *How he moved Lorilei. How he'd planned to move Wade, and probably me.*

Dex didn't know if he could stay on a bike, even one with three wheels. He staggered past it, and kept going. The lights and the crowd still seemed very far away, but at least they weren't getting farther.

He fixed his eyes on the Man. More fireworks were going off. Huge plumes of flame suddenly erupted on every side of it, reaching heights of a hundred feet or more, like oil wells igniting.

He kept shuffling forward. All he had to do was reach the edge of that crowd. How far away was it— half a mile? More? It was impossible to tell. The blood trickling down his leg tickled where it crossed the skin of his thigh. His hip hurt every time he moved his right leg.

It was hard to concentrate. Dust blew against his face, into his eyes. *Thirsty. Probably shouldn't drink, though—might not be safe. Might come squirting out between my fingers.*

Wonder how bad I'm hurt. Maybe I should have stayed at the Temple, waited for someone to find me. I collapse out here in the dark, I'll probably die before anyone finds me. Or runs over me.

Maybe I'll get lucky. Maybe they'll put me in the bed next to Lorilei's.

He kept going.

CHAPTER 19:

OUT ON THE PLAYA

Dex didn't know it at the time, but he was found by a wedding party. They were riding around on a mobile living-room suite—complete with couches, coffee table, console TV, and tacky lamps—celebrating the marriage of Tim and Laurie, who had tied the knot on the steps of the Man that afternoon. Everyone (except the bride herself) wore a wedding dress. They had arrived at the actual burning of the Man late, and so were on the edge of the crowd; therefore, they were among the first to leave when it was over. They had headed out on the open playa to have a few drinks and get out of the way of the rest of the crowd, and very nearly drove over Dex. At first they thought he'd just passed out—and then they saw the blood.

He opened his eyes in a tent. He was lying on a cot with an IV in his arm and a bright light in his eyes. He squinted, saw people moving around him and heard the clipped shorthand that medical professionals use when they're focused and in a hurry. His mouth was fuzzy and his head felt like it was out of focus.

A man in a bright yellow shirt was doing something to the IV. "He's awake," he said. "Hey, there. You're gonna be all right."

"I was stabbed," Dex croaked.

"Amongst other things," the man said cheerfully. He was black, with very short hair and thin, curving sideburns that almost looked drawn-on. "It's not as bad as it looks." A woman in the same kind of shirt was wrapping a bandage around his arm.

"How's it look?"

"Terrible." The man grinned. "But the blade didn't hit an artery or a major organ. Long as you don't develop peritonitus, you'll be fine."

"Terrific. Can I have some water?"

"Nope. But you can have all the saline you can handle." The man tapped the pole beside the cot lightly. "And we'll get some plasma into you at the hospital. The ambulance is gonna take you to the chopper as soon as it gets here."

Dex lifted his head and looked around. There were about a dozen other cots in the tent with him, half of them occupied. Several Burners were lying down with IVs in their arms, looking dazed or worried or bored; a woman in the corner was having her ankle bandaged. Near the door, four medics were trying to hold down a naked man covered in tattoos, who was thrashing and yelling incoherently.

"You picked a busy night," his attendant said. "And I think a few people are going to want to talk to you before you leave."

"I'll bet," Dex said.

Sure enough, the police arrived two minutes later—Sheriff Tremayne and two deputies. Tremayne walked up to Dex, looked down at him and said, "Dexter Edden?"

"Yes," Dex rasped. His throat felt like he'd been gargling with thumbtacks.

"I'm Sheriff Tremayne. You're a hard man to find," the sheriff said with a smile. He sounded like he'd appreciate Dex's vote in the next election.

"Am I under arrest?" Dex asked.

"Not yet," Tremayne said amiably. "But I am going to ask you a few questions before they bundle you off to the trauma center. It'd be in your own interest to answer them honestly."

He nodded at one of the deputies—a blond, fresh-faced man who looked as if he were still in high school—who pulled out a pad and a pen. The other one, the portly Latino Dex had seen before, hooked his thumbs in his waistband and tried to look intimidating.

"First off," Tremayne said, "you might want to tell me exactly what happened between you and the guy we found burned to death out on the playa."

"I don't know his real name," Dex said. "He called himself Moonman. He was camped at two-thirty and Vision."

"This the same guy that headed up the, what did they call themselves?"

"Acme Road Runner Guardians," the deputy with the pad said.

"Rogue-Runner," Dex said. "Rogue-Runner Guardians. Yeah, that was him."

"He was a real pain-in-the-ass," Tremayne said. "You probably had good reason to turn him into barbecue, right?"

"Self-defense."

"Uh-huh. How about Laura May Wilson and Wade Jickling? They self-defense, too?"

"I didn't hurt either of them. Moonman did."

"That's awful convenient, considering he's not exactly in any position to say otherwise."

"There's a trike, parked near the Temple of the Phoenix. If you look in the bin in the back, you might find something that'll link Moonman to Loril—Laura May Wilson's abduction."

"Or you could just ask her," a familiar voice said.

Captain Fun stuck his head around one of the deputies. "Hey, Mr. Urge. I just got word Lorilei's gonna be fine."

"Son, we're conducting an investigation here," Tremayne said. "You can talk to your friend later."

"I think you should listen to him," someone else said. The speaker stepped forward; it was the man in the white Stetson that Dex had talked to in the shack made of pianos. He was wearing blue jeans now, but otherwise he looked the same. "It'll change your way of thinking."

"Mr. Harvey," Tremayne said. He sounded a little less belligerent than he had a second ago. "This a friend of yours?"

"Everybody here is a friend of mine," Mr. Harvey said. "More to the point, though, is the fact that the Captain has information relevant to the case."

"Thanks, Larry," Captain Fun said. "Sheriff, you might want to check out the Airstream trailer at two-thirty and Vision as well as that trike. I'll bet you'll find some of Lorilei's blood as well as Moonman's DNA in either or both locations—and you won't find Dex's."

"Who the hell is Lorilei?"

"Laura May Wilson," Dex said.

"I just received an email from the young woman in question," Mr. Harvey said. "While she can't positively identify her kidnapper—he was masked the entire time—she can confirm that the person who drugged her is the aforementioned Moonman."

"Doesn't mean they weren't working together," Tremayne said.

"Except I don't have a motive," Dex pointed out. He shifted slightly and winced. "And Wade's son does. Once you learn Moonman's real name, you'll find out he and Rafael Tomasini know each other. When Rafe inherited Wade's money, Moonman was going to get a big cut."

"Looks like you were the one got the big cut," Mr. Harvey said. "A few of 'em, in fact."

"Still doesn't clear him," Tremayne said stubbornly.

"Of Wade's murder, no," Captain Fun said. "But he's got an alibi for the kidnapping. Lorilei was taken between eleven-fifteen and eleven-thirty. Dex was in my trailer, asleep, at that time. I've got two witnesses who'll swear to it."

"Who?" Dex asked.

"Cromagg and Sundog," Fun said. "Lorilei sent 'em to keep an eye on you, remember? They stuck their heads in the trailer, saw that you were asleep, and stayed outside. If you'd stuck around and talked to us, you'd know that."

"Sorry," Dex mumbled. "I wasn't really thinking straight."

"Well, sometimes thinking crooked is what gets the job done," Mr. Harvey said. "Long as you don't stop thinking altogether. You're lucky you have good people looking out for you."

"I know."

"Look," Tremayne said, "I've still got two corpses, a hospitalized woman and one suspect in custody. This whole thing smells like a scam that went wrong, with one partner turning against the other."

"Funny thing about partnerships," Mr. Harvey said. "They've got to be based on trust to work, and it's hard to trust someone when murder's involved. I'd guess Moonman and Rafe didn't trust each other much; since Rafe was the one getting all the money, I'll bet Moonman had a little insurance up his sleeve. Something along the lines of information to be delivered in the case of his death."

Tremayne gave Harvey a long, evaluating look, then grudgingly nodded. "If he was smart enough to think ahead, I suppose he would."

"It's not so much being smart," Mr. Harvey said, "as being aware of consequences."

Two men with a wheeled gurney came through the front door. "Looks like your ride is here," Tremayne said. "They'll take you to the Washoe County Medical Center, get you patched up. I'll be along in a few hours, take a full statement from you there."

"Take care," Mr. Harvey said. "Hope to see you next year." He turned and strolled away, the cops following.

"Uh—who *is* that guy?" Dex asked as the paramedics moved him carefully from the cot to the gurney.

Fun stared at him in surprise, then laughed out loud.

"Oh, man. I keep forgetting how green you are . . . That's *Larry Harvey.*"

Dex looked at him blankly.

"The guy who *created* Burning Man," Captain Fun said. "Head Honcho, resident of Camp One, the Impresario himself."

"Oh," Dex said. "Him."

They started rolling him toward the exit. "Wait," Dex said. "Before I go, there's one thing I have to know. Where did you go, all those times you disappeared?"

"Aw, hell," Fun said. "All right, I'll tell you, but you have to keep it to yourself, all right?"

"I promise," Dex said.

"I was checking on some art sites I set up. Replacing supplies, making sure they were clean, stuff like that."

"I don't understand."

"I'm 'Olaf,' okay?"

"Olaf? Olaf the Outlaw Outhouse Outfitter?"

"Yeah." Fun managed to look embarrassed and proud at the same time. "I don't tell people, 'cause it doesn't really fit with my image as a dashing superhero, you know?"

"Bullshit," Dex said. "You just enjoyed having a secret identity."

"Well—yeah, that, too."

"Time to go," the paramedic said firmly. They started to wheel him out.

"Say hi to Lorilei for me," Fun said. "And don't worry—Larry's got some really good lawyers. It'll all work out."

"I hope they work cheap," Dex said. "I'm unemployed."

"So what?" Fun said, walking beside him as they rolled the gurney outside. An ambulance was parked right next to the door. "Larry's got you covered. After all—you're a Burner, aren't you?"

"Yeah," Dex said as they loaded him into the ambulance. "I guess I am."

EPILOGUE: ASHES OF THE MAN

File Z (Playaboy66): You'll probably think I'm crazy, but my favorite part of Burning Man is Sunday.

I know, I know, it can't compare to the giddy rush of Saturday night, when the Man burns and everybody tries to cram as much partying in as they can before it's all over for another year; it doesn't have the same wild intensity of people letting go in a big orgasm of hedonism, as they throw the bash they've been planning all year, or burn the giant teddy bear they slaved over for two hundred hours and dragged five hundred miles to incinerate. If the rest of the week is foreplay, then Saturday night is the orgy.

And Sunday . . . Sunday is the afterglow.

Literally, in some cases. The Man is a big heap of coals, with people already starting to do cleanup. I usually go by and scoop a little bit of ash into a vial, as a keepsake; lots of other people do, too. I make mine into a necklace, wear it year-round as a touchstone. For me it's a reminder that anything's possible . . . and that I always have something to look forward to.

I'm sure it's just a trick of memory, that Sundays in Black Rock City are just as hot and have just as many dust storms as any other day, but I always remember them as being calm and just the right temperature. A week of acclimatizing helps, too; you can't really get *used* to Black Rock City, but you can reach the point where you'll accept almost anything.

Acceptance. That's a good word to describe the feeling you get, wandering around the city on a Sunday afternoon. Everyone's packing up, dismantling art installations and theme camps and getting vehicles ready for the road, and everyone seems to be smiling. People are giving away all the gifts they have left in a last-minute frenzy of generousity: ice cream, condoms, toys, joints, candy, jewelry, stickers, CDs, comic books, fruit, T-shirts, and a hundred other things. There's a general sense of satisfaction, of a job well-done. We came, we built a city, we celebrated. We survived, we learned, we grew.

I know so many people for whom Burning Man was a pivotal experience in their life. They went home and switched careers, or moved to another city, or changed their lifestyle completely. Do you know how many people get married every year in Black Rock? You can make all the jokes about desert romance that you want, but a lot of Burners find their partners out here. Bonding on the playa can be a powerful thing—it has the life-and-death intensity of the battlefield, but instead of guns and bombs and missiles you have art and drugs and sex. You can still die, but you'll probably die with a smile on your face and a beer in your hand.

One of my favorite things is the drum circle. It's a

more or less continuous jam, people coming and going all week, but never really stopping. To me it feels like the heartbeat of the city; when I'm playing, it's like being connected directly to the pulse of the Man himself. It's intensely tribal, but not in an exclusive way—it feels like we all belong to the same group.

I've heard Burning Man called the Gathering of the Tribes, and it's as good a description as any. Some people come out here and find their tribe; some people come out here with their tribe and discover all the others. Either way, it's a powerful experience. It touches something primal in you, something deep and primitive and basic, and you suddenly just feel more *human*. You see people with their civilization stripped away, and guess what? They're not the violent, ignorant savages we're all afraid we're hiding inside. They're loud and lusty and uninhibited, but they're also creative and cooperative and accepting. We don't have cavemen lurking inside us—we have children.

So I wander around on Sunday, picking up Moop on the ground where I see it, and watch the children play. They're tired, but they're happy. I watch the swing-dancers kicking up dust while a group of Klowns laugh their way through the mini-golf course. I watch the Santa's ho-ho-hoing their way from camp to camp—who but Santa can visit all the bars on the playa in a single night?—while the Death Guilders strafe them with machine-gun blanks from the back of a combat hearse. I watch the naked people painted blue, and the ones painted yellow, and the ones painted red and orange and green. I watch the stilters strut, and the motorized recliners roll. I watch the leather-clad and the latex-wrapped, taking their slaves for one more stroll down the Esplanade at the end of a leash. I watch fratboys talking to drag queens, robots playing with monkeys, tigers and lions and bears having a drink with Animal Control. I watch Rangers ride around on pirate ships, followed by the Devil and the Pope on a tandem bike and a Host of Angels in a flying saucer. Rows of dusty couches wait patiently to be hauled away, looking like a furniture graveyard.

But even though it's winding down, it isn't over yet. There's still one more important ritual left, one which acknowledges what fire leaves behind.

The Temple of Honor. It rises a hundred feet above the ground in three levels, columns tipped with minarets suggesting the Taj Mahal. It's covered in intricate black-and-white patterns and made entirely of paper, the individual pieces produced in a piñata factory and assembled here. But what it's made of—beyond being flammable and nontoxic—isn't what's important; it's what it represents. All week long, people have been placing things inside: pictures, poems, keepsakes. Memories. This is a shrine to the dead, to the people we love who are now dust.

And now, on Sunday night, it burns. David Best, one of the creators of the temple, walks slowly around the edges of the crowd, saying softly over and over, "It's not your fault. It's not your fault." People are weeping, holding hands, embracing. It is a time to grieve, but also a time to let go, to let the flames burn away your sorrow and loss. Mourning, after all, is about the suffering of the survivor; the dead feel no pain.

Burning Man means something different to everyone, but to me it's about transformation. The Man burns because everyone burns. No matter who you were when you came here, you go away different. If you survive the fire, what's left is stronger.

And will probably be back next year.

Not sure what to read next?

Visit Pocket Books online at
www.SimonSays.com

Reading suggestions for
you and your reading group

New release news

Author appearances

Online chats with your favorite writers

Special offers

And much, much more!

10421